KU-067-463

For my family

PROLOGUE

17 OCTOBER 2015

Collins walked across the bridge and saw them gathered on the distant quayside. He turned right, off the road, and passed the barrel-vaulted warehouses. The rigging on nearby yachts slapped against their masts, a sharp metallic sound.

Jim Dillon, the head of the Garda Water Unit, broke from the group and approached him, a phone to his ear.

'Detective,' Dillon said. He held his hand over the phone. 'I've called the hearse; it's on its way.'

Collins nodded and kept walking.

The wind picked up as he neared the cluster of men by the water's edge. It whipped at his ears and flapped his coat and pants. A bitter easterly, gathering chill and spite as it made its way up the river.

Two wet-suited divers squatted on the quayside, gathering their gear; two more stood over the closed body bag on the ground.

'Looks like that suicide, alright, Collins,' one of them said. Liam Mullins. A former international swimmer, he appeared as fit and healthy as ever, although he was in his early forties, the same age as Collins. 'Amazing how many of them we find around here.'

Collins licked his lips. He glanced up at the sign above their heads. PORT OF CORK. He lowered his right knee to the ground beside the body bag. A familiar genuflection.

He hesitated, then pulled the zip down half its length and drew back the two sides.

'Fuck,' he said. Something had eaten away her left eye. A small pool of water gathered in the raw socket. The colour of the flesh was no longer pink – it had turned a snot-coloured green.

It felt as if she were watching him with that eyeless hole. That she could look right inside him and see all that he had failed to do.

He closed the zip, stood up.

A Transit van backed up, beeping, and the divers began to load their equipment.

Collins looked at the river. The water chopped and spat at the limestone quay.

The door of the van slid shut and Mullins approached him, holding a clipboard.

'Em … can you sign here, Collins? We can't leave until we sign her over and there's a missing farmer near the river in Lismore.'

Collins looked at the form. He wrote the words 'Kelly Grace O'Driscoll' on it. He scrawled his name at the bottom and handed it back.

Mullins took the clipboard and hesitated.

'How are you keeping?' he said.

The question threw Collins – they hardly knew each other.

'I'm fine, Liam. I've had better days.'

'Oh, right. Well, see you so,' Mullins said. He sat into the van and it moved away.

Collins returned to the body bag, forlorn on the stone. He squeezed his eyes and grimaced to the grey sky.

'You useless prick,' he muttered.

Clouds scudded over his head, over the pale city all around.

The hearse arrived and Collins watched as they slid her into it. He signed another form.

He walked down Anderson's Quay, thinking about Liam Mullins's question. He wondered what Mullins had heard about the Butcher case – some of the rumours were ridiculous, but the truth wasn't much better. He wondered what Mullins saw when he looked at him. A lesson in what never to become, maybe: jaded and unfit, more rail thin than lean, losing his height to a stoop. Looking closer to fifty than forty. Burnt-out by the job, coming back after a mental breakdown, having clashed with a serial killer the previous year.

He took out his phone and made the call, looking at the Church of the Ascension in the distance and the water tower up on the horizon.

'Well?' June answered.

'It's her,' he said.

'Oh, Collins, I'm sorry.'

'I'm just about to ring Joe now, then I'll be heading up to the house with Liaison.'

'Are you sure?' she said.

'I'm sure.'

'What if Townsend's there?'

'Oh, I hope to fuck he is. But he won't be,' he said. 'Unfortunately.'

There was a momentary silence.

'Collins, don't do it.'

'I'll be back in ten.'

He hung up. Crossing the road, he felt the phone dig into his hand. He put it in his pocket.

He recalled the first time he'd met Kelly – twelve years before, at the Na Piarsaigh club grounds, after watching a Minor match with Paulo and Christy. One of those glorious August evenings that goes on and on, the air warm and dense with possibility.

They were drifting to the pub – slightly giddy already from banter and the promise of pints. Nobody could make him laugh like Christy. Dozens of children with hurleys were running around on the pitch in swarms, chasing white sliotars.

Their old teammate Joe O'Driscoll, known as Horse, waited for them at the gate, beaming. He looked well, he'd filled out a bit since he'd gotten off the streets and stopped drinking.

A little girl, maybe six years old, her back pressed against his thighs, squinted up at them. Her mother's button nose and chin. Her plump cheeks red from running, her dark hair splashed against her forehead. Dumpy arms aloft in the massive hands of her father.

'How's the going, Joe? How's the form?' Collins said.

'Grand out, Collins, how are you?'

'Oh, fine. Good to see you, boy.'

They shook hands and Collins bent down to the child. 'And what's your name?'

'Kelly, what's yours?' she said. She had a chipped front tooth, giving her a jaunty air.

'My name is Collins, pleased to meet you.' He extended a hand, which she ignored until nudged by her father. Her pudgy little hand. Her big blue eyes, like her mother's, bright as a morning sky.

He recalled the night in the club bar, just two years ago, hearing that Joe was back on the drink and things were bad between himself and his wife, Niamh. And that Kelly's half-brother, Jason Townsend, had returned from England bringing a heroin addiction with him.

Collins called in to a distraught Niamh, who told him the whole story. How Kelly, at only sixteen, had come under Townsend's influence. She started skipping school and getting into trouble with the guards. Before long, Kelly was taking drugs, too.

Niamh blamed herself. First she'd lost her husband to drink, then her son to drugs, and now her daughter was in a bad place.

Then Kelly fell for some friend of Townsend's and left home to live with him. She was seventeen by that time and there was nothing the family, or – when he got involved – Collins, could do. He tried everything: pleading, threats, intimidation, locking her up, locking Townsend and the boyfriend up. But Kelly was indomitable; nothing seemed to faze her. The health services were powerless. The boyfriend was controlling her completely.

Collins knew what the next stage of the story would be and he got the call one night from a colleague. She'd been picked up for soliciting. The boyfriend and Townsend had forced her into it to feed their habits. A further descent happened when the boyfriend died of an overdose and she came under the 'protection' of the main drug dealer and pimp in Cork, Dominic Molloy.

There was a big difference between selling yourself for drugs the odd time and being in one of Molloy's brothels, where you had to 'service' up to twenty men a day – every day. And Molloy was getting into what he called 'adult entertainment' – but what was, in reality, the vilest of hard-core porn. Collins dreaded to think what they had forced her to do.

Until, apparently, she could do it no longer, and there was a report of a young woman throwing herself into the river at Sullivan's Quay. Followed by a frantic call from Niamh, saying that Kelly was missing.

They went in two cars, turning into the tidy housing estate at dusk. The city was lighting up below, the harbour beyond fading into the dark. Collins and June were in the first, unmarked, car. June had insisted on driving him. Kate and Nora, the Garda Family Liaison Officers, were in the second. As they approached the house they noticed a small crowd gathered outside.

'They already know,' Collins said.

June parked on the kerb across the road, all eyes following them. The squad car pulled up behind.

'Right,' Collins said. He thought he saw pity in June's eyes and resented it.

As he got out of the car he remembered how nervous he'd always been before hurling matches, vomiting in dressing rooms, his knees jellied, hands trembling. And yet he still managed to walk out the door with the others, studs clacking on tile and concrete, running through the tunnel, into the light and the sound. That sound.

Nora and Kate were in uniform. They stepped onto the street, donned their caps and pulled the ends of their jackets down. Collins, in plain clothes, closed a coat button and then opened it again.

'The counsellor has been delayed, she won't be here for an hour,' Nora said.

'We can't wait that long,' Kate said. 'Collins?'

'I'll go first,' he said.

'Right,' Kate said.

The crowd outside the house watched them warily. As they went through the gate a few people on the path moved aside. He made eye contact with those he passed, searching for a particular face.

Alison, Kelly's aunt, stood at the open front door. She was the one Kelly had resembled most – they could have passed for sisters. She stared at him, eyes wild with pleading.

'I'm sorry, Alison,' he said and she slumped back on the stairs. He placed his hand on her shoulder and walked into the breathless living room. It was full of people, but he made straight for the small woman in the corner armchair, her face downcast, clutching a cardigan. He walked up to her and was about to bend down when she stood up suddenly and faced him.

'I'm so sorry, Niamh. They found her in the river an hour ago,' he said, looking down into her bloodshot, fearful eyes.

She lowered her head and put her hand to her mouth. Collins hesitated and then he held her. She was so small, and as he felt the tremors of her weeping, he could sense her fading into something tinier again.

Collins could not make eye contact with June when he sat back into the car. He tied his seat belt.

'I rang the morgue, they'll do the post-mortem in the morning,' she said.

'Thanks,' he said, rubbing the palms of his hands up and down his face.

'She was pregnant,' he said.

'Kelly? No.'

'Yeah, her friend Emma just told me.'

'Jesus Christ,' June said. 'Oh, for fuck's sake.'

'We should get back,' he said. 'Kate and Nora will bring her out there to identify the body.'

'Will we go for a drink?' she said.

'No. No thanks, June. You head home, it's nearly tea time.' He badly needed a drink and he would have welcomed his partner's company in other circumstances. But he wanted her out of the way.

Halfway down Shandon Street, June pulled the car into the side of the road. She turned to him.

'You're planning something, aren't you?'

'What do you mean?' he said.

'Don't mess with me, Collins. You're going after him, aren't you?'

'I don't know what you're on about.'

June glared at him.

'I'm not going to let you,' she said.

'What are you on about?'

'He's not worth it, Collins. Think of your career.'

'June, I'm not planning anything. I just don't feel like a pint. I'm heading home.'

'I don't believe you.'

Collins opened the passenger door.

'Thanks for coming up with me,' he said. 'I'm just going to head home. I'll hop out here.'

He paused for a moment, then closed the door.

'Don't do it, Collins,' she shouted.

He put his hand up in salute as he walked away down the hill towards the river.

A couple of hours later, Collins walked into the bar as if he owned it – something he had learned to do as a young garda on the beat. It was one of those places he hated, where you usually can't hear the 'music' they play because it's too loud, but you can't hear anything else either unless it's somebody shouting in your ear.

The pub was almost empty, just a few kids sipping cocktails on the high stools around a small square table. The owners had gone to some trouble doing the place up – an array of expensive-looking bottles of spirits were backlit behind the bar, giving it a feel of sophistication that it didn't merit. The music was bearably loud.

Collins saw the person he wanted behind the counter. Her name was Małgorzata Novak, but everybody called her Gosia. She'd come to Collins's notice for three reasons. One, she was a junkie, feeding a low-grade heroin habit. Two, she was fucking Pat Brady, a thug and sidekick of Dominic Molloy. And three, she had just made a big mistake. She was supposed to deliver a few kilos of Molloy's cocaine to a Dublin criminal by the name of Crilly, but she ended up high and horny when she shouldn't have been. When the Drugs and Organised Crime Unit raided Crilly's apartment a few weeks later and checked his laptop, they found a surprisingly high-quality video of Gosia and himself having some fun on his sofa. He must have had a camera hidden in the room.

Gosia had the fine bones and blonde hair of so many Poles, but she was pale and sickly looking. Collins stood in front of her by the counter as if he were a customer. She pretended he wasn't there. The bar manager asked him what he would like.

'I'd like to speak to her,' Collins said, pointing to Gosia, who had walked to the other end of the counter. She was trapped and Collins could see her dilemma, but he was low on sympathy. He followed her.

'I need to talk to you now, Gosia.'

'I don't know you,' she said. 'I don't say nothing to you.'

'You have a choice,' he said. 'Make up your mind quickly. Either I talk with you now somewhere quiet, or in five minutes three uniformed gardaí will walk in here and arrest you for possession of drugs for the purpose of sale or supply. And then they'll take you out in handcuffs in front of your boss and all the customers.'

She stared at him, hatred radiating from her like heat off a fire.

'Not here,' she said and marched out the back of the bar. Collins followed.

She led him to a small, dark storeroom that she opened by tapping in some numbers on a keypad at the door. She went through and faced him, folding her arms across her chest.

'You not scare me, Collins,' she said and smiled darkly, her cheeks reddening. 'Yes, I know your name.'

Collins closed the door behind him.

'I'm looking for Townsend. Where is he?'

'I don't know no Townsend.'

Collins took five photographs from an inside pocket. He shuffled them slowly, examining each one, smiling as he did so. Gosia shook her head.

'What?' she said.

He handed her the top photo. The quality was poor, giving a pornographic tone to the already seedy content.

'Impressive show, Gosia,' he said. 'We have a video too. The whole works, sound and vision. The lads in the station really enjoyed it.'

Gosia said something in Polish and grabbed the other photos. She looked through them quickly and tore them all up into small pieces. She reached for a coat hanging from the wall and took out a lighter. She placed the pile of torn paper on the ground and lit it.

Collins stepped back and watched her.

'Do you know what your boyfriend will do when he sees those? And the video?'

She put her face in her hands and moaned quietly.

'Where you get these?'

'There's a video of the whole thing, from start to finish. It's a long video – coke, eh?'

She groaned and turned away. She took a box of cigarettes from her coat pocket, lit one and sucked hard. She shook her head, vehemently.

'If I tell you anything, he will kill me,' she said, her chest heaving, her nostrils flaring. She pulled hard on the cigarette.

'No, he won't, Gosia, because he'll never know. This is just between you and me. Nobody else in the station knows I'm here. Not even my partner.'

Collins pressed on – he had to get the information before she could gather herself.

'And I only want Townsend, the little shit. Not Molloy, or Brady or anyone else. Nobody will *ever* know.'

She was shaking. 'I wish I never come to this country.'

'Where's Townsend? Tell me now and I'm gone and the video is gone.'

'Where's Townsend, where's Townsend? All you ask. What about me?'

'Where is he? Just give me an address. Nobody will ever know.'

She stared at him with disgust.

'Okay, but if I tell you where he is, that's it? No more photos? Nobody knows?'

'Absolutely. That's all I want. Nobody knows,' Collins said, putting his two hands up in a surrender sign.

She took another drag from the cigarette and tapped a shoe on the ground.

'What I do? I sick of this shit,' she said, and stubbed out the cigarette viciously. 'Okay, okay. I tell you where is Townsend. But that's all.'

Collins appeared solemn, as though he respected her decision.

An hour later, he was parked in an unmarked car on Fort Street, just under the old fort wall, with a view up Vicar Street Lane. Townsend would turn up eventually. He liked his home comforts, did Jason. Collins held the Taser in his lap and checked the packing tape and cable ties in his pockets.

As he sat there, he had a vision of himself and where he was headed that night. Standing in river shallows a few miles outside the city with Townsend on his knees before him. A figure in dark clothes with an implacable hold on the neck of the small, bound and struggling man, pushing his head towards the water. Townsend's pleading eyes trying to meet his, the moans behind the tape bound around his mouth and head. The pebbled bankside, the riverbank trees, the moonlight and the sodium-lit road across the fields. Collins could see the indifferent city's glowing sky in the distance. He could feel the freezing water swirling around his shins and hear the quiet shuffle of a bullock behind the reeds. He could hear his own voice, sounding strange and unreal.

'You shouldn't have put your kid sister on the game, Jason. You shouldn't have got her hooked to keep her there. You fucked up, Jason.'

He could feel the shuddering of the weak-willed loser in his grasp under the water, his bony neck scrabbling to be freed. Bubbles, struggling, then stillness.

As he sat in the cold car, waiting, he wondered: *Will this be it for me now? The moment I read about in that Frank O'Connor story in school? Will anything that happens to me after, ever feel the same again?*

The sick rose up towards his gullet. He gripped the steering wheel as if his hold on it was the only thing saving him from an endless fall. He clenched his teeth and roared until he could feel his face about to burst. His ragged breathing burned his chest and throat. He could feel the blood pounding inside his skull.

He looked up the alley one last time. He licked his lips. He lifted his face to the roof of the car and groaned.

'You useless fucking prick,' he said, pressing his head against the side window.

He started the engine and drove away.

PART 1

11 AUGUST 2016

1

Dominic Francis Molloy, who liked to be called 'The Dom', looked at the laptop screen. It showed a video of a small man smoking a cigarette in the back of a van. The image was murky. The man was just sitting there, leaning against the side of the van, his knees bent, his arms resting on them. He wore a dark tracksuit, a jacket that appeared to be a couple of sizes too big for him, and white runners. He took another drag from the cigarette. He seemed bored.

The laptop was on a low rectangular table, in a small, empty bar with a curved counter. There were three glasses on the table. One, from cut crystal, was half-full with golden liquid and ice cubes. The others were pints of lager. A shout came from the adjacent room, a busy bar – there was a match on the television.

'And that's live now?' Molloy said, in a strong North Cork accent.

He picked up the crystal glass and took a sip. He tucked the tie inside his suit jacket. He wore suits from time to time – to show the fuckers what a prosperous businessman should look like. He was clean-shaven and his hair was neatly cut and parted on the left. He was proud of his leanness and good looks.

'Yes,' the man on his left said. A bulky man, with Slavic features and short fair hair. They called him Alex; his full name was unpronounceable. 'Is live streaming. And is backing up on cloud.'

Molloy didn't like asking questions, he thought it made him appear weak. But the Poles tended not to offer information unless prompted.

'And is it on battery?' he said.

'The mobile Wi-Fi is plugged into cigarette lighter on the dash and hidden under passenger seat,' Alex said. 'That way battery cannot die. Otherwise is a risk. And camera is linked to that.'

'Right,' Molloy said. He picked up the glass again and sat back, satisfied. 'And the camera is where?'

'Camera is hidden in panelling behind driver's seat. Completely invisible.'

'What do you think?' Molloy said to the other man, whose features were picture-perfect and resembled those of a striking male model, with sallow skin, night black hair, impossibly blue eyes and a perfectly symmetrical face. He pursed his lips. His name was Tomasz Mazur, or that's what he'd told everyone. Molloy couldn't care less what his real name was.

'Is good,' Mazur said. 'If he comes in the van, we will get a video and post all over Web. He is finished.'

'Sound is perfect, too, so we will hear everything he says,' Alex said. As if on cue, the man in the van coughed and they could hear it clearly.

Alex pressed some keys and a series of figures and a volume bar appeared on the screen. He adjusted something. He was a technical expert, something that Molloy valued, with knowledge of Apps, smartphones, Internet banking, surveillance and the Dark Web. Porn and cybercrime were the coming things; they would eventually put drugs and prostitution in the shade, and involved no hassle with needles or street crime.

He swore by those Poles, did Molloy. They were cheap, quick to learn, and disciplined. They didn't use, unlike most of his own clueless fuckers. They obeyed orders, didn't ask stupid questions, and above all, they were ruthless. They laughed at the restrictions that Irish law placed upon the gardaí and came up with innovative ways to get around them. They had contacts in Eastern Europe to source guns and they even knew some Russians who could launder money in Cyprus.

Molloy sipped his whiskey, satisfied with himself.

Collins was sure to act out and attack Townsend, and the camera would get it all. That would be the end of the prick, trying to stop a businessman from doing his job with his pathetic vendetta.

With him out of the way, the place would be wide open for the benzos and synthetic opioids – they were already taking over and had stayed under the radar.

He'd bring the Poles with him to Spain for sure. Technology was the way to go.

2

Collins entered the hall of his third-floor apartment and closed the door behind him. He left his keys on the coat hook and went into the living room. The usual soft light seeped up from Pope's Quay and Lavitt's Quay below. He paired his phone to the Bluetooth speaker and selected 'The Safety of the North'. The elegiac notes swelled and filled the room. The satisfying welcome home of familiar music.

He took a bottle of pale ale from the fridge, flicked off its cap, picked a glass from the shelf and stood in front of the painting in the corner. Its broad teal strokes seemed more blue than green in the faint tawny light. The outline of a pillow on a bed could be seen in the abstract image, which was more about colour and texture than what it represented.

He sat down in his father's old armchair in the bay window. It faced to the north-west, towards Gurranabraher. The Church of the Assumption, impassive at night, stood elemental above the rows of small sleeping homes scattering out around it. In the distance the headlights of a solitary car appeared and disappeared, almost magically, crawling down Cathedral Road.

As he poured the beer, he noticed, in the corner of his eye, a brief orange flash from the back of a van parked on the street below. With its dirty rear windows faced directly towards his apartment.

Young lovers, maybe; surely they could have found a better spot. Or some guy down on his luck, homeless. But he recalled how a retired colleague had phoned him a couple of days previously, saying he *thought* he'd seen Jason Townsend 'hanging around' on the same street. Collins had put it down to mistaken identity or coincidence at the time. There hadn't been sight nor sound of Townsend since Kelly's death.

He placed the glass and bottle on the small table, moved away from the window and paused the music on his phone. The sudden silence was grating, putting him on edge. He picked up the binoculars from the low bookshelf and, standing as far back as possible from the window, he focused them on the van. The tiny but unmistakable glow of a cigarette being pulled-upon shone and faded.

He noted the registration number and called the station.

'Mick? Collins here,' he said.

'Detective Collins,' Sergeant Mick Murphy said, with clipped asperity – his voice as tight as new rope. They went back a long way and the road had been rocky. Collins pictured his thin lips pursed in disapproval.

'Mick, can you run a number for me please? A Ford Transit van. White, maybe cream. 02 C 97412. It's parked across from me on Pope's Quay.'

'Right. I'll call you back,' Mick said.

'Thanks.'

He put the binoculars to his eyes again and waited for the call. The phone rang.

'Collins,' he answered.

'It belongs to a garage off Blackwater Road. Seanie McDonagh runs it. Remember him? We got him for procuring a few years ago.'

Collins winced. He tried to think. He watched the van; it seemed so innocuous.

'Is there a problem, Collins?' Mick said.

'I'm not sure,' he said. 'There's somebody inside it. Yeah, I remember him alright. Thanks, Mick. Are the traffic cameras live on Christy Ring Bridge? The one facing west, down Pope's Quay?'

'I think so, I didn't hear of any problems.'

'Good, thanks. I'm coming into the station to have a look. Will you send a car around, please? It's probably nothing, but still …'

Collins hung up. Seanie McDonagh. Not good. He glanced at the beer on the table. He knew he had to check the video immediately or it would eat at him through the night.

He thought about going down and confronting whoever was in the van but decided against it until he knew more. If it *was* Townsend …

Collins looked across at St Mary's Church on the opposite side of the river. The statue of the Blessed Virgin Mary stood above its Ionic columns and portico. He knew her well; they have had many a staring match. She won every time.

The statue, high on its plinth, faced south, to the hills beyond the city where the lights of the airport shone out at night. A pale green mould had begun to mottle her face, neck and white robe. Splotches of it grew over her eyes, giving the impression of an ancient affliction. She held her left hand out, low and open, as if in acceptance of her fate. Her right hand was higher, palm up, showing more authority. Her fingers pointing towards the hillside to the west.

He noticed his face half-reflected in the window, scowling. He softened his gaze.

An abiding dreariness pervades a garda station late at night. Collins felt the familiar gloom as he walked through the doors of Anglesea Street Station.

A fraught middle-aged couple sat on the mock-leather bench across from the main desk. Waiting for a drunk-and-disorderly son to be released. Or for news of a daughter who has been missing for days – probably taking drugs and having sex with a man they fear and despise.

He strolled past the main desk and saluted the night-duty garda.

'Quiet, Tom?' he said.

'Hectic here, Collins.'

Sergeant Mick Murphy and Garda Paddy O'Keefe sat before the large bank of monitors in the video room. Most of the screens displayed empty streets or light traffic. Mick adjusted the control panel to isolate a specific recording on the main screen. He was already rewinding the images when Collins entered the room.

'Is that it, down near the church?' Mick said.

'Yeah, did you see when it was parked?' Collins said.

'Not yet. I'm nearly back as far as seven o'clock.'

He continued to rewind. When the clock reached 16:30 a small male figure emerged from the van, walked quickly backwards towards the camera, and then out of view. Collins stiffened. That shape and walk, that *gatch*, even backwards, was familiar. The figure suddenly reappeared from the same spot, this time facing forward.

'Here he is,' Mick said. 'I'll pause and close up on his face. Fuck!'

Mick's eyes widened with shock. The two men exchanged looks.

Collins sat down resignedly, and tried to think. He glanced at the still, blurry image on the screen. There was no doubt. It was Jason Townsend.

'The little prick. Will we bring him in? This is way out of order,' Mick said.

Collins tapped his left forefinger against his lips before answering.

'No. Leave it for now, Mick. Sure what harm can he do? I'll talk to June and the Super tomorrow. We might be able to use it against Molloy if we play our cards right.'

'Are you sure? The fucking cheek of him. They're not planning something, are they? On you?'

Collins laughed. 'No, Mick, I'm sure it's nothing like that.'

'Will I keep an eye on it, overnight? We could park a car down the road, or drive around. We can't let this go, Collins. I'll have someone watch the video here at least.'

'No, no, there's no need. Sure, it's recording away. Can you go live again? It's probably gone already.' Collins wanted that face to be removed from the screen.

The van was still there, grainy and now sinister.

Collins stood up to leave: 'Thanks, Mick. I'll give you a shout in the morning before eight if it's still there. See you, Paddy.'

'See you, Collins,' Paddy said.

Collins left the video room. He tried to fix his body language to make himself appear calm. It wasn't easy. He stopped to chat and joke with a young female garda whose name he could never remember, who was bringing a tray of mugs of coffee and tea to colleagues.

Collins sat for a long time in his father's armchair that night, staring at the van.

The beer lay stale and flat on the small table by his side. Eventually, he pulled himself out of the chair and dragged himself to bed.

3

The following night, Collins stepped briskly through his apartment building's front door, out to the riverside street. He wore dark running gear, a hoodie, a cap and gloves as he jogged across the road at an angle. During the day, Lavitt's Quay is a busy four-lane artery for traffic traversing the city, but now it was empty, as he'd hoped it would be, at three in the morning on a damp night.

He ran slowly across the bridge and paused to check that the high traffic camera was facing the wrong way, as arranged. It was. As a couple were passing by, he put his hands on the wet metal railing of the bridge and feigned some stretches.

Flecks of rain etched the still, tide-bound river water below.

He went left onto Camden Quay and stepped over the plastic railing surrounding some building materials by the river wall. He picked up two large rust-coloured bricks from a pile and stalked alongside the parked cars, towards the van. A look up and down the quays and across the river showed no sign of life.

He walked on, along the footpath beside the river, the bricks held low. They each had two curved ridges on one side. He placed them on the ground beside a car. Crouching down, he pressed a hand against the door and squeezed his eyes shut.

Don't lose it in there, he thought. *Jesus, don't.*

He forced himself upright and picked up the bricks. He checked up and down the quays again. Nothing. He crossed the road.

He listened outside the van. Stillness. Silence. He peeked in through the grime and saw a figure lying huddled up in a sleeping bag.

Glancing left and right, he stood away from the rear-end of the van, stretched back his arms and flung the two bricks through the windows. He put his hand inside the broken right window and quickly opened the door. Townsend was rising slowly, moaning. The brick on the left had met its mark.

Collins hopped into the van, took out a flashlight from inside his hoodie and closed the door behind him. He recoiled at the smell. Detritus lined the floor. Broken glass crunched under his feet. He shone the light into Townsend's face. A familiar, pathetic face, wasted by addiction and self-neglect. Blood poured from a cut on his temple. Collins held his pointed, stubbled chin sideways, examining the wound.

Townsend moaned, pressing a hand to his head.

Collins put the light down, turned him over quickly and tied his hands behind his back with a plastic tie.

'*You*,' he said, picking up the two bricks. 'After what you did to your sister …'

Townsend cowered beneath him.

Fifteen minutes later, Collins opened the door of the van and pulled Townsend to the edge, letting him sit there. Still all quiet on the street.

Collins wrapped the sleeping bag around Townsend's shaking shoulders – shock was setting in. Townsend's head hung down into his chest and he began to weep. The gentle rain descended silently, moistening his hair and downturned brow.

'Don't move, Jason. I'm calling an ambulance. They'll fix you up. They'll give you plenty of painkillers, as much as you want. OxyContin, the works. Just sit there, I'm calling the ambulance now. We'll say you fell and hurt yourself. It's all over now.'

Collins moved to the wall by the river and took out a small mobile phone and dialled a number.

'Hi, Paddy.'

'Collins.'

'How's your mam, Paddy, any change?'

'Not much. Still sick as a dog. Mairead says she's like death warmed up.'

'I was going to call in at the weekend, would she be able for a visitor?'

'She'd love to see you, Collins. Any time.'

'Okay, I'll do that so. I'll ring you beforehand to check.'

'Do. She might get worse when the chemo kicks in.'

'Poor thing. Listen, Paddy, you can point those cameras down Lavitt's Quay and Pope's Quay again in thirty minutes. Thanks for that.'

Hesitation.

'Okay, Collins. Come here, everything all right there? You don't need backup or anything?'

'No, no. Long story. Keep this to yourself. I'll fill you in at the weekend. Grand, thanks, Paddy, talk Saturday. The station quiet?'

'Yeah, dead quiet. Okay. I'll do that. Half an hour, you said?'

'That's it. Thanks, Paddy.'

Collins switched off the phone and put it in the right pocket of his hoodie. He took out another phone and dialled 999, asking for an ambulance, giving the location. He opened his penknife and cut the cable tie from around Townsend's wrists. He took a heavy plastic bag from inside his hoodie, picked up the bricks from the van and put them into it.

He lifted Townsend to the bench on the side of the road. He weighed no more than a child. Townsend kept his eyes closed, as if by not seeing what was happening meant it did not happen.

'They'll be right here, Jason. Ten minutes max. I told them it was an emergency. Just sit down there. Keep your leg up over the edge of the bench there.'

Collins went back to the van, took out the bag with the bricks and closed the door. He jogged along the footpath, past the church, upriver. He turned at the pedestrian Shandon Bridge towards the Coal Quay, and looked around carefully. Nobody. He threw the bag, the 999 phone and the cable tie into the water as he ran. Going left again, he looped back towards his door.

Entering his apartment block, he glanced towards the van, but the view of the bench was obstructed by the riverside wall. He climbed the stairs and fumbled the key into the door lock.

In fifteen minutes he saw the ambulance arrive from his sitting-room window, lights flashing – no siren needed at that time of night. He watched as they lifted Townsend inside the vehicle and drove away.

Collins slumped into the armchair. He held his head in his hands and tried to slow his breathing. He told himself that it was about bringing Molloy down, that it wasn't just placating his own guilt, or getting revenge for Kelly.

'Jesus Christ,' he said.

He jumped up, rushed to the cabinet and took out a bottle of whiskey. He poured a large measure, already feeling the satisfying burn in his throat. He stared at the golden liquid, then poured it down the sink, rinsed the glass, filled it with water and sat at the table in front of the notebook he had earlier placed there.

He stared at the blank page, thinking hard.

He began to write.

As he was writing, the tide turned. The river water outside

his apartment began to swirl, then flow. It flowed under Christy Ring Bridge, and under Patrick's Bridge, and under Brian Boru Bridge, past the city's buildings, streets and docks. Past the PORT OF CORK sign, the high houses to the north, and the Marina's broad-leaved trees. Past Blackrock Castle out into the harbour, flowing on. Flowing past islands and headlands, past all land, out into the deep waters, into the wide-open cold black sea.

4

Collins woke to the sound of his phone ringing. He was still sitting at the table, his head on his arms, the glass and notebook before him. The room was grey with dull early morning light.

He saw the number and winced.

'Hello,' he said blearily.

'Collins, what the fuck did you do last night?'

'What? Is that you, Mick?'

'Collins, Jason Townsend was picked up by an ambulance across from your flat a few hours ago with a fractured ankle, lacerations and bruising to the face. Now don't tell me you know nothing about it.'

'Townsend? In an ambulance?' Collins said.

'Who are you trying to cod, Collins? You *told* me you weren't going to do anything. You *told* me not to pick him up, that you were going to talk to June and the Super about it. You *told* me not to keep an eye on the video. And, you got Paddy to point the cameras away. So don't play the innocent here, alright?'

'Mick, when I went to bed last night –'

'"When I went to bed," would you listen to yourself. Collins, you're a law unto yourself – or at least you think you are. If you think a few All-Irelands and a big case allows you to do whatever you like, and walk over everyone in this district, or this division, you have another thing coming. I'm going to the Ombudsman with this, I don't care anymore.'

'Mick, will you let me explain?'

He heard the tone of a phone hanging up.

He redialled the number. It rang and rang. A voice message began. He hung up.

'Shit,' he said.

He tore the top sheet from the notebook, picked up the glass and rose from the table. He looked out the window and saw that the van had gone from across the river. He put the glass in the sink. He read his page of notes, tore it up into little pieces and threw them into the compost bin. He plugged the phone into the cable at the kitchen counter and half-staggered towards the shower.

Opening the bathroom window, he heard two herring gulls crying raucously somewhere high above the building.

June Carroll walked into Café L'Atitude, on the corner of Union Quay and Anglesea Street.

Morning sunlight slanted through the windows, illuminating the dust motes floating over the old table. Collins was sitting, back to the wall, facing the room. He glanced up to see June scowling at him and he smiled palely. She pointed at his empty coffee cup and he nodded. She went to the counter to order. Collins watched her.

His partner had been full of enthusiasm once, ambitious and keen. He remembered that bright, lively and bold young detective. She was as good as anyone in the station, those days. Better. Never gave up on a case, incredible persistence and dedication, a huge conviction rate. Go through a suspect as soon as look at him.

Not anymore. Fifteen years of serious crime – wave after wave of filth washing over her – had taken its toll. What with having two children – one sick with Crohn's disease – and drinking the best part of a bottle of wine most nights, June's engagement with the job had diminished. Collins didn't blame her for it. Superintendent John O'Connell turned a blind eye to her absenteeism and Collins was happy to cover for her. He was also glad of the freedom, though he did miss her company and the opportunity to bounce gripes off her.

She had always acted maternally towards him, even though he was a few years older. Trying to shield him from recrimination and to reel him in from his own worst excesses on the job. After a few pints one night, after she'd given him another telling-off, he told her that she was the district's lioness, the protector of the pride. She replied that he needed protecting alright but mostly from himself.

She sat down opposite him, then beside him, away from the sun's glare.

'And when were you going to tell me?' she said.

'I'm telling you now, sure.'

'No. Mick Murphy told me, in no uncertain terms, this morning. And this is Wednesday. You saw the van on Monday. Why didn't you tell me yesterday?'

'Well, we were busy with that stand-off ... and it was Tuesday morning really, after midnight.'

'Collins –'

'I didn't want to implicate you. I was up half the night thinking about how to handle it. If I told you and anything happened, you'd be in the shit too. Anyway, you'd only have tried to talk me out of it. In fact, you probably would have talked me out of it.'

'As if. You always do whatever *you* want to do, Collins. Always have.' She looked at him appraisingly. 'And you look like shit.'

The coffees arrived and she took a sip. She drank it black and strong, as did he. She exhaled with the pleasure of it, then ordered a croissant and asked if he wanted one. He didn't.

'What do you think Jonno's going to do?' she said.

'Cover his ass, as usual. If he thinks it won't get out, he won't do much. Rap on the knuckles. It's down to Mick, really. He's seriously pissed off and that's fair enough. If he goes to the Ombudsman …'

'He won't do that, surely.'

'He's old school, June. He … we go back a bit. You know the story.' Collins recalled the betrayal in his old colleague's voice that morning. New regrets to keep the old ones company.

'What the fuck were you thinking? I mean, a broken ankle?'

'Jesus, that was an accident, June.' Collins sipped his coffee. 'He made a go for me and I stamped down on his leg to stop him. I wanted to scare him, yeah, and try to get some answers, but it wasn't planned or anything. I didn't even know I was going over there until the last minute. *And* I was pissed off.'

'Yeah, well, I don't blame you for that.' She paused and put her cup carefully on its saucer. She picked up the croissant from the plate and put it back down.

'Collins, what happened to Kelly wasn't your fault.' She put her hand on his arm and tried to meet his eye. The light in the room had changed, the sunlight gone. 'You can't save them all, boy.'

He held his head rigid.

'Collins?'

He shook his head. He did not reply. What was the point?

'Anyway,' June said. She removed her hand. 'If Jonno gets a sniff of a newspaper, you're in the shit. He'll throw the book at you. Geary won't bail you out this time, either.'

Collins smiled ruefully.

'No, he won't.' He scratched the side of his head. 'I don't think Mick will take it further, when it comes to it. But I will get a good bollocking,' he said. 'Deserve it too, probably.'

She didn't disagree with him. They sipped their coffees. She ate her croissant. Collins watched a man at the corner of the bar nursing a sick-looking pint of lager. He shuddered and stood up.

'Might as well get it over with,' he said.

'I'm going in with you.'

'You are not.'

'I am.'

She went to the counter to pay. Collins walked past her, out the door of the café. A young waitress stood outside, smoking, and his longing for a cigarette was like a blow to the chest.

On the street, when June caught up with him, Collins laid out his case.

'June, I fucked up. I broke his ankle. And nobody is going to believe it was an accident, so that's on me. Not you. You didn't know the first thing about it. He won't let you in, anyway.'

'He has no choice. You're my partner.'

Collins smiled. The lioness.

'And slow down, will you? My back is killing me,' she said.

He reduced his pace.

'One question before we get there,' she said, grabbing him by the elbow.

'What?'

'What did he tell you?'

'Townsend?'

'Who the fuck else, Collins?'

Collins held up his hands. 'I'll tell you later.'

'You'll tell me now.'

'On the side of the street?'

'Yes, on the side of the street. Now.'

'Okay, okay,' he said, looking around. He had prepared this too.

'Three things really. One, there's a big shipment of coke coming in – he says he doesn't know how, but I think it's by boat. Two, Molloy has gotten into bed with the Keaveneys. We kind of knew that anyway, but it seems they can source the coke and Molloy can ship it in. I think the up-front money is theirs too – they'll probably take the bulk of it for Dublin. And three …' Collins stopped and turned around again. A businesswoman talking into a phone passed by. 'Something about a dentist,' he said, when she had gone from earshot.

'A dentist?'

'Yes. You know, somebody who fixes teeth.'

'I know what a dentist is, Collins, but what's that got to do with Molloy?'

'I don't know. I don't think Townsend knows either, but Molloy keeps joking about it. "The dentist will sort it all out. The dentist will make us all rich, boys,"' he said, mimicking Molloy's accent.

'A dentist?' she said.

'I know.'

What Collins told her wasn't as important as what he didn't say. To June. To his own partner. On that sunny August morning. On that busy street.

What he did not tell her was that he had a fair idea who that dentist might be. He would have to think about that one very carefully, and go after him alone, for now.

Especially in light of the other thing Townsend had told him. The other thing he had not shared with June.

Amid his muffled screams, Townsend told him that there was a source inside Anglesea Street. There was a garda tipping Molloy off, telling him about everything that happened in the station, everything they knew, everything they intended to do.

Collins believed him because he had suspected as much. Three times they had planned to move against Molloy and each time he was ready for them, expecting them. They thought they could pick apart his alibi for Jimmy Cummins's murder the previous year, but he had it fixed by the time they questioned him. They had turned one of his pushers, Johnny Cadogan, until – the following day, before Molloy should have known – Cadogan was admitted to the Mercy Hospital with severe burns and refused to talk. Every time they found out where Molloy's brothels were, they suddenly upped and were gone. It was all too much.

Collins didn't tell June because he couldn't trust her. He could trust nobody in the station.

5

Collins knocked and heard the 'enter'. He went through. He could see, even from across the room, the rage in Superintendent John O'Connell's face. He was not faking it just to make a point, as he sometimes did. He didn't even wait for Collins to sit down before he let fly.

'Don't you want to be in the force anymore?'

'Of course I do, Superintendent.'

'Well you've a funny way of showing it. Breaking his ankle? Jesus Christ, if anybody saw you. They all have camera phones now, Collins. It could be all over the *Examiner*. Every paper in the country. The Internet. A video? Can you *imagine* the damage?'

'I didn't mean it. He made a go for me.'

'"I didn't mean it. He made a go for me." Would you listen to yourself? He's about half your size, doped up most of the time. And another thing,' Jonno said, tapping a forefinger on the desk. 'Did you ever stop to think why Molloy sent that prick Townsend to watch *your* apartment? Did you ever think about that?'

'To goad me, or threaten me, I suppose. Or just to make a point – who knows with that scumbag?'

'Yeah, yeah,' Jonno said. 'But why Townsend? Why *him*, of all the little fuckers he has to hand?'

Collins went cold. A wave of realisation washed over him.

'Because of Kelly and Joe,' he said quietly.

'Exactly. Because you had a personal tie to that family. I was surprised you didn't have a go at him last year, when that poor misfortunate drowned herself. He was probably expecting that too.'

Collins remembered how close he'd come, what he had planned and almost carried out.

'It could have been a set-up, Collins, did you ever think of that? There could have been a camera on you the whole time. There *might* have been, for all you know. Did you check?'

Collins shuddered. He had not checked the van, nor even thought of the possibility. It could easily have been something Molloy would do.

'He likely wanted you to lash out, Collins, and attack Townsend. He played you, boy.'

Collins's mouth was dry. He tried to swallow, to generate some spit. He could feel his face redden. He'd underestimated Molloy. And Jonno too – a man doesn't get as high as him in the gardaí by being stupid.

'And you obliged him,' Jonno said. 'Although, in fairness, you covered your tracks well.' He read through the page at the top of the file on his desk.

Collins was silent. He was not used to feeling stupid.

'That's another thing, Collins. Redirecting those cameras.'

'I deny that, sir, I wasn't even in the station.'

'Collins, have a small bit of respect. We both know that there were ten people in the station last night who would have moved those cameras for you. Jesus, if it ever gets out.'

'Superintendent …'

'Shut up. Okay? Just shut the fuck up. You and your precious vendetta.' Jonno glowered at him. 'Like you're the only one who's trying to put him away. I've more men on that scumbag's case than anyone else since the IRA were on the go, and it's still not enough for you. Well it ends today and that's that. Right?'

Jonno slammed the palm of his hand on the desk. Then he sat

back and paused, making an effort to calm himself.

'Listen, I know you want to get the drugs off the streets. Jesus, we all do. We all do, Collins, it's a mess. But there is a place called stop. And this is it. And what am I going to do with Mick Murphy? Would you answer me that?' He held up the sheet of paper – Mick's complaint, obviously. 'I've never seen the man so angry. And some members will take his side too. God knows you've made enough enemies around here. Somebody could go to Chief Superintendent Geary, and if they do …' Jonno shook his head.

'I already apologised to Mick. I don't know why he is so upset to be honest. He'll come around, we go back a long way.'

'You stay away from him, do you hear me? I'll sort him. You're lucky he didn't go to the Ombudsman. And he will the next time, Collins, and then we're all in the shit.'

Jonno sat back in his chair. He scrutinised Collins.

'My father worshipped the ground you walked on. Did I ever tell you that?' Jonno sighed, as he often did when he thought of his father. ''95, when you scored that goal? Jesus, I don't think I ever saw him so happy.' Jonno's face softened for a moment. 'But I'll tell you this, and I'm telling you for the last time. You mess up again on my watch and I will throw the book at you. The fucking book. I'm sick of it. You won't bring down the reputation of the force in this district or this division, or *me*, just because you feel like it.'

Jonno closed the file and moved it to his left. He looked at his diary.

Collins said nothing. It was not the time.

'And if you're going down, you'll do it alone. D'you hear me? I guarantee you that, Collins. You'll be directing traffic on Achill, while I'm enjoying my retirement on the beach in Lanzarote. Now get out.' He picked up the phone on his desk and tapped some keys.

Collins rose and left the room.

He saluted the desk sergeant as he left the station.

'Quiet, Tom?'

'Naughty, naughty, Collins.'

6

Molloy strode back and forth from the window to the end of the counter in the small bar. The Brady brothers, Sean and Pat, and the giant Jim Corcoran were sitting at the table beside the back door. The main bar was still closed; it was early in the morning. Corcoran had his head bowed, as he sometimes did when he didn't want to engage – it made him appear as if he were asleep.

The three Poles: Tomasz Mazur, Alex and Alex's brother, Karol, were sitting erect at another table with the laptop in front of them, along with the mobile Wi-Fi device, the webcam and some cables.

Townsend, his leg in plaster and his crutches laid out before him, sat snivelling on his own. He was shaking slightly, he'd taken too many painkillers and his eyes were wavering and closing despite the furious tension emanating from Molloy.

'The one thing we told you,' Molloy said. 'The one fucking thing. Make sure the Wi-Fi is plugged in.'

'I …' Townsend tried to speak, but Molloy drowned him out.

'We had him! We had the cunt, lock, stock and barrel. Jesus fucking Christ!'

Molloy approached Townsend, his fists clenched, his face bulging red. 'What. The fuck. Happened?' he said, through gritted teeth.

'I didn't do nothing,' Townsend said. 'I didn't touch it. Them langers must have fucked it up.' He pointed to the Poles.

'It was working,' Mazur said quietly. 'We have video until you disconnected Wi-Fi at 1.28.'

'Show him,' Molloy said. Alex opened the laptop and pressed a key. The video came on. It showed Townsend sitting in the van, from behind, over his left shoulder. The time in the corner of the screen was 01:26. Townsend removed a packet of cigarettes from his pocket and took one out of the box. He tried to light it, but the lighter would not work. He shook it a few times and it sparked but did not flame. Townsend threw the errant lighter away and got up and turned to his right. He went out of picture for a moment and then the video went black. Nothing.

'You plugged out the fucking thing to light a fag,' Molloy said, his face inches from Townsend's. 'And you never put it back in.'

'I … I …' Townsend mumbled. 'I dunno.' He stared at the laptop screen, as if it were about to come back on and show the missing video. He shook his head. He blinked a few times.

'I dunno, Dom,' he said, making the mistake of looking up. Molloy pulled his head back a few inches and head-butted Townsend on his nose, producing a wet, fleshy sound. Townsend's head recoiled, blood spurting on the table and floor. He moaned dully, lay on his side, and pulled his hands up to his face.

Molloy leaned on the Formica bar counter.

'Give him something,' he said to the Bradys. 'He's making shit of that seat.'

Pat Brady pulled a worn tissue from his jacket pocket and gave it to Townsend, whose moaning seemed to be progressing into a whine, and who pressed the paper against his nose. It soaked up the blood almost immediately and began to drip.

Molloy gathered himself. He pulled over a stool and sat on it, his face only inches from that of Townsend.

'And what did you tell him?' he said, more quietly now.

Townsend mumbled into the tissue and then removed it. Blood

poured down his face, around his lips, giving him the frightful appearance of a cannibal.

'What you told me to say,' he said, and replaced the tissue under his nose.

'And that was?'

'That you were out of the game, that you'd sold up to the Keanes and were off to Canada with the money.'

'Right,' Molloy said. 'And what else?'

'Oh, that you were a legitimate businessman with, with, with – an online IT business now, with new partners from …'

'From where?' Molloy said.

'From …' Townsend looked at the Poles, as if for a hint. 'From Hungary,' he said, triumphantly.

'And what did he say?'

'He didn't say nothing. He only said he'd break my other leg if I told anyone.'

'And he broke your leg.'

'He did,' Townsend moaned. 'I'm bolloxed, like.'

'You are, you dopey cunt. You may be sure of it,' Molloy said. He nodded to the Bradys and Corcoran. 'Take this article home.'

Corcoran came over, all stooped. He bent down and put his left arm under Townsend's legs, his right under his back. Townsend recoiled. Corcoran picked him up, carried him to the door and stood there. Pat Brady opened the door and went out. Corcoran turned sideways and followed him. Sean Brady picked up the crutches and went out last. They were glad to get out of there. They were all glad that somebody else had fucked up and not them.

Molloy slammed the door after them. The three Poles sat impassively, their eyes downcast.

He reached across the counter and took out a glass and a bottle of whiskey. He half-filled the glass and took a large drink from it. He gasped and said, 'That's the kind of eejits I have to put up with.'

Mazur shook his head. 'I don't think he is so stupid as he pretends.'

'Oh, he's stupid alright,' Molloy said, taking another sip of whiskey. 'Thick as two planks.'

'I will watch him,' Mazur said.

'Never mind him, I want that bastard Collins off my back. I'm sick to death of his interfering, and all because of that stupid young one. I still owe him for putting Bobby away, too.'

'I have idea,' Mazur said. 'He goes to that café on Saturdays. I can get a waitress in there.'

'Go on,' Molloy said. He pulled a small bag of white powder from a pocket and sprinkled some on the counter. He chopped at it and pushed it into two lines with a credit card.

7

Collins walked out onto a busy, rain-swept Anglesea Street. He crossed the road, shoulders hunched against a squall. At an Asian restaurant, Ramen, nearby, he ordered the sweet chilli coconut and sat down. He needed to think, but not on an empty stomach. He took out his phone and made a call.

'Hi Rose, Collins here.'

Sergeant Rose O'Grady worked in Garda Headquarters in Dublin and had access to all the information it was legally permitted to know about everyone in Ireland. And some information it was not legal to know. She and Collins had shared a flat in Dublin, in Kimmage, for two years when he was a new recruit stationed at Store Street. Rose was a lesbian and had to keep it quiet in the force at the time. Collins had pretended to be her boyfriend at some events and a family wedding in Louth. They'd had fun that night making sex noises in a hotel room, jumping up and down on the bed and banging the headboard to shock her cousins in the adjoining room. Now she had a partner, Alice, and they had adopted a girl, Suzie.

'Hi Collins, heard you're in the shit again.'

'What? Already? Who told you?'

'Oh, I never divulge my sources, but come here, did you really break his leg in five places?'

'What? No, I did not. I think it's just a ligament or something. The fucker made a go for me and I thought he had a knife. He was staking out my apartment, for Christ's sake. I just kicked him, that's all. Jesus, the way things get legs around here. Don't tell me it's common knowledge in Dublin too.'

'No, no, I just heard this minute. Ha ha, "the way things get legs", I like that.'

'Hmm. Well, I'm actually looking for some information myself. On the QT but quickly. Would you have a few minutes?'

'Sure, fire away.'

'A dentist based in Cork by the name of Eric O'Donovan. Also stuck in property, owns a few apartment blocks, I hear. The full works if you can. Foreign assets especially.'

'He sounds familiar, isn't he …?'

'Yes, yes, his wife is the Minister's sister. She's a famous painter. I know, but this is important, Rose. I think there's a son too, maybe early twenties.'

'Jesus, it better be, Collins, and you heard nothing from me. They track the numbers of callers here you know.'

'Sure, sure, ring me back. How's Alice and Suzie?'

'They're fine, Suzie's in the Naíonra now, can you imagine?'

'Jesus, she's only two, Rose.'

'She'll be four in March, Collins, get with the programme.'

'Four? Seriously? Wow. I'll call up soon, I promise.'

'Yeah, right. Heard that before. Buzz you in twenty.'

8

Two hours later, Collins sat alone in an unmarked car outside two new, ugly and ostentatious houses in an exclusive estate in Douglas. He had told June he was going to visit his mother to cool down and she agreed it was best to stay away from the station, except when did his mother ever help him to cool down?

The two buildings were Celtic Tiger monstrosities, completely out of keeping with their conservative and old-school neighbours. The wooden exteriors, curved roofs and walls, bare concrete and glass made the houses appear unfinished and more like small avant-garde office blocks than homes. The *pièces des résistance* were five hook-like curved metal spikes that protruded from the roofs. Each house was the mirror image of the other. Collins stared at them in amazement, wondering how they had managed to get planning permission before remembering that the brother of both women in the houses was a government minister.

He checked his notes from Rose and walked to the nearer house. He pressed the buzzer and waited.

A fuzzy female voice. 'Hello, can I help you?'

Collins held up his badge to the camera.

'Miss Jameson? I'm Detective Garda Collins from Anglesea Street Garda Station and I'd like to talk to yourself or Mr O'Donovan about a security issue that has arisen.'

The intercom turned off and after a moment the gate began to slide open. It was strangely plain-looking in front of such a garish house. The front door was at the side of the building, another incongruity. A Porsche Cayenne was parked in the drive.

Collins stood before the peephole. He saw movement behind it. The door opened to reveal a thin, sharp-featured woman in painter's overalls. She looked in her thirties, but he knew she was forty-four. He knew a lot about her. Perhaps her short pink hair, with a rounded fringe, and the four hoops in her ear made her appear younger, but there was no escaping the spirit behind those eyes.

'You called me Miss Jameson. Everybody calls me Mrs O'Donovan. How did you know my real name?' she said.

Collins thought for a moment.

'One, I'm a detective. I detect. Two, I own one of your paintings. A small one from the *Pillow Sequence*.'

'You do? Really? On a guard's salary? Oh, is that rude?' She scrutinised him. 'But besides the cost of it, why?'

'Why did I buy it?' Collins paused. 'Well, I was left a lot of money some years ago and I decided to get something beautiful with it. And I see that painting every day, and I'm reminded every day that I did the right thing. So …' He shrugged.

'Wow. I'm sorry, but I didn't expect that from a guard. Oops, rude again. Stereotyping. You better come in. I'm intrigued. Collins? Do you have a first name?'

'Collins is fine. And is it Susan?'

Her eyebrows arched. '*You* can call me Sue. Today, at least.' She glanced out the door as he passed her into the hall. 'Are you on your own?'

'All alone,' Collins said, soaking up the décor.

The inside of the house was more impressive and tasteful than the outside. Warmer, with a huge, centrally set rug in the hall, and soft pastel-like paint on the high-ceilinged walls. As they passed the living-room door, Collins did a double take. Two large Le Brocquy paintings hung above a sideboard.

She saw him gape.

'What do you think?' she said, smirking.

'Le Brocquy.'

'Yes. Come in. Take a closer look. The light is awful but still. Are you really a guard?'

'Yes, of course.'

She led him into the large room. She smelled of paint and peaches. Her loose canvas shoes flapped when she walked. She wore no socks. He noticed a splash of teal on her ankle. It was the colour for which she was famous. The colour that lit up one little corner of his home. How could a painter get paint on her ankle?

'But what do you *do*?' she asked, genuinely puzzled.

Collins hesitated, distracted. 'I told you: I'm a guard.'

He had been taken aback by the huge Shinnors painting behind the door; its vast scale dominated the room. White swathes rising out of darkness, a red slash, shocking, like arterial spray. He found it difficult to take his eyes from it.

He moved away from the large canvas to take it in.

'Shinnors,' he murmured. 'It's big.'

'In more ways than one,' she said. 'The emotion is too much, sometimes. If anything. His work is too much. All about emotion. Not enough about colour, light and shade.'

'That red is colour enough for me,' Collins said. 'Hard to look at it, or not to look at it.'

'It's not so much the red. It's what it means,' she replied. 'It's too much. But as you said. Every day it shows me what's possible. With paint and canvas. Will you have a coffee?' She moved into the kitchen.

'Yes, please,' the standard policeman's answer, buying time and a cosier environment. Collins scanned the room for photographs, but there were none. Not one. He noticed her strange, staccato way of speaking, but he'd leave thinking about that until later.

'Is this a Turner?' he said, raising his voice, looking at the small vivid yellow depiction of a sunset over water in an ornate gilt frame. It was all a bit off-putting, and he tried to concentrate on the job in hand.

'Yes. Not great, to be honest. But nice to be able to think that paint he actually touched is in this house.'

Collins went through as she spoke.

The kitchen was full of light, admitted by two tall, south-facing glass walls. Outside, a hedge, some grass, a deck. Bright plastic chairs. Three bins to one side, surrounded tastefully by a wooden fence. The three sentries to the modern Irish home.

Again he looked around for photos. But they were not there.

Why no pictures of a precious son? Smiling on a beach, chubby, shovel in hand; riding a new Christmas bike; a Holy Communion with proud, handsome, young parents, still full of hopes and dreams for his future.

Might as well get this done, Collins thought.

'Can I use your toilet?' he said.

'Sure, first on the left in the hall there.'

Once in the bathroom, Collins quickly removed the top of the toilet bowl cistern and placed it with care on the seat. He took a screwdriver out of his pocket and began to loosen a rubber seal at the bottom of the cistern. In moments, the seal had been eased free and a steady trickle of water was flowing onto the tiled floor.

'Looks like you have a leak in there,' he said as he re-entered the kitchen.

'Shit. Really?' She passed him to see.

'It's the cistern,' Collins said. 'It should stop when it's empty, as long as we can tie up the ballcock. Do you have some twine or a coat hanger?'

'Shit. Shit shit shit. And I'm right in the middle of a sketch.'

Collins tied up the ballcock while Susan mopped up the water. While she was phoning her husband to arrange a plumber, he asked if he could use the bathroom upstairs. She nodded.

He stuck his head into the first room at the top of the stairs. A bedroom, airy and bright, with a double bed, a bookshelf, a desk and chair, a large wardrobe. He opened the wardrobe: men's clothes. The son's room. He was tempted to look at the books, but no time.

The next room was the bathroom. The door of the room after that was slightly ajar. He pushed it open quickly to prevent a squeak. Inside, a mess: papers, sketches, canvases and books strewn over the floor and an old dark desk.

He searched for a document holder, a set of folders, or filing cabinet. None. He tried the drawers in the desk, from the bottom up. Nothing. There was a MacBook Pro on the desk. He opened it and it lit up, no password required. The stupidity of people when it came to their computers and phones never ceased to amaze him. No respect for information. He closed the computer again.

He went into the bathroom, locked the door and raised the Venetian blinds in front of the window. He opened the window half an inch. Hega had been specific about which window he would enter from, because it wasn't visible from any neighbouring houses and the single-storey kitchen roof beneath would give him access.

Hega – Philip Hegarty – owed Collins for keeping him out of Cork prison on more than one occasion and Collins called in a favour every now and then to remind him. Hega was working more or less full time for his father these days, repairing electrical goods. More or less – Collins suspected an illicit sideline or two, but he didn't want to know.

He flushed the toilet, washed and dried his hands and went back downstairs.

Susan had made the coffee for him but none for herself. She wanted him gone. Fine by him.

'You mentioned a security issue. What issue?' she asked, as he drank half the coffee in one gulp. He looked her in the eye. Always best when lying.

'Oh, it's about the car that was seen outside your house a few months ago. The person in it was known to us. He has … associations with serious crime.'

'Yes, I remember that. Has something happened?'

'Not really, but we just wanted to follow up on it. Have you or your husband noticed anything unusual since? Any other people hanging around, or any strange contact lately?'

'No, nothing. I don't think so, anyway. Eric didn't mention anything either and he would have. You lot thought he was staking out the houses, or something like that.'

'Yes, it was probably nothing. These people turn up from time to time, but we just wanted to follow up and reiterate that if you do notice anything, however small, to get in touch. This person is of interest to us.'

'Right,' she said. 'Do you have a direct number?'

'Sure, I'll text you and you'll have it. What's your number?'

She gave him the number and he texted her the word 'Collins'. He did not hear a beep. He guessed she painted in the adjoining garage-type building and would like to have seen the space. Not that it mattered; he had what he wanted.

They shook hands formally at the front door. As he walked away, he phoned Hega.

'It's open now. I think she'll go back to the garage on the southern side of the building, but be careful.'

'I see it. There's an alarm system, was it on?'

'No, fairly sure it wasn't on earlier, but I've just warned her about security so be careful. And there might be a plumber on the way. There are files and a laptop in the room to the right of the bathroom, probably your best bet.'

'Okay,' Hega said and hung up.

Collins stood outside the electronic gate as it slid shut behind him with a rattle. He looked around the leafy spacious surrounds of the homes in the park. It struck him that the neighbourhood was dreary and tired.

He had gone out with an art student when he was in college. It was through her that he first became interested in art. K. D. – a wild and scattered thing. She would come up with a hundred ideas in a minute and have forgotten all of them a minute later. He could no more have held on to her than he could have held his hand in a fire. But if she had kept him on, what and where would he be now? In what kind of life? Not a guard in Cork, that was for sure.

K. D. ended up with another sculptor in Dublin, an alcoholic abuser. It took her twenty years, a broken heart and several broken bones to leave him. Collins shook his head at the memory of her diffuse power.

He thought of another life that might have been his, too, in different circumstances. Among the Douglas elite, born to rule and control. A life full of entitlement and ease; with confidence in the future, assurance that this was the way it was meant to be.

No, he thought. Whatever about being with an artist, that was definitely not him.

9

Collins walked home from the station after returning the car. He left the building immediately, out the back, making sure to avoid Mick Murphy. The light was fading, and the lowering sun brought brilliant crimsons and auburns out of the clouds in the west, as it often does in Cork. He bought food for dinner in Marks and Spencer and went to The Bierhaus pub on Pope's Quay, across the river from his apartment. He ordered a pint of red ale, brewed in Templemore, for old time's sake. Templemore, that grey old English-looking Tipperary town where he had trained as a garda all those years before. He remembered his mother's pride and his father's unease on the day of the passing out ceremony. His own detachment, even on that day.

He sat on the barstool at the end of the counter, back to the wall, the favoured seat in any pub, and checked his phone. There was an email with an attachment, just arrived from one of the accounts that Hega used. How could he have found something that quickly?

The document was long and written in formal medical language. It outlined, in great detail, the paedophilic ideations of one Shane Eric O'Donovan, date of birth 21 May 1995, and the long-term treatment he was undergoing in a specialist in-house unit in Co. Kildare.

Rose had unearthed some shadows of rumours in a file about a hushed-up incident when Shane was seventeen in a playground in Ballinlough. She had given Collins the names of two clinics that specialise in paedophile treatment programmes.

He phoned Hega.

'Got that, thanks. Did you copy the whole drive?'

'Yeah, like you said.'

'Can you get that to me? I want to check for some other stuff too.'

'Sure thing, Collins. Over and out.'

Collins smiled. Hega liked to think he was a spy or something, but Collins was wary of providing him with access to such information. He'd have to give Hega a good warning when he saw him.

A drunk approached him at the bar. Tony Counihan, an old parishioner of his from Togher, off drugs now, but rarely sober. The barman had gone to change a barrel; otherwise he would never have gotten past the door.

'Collins? Collins, sub us a pint would ya? I'm dying here, man.' His voice was as rough as grit. He had a cut just above his left eye that was going septic.

Collins took a five-euro note from his wallet and held it out. He glared at him and said, 'Get out, Gandhi.'

This was the drunk's nickname since he had been a young hurler – he had never taken the non-violent option during a game. Collins always thought: *There but for the grace of God.*

Gandhi grabbed the note.

'Thanks, man. Any fags?'

Collins really glared at him and Gandhi got the message, turned tail and, failing to see any unattended drinks on tables, shuffled out the pub door. At the word 'fags', Collins felt the familiar itch in his fingers, the shift in his heartbeat. Some young men had been smoking outside the pub as he entered. He thumbed the condensation on his pint glass.

The report on his phone confirmed his suspicions. Three months previously Sean Brady had been seen sitting in a car watching the house that he had just visited. Brady never did anything without Molloy's go-ahead. Collins was sure now that O'Donovan was the dentist mentioned by Townsend. Molloy must have gotten some proof that Shane was a paedophile and blackmailed the father with it. He may have set up a sting with an underage girl or boy in one of Tommy Tan's brothels. But Collins did not have any proof – and knowing was not the same as proving. He needed to talk to Shane and get an admission from him. That would not be a problem now that he knew where he was.

But he couldn't use the information yet, at least not formally. Especially with a traitor in the station.

He went back to his apartment and checked his watch. Violette would arrive soon, not that she was ever on time.

He'd begun dating Violette after meeting her at a lecture about the history of film in Cork at the Triskel Arts Centre in May. She was in her early forties, recently separated from a husband she hinted had been doing the dirt on her. So she said, anyway. She didn't give any more details and he didn't ask. There were no children, as far as he knew.

She was small and very French, with a temper like a whirlwind, which he had only witnessed once when a waiter had 'disrespected' her. She rolled her own cigarettes, and he liked to watch her make them and to smell the smoke when she exhaled. She was messy and never cleaned up after herself, which drove him crazy.

She had ostensibly come to Ireland to do research in UCC for a PhD on ethics. But Collins wondered if it was to get away from Paris, make a new start and have an adventure. Nothing serious or permanent, for sure. So it suited them both.

He went to the small, dark, painting in the corner of the living room. He stood before it, savouring its lush surface.

While preparing the food for dinner, Collins thought about the weekend ahead. It was going to be a good one, he could just feel it.

Liverpool were playing Everton in the Merseyside derby on the following day. He was all set to watch it with Christy and Paulo in the back bar of The Harp. This year Liverpool were definitely going to make the Champions League.

Dinner and probably sex tonight. A nice lazy morning, reading the paper over brunch in The Tavern the following day, followed by the match and few pints. Maybe a walk on Sunday.

It was going to be better than good; it was going to be a bloody great weekend.

10

Kyle Buckley, aged fourteen, sidled up to the counter of Tony Mulcahy Meat Providers in the English Market. He was hot after running down Tarrant Road, then Shandon Street and along the Coal Quay to the Grand Parade, but hardly puffing at all. He was really fit, and he loved his new Nikes. Even though it was Saturday, the market wasn't busy – usually there was a load of people before him in the queue.

He stood impatiently, shuffling from foot to foot as an elderly woman with bright purple hair recounted the horror of her chilblains to the butcher.

'Epsom salts, Mrs O'Mahony,' Tony said. 'My mam swore by the Epsom salts.' He glanced at Kyle and winked.

'Oh I know, Tony, but they're desperate dear.'

'Do you know where you'll get them cheap?' Tony said. 'That Nigerian shop on North Main Street, near the bridge.'

'Oh God, I couldn't be going in there,' Mrs O'Mahony said, affronted. She turned, pulling her little message trolley behind her, and shambled away.

'How's the going, Kyle?' Tony said, showing an array of crooked teeth. 'How're them bitches of yours, hah?'

'Grand, thanks,' Kyle said. 'Have you a few spare bones?'

'Oh, we do, we do. Seanie, get some bones for the young fella there, will ya? In the back fridge – the good ones.' He leaned on the glass counter, his rosacea-scarred nose shining in the fluorescent light. He grew serious and lifted his two fists to his face.

'Come here, boy? Are you keeping your guard up?'

'I am,' said Kyle. 'I've training Tuesdays and Thursdays.'

'Did you run down like I told you?'

'I did, I've new runners. Nike.' He showed them off, they were bright blue.

'Oh, sound,' Tony said. He handed over the red-and-blue-striped bag of bones and bits of meat. 'Wait, I'll double bag that for you. And here's a few chops for later. How's your mam?'

'She's fine,' Kyle said and lowered his head. His shuffling intensified.

'Mind yourself, Kyle,' Tony said and turned to a customer, a small Asian woman with a headscarf. Kyle jogged away out the door of the market. Tony glanced after him and shook his head sadly.

Kyle reckoned he could run home in a new best time if he took it handy until the top of the last hill and then sprinted from the bookies all the way to the gate. He set the timer on his phone and took a good hold of the bag of meat.

11

Collins wandered through the farmers' market in Cornmarket Street, a regular Saturday amble.

He strolled over to the window of McCarthy's iconic clothes shop. He recalled the day he went through that door, aged thirteen, to buy his first Doc Martens; putting his old shoes into the box and walking out the door a new man, flaunting a pair of eight-eye oxblood beauties – a defiant announcement to the world. Or so he thought at the time.

He looked at the range of boots now in the window and was amazed. A middle-aged man passed behind him. Collins glanced back, making eye contact. Mistake. He knew him from somewhere. A hurling club, he thought, in the city. St Finbarr's. The man turned around and made a beeline for him. No escape.

'How's the going, Collins? How's tricks?'

'Hi, how are you? How are they all in the Barrs?' Collins replied.

''Yerra, all right boy, all right. Shocking bad hurling team again this year, but the Minors weren't too bad, like. The footballers are going well, though.'

'Micky Hal still involved? I haven't seen him for a while.'

'Micky Hal? Micky Hal? No, boy, we don't see Micky no more. I dunno, I think he's out in Carrigaline or somewhere. Jesus, the two of ye had some battles, hah? The county final in '91? Fuck me, I thought ye were going to run out of ash to break off each other.'

'Ah, Micky is sound. We always left it on the pitch.'

'Come here, the Cork Seniors could do with someone like you

now, Collins? A bit of steel? They're gone fierce soft altogether, hah?'

'Ah it's different times, too. You can't do the kind of stuff we used to do anymore. With all the cameras and the CCCC, you can't get away with anything, these days.'

'Yeah, yeah, but they're fierce soft. They give up, Collins. They give up too easy altogether. I dunno, boy.' He shook his head.

Collins would bet he'd never pucked a ball in his life, nor faced down a man swinging a hurley at him.

'Different times, Teddy, different times. Mind yourself.' Collins had remembered the man's name, and made to move away on the strength of it.

'But come here, Collins. One question. One question. I have to ask it. We were talking about the '97 All-Ireland the other night in the pub …'

Collins tensed, then bristled. That fucking question.

'See you, Teddy. Tell Micky Hal I was asking for him.' He moved away towards a food stall.

The thin young woman behind the stall, with the obligatory nose ring, wearing colourful hippy clothes and an extravagantly concocted woollen headpiece, railed against the fluoride in water and the additives in processed supermarket food. Collins blinked, trying to keep up with her, as she denounced in rapid succession: artificial sweeteners, genetically modified food, monosodium glutamate, food dyes, additives, pesticides and trans fats. He smiled and sidled away.

He noticed Kyle Buckley jogging towards him in the morning sun. Kyle Buckley, younger brother of Dinny Buckley, murdered by Molloy when he was only twenty-two. Dinny had been stupid and greedy, as addicts usually are, and one miserable March night, he made the last mistake of his life. He snorted the cocaine he was supposed to sell and then he lied about it.

Dinny told Molloy that he had been jumped by a couple of local thugs and his stash stolen. Before the day was out he was eagerly admitting everything and he no doubt ended his miserable life begging for mercy and forgiveness. Neither of which Molloy possessed.

Dinny was dead and buried in a bog or forest somewhere, and was mourned every day by his mother, Jacqueline, who had doted on him. She mostly did her mourning in the Soldier's Rest when she had the money – a dreary, dirty pub around the corner from her house.

Dinny was no longer mourned by his sister Jackie, a prostitute and heroin addict – she was too busy making the money to get herself high. Collins had never met anyone with such single-mindedness and dedication. She looked forward only, never backwards. He knew that she sometimes put money aside for Kyle. Collins wasn't sure why he kept an eye out for the Buckleys more than other families – maybe because Kyle could still go either way. Or maybe because he reminded Collins of himself at that age.

'Hello, Kyle,' Collins said kindly.

Kyle recoiled when he recognised him.

'Oh, eh, hi.' He looked around in the hope that somebody could save him.

'A few bones for the dogs?'

'Eh, yeah, I have to go and feed them.' He made to move, but Collins put a hand on his shoulder.

'Have you two or three now? I forget.'

'Four now, I got a new bull terrier bitch off me uncle.'

'Going to breed off her?'

'Yeah, there's a good dog over in Farranree I can get fairly cheap when she's old enough. She has to be a year old before I can register her.'

He pronounced the word 'register' emphasising the second vowel – a likeable habit of Cork city people.

'How's the boxing going?' Collins said. 'I heard you have a handy left hook.'

Kyle grew an inch taller.

'I won the Under–14s in July in the Lough,' he said.

'Did you? Nice one. You should keep it going so. And how's your mam, Kyle? I heard she was in hospital.'

'She's out now, she's grand, like. I have to go.'

'And Jackie?'

'I … I dunno. I dunno nothing about her.' Kyle looked up boldly and Collins was glad to see it. He hoped that Kyle would be as defiant when the lure of the high came calling, which it definitely would – if it hadn't already.

'That's okay, Kyle, I'm just wondering how's she's doing, I haven't seen her for a while. Will you tell her and your mam I was asking for them?'

Kyle nodded and darted away towards Shandon Bridge. Collins wondered what his own life would have been like without his older brother, Paul. Maybe Kyle was better off. Dinny had been a foul and violent thug and would not have hesitated to draw the boy into his grimy dope dealings. But if Dinny were still alive, Jacqueline might be in a state to protect Kyle. She had failed Jackie and she was failing Kyle now.

Collins did not give the boy much of a chance, notwithstanding his defiance and his dogs and his boxing.

The sign at the food stall said, 'Mushrooms fresh from the Ballyhoura Mountains'. Even though he had been raised on a farm Collins had never seen some of the fungi and quizzed the stallholder.

'Hi, what's this one?' he asked, pointing to some of an interesting chestnut colour.

'Those are Bay Bolete,' the stallholder replied with an East European accent. Latvian, maybe. He was muscular and round-faced, with a sharp intelligence in his eyes. 'Wild mushroom, very good.'

'Ah,' Collins said. 'I see. A bit early, isn't it? In August?'

'It was a wet summer,' the stallholder said. 'These are an early species.'

'Okay. Give me one hundred grams. Can I just fry them or put them in an omelette?'

'Yes, of course. Very good to fry with garlic. Or with risotto. Or you can make soup. Many things.'

'They won't poison me?' Collins joked.

'No no, for sure. These ones very safe, very nice. I promise.'

'Okay, I'm only joking, I'm sure they will be great.'

'Collins?' A gentle voice behind him asked, and he turned.

Deirdre's cheeks glowed and the bump underneath her woollen coat put her at seven or eight months pregnant. She wore a knitted, bobbled green and white hat and Collins could hear the clicking of her needles in front of the fire, her feet tucked up underneath her.

'Deirdre,' he almost whispered, rigid with memories.

'Hello, Collins. It's nice to see you.'

'And you. And this is …?' he asked, bending and smiling to the boy of four or five who clutched his mother's hand. He had a solemn expression and a darker version of his mother's eyes.

'This is Jack. Say hello to Collins, Jack.'

'Hello,' a faint voice complied.

'Hello, Jack. Will you shake hands? Even though I'm a Liverpool fan and I don't know if I should shake hands with an Arsenal supporter.' Collins smiled, glancing to the boy's bright red Gunners hat.

The boy reluctantly withdrew his hand from his mother's and put it carefully into the long-boned and gnarled paw extended to him. Collins gently gripped it and formally shook it up and down three times, before letting it go, smiling all the time. The boy immediately regripped his mother's hand and pressed himself further into her coat.

'Jack, Collins won three All-Irelands with Cork. He was a great hurler, and he played with your Uncle Dermot.'

The boy's eyes widened.

'Did ... did ye beat Kilkenny?' Jack ventured, emboldened by this momentous news.

'We did, Jack. And will I tell you a secret?' Collins looked left and right, as though watching out for an interloper. He leaned forward and whispered: 'It's a *very hard* thing to do.' He put on his most serious face to emphasise the point.

He smiled at Deirdre, his heart racing. Her face was a little plumper with the extra weight. But her skin ...

'And Jack is going to have some company soon, I see.'

She laughed, and Collins remembered how that laugh had once lit up his young world.

'Yes, in six weeks or so, all going well.'

'And all is well? You're well, Deirdre? You haven't aged a day.'

'Very well.' She smiled. 'Thank you. This little man keeps me busy, don't you, buster?' She shook the boy's arm.

'How's Richard?' Collins ventured, more because he should than because he cared.

'He's fine. Busy as ever on the farm. And you? I saw your name all over the paper last year. What a horrible thing, I don't know how you did it.'

'Oh well. Somebody had to, I guess.'

'Yes, but …' She stopped herself. 'Well, we better be going. How's your mam?'

'She's good, Deirdre, thanks. Yeah, Mam's fine, same as ever.'

'Tell her I was asking for her.'

'I will, of course.'

Collins kissed her cheek. She patted his arm.

'Take care, Collins,' she said as she turned and walked away.

He blurted: 'Good luck … with everything.'

Jack looked back to examine Collins one last time. Deirdre kept walking.

12

Tomasz Mazur kept his distance. He knew how to do this. He'd perfected it long ago.

There were lots of people, the market stalls gave him good cover, and he could keep one eye on Collins and the other pretending to be interested in the wares on display. His earphones meant that people thought he was listening to music and they didn't engage.

He stayed patient. He was confident. If he lost Collins, he knew that he would find him again. The easiest way to be spotted was to panic, to get jittery, to chase the quarry and get too close. Tomasz Mazur did not get jittery.

In the Gymnasium they gave him the nickname *Lodziarz* because he was never fazed, he never lost his cool, even at that young age. Papa used to test him, sneaking up behind him and clapping his hands, or telling him a terrible story such as everybody on the street had died from gas, or there was a new war with Germany. In the end, before Mazur went off to *Wojsko Polskie*, to the army, on his eighteenth birthday, it had become their game. But Papa was weak, he let Mama tell him what to do, and he worked for his own brother instead of being the boss. And now Papa was dead to him, or he was dead to Papa, which was the same thing.

His face had gone against him in the WP; the queers wanted him and the straights wanted to scar him or break his nose. He had to learn the hard way to defend himself. He had to cut some of them, which he did. Until that stupid *podporucznik* went and bled out and there was hell to pay, and he was discharged. But it was worth it to see the look on the faggot's face when the knife went in, that sweet stare of shock, of disbelief. By then he'd done his tours of duty, he'd seen it many times. He'd learned how to use his 1996 Beryl, he'd learned how to kill, and he'd wiped out at least a dozen Iraqis and fifteen Afghan towelheads.

Mazur was never going up the ranks, anyway; his accent and his lack of friends among the officers would have seen to that.

But he'd made other friends, who had been more than helpful when his tours ended. That private job in Iraq, outside Mosul, was a kind of heaven. What a buzz, what fun, and €500 per day. He'd have paid *them* to 'question' the prisoners, not the other way around. That American slob, Chad, had been squeamish at first, until he realised how much information Mazur could extract from them. With a price tag of $10,000 per jihadi, he wasn't so squeamish then, was he?

But that all ended too, when the Americans went home. He was on the wrong side of the turf war at home in Lublin, and he didn't have any contacts in London, so Ireland would have to do. And Cork would have to do – for now.

Collins was talking to a pregnant woman and a boy. He bent down to the boy to shake hands. Collins was weak; men don't bend down for anyone. They said he was tough, but he was soft, and today Mazur would watch him die. Collins had been lucky the webcam did not work, with that stupid druggie plugging it out. He could not be lucky every time.

Mazur smiled. He could not wait to get out of this shithole to Spain. Spain would be good, lots of fun. Lots of Romanians and Moldovans and Chechens. African refugees. Undocumented losers, nobody to come looking for them. He liked the women best, the way they squealed. He began to fantasise about the pregnant woman Collins had been talking to. He'd love to do a pregnant one, to hear her beg for her baby. He could feel his cock stiffen, but then Collins came closer, so he forgot about her and moved away.

Collins went into the café and Mazur took his phone from his pocket.

'He is gone into café, I follow now.'

'Right,' Molloy said. 'Is your woman in place?'

'Yes, they gave her job last week. She works every day.'

'Does she know what to do?'

'Yes, I train her. She knows.'

'Okay, let me know when it's done,' Molloy said and hung up.

Mazur approached the café and opened the big door. He was met by a blaze of noise and heat. He looked around, as though for a free table. He didn't want to sit too close to Collins, but he did want a good view. He could see Katarzyna approach Collins and take his order. She seemed nervous. She had better do it right, or she would suffer.

He sat at an empty table about four metres from Collins. It was not close enough for witnesses to notice him; he was just another person in a café.

He smiled. This was going to be good.

13

Collins liked The Tavern, especially at weekends. Its high ceiling and its brightness and the buzz of conversation. He thought of it as a haven, full of confident young people from all over the world, speaking so many different languages. At the junction of Cornmarket Street and Kyrl's Quay it was just around the corner from his apartment, and he usually brought the newspaper there on Saturday mornings.

He had wandered into the café in a stupor after meeting Deirdre, thinking hard about their break-up. Thinking about his loss and the gain of Richard Cahill, a dairy farmer with more than five hundred acres outside Fermoy. Thinking about how he had not fought to keep her and why.

He recalled their last fraught night together, almost ten years ago now, when she cried and raged at him, their anguished greedy sex, both knowing it would be their last time.

'It's all gone now,' she had said, after she stopped crying and came down the stairs; looking, one last time, around the house in Ophelia Place that they had shared for three years, her bags at her feet by the front door. Leaving on that miserable Sunday morning, to go home to her parents. To never come back.

'All our time here. Everything. Is it all gone, Collins? Is it really over?'

She had gazed at him imploringly that day, willing him to say 'no', to say 'stay'.

'You're the one leaving,' he had replied.

It is all gone, he remembered thinking, after she closed the door.

Now there's only me.

He had wanted to put it down to how he reacted to his last injury and the end to his hurling, which happened a few months before they broke up. An end to the glory and the high of being a player, being the whole man. But it wasn't that either; it was something else, something rotten inside him that he had to wrap up tight and stamp down deep.

He had gone to a pub that day, then another one. Two weeks later, his old boss, Quirke, found him and dragged him out of the Mountain Dew, sobered him up, told him some home truths, and brought him back to work in the Bridewell Garda Station. Like a whipped dog, Collins had taken it and returned to the pack.

A waitress took his order of strong black coffee and the Tavern brunch. She appeared drained, her pen shaking as she wrote on her small notebook. She brought the coffee, holding it with two hands, almost spilling it.

He took a sip of the coffee. It tasted bitter. He smelled it, and caught a hint of chemicals. There was a buzzing in his head. He looked around for the waitress, to order a replacement.

A strikingly handsome young man a few tables away was staring at him, unabashedly, and smiling. Or was he? No, he was.

He was more beautiful than handsome, fine-boned and dark-eyed. Collins had never seen him before but immediately recalled something June had told him a few weeks earlier.

'Molloy has some new "helper" apparently,' she had said as they were driving down Horgan's Quay. 'A total babe, Collins, you'd want to see this fella. Polish. Could be a model no problem; talk about hot. A bit mad, Jackie Buckley said.'

Collins stared back at the man, his vision blurring. Something was wrong. He couldn't breathe and his heart was hammering in his chest. He saw the man take a phone out of his pocket, bring it to his ear. He was still looking at him, grinning.

Collins made to rise but flopped back down into his chair. He tried to shout, but no sound came out. Something was wrong with his breathing, there was no air. The table, the table was in his way. The door, he had to get to the door and escape. If he got outside, he'd be safe.

He put his hands under the table and with one absolute effort he turned it over. Then he fell to the ground beside it.

His cheek was pressed to the tile floor. There was liquid nearby, a puddle of it, moving away from him.

There was chewing gum on the underside of the table. Three pieces. And writing. He tried to read it.

Someone shouted, a woman screamed. People began to crowd around him, talking. He tried to make out the numbers written on the table's underside. There were letters too. An M, he could see that. And a P, a long slash but back to front, a 4 and a 5 – a 5 for sure – and the last one was a 6 or maybe a zero. Or maybe an O. It seemed important for him to know what it was. Somebody was tapping his cheek, a heavy-set young man. Collins could see his face, his mouth moving. He heard the words 'heart' and 'ambulance' but only faintly.

Only faintly because Collins was back on the family farm again, back home. On a warm glowing day, a day full of the abundance of summer. The yard was spotless; he must have cleaned it. Even his father said he cleaned the yard the best – *'tis shining, boy*. His mother's flowers vivid on the windowsills and by the gate, and the low sweep of the house martins and the high *cheep* of the barn swallows all the day long. And the grass lush behind the barn and the buzzing of insects in the fields. And the slow pendulum swing of the cows' udders when he brought them in through the dew for morning milking, the air cool and fresh. And the sweet taste of cold water from the hose.

He was fifteen, and, with the exhortation of Joseph Conrad, whose books Brother Thomas loaned him, he had learned to hope and love and put his trust in life.

And so, with hope and love and trust in life, he ran. And he ran. And he ran. He ran *ar nós na gaoithe*, as his father would have put it. The grass was not deep here; it did not constrict his legs. He ran through the Back Field beside the road to Ballydavid, along by the low ditch, and his father drove the tractor on the road. Collins raced him. Eddie Power, the farm worker, stood up in the trailer and made a mock commentary.

'We have you now, Timmy, here's the ditch. We have you now, boy.'

But they didn't have him because he had taught himself to jump onto the concrete water tank and propel himself off it over the ditch behind. And the ground was firm around it, and he didn't have to slow down. So, jump he did, over the tank and its scummy water and over the gorse-filled ditch and its smell of coconut, and over the hawthorn and the electric fence, and the green grass and the green fields and the farm like a crocheted blanket and all the land of the bright earth lit up with life. Up into the blue sky, and up and up and up he jumped. He flew.

Blackness.

PART 2

20 AUGUST 2016

14

'Who's got the smartest daddy?' Molloy said, holding Luke's chubby hands out, as the toddler negotiated unsteady steps through the deep living-room rug.

Mary Brady, Molloy's partner and Luke's mother, watched, smiling. Luke had his determined face on, the one that Dom liked so much and, if Molloy was happy, everyone was happy. She relaxed and smiled a thin smile.

'Who got rid of that bold man?' Molloy said, sweetly. 'Hmm?'

Luke took another step.

'Ah,' Luke said.

'That's right,' Dom said. 'Say Daddy. Say Dad-ee.'

Molloy turned to Mary and she smiled back. She'd never seen Dom so happy, sober. She had bided her time as he discarded one pretty young thing after another, until he realised that what he wanted was somebody long-term whom he could trust. She wasn't stupid enough to think that he didn't have sex with other women, but he knew, too, that she provided him with the stability he needed. Getting pregnant was a godsend – he was tied in now – though she'd made sure to get her shape back after the birth, going to Pilates and Zumba classes three times a week.

She had to drag those two feckless brothers of hers up out of the poverty they'd been steeped in. That useless so-called father was long gone, her poor mam dead from cancer these eight years. Sean and Pat were serious players now, Dom's right-hand men. No more selling drugs on the street. No more prison, either, if they stayed smart and disciplined, and she was determined to make sure that they would. No going back now. No way.

Molloy picked up the child, who whinged until he was passed to his mother. Mary laid him in her lap and snuggled kisses on his neck, tickling him.

'Sky's the limit now, girl, with him out of the way,' Molloy said, sitting in the armchair by the fire and picking up the glass of whiskey. 'Ye'll love Spain. Luke can paddle in the sun – no more miserable cold and rain.'

Mary worried about Spain. Luke was so fair – he could burn easily with all that sunshine. She'd have to watch him like a hawk.

'Oh, I got something for you,' Molloy said and gave her a small box with silver wrapping paper and a white ribbon.

'What is it?' she said, taking it. Luke stretched out a pudgy hand and she pushed it away.

'Open it and see,' Dom said, pleased with himself.

She untied the ribbon and opened the paper. A small black box with the Brown Thomas logo.

'Is it a voucher?' she said. She gave Luke the paper and the ribbon, which he tried to put into his mouth.

'It is,' Dom said. 'Have a look how much.'

She lifted the card from the box and read the receipt underneath it.

'Ten thousand?' she said, her eyes wide.

'Yeah,' he said. 'All for you, girl. Buy some nice outfits for Spain. But don't say nothing to the lads.'

'Oh, sweet Jesus,' she said. 'Thanks, Dom.' She stood, Luke still in her arms, and kissed him.

'Mind him,' Dom said, pointing his glass at Luke.

She readjusted the toddler and re-read the card. She could get anything she wanted with that kind of money. Anything. And them snobby shop-assistant bitches wouldn't be looking down their noses at her then, would they? They fucking would not. She rocked Luke up and down in her arms, humming, as though dancing with him around the room.

The doorbell rang and Molloy stood up.

'That's the Poles now. You stay here, I'll talk to them in the kitchen.'

In the kitchen Alex stood back and let Mazur do all the talking. The whole thing had been his idea.

'Wait. You're saying he isn't dead?' Molloy said, pointing at Mazur.

'We don't know for sure. Karol is at hospital, trying to find out.'

'You said that stuff was guaranteed.'

'Yes, yes, that's what they told me.'

Molloy walked back and forth, kneading his hands together, trying to think.

'Are you sure they can't hear us?' he said.

Alex took his phone from an inside pocket.

'Yes,' he said. 'Sonar blocker is working fine, they cannot hear.'

Molloy glared at Mazur. 'I thought he was dead. One of my sources said he was dead on arrival at the hospital.'

'Even if he isn't,' Mazur said. 'Is only a question of time. He will be a vegetable. They told me.'

Molloy shook his head.

'You better be right, boy.'

He turned to Alex. 'Have ye hacked into the CAB computer system yet?'

Alex squirmed. 'Russians say is very hard to get past firewalls.

New system is very strong. They will keep trying, day and night.'

'Get it fucking done, right? I want to see what they have on me before I go to Spain.'

Alex and Mazur looked at the ground.

'Alright,' Molloy said. 'Let me know when you hear anything. Tell the Russians I want more people on it. Give them another twenty grand, but that's it. You can leave by the back door, there.'

Molloy returned to the living room and stood by the door.

Mary could see his anger and was on guard.

'Top up?' she said, and pointed at the glass.

Luke, propped in the corner of the sofa, raised his arms to be picked up, and said, 'Ahh, ahh, ahh.'

'I'm going out,' Molloy said, and left the room.

Mary sat on the edge of the armchair and watched the baby in case he lost his balance and fell.

15

There were beeping noises and some kind of hissing. A loud insistent alarm. It wouldn't stop. Then it stopped. Then it started again. Voices. Some kind of trolley squeaking. A telephone, a voice. A moan. Somebody running. That alarm again. *Would it just fucking stop*. Pain. Pain in his chest, pain in his throat, pain in his stomach, pain in his head. Buzzing. Beeping noises and some kind of hissing.

Something was catching at his arm. It pulled when he tried to move it and hurt his hand. There was something on his face.

A shadow, the light fading. A voice, closer now. Attention on him. He could see the face of a dark-skinned man. Thin. He wore a blue cap and overalls.

'Hello, Mr Collins. Hello, can you hear me? Timothy? My name is Doctor Gandapur.'

Collins closed his eyes. Sometime later, another voice. A woman's. Insistent. A hand on his shoulder.

'Hello? Hello? Time to wake up now.'

Collins opened his eyes. A woman with the same blue cap and overalls as the dark-skinned man was smiling at him, her eyes kind.

'Well, hello,' she said. He looked at her, blinking.

'Tim, my name is Norma, you're in Cork University Hospital, and I'm the Clinical Nurse Manager here in the Intensive Therapy Unit. But you're okay, you'll be fine, alright? You're going to be fine. Can you hear me? Just nod if you can hear me.' Her voice was gentle.

Collins tried to speak, but the mask on his face prevented him. He tried to lift his hand to remove it, but it caught on something.

He tried the other hand. The woman helped him take it off.

'That's better. Annoying things, but you need a bit of oxygen to help your breathing right now. Here, take a sip of water – just a small sip and you might be able to speak. Okay?'

Collins took a sip of water through a straw. His throat burned as it went down. He tried to speak again.

'What happened?' he croaked and winced.

'Okay,' she said. 'Well, Tim, you've had a bad shock to your system and that's why you're in hospital. You suffered toxic poisoning. We're not sure exactly what it was yet, something organic it seems, but it was very strong. We got most of it out of your body and you're going to be okay. It has affected your heart and your breathing, so we have to give you a bit of help with that for a while. Now I want you to sleep for a bit and I'm going to put the mask back on. Don't speak anymore now, just close your eyes. Good man. Is that okay, Tim? Or is it Timothy?'

He closed his eyes and swallowed.

'Collins,' he said. 'You can call me Collins.'

He woke up. His eyes kept closing. He tried to focus.

'Collins.'

June was standing by the bed. He tried to smile, but it felt crooked.

'Good to see you, Collins – you gave us a fright there, boy.'

He blinked. *Yes. Good to see you too.*

'Oh, Collins. I'm so sorry this happened. I can't stay, the nurses keep throwing me out. But you're going to be okay, right? And Collins, we're going to get the fuckers who did this. You can be sure of that.'

He believed it. The lioness. She squeezed his hand.

'I'll see you again, soon. I'll be back in the morning. Okay? Don't worry about anything. You're going to be fine. Okay, Collins? You're going to be fine.' Her eyes misted and her voice caught at the final words.

Collins closed his eyes.

Beeping. That fucking beeping. *Will it ever stop?*

He remembered.

The beautiful young man grinning. The tremulous waitress. Lying on the ground, looking at the underside of the table.

He tried to calm himself and pressed the button to release more drugs.

His mother was sitting in a chair beside his hospital bed. A little old lady. Her lips were pressed tight, her brows furrowed, her eyes down. Her features were edged in exhaustion. He could hear her hum one of the songs from *Maritana* that she liked. She only sang, he knew, when she was upset or worried.

As boys, when they came down for breakfast, if she was singing in the kitchen, he and Paul would know what kind of humour their father was in, and what they could face when he came in from the morning's milking. Any music was an alert, and they would immediately be on guard and careful when the sound of the milking machine stopped.

Collins looked at her small frame in the chair, the spectacles perched on her nose, her spindly legs and brown tights. How could she have gotten thinner in just a few weeks? And when did she get so old?

The years of discord between her and his father. His impossible father, mercurial, fraught and bitter. How she had stayed cheerful, at least outwardly, through his long bouts of depression. Enduring the long silences, and then the relentless haranguing. How she had often defended her sons from him, and suffered the consequences. Later, taking his side when they were old enough to challenge and confront him.

Then nursing him, the suddenly weak old man fading away from his stroke. His decay to an early death. At home, of course – no hospital for him. All borne on the slight shoulders of the slip of a thing sitting right there. Collins wondered who had told her. June, he presumed.

When she felt his attention, she raised her head and smiled and her face was transformed. The years poured off her, light teemed into her brown eyes, and she was his mother again. He was her boy again. A sick boy who needed his mammy.

He tried to pull his lips into what was probably an insipid smile. He fought back the tears. *No fucking way.*

She stood up and put her hand on his arm.

'Timothy.' Her voice was almost a whisper. He could see her effort to guard herself against crying, to stay in control. He was shocked. He'd never seen her weep, not once, and he thought he never would.

'Oh, Timothy,' she said. Her expression hardened, her eyes boring into him. 'You're going to be fine. You're my rock, you always were. And nothing can break you. Nothing. Do you hear me, Timothy?'

Collins nodded. He heard her. He closed his eyes.

He awoke to voices being raised.

'No, no, Mrs Collins, I'm very sorry, but you can't stay here all night. That's not allowed I'm afraid.'

'Sure I'm no trouble, I'll just sit here. I won't make a noise. He might need something during the night.'

Collins watched the pair. Norma was twice his mother's size and exuded resolve and authority. But he also knew his mother's quiet and understated obstinacy. It had driven him to distraction for years. He smiled, sleepily.

'If he needs anything we'll bring it, Mrs Collins. Have you nowhere you can spend the night?'

'Ah sure I don't, I came straight away. I suppose I could sleep in the car, if that's what you wanted.'

'No, no, of course not. But we have a visitor's room down the hall and you could go there if you like.'

'Oh, that's very kind, sure I'll take a look, so.'

When he woke again some time later, his mother was back in the same chair, dozing, slightly snoring, amidst the beeps and the hissing and the patina of dulled pain transfusing the airless room. There was a blanket over her, covering her from bony shoulders to sensible black shoes.

Norma attended him in the deep of the night, taking his temperature and blood pressure. Giving him some more tablets, she glanced to her right and said, 'She's some operator, wherever you got her.'

'Hmm,' he said.

She placed the cup and straw back on the bedside locker and wiped his mouth with a tissue.

'But if it was me, I'd want my mother to do the same,' she said, writing on his chart. 'And if it was my son in the bed, it would take the army to shift me.'

'I'd pay money to see that,' he mumbled, his voice still raw.

She appraised him, an eyebrow arched.

'I think we'll be able to move you out of ITU soon,' she said, tidying his bed. 'Cheek is always a good sign.'

He closed his eyes and tried to let the drugs take him. But all he could see was Pretty Boy's malevolent grin, until finally he drifted away.

16

Two days later, they moved him to a small private room down the corridor.

He tried to eat some lunch. The toast felt like sandpaper in his mouth. The soup was beyond him. He drifted off to sleep.

When he awoke, his mother was knitting, with the blanket folded over her knees. He wondered what time it was, how long he'd slept. She was humming again. He closed his eyes. He had dragged her into this mess. She should be at home in her kitchen, listening to the radio, making a list of shopping, or getting some food ready for her dinner.

O'Regan and Clancy entered the room cautiously, as though they were walking into a trap. *About fucking time.* Collins had been wondering who Jonno would send. He was glad.

O'Regan towered over his partner, leading to the inevitable nickname of Mutt and Jeff. But Collins knew who he would pick to get him out of a tight corner. Clancy said little, scowled for the most part, was small in stature and had a thin, pale, pinched face. He liked to let the gregarious big man get all the attention while he looked on.

'Collins,' O'Regan said, awkwardly.

Clancy looked around the room, casually taking it all in.

O'Regan stretched down his hand to Collins's mother in the armchair, towering over her. She stood up.

'Mrs Collins, I'm Detective John O'Regan and this is Detective Sergeant Jack Clancy. We're colleagues of, eh … your son here, in Anglesea Street.'

Clancy shook her hand, smiling his sardonic smile. There was an awkward pause.

'Mam, I wonder if you could give me a few minutes with Detectives O'Regan and Clancy? We have to talk a bit of business.'

'Of course I could, Timothy. I'll go down to the chapel for a bit. Don't tire him out, please,' she said to the two men. She put her knitting into a deep cloth bag, and left the room.

O'Regan seized upon the armchair and quickly pushed it closer to the head of the bed; he dropped himself into it.

'Jesus, you're in some mess, Collins.'

'Nice to see you too, Regan.' He did not acknowledge Clancy, nor was he greeted in return.

'The doctors say it's poison. From some plant. A toxin, whatever that is. What did they call it?' O'Regan said. He glanced at Clancy.

'Of an indeterminate nature,' Clancy said.

'That's it. "An organic toxin of an indeterminate nature." Poison, basically, to you and me. Fatal if they didn't get you to a hospital quick enough.'

'I only took a sip,' Collins said. 'That's what saved me, I think.'

'Can you remember anything?' Clancy asked. Straight to business. 'June told us what you told her, but I wanted to hear it direct.'

'Yes, I think I can remember everything up until the time I lost consciousness. There was a waitress, Polish I think. She was very nervous. I think she knew what she was doing, what was in the coffee. It was the coffee, for sure.'

Collins drank some water and cleared his throat.

'She was about five-five, good-looking, pale, blonde hair tied up, thinnish. A star tattoo on her left wrist. Blue eyes. I've never seen her before in there and I would have noticed. And there was this pretty boy at a table. He made a phone call just after I drank the coffee. I think June might have some information on him. He's Polish too, apparently. Did you talk to the waitress?'

'No,' Clancy said. 'But our description matches yours. She only got the job a few days before and left straight away after the ambulance came. Seems like she used a false name and address. Another Polish guy there reckons she was from the north of Poland, maybe Gdańsk. He thought she was on something a couple of times, a bit wired. Can you describe the man?'

'Like a model, all cheekbone and chin. Straight nose, slicked-back dark hair. Big lips, kind of effeminate looking. Five-ten, maybe, but he was sitting down.'

'Gay? Is that what you're saying?' Clancy said.

'I don't know. "A pretty boy", June described him as – one of her informants mentioned that Molloy had a new lackey with that description. She's trying to get a name for him.'

'How can you be sure he's one of Molloy's?'

'I can't, but when I said it to June, she said it was definitely him,' Collins said.

'I know you want to pin this on Molloy, Collins, but this is a stretch.'

'Who else could it be? Either way, this Pretty Boy is the key – he probably set it up. He'll be on the CCTV, and if June can't ID him, she knows someone who can.'

'But how do you know he was even involved?' Clancy said.

'I just do, alright? It was the way he was grinning at me. He *knew* what was happening.'

Silence. The two detectives looked at him sceptically.

'You sure about this, Collins?' Clancy asked. 'Totally certain?'

'I … I'm fairly certain.'

'How far away was he?' Clancy said.

'I don't know, maybe ten feet.'

Clancy shook his head.

'Isn't there any CCTV?' Collins said.

'This Pretty Boy,' Clancy said, ignoring the question. 'Do we know anything more about him?'

'I don't, maybe June does. Why don't you bring him in?'

'Oh, we will,' O'Regan said. 'Problem is, there's no CCTV. It was wiped.'

Collins stared at him, horrified.

'What? How?'

'We don't know,' Clancy said. 'It might have been out of order anyway.' He scratched his chin. 'Any suggestions?'

'It's Pretty Boy and the waitress, I guess, and links to Molloy,' Collins said. He had been thinking about how he would have proceeded if he were the investigating officer. 'She could be toughing it out somewhere local. Worth chasing her down a bit. Who got her the job? Any references? Any witnesses in the place? Somebody surely noticed Pretty Boy. Any CCTV on the street?'

'We're checking those. Anything else? For Molloy I mean?'

'I dunno. He's normally careful, but this is a big step up,' Collins replied. 'Killing Buckley and Cummins is one thing, but a garda? If you could get at one of the Bradys or Corcoran, they might be in the know. He might brag about this. But that's different from proof. Maybe the poison. Any trace of that left?'

'No, they cleaned up straight after you. The coffee was out of a machine, so that waitress must just have dropped something into it,' Clancy said.

'Is this retaliation for Townsend, Collins? Poisoning a garda? Fuck me.' O'Regan blew through pursed lips.

'You surprised at anything he'd do?' Collins said. 'Who do you think we are talking about here, Mother fucking Theresa?'

'All right, all right,' O'Regan said. 'Don't give yourself a heart attack as well.'

Collins racked his brains. His head throbbed, a bad headache was coming down the tracks.

'Look, if you can't get him for this, maybe you can get him for something else. What about the drug money? It has to be laundered somewhere.'

Clancy shook his head. 'That's a whole other investigation, Collins, and you know it. CAB have been all over him already and got nothing. We all know Molloy killed Cummins and Buckley, but they were scumbags and without a body or an informer we won't get him on those. This is an attempted murder of a member of the force. If it is him, we'll get him.'

'There's no "if" about it,' Collins said. 'Who else could it be?'

'You've put away your fair share of scumbags. Could be one of those who got hold of some poison, somewhere.'

'I can't see it.'

Clancy's face softened.

'You know what?' he said. 'For once, I'm inclined to agree. I think this has Molloy written all over it. I'll talk to Jonno and we'll get going. Okay. If you think of anything else, let us know. I'll send somebody in to take a formal statement. Mind yourself, Collins.'

He turned abruptly and left the room. O'Regan rose from the chair. He winced and tried to straighten up to his full height. 'My fucking back, I'm killed from it.' He shook hands with Collins and smiled. 'Come here, don't mind him. You know what? I think he's a bit jealous it was you and not him.'

He grabbed some grapes from a bowl on the overbed table and limped out the door.

17

In one moment Collins was alone, in the next, his older brother Paul was sitting in the hard chair close to him, his hands on the side of the bed, eyes firm on his, intense with will. Handsome and urbane in a tweed jacket and cords. Rangy and easy in his skin. Professor of English and Comparative Literature at Columbia University, no less. Collins's pride and joy. What he could have been, himself, in a different life.

'Nincompoopery,' Paul whispered. But Collins could see that his heart was not in it. Paul rested his hand on Collins's arm, as if to feel for life there.

Collins held his gaze. 'Balderdashery,' his stock reply. Tough this out, he told himself. *Do it.*

'Poppycockery.' Paul was trying, Collins had to give him that, but in the end it was too much. Paul bowed his head, then raised it, wiping tears from his face.

Collins made a stab at 'Cockamamie' but failed. He pushed the back of his head into the pillow – as if that would work. Paul stood and held Collins's face in his hands. He pressed his forehead to his brother's, then smiled and shook his head at him.

'Well, here's another nice mess you've gotten me into,' Paul said.

'Sorry about that, chief,' Collins said. He was sorry for dragging Paul across an ocean and into his dirty world. But he needed him too – deep down, who the fuck else did he have?

Paul asked what had happened and Collins told him. Almost everything. He told him what he told June about Townsend and the van. *He made a go for me, I stood on his foot.* He told him about Molloy's source in the station.

'Is there nobody at all in the station you can rule out?' Paul asked.

'I can rule several people out each of the three times I'm sure he was tipped off. They didn't have the information. But what else has he been told that I don't know about? And the very people who can really help me are the senior detectives, inspectors and superintendents who did know about those murders *and* the evidence we had, *and* the raids that were planned, which he clearly knew about in advance. So it's probably someone senior. And I think there might be more than one.'

Paul leaned forward conspiratorially and lowered his voice.

'Two things,' he said. 'One: the poison may have had nothing to do with the thing in the van. It seems to me that the timeline is too tight. For example, had that waitress been in place *before* the Townsend incident? And what's the rate-determining factor to set up something like that? It would take a lot of forward planning. To get the toxin, get the waitress in place, get the toxin to her, make sure she knows you, make sure she serves you. That's not a spur of the moment revenge thing, it seems to me.'

Collins noted the euphemisms, and was grateful for them. And for Paul's perspective.

'Secondly,' Paul said. 'Of course there could be more than one informer in the station. Or ten, or twenty. But all you know is that Townsend *thinks* there is one. He may have been lying. Or he may have been fed that information falsely to get it to you. It isn't beyond doubt that Molloy could have set up Townsend in that van with incorrect information knowing you would confront him and question him. So it could be there is no informer and it's all to mess with your head. There's no guarantee there is any informer, let alone more than one.'

Collins nodded. He didn't really want to think about it anymore.

'There's one thing I want to ask you,' Paul said. 'Why is this Molloy character so fixated on you? Why you, given there are so many guards on his case?'

'Three reasons, I think,' Collins said. 'First of all, I put away his brother Bobby for manslaughter a few years ago and he never forgave me for it. I thought we had him for murder and I pushed hard – it *was* murder too – but the DPP eventually settled for manslaughter and we got the prick for that. He got eleven years and he'll probably do eight or nine. Molloy idolises him and he's very bitter about it.

'Another reason is this: I lost my temper with him once and humiliated him in public. He was with a few of his cronies in a pub in Barrack Street one night and, as we were leaving, he made a comment about the woman I was with. I marched up to him and slapped him across the face. Crazy stuff, I was well out of order. He was so shocked he didn't react; he just sat there with his mouth open. They all knew me and I expected them to pile in and give me a kicking, but they just sat there, waiting for his lead. When Liz and I left the pub, there was a taxi passing and we sat into it. We were just pulling away when they all rushed out, but by then it was too late.'

Collins picked up the medical cup from the locker beside his bed and took a sip from it.

'But I think the main reason he wants to get rid of me is because he knows I'm the best chance we have of putting him away. He knows he can't bribe me and he knows I'm not going to let up. Eventually it's going to come down to me or him.'

Paul was smirking.

'I know, I know,' Collins said and he gave a wry smile.

'Then there's the other question,' Paul said. 'Are you okay to talk, you sound a bit hoarse?'

'I'm fine, my throat gets a bit raw.' He took another sip of water. 'Do you mean why am I fixated on him?'

'Yeah. If that's the word. I was thinking more "focused",' Paul said.

'"Focused." Yeah, well. He holds that whole organisation together. All the killings, the drugs, the trafficking – the whole works. It all revolves around him. If he goes down, the Bradys would revert to type and we'd have them in a week. Their sister is the brains in that family; they're too thick to even see that. Molloy's brother is away and his two sons are no more than thugs. He has some Poles in tow now, but they can't take over, the locals wouldn't have it.

'So,' he said. 'If we get him, the whole thing crumbles and we can really put a dent in the misery.' He paused. He was about to say something about Kelly, how much he'd been thinking about her, too. But he decided against it.

'Cut the head off the snake', Paul said. 'I get it. Well, if it comes down to you or him, make bloody sure it *is* him so.'

The following morning, Paul made his pitch.

'You remember Connie's dad, Ron?'

'Yeah, big Reagan/Bush fan, right?'

'Yeah, but he has contacts in the security industry. Easy money, he said, travel, nice suits, nice hotels.'

'What's this about, Paul?'

'He said he could get you a job there, no problem. Ex-cop

and all. Green card, the works, a hundred and fifty K a year plus expenses. You could be out and set up in ten years.'

'Paul,' Collins said, shaking his head.

'Start a new life. You'd love New York, you fucking know you would. Or Los Angeles – imagine the sun. California dreaming. Get away from all this shit, these scumbags. You might not be as lucky next time.'

Paul looked at him earnestly.

'Thanks, boy,' Collins said. 'I appreciate the offer. Tell Connie and Ron I said thanks too.'

He thought about it all that night. To live in New York City or Chicago. The sunshine in LA, the Pacific coast. The endless possibilities. Another life.

The following day, after a lecture about staying out of trouble, Paul said his goodbyes and was gone. As suddenly, it seemed to Collins, as he had come.

Now who could he talk to?

But he was glad, too. Paul belonged back in his safe and cultured academic world. That was all there was to it.

18

Two days later – eight days since the poisoning – Superintendent John O'Connell strode into Collins's room in full dress uniform with a tall distinguished man in his early sixties, also in formal senior garda attire. Collins recognised him immediately.

His mother stood up, in awe of the uniforms and the eminence the men projected. Jonno reached out his hand to her.

'Mrs Collins, I'm Superintendent John O'Connell and this is Deputy Commissioner Denis Sweeney. We just called in to see your son for a minute and to enquire how he is doing.'

'Mrs Collins, Denis Sweeney,' the Deputy Commissioner said. She shook his hand deferentially. He smiled.

Collins noticed his perfect pitch: solemn but charming; grave but determined. A formidable man.

Jonno turned to Collins. He shook his hand, making way for Sweeney to do likewise.

'Detective.'

'Deputy Commissioner. Thanks very much for your visit.'

'Not at all, I'm only sorry I couldn't come sooner.'

Jonno jumped in. 'How are you, Collins? I hear you're on your way home soon. I'm sorry I couldn't come to see you sooner, but I'm personally co-ordinating this case and I couldn't get away.'

'I'm on the mend, Superintendent, thanks very much. And thanks for visiting me, I'll be back at work before too long.'

'No you won't Collins, no you won't.' Jonno shook his head. 'You will take your time and recuperate fully. I'm sure your mother will be glad to look after you.' He smiled at her.

'Collins, I want you to know,' Jonno said, 'and you Mrs Collins, that we are putting every resource at our disposal into this case. *Every* resource. It will not stand. A member of the force, one of our own. By Christ it won't. Excuse me, Mrs Collins.'

Sweeney then said his piece. It was almost as if they had rehearsed.

'Detective Collins, I want you to know that we are taking this case most seriously in the Phoenix Park too. I have spoken to the Commissioner about it and he has assured me that Superintendent O'Connell will have every resource he needs to bring this case to a resolution. We're going to get whoever did this and we are not going to stop until we do. I just wanted to reassure you of that fact. And the Commissioner specifically asked me to pass on his best wishes for a speedy recovery.'

'Thank you, sir. I got his letter. I'm very grateful.'

'I want you to know this, Collins, it's very important,' Sweeney said. 'You're one of us and we look after our own. The Minister has been informed and he is fuming about it. He's told us to do whatever we have to do – within the law, of course. We're absolutely committed to bringing this to a successful conclusion. But you concentrate on getting your health back. That's your role in this for now, Detective.'

'Yes, sir,' Collins said, thinking 'for now' indeed. 'Superintendent, I'd like to be kept informed about developments in the case. I know I can't be directly involved, but I would like to know what's happening and maybe to give advice from time to time.'

Jonno frowned. 'Yes, yes, of course we'll keep you fully informed, Collins, I'll get June to update you regularly. But no involvement. No input. Your job now is to get well again – and take your time doing it.'

Sweeney looked at Jonno and tapped his forefinger on his watch.

'We have to go,' Jonno said, donning his cap. 'I'm sorry not to stay longer, but we have a meeting with some TDs and councillors in County Hall, and we're already late. Mrs Collins, very nice to meet you again. You'll take good care of him I know, though I don't know how you put up with him.'

Jonno smiled, Collins's mother smiled, Deputy Commissioner Sweeney smiled. Collins did not smile.

'I will, of course. It will be nice to have a bit of company for a while,' she said.

The two men departed quickly.

Collins regarded his mother and smiled apologetically.

She glared at him.

'A letter from the Commissioner? You never told me that.'

19

Time seems to pass quickly in a hospital. Or not at all. A day doesn't mean much in a hospital.

No getting up, no dressing. No undressing, no going to bed. Nothing really between one darkness and the next. It's a vague passage, a road in the fog. You look back and you look ahead, but you can't tell the difference.

There is light through the windows during the day. Doctors and nurses visit more. Some days there are visitors, welcome or not. Meals come and go, mostly picked at.

The world is happening outside. Your world is the distance from the bed to the toilet when your stomach starts to cramp. If you don't have the runs, you're constipated.

The windows are dark during the night. The odd nurse checks in on you.

You try to sleep and mostly fail. You look forward to the first cup of tea in the morning.

When you do sleep, the nightmares keep you busy. The sense of people standing over your bed, but you can't move. You know they are evil and mean you harm, but you are stuck there, rigid. You know it's a dream, but you can't awaken.

The quotidian cycle of boredom, drugs and sleep.

The drip being replaced and eventually removed. The cannula being taken out of the back of your hand.

An ever-patient, ever-present mother.

The vomiting scrapes your throat raw. It makes you breathless and brings on headaches.

The anger, growing like a tumour in your chest, in your head. Consuming everything, except the shame.

Then you are discharged.

20

Collins liked his mother's house in Bandon. The kitchen/dining room was L-shaped, sweeping and spacious, with windows its whole length, facing out onto a stepped, ordered garden. There was a sofa and two armchairs where the room opened into a conservatory-type space, which was full of low winter light on sunny days. Everything gleamed; everything was in its place. Collins had inherited his mother's fastidiousness – it just felt right to him when countertops and tables were clear of clutter and debris.

He took to sitting in the armchair in the early mornings, listening to music and trying to read, looking out the window for the first signs of sunrise. June had brought him his Bose headphones and Bluetooth speaker. He had downloaded forty books to his Kindle. The days were long, but he slept frequently thanks to the drugs.

His mother's estate, just outside the town, was twelve years old, and small, with nine detached houses in a cul-de-sac and a large green in the centre. She had moved in there after his father died and she sold the farm. It wasn't far from her friends and there was a SuperValu down the road.

There was an old Sitka spruce forest behind the estate and he sometimes strolled there; it was quieter and more sheltered than the road and he liked being among the trees. He was self-conscious about meeting people on the street, having to make up lies about 'stomach problems'. From their reactions, most of them seemed to think it was cancer. Two people had commiserated with his mother, as though he were already dead.

He tired easily, his lungs blowing thin and quick. It discouraged him and made him irritable. He ached all over, his joints creaking like those of a seventy-year-old. He had to caution himself against taking his frustration out on his mother when she fussed over his comings and goings.

The pain in his stomach had subsided and he began to eat more often, but he could still manage only small amounts of food at a time. He'd never eaten so much white toast, but it did the job. He could not drink coffee, but he still made an espresso in the morning, holding the cup under his nose so that he could at least smell the benevolence of the roasted beans. On some mornings he woke in a panic, reliving the poisoning, and headaches soon followed. Paracetamol eased them, but their remnants lingered until after noon.

He practised his mindful meditations, fearing a lapse into the torpor he had endured the previous year after the Butcher case, when he had struggled to get out of bed for almost nine weeks.

He got up earlier and earlier and went to the kitchen and switched on the Nespresso and the lamp by the wicker armchair. Until his mother would shuffle in and tut tut and berate him for not putting on the main light.

'You'll ruin your eyes, Timothy, and you have great sight. Sure 'tis nearly dark in here.'

After a fortnight out of the hospital – five long weeks after the poisoning – as his strength increased, he was walking every day. His mother fretted and muttered about it being 'desperate wet' and 'bitter out'.

'I have my umbrella, Mam, and it isn't cold. Stop fussing. I'll be fine.'

'You'll catch your death, you're still not a hundred per cent and the doctor told you to take it easy.' She hovered by the door, frail and powerless.

'I'm only going down the road, and if it gets heavy I'll step in somewhere. I might go for a cup of tea in The Dock. It's just to get out for a half an hour. Don't be worrying, it'll only give you wrinkles.' He gave her his best smile, such as it was.

'Oh, there's no talking to you anyway. You're like your father.'

One day, he bought cigarettes and a lighter in SuperValu and lit up just outside the shopping centre. But he immediately felt dizzy and sick and he stubbed out the cigarette and threw the lot in the nearest bin.

When his mother played her daytime radio, he withdrew to his bedroom to sleep or read and listen to his music. He listened to ambient music: Brian Eno, Max Richter, Hammock, Epic45. Rock or ballads didn't seem to do it for him, somehow.

To pass the days, he did odd jobs around the house. Painting and keeping the garden tidy of weeds calmed him. He loved setting the fire every afternoon. He allowed himself to snooze after lunch some days, but he woke up groggy and cranky, feeling old.

His mother's television was in the living room, so he would stay in the conservatory when she watched the news, the current affairs and the soaps that she liked. She nagged him to come in by the fire, but he said he was happy to read where he was – and he was. He joined her every now and then, making her tea and pretending to be interested in the state of the nation or the dramatic storylines of the soaps.

He was especially content to sit with her when she switched the TV off, and to listen to the flap and sputter of the fire and the rhythmic click of knitting needle on knitting needle, while he read. When she went to bed, he would sit longer and watch the dying embers. They seemed to whisper faintly from the past before they dimmed from orange to red to a grey coldness. Finally, he would go to bed, praying for the drugs to kick in quickly.

June called each week, and his mother fussed over her, asking about Maeve's health in hushed tones. Paul had contracted meningitis when he was eight and she liked to speak of it whenever she could, bonding over the shared trials of motherhood. She served them tea and queen cakes in the living room, from a tray with her good Royal Tara tea set – a treasured fifty-year-old wedding present.

June gave him what little news there was of his case. Jonno was ranting and raving around the station, demanding a breakthrough. Some journalists had heard that a guard had been attacked, and were sniffing around, but if they knew the details, they had not yet fully pursued it. Collins had received four calls from journalists, with voicemails asking to ring them back – which he ignored. There were hints on social media, but with no proof and no quotes, the media had held the story back, for now.

Collins didn't want it made public unless there was a prosecution. He didn't want to give Molloy the satisfaction and it would also have been a blow to his own pride and to the pride of the force. Division Chief Superintendent Sean Geary wanted it kept under wraps, too. There was enough pressure about the 'epidemic' of drugs in Cork without more negative publicity. Geary privately used the poisoning to cajole the Commissioner for more resources, but publicly, there was official silence.

Collins reckoned that favours were being called in, or threats were being made, for editors to keep it quiet, but he was still surprised that somebody had not broken ranks and leaked the story. June had heard about an injunction.

In October – two days after Collins had phoned Niamh on Kelly's anniversary – June told him that Clancy had been inexhaustibly chasing leads and harassing junkies, drug pushers, Molloy's nephews and other lackeys, dragging O'Regan around behind him. She said that he ate, drank and slept the case, except there was not much sign of sleeping. Collins had phoned Clancy five times for updates and to pass on suggestions, but Clancy took the call only once, to say: 'Can't talk now, Collins, nothing to report. Talk to your partner,' before hanging up.

'I don't think he ever goes home,' June said. 'Or washes, either. Jesus, some days he's reeking.'

Collins smiled. He'd worked with Clancy on the Dinny Buckley murder and personal hygiene was not high on his agenda.

'He doesn't like to get beat, Mr Clancy,' Collins said. 'And because it's me, he really won't want to fail, to have it said. He'd like to have it over me.' Collins looked into the fire. 'But he won't. And Jonno won't rock the boat that much, when it comes to it, whatever tough talk he had in the hospital.'

He sipped his tea.

'Those two could be anywhere now. South of Spain. London. Anywhere,' he said. 'Listen, June. If you were working abroad – say London. And you did something, broke the law. Even something small. Would you go home afterwards? To bring the shit to your own doorstep? They might be in Poland, but they won't be near home. What amazes me is that we haven't identified them yet. Do we even have names?'

'Oh yes, I meant to tell you. We have a name now for Pretty Boy: Tomasz Mazur. He has a record as long as your arm, the

Poles sent over a magistrate to be briefed by Jonno. The waitress went by the name of …' She checked her notes. 'Irena Milczarek. They reckon the name was false, and the PPS number was fake too. She was never going to stay around long enough to pay tax or anything.'

'What's Mazur wanted for?'

'Attempted murder, extortion, assault, you name it. There's even something about stuff when he was a soldier in the Middle East. Bit of a psycho, apparently.'

'Fits right in with Molloy so. How did ye get his name?'

'An anonymous call would you believe, but it checked out.'

'Wow,' Collins said. 'Somebody on the inside doesn't like him, we might get lucky there.'

He poured more tea.

'Is Molloy going to be brought in?'

'I think so.'

'Will you get me a tape of the interview?'

June looked up, annoyed. 'No!' she said. 'For God's sake, Collins.'

'I'n oney askin',' he said, in a child's voice. This was a shared joke they had, though he could not remember the source. Perhaps one of her children used to say it to her and it caught on.

'Yeah, well. Main thing for you is to get better. You're putting on weight, I think.'

'You were always a bad liar.'

'Yeah, well, you were always too fucking good at it.'

Collins laughed.

'Good to see you laugh, Collins.'

'Not much to laugh at around here. Jesus, that radio. I never heard such doom and gloom. This country is in a perpetual state of self-pity.'

'Mícheál only listens to Lyric now. Can't stick it.' She shuffled. 'Listen, Collins, I'm thinking of taking some time out. From work.'

Collins tensed.

'Is Maeve okay?'

'No it's not that, she's managing away. It's just … I'd like to be there more for her. Just for a while.' She looked at him sheepishly, as if she were betraying him.

'Of course, June. Jesus, you don't have to explain anything to me.'

'I know, I know. It's just …' She paused. 'It's for me too. I … I've been struggling a bit myself, what with everything.' She was fighting back tears. She lowered her head. Elbows on her knees, she folded and unfolded the crinkled baking paper from the queen cake.

Collins put his hand on her arm.

'You take care of *yourself*,' he said. He forced her to meet his eye. 'Hey? And Mícheál, Maeve and Jack. They always come first. Anyway, Clancy will come and visit me, I'm sure. And keep me updated.'

'Fuck it, Collins, I'm not here to update you. I'm here to see you. Is that all you care about?'

She squeezed her eyes closed and kneaded her forehead with the fingers of her left hand.

'I'll still come and see you, Collins. You're sick, remember?'

'I know you will, June. And I appreciate it.'

Their eyes met and she began to cry. He felt teary himself. He got out of his chair, leaned over her awkwardly and put his arms around her. She tried to gather herself. He half-expected his mother to come in and think they were having a lovers' quarrel.

'I'm okay, I'm okay. Sorry. Sorry about that,' she said. She wiped her eyes with a tissue. 'It's just that …' She faced him again. 'When I heard. And when I saw you in the hospital. I thought you were dead. Only for that mask, and the stuff inside it. I thought you were dead, Collins. And, and …'

'It's okay, June, it's okay.'

'I couldn't take that, Collins. I just couldn't take it.' She looked at him pleadingly. 'Do you know what I mean?'

'I do, June. I do. Nobody should have to see that. Take a break, for God's sake. Do that course in Ballymaloe you're always talking about. Head away to France with the lads for the summer, sure Mícheál has great holidays. Take some leave. Do.'

She hugged him at the door of her car. He had a strange idea that he would never see her again, and then he chided himself for being maudlin. But it was one more thing to feel guilty about. If she took a leave of absence, he had a feeling she would never come back. Never work as a garda again. Was that down to him?

He couldn't help but consider that if she were Molloy's source, it would be a good time for her to get out. Perhaps she felt guilty about him, and that's why she was so upset. He shook the thought aside. What the hell had he become? What he was capable of thinking?

He went to An Teach Beag that night and got drunk. He vomited on the way home, and woke his mother getting into the house. She made a fuss and he could tell by her worn-out appearance the following morning that she had not slept well, if at all. She did not speak to him for most of the day and he was glad of it. He spent much of it in bed, brooding, hung-over and full of self-pity.

The first frost came and Collins went in search of an old overcoat of his in the spare-room press. He noticed his box of hurling medals under some blankets. He closed the door of the room and picked up the box – an old Jacobs USA Assorted Biscuits tin – and laid it on the carpet.

It opened with a soft metallic scrape and there they were. Dozens of small red cardboard and plastic boxes, each one, he knew, containing a small piece of metal wrapped in cotton wool. He sought out one in particular, the one when he was captain of Cork and they'd beaten Galway in the final after a replay. He had to open five boxes before he found it.

It was of a darker, more burnished gold than the others – the captain always received a different medal. He looked at the symbols of the four provinces and the harp in the centre, the fine etching of its strings. The medal felt so light in his hand, and seemed so small. How could something so apparently insignificant, just a tiny piece of metal, mean so much to so many people? And to him?

He turned it over and pressed his forefinger across the tiny letters engraving the word: *Captaen*. When he heard his mother in the hall he put the medal back. He closed the lid of the biscuit tin, placed it on the floor of the press and covered it with the blankets.

21

Molloy put on his best sneer as he entered the interview room. He'd done dozens of these and they'd never got a single thing from him. Not once. This would be no different. They'd never learn. Muppets.

His solicitor, Derek O'Callaghan, walked beside him, a file of notes in his right hand.

Clancy and O'Regan followed them in and sat on the opposite side of the table.

O'Regan pressed a button on the comms panel and spoke.

'Interview on Friday twenty-fifth of November, 2016, 11.45 a.m. at Anglesea Street Garda Station, Cork. Those present: interviewee Dominic Molloy, his legal representative Derek O'Callaghan, Detectives Jack Clancy and John O'Regan.'

Molloy didn't even look at them, he wouldn't give them the soot of it. This is why O'Callaghan got paid the big bucks.

'Mr Molloy,' Clancy said. 'Where were you on the morning of August twentieth last?'

'Detective, we've been through this,' O'Callaghan said. 'My client has already answered that question, several times. This is harassment, pure and simple, and I insist this interview be brought to an end right now.'

'It will end when your client answers our questions,' Clancy said. 'Unless he has something to hide.'

'My client has co-operated with your investigation fully and holding him in custody for this long without a charge or *any* reasonable due cause is in breach of his constitutional rights.'

'Mr Molloy,' Clancy said, 'do you refuse to answer the question?'

'Detective –' O'Callaghan said.

Molloy cut him short. 'I already told you. I was with my partner, Mary Brady, and our son, Luke.'

'Is that the Mary Brady who is the sister of your known associates Pat and Sean Brady, both of whom have done time for serious crimes, as have you?'

'Detective, that is hardly relevant,' O'Callaghan said. 'Unless you are trying to impugn the character of a completely innocent woman. Is that your intention?'

'Mr Molloy, will you answer the question?' Clancy said.

'Yes, I know Sean and Pat Brady. Is that a crime now too?' Molloy said.

'And what is your connection with a Polish national by the name of Tomasz Mazur?' Clancy said.

O'Callaghan began another interjection. Molloy thought: *How boring is this? What a waste of time.*

Spain can't come quickly enough. An end to this rubbish. Building up a proper empire. New partners coming on board. The piles of money accumulating.

And Luke growing up to inherit everything. Toughening him up and getting him a real education to prepare him for the life he's destined to live. Not this shit, but making everything legit, like the mob did in the States. It's all about Luke now and his future, never seeing the inside of dumps like this.

Molloy smiled, ignoring another question from Clancy.

Thinks he's smart and tough, Clancy does, just like Collins. It isn't over with him, either. Mazur isn't going to let that prick have a moment's peace. Like a dog with a bone, Tomasz.

22

Late in November, Collins picked up Violette from her flat on Blarney Street after he'd dropped his mother to the bus station – she was visiting her sister Máire in Galway for a long weekend. He drove quickly back to Bandon, where they immediately had sex in his bed. He felt like he'd never needed it so badly, weak and all as he was. He promptly fell asleep and by the time he awoke, she had unpacked her bag, lit a fire and put the dinner in the oven.

He came into the kitchen to the smell of lasagne and Violette incongruously wearing his mother's apron, drinking a glass of wine and dancing to 'The Jean Genie'.

'Make yourself at home, why don't you?' he said, smiling.

'I brought this bottle, Collins,' she said. *Zis bottil.*

He laughed. 'I'm not accusing you of anything, Violette, it's just funny to see you there with my mam's apron and everything.'

'Yes, but you must eat, and I don't want my dress to get dirty. You will need all of your strength, you know,' she said, archly, and kissed him.

'Well then, give me a drop of that so.'

Later, before they went to bed, he told her they were going out for a short walk.

'What? Now?' she said.

'Yes, but not far and it's a lovely night.'

He gave her his mother's Wellington boots in the utility room and he put on his own old working coat and boots.

'Where are we going, Collins?' she asked, as the cold hit her outside the back door.

'It's a surprise, but you have to be quiet, okay? I want you to meet some friends of mine.'

She shrugged her Gallic shrug.

They went around to the front of the house and down the path at the end of the drive, past cars with frosted roofs and windows. The high clouds had cleared, showing a gibbous moon and the silky spine of the Milky Way. They passed through the gap and into trees. He took out his phone, lighting the path and their breaths in the cold air. She held his arm.

'Why don't you have a hat on, Collins?' she said.

'Shhh, we have to be quiet.' They followed the path to the car park and turned left, deeper into the forest. The ground, mounded and blanketed in spruce needles, dampened the sound of their feet. They came to a gap in a ditch where an electric fence pulsed at the edge of a field.

'You go under,' Collins whispered. 'Mind, it's live.' Violette crouched down and nimbly slipped under the wire. Collins stepped over it. They walked alongside the fence, their way lit again by the moon and stars. The grass was crisp, giving a creaking sound on each footstep. The land rose and then dropped and they followed it down to a metal cattle trough with muddy bare soil all around it. The surface on the water was filming to ice.

'Oh, my God, the stars,' Violette whispered.

'Yes,' Collins said. 'Here.' He pointed to a small bank beside the trough, under a bare ash tree.

'What now?' she said.

'Now, we wait,' he said, taking a clear plastic bag from his pocket, full of sausages, cut into pieces.

'What is it?' she said.

'Wait,' he said. Already he could see something in the field above. He nudged her. 'Look.'

'Oh.'

The vixen came closer, then stopped and sat about fifty metres away. There was movement behind her, indistinct at first and then clearer. Four cubs. They sauntered forward and halted at the sound of a car in the distance. They approached again, two of them jostling and nipping at each other. They stopped and sat by their mother.

The vixen stood up and approached. Collins opened the bag of sausage pieces. He threw two towards her. She paused and the cubs ran away. She approached again, to within a few metres, picking up first one piece of meat and then the second. She turned around and the cubs ran to her. She gave the meat to one of them, the runt, and pushed the others away, snapping at them. She sat down again, facing Collins and Violette. Three cubs, but not the runt, came closer. Collins threw a piece of sausage, and one of them took it and scarpered away. He gave Violette the bag.

'What?' she whispered.

'Throw another, but not so far.' The cubs were looking intently at them, pulled by hunger, pacing back and forth, sniffing the air. Violette threw some sausage – just a couple of metres away – and a cub, the bravest one, picked it up and gulped it down. She threw a piece to another cub. His colouring was different from the others – his flanks were of a lighter hue, his rump was also pale and the tip of his tail was white.

'Bend down slowly and hold one out,' Collins whispered.

Violette crouched down on her haunches and stretched her fingers out as far as she could, her hand trembling slightly. The brave cub came close then shied off. He approached again, snatched the meat from her hand and bounded away. She took out another piece. The brave cub neared and she threw the meat behind him, towards the other two, who fell upon it. The runt watched on from his mother's side, sitting, then standing and crouching, whining and circling her but never coming closer. Violette threw the next piece towards them, but it fell short and one of the other cubs rushed and took it. The brave cub took two more pieces from her hand, and then the pale cub came and took one. She held out her hand empty, the fingers outstretched and the brave cub licked them. The last piece she threw overhand, right at the vixen and runt, and the vixen caught it in her mouth and swallowed it, the cub jumping up and licking at her lips.

'*Merde*,' Violette whispered. 'Why didn't she give it to the little one?'

'Instinct, maybe,' Collins said and stood up and stretched.

The foxes, knowing there was no more food, turned away and ambled up the field.

'What will happen to the little one?' Violette said.

They moved along the fence again, towards the gap.

'It will probably die,' Collins said. 'Nature is red in tooth and claw.'

'Oh, Collins.'

'Pretty cool, though,' he said. 'Feeding the foxes like that. You weren't afraid?'

'I am not a pussy cat,' Violette said. 'But it was cool. Thank you.' *Sank you.*

'You can thank me later,' Collins said, moving off.

'Think you can survive it?'

He pulled her close. 'Only one way to find out,' he said. 'Be a nice way to go.'

23

The doorbell rang and Collins's mother came into the living room, beaming.

'Look who's here, Timothy. Paul and Christy.' And there they were.

Collins rose unsteadily from the low sofa to greet them and they almost managed to hide their shock at his appearance. He had not seen them since July at an Under–16s hurling match when Christy's youngest boy was playing for Na Piarsaigh. When Collins had been tanned, several kilos heavier, and didn't look like he was verging on old age.

'How's the going, boy?' Christy said, his eyes twinkling blue.

'Collins, good to see you.' Paulo smiled his lovely smile.

'Now, lads, ye'll have a cup of tea. And a queen cake?' Collins's mother said.

'No thanks, Mrs Collins,' Christy said. 'We can't, unfortunately. We were hoping to take Collins out for a spin; I've to check out a dog over in Ballineen and we're dead late. Would you mind at all if he came with us for a bit of a spin? Get him out of the house.'

'Oh no, that would be grand, Christy. Timothy, take your heavy coat and scarf, 'tis bitter out there today.'

'Yes, Mam,' Collins said, like a child, rolling his eyes at his friends.

He was surprised at his giddy joy to be getting into Christy's battered old Opel with Paulo sitting in the back, scattering debris to make room. Christy sat into the driver's seat. Collins closed his eyes for a moment, remembering how often the three of them had ventured out together, boys and men.

'Where to, lady?' Christy said in his best New York accent.

'That bloody, bloody, bloody,' Paulo mimicked from the back, recalling the time they were all nearly killed in Hell's Kitchen when another cab ran a red light and their Indian taxi driver cursed all the way to the Bronx, with 'bloody' – apparently the only swear word he knew.

'Bloody bloody,' Collins repeated in an Indian accent, rolling his head as the driver had done all the way uptown.

'Bloody bloody bloody bloody,' Christy said angrily, shaking his head.

Collins found himself bursting into song.

There was a wild colonial boy, Jack Duggan was his name
He was born and raised in Ireland, in a place called Castlemaine
He was his father's only son, his mother's pride and joy
And dearly did his parents love the wild colonial boy

Christy looked at him for a moment, bemused.

'Right,' he said, and put the car in gear. 'That's that, so.'

They settled down in their third pub, The Carbery Arms, Collins's favourite in Bandon. It served some craft beers and the music was down low, and the television was silent. Its wooden bar, tables and seats were washed almost to a cream colour, reminding him of New Zealand, where he'd gone during two months off in 2003. He liked it especially during the day, with the sunlight bright on the pale furniture and the smell of real coffee from the espresso machine. Katie, the Antrim woman who ran it, was fiery and striking, her diastema reminding him of a darker Anna Paquin.

Collins was drinking slowly and could not keep up. Christy was merciless.

'Fuck it, sure a few beers would be good for you. Put on a bit of weight, like.'

'I wish I could, Christy, but with the tablets and everything …'

'Ya big wuss. What happened you anyway?'

'Some kind of toxin, they said in the hospital. Poison. They put it in my coffee.'

'Who's they? Jesus, Collins, you're making a habit of this stuff,' Christy said.

'I know, I know. A scumbag drug dealer.'

'Will they get him for it?' Paulo asked.

'No, but I fucking will. That's for sure,' Collins said. 'My round. Same again?'

The two men watched him rise clumsily and go the bar.

When Collins had ordered the drinks, he glanced back at them. They were talking animatedly and both turned to look at him at the same time. It didn't take much imagination to figure out what they were talking about.

He turned back to the bar and fixed a tight smile on his face.

That night, before Collins fell asleep, he realised that, apart from his brother Paul, Christy and Paulo were his only two real friends. Even though he had not met them for months, in minutes it was as if they'd never been apart.

He wondered if having so few friends was a sign of a life badly spent. All those schoolmates and teammates, all those work colleagues. Even June, even after all they'd been through, all the time they'd spent together.

Maybe two was enough, he thought, resolving to spend more time with them, on more nights like the one he'd just had, laughing and reminiscing.

24

Collins looked at the bedside clock, its green glow. 05:02. He switched on the lamp, dragged himself out of the bed, put on his slippers and dressing gown and shuffled into the kitchen for a cup of tea.

By the sink he saw a movement to his left, outside the window. The unmistakable form of a man jumping over the back wall of the garden into the field. He froze and tried to think. There was no good plausible reason for a man being in his mother's garden at this time. He felt for his phone in his dressing-gown pocket. He thought of the layout of roads nearby, where the man could be headed. The car park in the forest.

He put down the kettle and went to the front door. He tied his dressing gown tight, picked up the old hurley in the corner of the hall and closed the door quietly behind him. He jogged the first few metres on the front path. The cold air bit into his chest. His slippers flapped and he cursed them. He went left at the gate and moved to the centre of the road. He ran, trying to up his pace, closing his eyes every third stride and gripping the hurley further up the shaft. He was soon panting, a pain in his side, but he pushed himself on.

Just before the opening into the forest, he bent lower, spreading out his arms. It became dark almost immediately, away from the streetlights. He slowed, and narrowed his stride, counting his steps. After three hundred he was staggering rather than walking, the blood roaring in his ears. He thought he might vomit, and tried to breathe it away.

He saw the dim outline of a vehicle at the edge of the car park. Ducking behind a bush, he forced himself to take long draughts of air. He felt light-headed and had to steady himself against a tree trunk.

The form of the car became clearer. There was no sign of movement, no sounds except the ones he made himself.

It looked like a Nissan Qashqai but he couldn't see the registration in the dark. He approached it, bent low. His dressing gown snagged on a branch and he had to tug it free. He quietened his breathing and crouched behind a forest sign just yards from the car, on the driver's side. He prayed whoever it was would approach from the other side, from the direction of his mother's house.

His mouth was dry and he ran his tongue around it and leaned on the hurley. He bowed his head low and looked under the car. He heard the footsteps before he saw any sign of movement. For a moment he couldn't tell which direction the sound was coming from, but the car's lights came on to the clunk of it being remotely unlocked. He bent into a crouch, hurley upright, and drove at the figure.

The first blow was a jab to the temple – Collins didn't want to risk a big slow swing. The man went down with a grunt. The second blow was a chopping cut with the heel of the hurley's *bas* onto the balaclava-covered face. Collins hit him twice more to the head, hard, then smashed the hurley down on his gloved right hand, which had been holding the car keys. He stood over him, pressing the hurley to his neck, waiting for some movement. There was none.

Collins pulled off the balaclava to reveal the face of Pretty Boy in the headlights. It was undoubtedly him, even with the smashed and bloody nose and the swelling of what seemed like a ruptured eye socket.

'Well, well,' Collins said, breathily. He felt sick again and bent over and retched, keeping his eyes on the prostrate man. He put the car keys in the pocket of his dressing gown, knelt on Mazur's right arm and fished through his pockets. A wallet with a Polish ID card: Robert Jankowski. Fake. He found a large hunting knife in a shoulder holster, outside his dark T-shirt. He took it out of the sheath, with the tips of his fingers, and stood back.

Collins dropped the knife, knelt down and lifted the unconscious man by the chest of his jacket.

'You bring this *here*!' he shouted, slapping the flopping face. 'Here!'

He tightened his grip and bunched a fist. He pressed the fist against Mazur's distended cheekbone and pushed it until the back of his head was being ground down into the gravel. Collins groaned and then roared.

How easy it would be to throw this piece of shit in the boot of the car, drive up past Gortadubha bog and tip it over the cliff into the quarry pond. Jimmy Cummins and Dinny Buckley had been buried by Molloy in some woods or a bog somewhere. Kelly O'Driscoll was dead, under the ground, too, along with her baby. Jacqueline Buckley was sleeping off a bender in somebody else's bed; Kyle, probably alone in the house in St Colman's Park, wondering if his mother would come home before he went to school; Jackie, high on heroin, in some druggie shithole. There were reports of prostitutes gone missing. How many others had Molloy and Mazur killed?

Collins inhaled and exhaled deeply through his nose. He put his hand on the car for support and the lights went out. He reached for the keys and pressed the remote. The lights came back on, illuminating Mazur again.

Removing a glove, he put the knife into Mazur's immobile right hand. He gripped his own fingers around Mazur's fingers, then threw the knife under the car.

He removed the phone from his dressing-gown pocket, tapped in the code, and found Clancy's number.

It was just before dawn when Collins got back to the house, exhausted and cold. June drove him, though it would have been quicker to walk. His mother was standing at the small front gate, looking tiny, her face ashen, flanked by two uniformed gardaí that he had told June to send there. Collins had phoned his mother to tell her what happened, and to stay indoors – so he knew she was safe. He was surprised to see her outside.

One of the gardaí approached him when he got out of the car.

'We tried to get her to go inside, Collins,' he said, hurriedly.

'Not fucking hard enough,' Collins snapped. 'Mam? Mam? Come on in out of the cold, no need to be standing here.'

She stared at him, her face lined, her eyes wild with emotion, of what kind he didn't know.

'I have to show you. I have to show you,' she said, hoarsely.

'It's okay, Mam. It's okay, let's go inside.'

He sat her down in the kitchen and she began to shake.

'It's okay, it's okay, Mam,' he said, rubbing her arms. June came in behind him. 'June, will you phone an ambulance? I think Mam is in shock.'

'No!' his mother shouted. 'No, I don't need an ambulance. I just have to show you. It's in the bin. I put it in the bin.'

'What, Mam? You put what in the bin?'

'In the bin, in the bin,' she said, pointing out the back of the house, where the wheelie bin was.

Collins got up. His mother was staring straight ahead of her.

'It's okay Mrs Collins,' June said. 'We'll have a cup of tea, you got a bit of a shock. I'll put the kettle on.'

Collins rushed out through the utility room and into the back yard. He pulled open the lid of the wheelie bin. There, on top of some ashes and garden waste, was a large white bag. It was open and messy with red liquid stuck to the plastic. He looked inside. At the heads of four foxes, one large, the other three small. Their eyes were open, their tongues were hanging out, their mouths and teeth set in a mocking grin.

25

Collins was sitting at one end of a large conference table in Meeting Room Number 1, in Anglesea Street Garda Station, with eight other people. He was trying to control his temper. He had insisted upon the meeting, repeatedly phoning Jonno and Clancy in the days after Mazur's arrest. Each unanswered call was followed by a more belligerent one.

Michael O'Leary, his Garda Representative Association officer, who sat beside him, tapped him on the side of his foot. Collins looked at him and Michael nodded down. Collins saw his own knee bouncing up and down under the table. He had been unaware of it.

The others at the table were June – she had insisted; Clancy and O'Regan as chief investigators; Gerard Brennan, a self-important inspector to whom Clancy and O'Regan were reporting, and who was Jonno's usual go-between; another inspector, Sheila Thompson, who was the head of Human Resources and who really shouldn't be there for this issue, but Jonno liked to keep meetings top-heavy with his cronies; and finally – and this had thrown Collins – sitting beside Jonno was John Doyle, of the Killarney District, in his resplendent superintendent uniform. He, with his shining pink face, and his three chins flopping out over a tight collar. He was obviously proud of his fine head of thick black hair, he kept it so slicked and well-barbered.

Collins was not sure why Doyle was there, he didn't have anything to do with the case or with him. It must have been some management issue, or Jonno wanted to cover his ass. Not knowing, or even having a viable theory, rankled with Collins, along with a lot of other things.

Jonno was droning on about staff cuts and new priorities and all the usual filibustering stuff that he came up with in order to avoid talking about the point at hand.

'Superintendent,' Collins said, 'I just want to know when this guy will be charged.'

'Yes, but that's the problem, Collins,' Jonno said. 'Charged with what?'

'The knife, for starters,' Collins said.

'His prints were on the knife, but he's denying he attacked you,' Clancy said.

'Of course he's denying it,' Collins said. 'What did you think, he'd confess?'

'Yes, but these Europol Red Notices are very serious,' Jonno said, waving some sheets of paper before him. 'The Polish Embassy has been plaguing the Deputy Commissioner about it.'

'Hold on,' Collins said. 'Since when does an attempted murder in our jurisdiction *not* take precedence over a European Arrest Warrant?'

'We'll never get him for attempted murder, Collins, even with the knife,' Clancy said. 'You know the DPP wouldn't touch it with a forty-foot pole.'

'Not if we don't fucking try,' Collins said, realising he'd gone too far.

'Calm down, Collins,' Jonno said. 'We all want this animal behind bars. Now, I got a phone call yesterday from the Chief Prosecutor in Lublin and he guaranteed me ...' Jonno tapped the table with his forefinger for emphasis. 'He *guaranteed* me that this guy, what's his name?'

'Mazur,' Clancy said. 'Tomasz Mazur.'

' ... Mazur, would be going down for twenty years minimum. Might even be more,' he said, 'there's talk of war crimes in Iraq, for Christ's sake.'

'I wonder would you be of the same opinion, Superintendent,' Collins said quietly, 'if this person had arrived with a knife at *your* mother's house in the middle of the night? And not mine?'

He glanced at June and her eyes were wide, warning him to calm down. There was a long silence until Jonno coughed and spoke.

'You know what, Collins?' he said. 'If it was my mother's house I might feel different. But the fact is that it wasn't. And the fact is that these Red Notices are for murder, attempted murder and extortion. And they are cut and dried, while all we have at the moment is an accusation of assault from O'Callaghan on his client, Mazur, against *you*. His list of injuries is very extensive, I must say.'

'Don't we have a witness who put him in the café the day I was poisoned? And he's a known associate of Molloy,' Collins said.

'That witness withdrew her statement a couple of weeks ago,' Clancy said.

'Why wasn't I told?' Collins said. 'What reason did she give?'

'She said she wasn't sure anymore,' Clancy said. He threw up his hands. 'Nothing we can do.'

'That's 'cos they got to her,' Collins said.

'I put that to her,' Clancy said. 'Forcefully. But she's adamant.'

The question that Collins really wanted to ask was how Derek O'Callaghan, Molloy's pet solicitor, was waiting for Mazur's ambulance at the hospital and was by his side the moment he fully regained consciousness. Collins was certain that Mazur was faking his grogginess after the paramedics arrived – he just wanted to buy time. Who had called O'Callaghan? And, how had they gotten his mother's address in the first place? Which bastard in the station had told Molloy? That's what he really wanted to know, and when he found out …

He said nothing, trying to keep his control. Whatever he let people know about that issue would not do him any good.

'Was there blood on the knife?' he said.

'The results are just in,' Clancy said, reading from a sheet of paper. 'Yes, foxes' blood and human blood.'

'Human blood,' Collins said. 'What about that?'

'Collins, we can charge him with some petty crime if we want, but what good will that do us?' Jonno said. 'This way we get rid of him and he's away for a long time. He might even be tried at The Hague when he gets out.'

'What about the poisoning?' Collins said. 'Where are we on that?'

Clancy coughed and shuffled in his chair.

'Not very far,' he said. 'We can't link Mazur to it, let alone Molloy, and there's still no sign of the waitress. We've no CCTV, no forensics, and without that witness …' He shrugged. 'We've nothing, really, not even circumstantial. And we've no way of linking them to the poison either.'

'*I* saw him there,' Collins said. 'And now he's at my mother's house with a deadly weapon.'

'He has an alibi for that date,' Clancy said. 'It's your word against his, and even if Mazur was there, what does it get us? You had just swallowed poison. You know what a barrister would do with that if it ever came to court – which it won't.'

Collins threw up his hands. There was another long silence.

'Alright. Alright,' he said, defeated. The whole thing was a fucking joke from start to finish. 'The next thing I want to talk about is coming back to work.'

'Right,' Jonno said, and he opened the second file before him. 'Detectives, can you leave, please? Michael? And you, Gerard; and you too, John, if you don't mind. This is a private HR matter relating to Detective Collins.'

Collins kept his eyes down as the gardaí left the room. Michael, beside him, wrote '2 weeks?' on the top of his pad and showed it to him. Collins nodded.

'Michael,' Jonno said. 'This isn't really a GRA matter, is it? I don't think you need to be here.'

'I want representation, Superintendent,' Collins said. 'I think I'm entitled to that, at least.'

'Are you okay with that, Sheila?' Jonno said.

'Fine by me, Superintendent,' Sheila said.

'Thank you,' Collins said.

'Superintendent,' Michael said. 'Collins here has the complete backing of the Association to return to work immediately. Full duties. And he has a letter from his GP, too, indicating ...' he read from it, '"major physical improvement, weight gain, bloods showing no abnormalities, no apparent mental health issues". He's completely fit for duty.'

'Now, Michael, you know that's not an option,' Jonno said. 'Sheila here will fill ye in.'

'There's two issues,' Sheila said. She had an unusually hoarse voice, one that other officers mimicked. 'There's the physical fitness to work issue – you nearly died, Collins.'

'I'm aware of what happened, Inspector, and my medical situation. My GP is happy I've made a full recovery.'

'And then there's the psychological issue,' Sheila said, ignoring the interruption.

'What psychological issue?' Collins said. 'I was passed fully fit and recovered twelve months ago.'

'I'm not talking about The Butcher,' Sheila said. 'You nearly died, Collins. That's a seriously traumatic event. We've had advice that you need another psychological evaluation.'

'This is bullshit,' Collins said.

'Calm down, Collins,' Jonno said. 'I won't tell you again. This is medical advice, we can't go against it.'

'Superintendent,' Michael said. 'Detective Collins is offering to undergo a physical and psychological evaluation this week. We want an appointment with the Chief Medical Officer immediately. If Doctor Laker approves – which she will, I'm sure – I presume he can return to work straight away, full duties.'

'Desk duties,' Jonno said. 'I'm holding firm on that.' He paused for a moment. 'For now.'

'The Association will act on that, Superintendent,' Michael said. 'It could be seen, externally, as punishing a hero, a man who has been the victim of a vicious attack. A winner of the Scott Medal only last year. I'd say the public would approve of a promotion, not a demotion.'

'This is not a demotion, or a public issue, Michael,' Jonno said. 'And it's not a GRA issue either, as I've already pointed out. I hope you're not threatening to go to the media with it.'

Michael blinked. Jonno and Sheila exchanged glances. Collins said nothing.

'Jesus, Collins,' Jonno said. 'Would you not wait until the new year at least?'

'I'd prefer to be back at work, Superintendent,' Collins said.

'Making a contribution.' This was a pet saying of Jonno and the Superintendent now stared at him with hostility. Collins was close to burning bridges, but he didn't care anymore.

'Very well,' Jonno said. 'Sheila, will you arrange that with the CMO, please? Collins, if she approves a return to work, desk duties for two months and we'll reassess. Take it or leave it.'

Collins stared him down. He didn't want to be stuck at a desk, like a piece of furniture.

Jonno cleared his throat. 'If you do have some spare time, I might be able to reassign you to the odd case.'

Collins looked at Michael and nodded again.

'Thank you, Superintendent,' Michael said. 'Inspector.' He smiled, stood up and closed the file before him. He patted Collins on the shoulder.

Collins tried to smile but couldn't.

26

Three days later, Collins drove his mother to Shannon to board a flight to New York City. He and Paul were surprised at how little she had resisted the idea, especially with Christmas only a few weeks away. Paul's wife, Connie, had sealed the deal, talking up the snowy walks in Central Park, how her grandchildren wanted to show her the Rockefeller Centre, and what a lovely time they would have. But the real reason for her trip gnawed at Collins. She was afraid – in her own home. Since the night of the foxes' heads she had looked wretched and agreed to take sleeping tablets – for the first time in her life.

She tried to be cheerful and chatty on the drive, but the residue of the sleeping tablet meant that she was nodding off until Limerick. She was nervous, fussily checking her ticket, passport and ESTA form in her bag every twenty minutes. They put her in a wheelchair at check-in and it broke his heart to see her being wheeled away into the maw of the security area. He drove back to Cork in a temper, teeth gritted, pushing the car hard.

He moved back in to his apartment. He walked further and further around the city every day and his strength and endurance improved. He told himself that being back at work would improve things, that he'd have direction and people around him. He tried to convince himself that he would pass the CMO medical examination. He tried to eat more.

Violette stayed with him most nights, though she was so untidy that he had to fight a constant battle with himself not to chide her.

But she opened the front window by the balcony to smoke, and he liked having the company and the sex.

On a bright, chilly morning he decided they would get a taxi to Blackrock Castle for brunch and then walk it off, back along the river. He wanted to push himself on a long walk and to tell her something that had been on his mind.

The castle restaurant was bright and warm and Collins wore his shades and basked in the milky sunlight. Violette ate her full Irish breakfast quickly and with gusto. Afterwards, the fine bones of her face were lit with pleasure, her fingers wrapped around her third cup of coffee. She hummed, as she sometimes did when gratified.

'Come on, Collins, hurry up, why do you eat so slow?'

He enjoyed the way she said his name, emphasising the second syllable.

'I always used to eat slowly, even before I became a stick insect that can only nibble,' he said.

He examined the sunlight on the tea in his white cup. How could he never have noticed the dusky, exotic colour of sunlit tea before?

'Okay, let's go,' he said. 'I'll never finish this anyway.'

He said hello to a retired colleague, Tony Kinsella, and his wife, Margaret, on his way out. Collins hadn't met him for eighteen months. Tony shook his hand, speechless. Margaret spoke up.

'Collins, what happened you? You're skin and bone, lad. And as pale as a shroud.'

'Margaret,' Tony said, in admonishment.

Collins smiled, though he was stung. 'Yes, I was sick there for a while. Stomach troubles, Margaret, but I'm on the mend now. I should be back at work in a week or two. This is Violette. Violette, this is Tony and Margaret Kinsella, I used to work with Tony, back in the day.'

Margaret smelled a bigger story about his hollow look, and wanted more details, but Collins prevaricated.

He paid and left, resolving to eat more and get some sun. Maybe a trip to Italy.

From Castle Road he showed Violette one of his favourite views of the river, with the city off in the distance. The Marina on the south bank, its trees winter-bare, and the fine houses of Montenotte on the hill to the north.

As they walked along the Marina, two scullers pulled their oars steadily in the calm water and Collins pointed out Páirc Uí Chaoimh, the stadium where he had trained and played so often. It was being redeveloped, and the bright new terrace and stand towered above them.

'You?' she said, disbelieving. 'In this stadium?'

'I told you I used to play sport. When I was on the county team it's where we trained. But they have some local club games here too. Well, the big ones. Of course there won't be any matches played there now until it's finished next summer.'

He thought about all the matches he had won and lost there and, unusually for him, he felt a wrench. When he had stopped playing, when his knee could take no more injections, and he couldn't train properly, and the great coach Canon Con had been ousted by the County Board, Collins had just walked away without a glance over his shoulder. It had seemed natural, the right time, even with what the psychotherapist had told him later. He'd had enough, been lucky for the most part, done his bit. No regrets. But just then, he remembered that feeling. The sound of 60,000 people in Croke Park, when you score a goal.

They walked back into the city. It was one of those still, perfect, sunlit winter days. Violette snuggled into him for warmth and he enjoyed that, his arm around her.

At Brian Boru Bridge, he glanced to his right. He could hear hip-hop blaring out of a Golf GTI, stopped at the lights. It was full of teenagers. He recognised the two in the front, they were Tomás and Kevin Molloy, sons of Bobby, Molloy's brother. Collins had almost gotten them on a possession for sale or supply charge. They were dealing for their uncle and the car was a good indication of how lucrative it was.

'Stay here,' Collins said to Violette and he went onto the road towards the Golf. The Molloy brothers saw him approach, in alarm. The lights changed and the car shot forward and Tomás, grinning in the passenger seat, gave him the finger. Collins could see the kids in the back now, too. Sitting in the middle was Kyle Buckley, a guilty expression on his face.

A car beeped and Collins glowered at the driver and stepped back onto the footpath.

'You know them?' Violette said.

'Unfortunately,' Collins said, and they walked on.

They continued west along Patrick's Quay and Camden Quay, noisy and ugly with cars and buses.

Collins glanced at St Mary's Church as he passed, and up at the statue. He was trying not to think about Kyle in the back of that car. He told Violette about the Lavitt family, French Protestant property developers from the eighteenth century. He pointed out the different seabirds perched on the river's limestone quay walls.

They crossed to the North Mall, where railings replaced the walls. It was one of Collins's favourite streets, a pleasant, leafy, shady stroll in summer, lovely with evening sunlight on the river, the trees on one side and the tall residential Georgian terrace on the other.

'This used to be the red light district of Cork a hundred years ago, to service the British Army. Wherever you get soldiers, you get prostitutes.'

'Really?' Violette asked. 'Where is it now?'

'What, the British Army?'

'No!' She punched his arm. 'The red light district. Is there one?'

'Now the red light district is everywhere. The Internet saw to that. Unfortunately.'

'Why "unfortunately"?' she asked. 'Is it not good for the sex workers to be in better places than the streets? Now they can work in their own homes if they want. At least they have some control.'

'Hmm. Maybe, for some.' He rubbed his chin; he didn't like talking about work. 'But most of the prostitutes I come across are either trafficked women from Eastern Europe or Africa, or drug addicts being exploited and abused every day of the week for a pittance. The pimp takes most of the money and little of the risk. One particular drug dealer runs the prostitution in Cork and he has a guy checking for freelance operations on the Internet. If he finds any, he hurts them – badly – unless they agree to work for him. Hospital badly.'

Violette shuddered.

A grey heron flew upriver and Collins watched its old, slow grace.

In Fitzgerald Park they sat outside the café in the shaded cold so that Violette could smoke. Collins was glad of the rest. He would have to bluff his way through the physical exam with the Chief Medical Officer the following week, but most gardaí his age would struggle with that. He drank herbal tea and smelled the smoke longingly.

At the end of the Lee Fields they were almost in the countryside, and they stopped to turn around. The river was handsome there, bordered by tall willows. Collins readied himself for what he wanted to say.

She sensed the change in him.

'Collins?'

'I was just thinking that you might be in danger,' he said. 'The man behind the poisoning and that thing with the foxes wouldn't hesitate to attack you to get to me. I won't hold it against you if you choose not to be with me.'

She seemed startled and hesitated before replying.

'No,' she said, shaking her head. 'I am not afraid of him.'

But Collins was not convinced. He kissed her and held her. He bowed to smell her hair and feel it with his lips. He watched the swirling water, murky and deep.

27

They stopped into The Bierhaus on the way home. Collins felt he deserved a drink, even in the afternoon. The low sunlight was shining into the pub, lighting up the array of beer bottles behind the bar. He ordered a golden ale made in west Kerry called *Béal Bán*, after a favourite beach there in Smerwick Harbour. He remembered a glorious day with Deirdre watching horses racing across its sand, in a different life.

Violette had her usual pint of Beamish. They took their first sips, savouring. He told her about Corca Dhuibhne, the most beautiful place in the world, and promised to bring her there. She didn't know the film *Ryan's Daughter*, which amazed him.

She went outside for a cigarette, taking her stout with her.

He thought about the lyrics of a Bruce Springsteen song: *Is a dream a lie if it don't come true/Or is it something worse?* All those dreams. He vowed to himself that he really would bring Violette there, and look out at the *Fear Marbh*. He tried not to read too much into her hesitation before saying that she was not afraid of Molloy, out in the Lee Fields.

She returned to the table with a small excited man in tow.

'Collins, this is Eamonn. He wants to say hello and get a selfie, is that okay?'

Collins extended a hand, half-standing. 'How's the going?' he said.

Eamonn was gushy.

'Jesus. Tim Collins, what an honour. My brother won't believe this. Fuck it, legend. Thanks, thanks very much. Eamonn

O'Sullivan, Valley Rovers. You played against my dad in the county final in '99. Seamus, Seamus O'Sullivan.'

Collins smiled and beckoned him in for the photo. He seemed to take several. Collins put on his solemn expression for photos, trying for James Joyce inscrutability and failing, as usual.

Eamonn hesitated. He seemed torn between boasting to his two friends near the door while putting the picture up on Twitter and Facebook, and trying to initiate a proper conversation and stay.

He shook his head again and said, 'Jesus, Collins, you owe us nothing, boy.'

'Thanks, Eamonn,' Collins said, quietly.

Eamonn offered to buy them drinks. When Collins demurred, he returned to be with his friends and seek out his social media likes.

Violette scowled at Collins.

'What?' he said. 'I let him take the photo.'

'You never told me you were this … this legend hurler.' *Legande hurlare.*

'I told you I played in Páirc Uí Chaoimh earlier. I thought you said you googled me in June before our first date? Surely there was something there about me being a Cork hurler?'

'Yes, but he said you were this famous hero to all of them. In all of Cork. You won three big Irish championships. He said you were the best he ever saw, Collins.'

'He didn't look hard enough.'

She was still not happy. 'What did he say at the end? I didn't hear him. You said "thanks" to him.'

Collins had to think to remember. 'He said that I didn't owe them anything. It's something we say. Men, especially. It's a kind of euphemism. We're not good at compliments. It's something we say to a person who has done some … service. Who has …' He was suddenly moved. 'It means he thinks I've done well. For my people, my county.'

He paused.

'It *is* nice when somebody, a hurling man especially, says something like that,' he said. 'I do appreciate it. And I don't owe them anything, I suppose.'

She shook her head. 'You are so strange, Collins. Most men would be boasting about this all the day long. Why not?'

'I don't know. It was a long time ago, Violette. It's over and done with.'

'Not to him!' she exclaimed, pointing.

'I know, I know. I … I was getting some therapy early last year for a while, after a case. I had post-traumatic stress after I'd encountered this murderer. A serial killer. Anyway,' he continued, not meeting her gaze, 'the psychotherapist kept asking me about the hurling, and I couldn't understand why. She knew about me and who I was, but she kept bringing me back to when I stopped playing.'

Collins moved closer to her, he didn't want anybody else to overhear.

'She said that sometimes a recent trauma rekindles older, more serious traumas that have not been resolved and they join forces together, and attack you *en masse*. She thought I had never come to terms with not being able to play hurling anymore. And that's why I didn't talk about it. She said it was common, and the higher the level of the sport, especially professional sport, the worse the potential loss.' Collins sipped his pint. He was sorry now he'd begun this conversation.

'I didn't believe her, but I'm not so sure now,' he said. 'So when people like Eamonn say nice things about my hurling, yes, it's a validation of sorts. Because I often get criticised too, especially about one incident in my career, one match.'

He caught the barman's attention and pointed to the two glasses, indicating more drinks.

'What happened?' she said.

'It was in the All-Ireland final of 1997. We had won the previous two years, so we were going for three in a row – that's a big deal, even for Cork. And I had been man of the match the previous two years in the final, so a lot was expected of me. Anyway, it was all going well, we were winning by a few points when early in the second half, one of the Kilkenny backs – defenders – hit me off the ball.'

'What does it mean?' Violette asked. '"Off the ball?"'

'Oh, it means when the ball is not nearby. Sometimes you get hit when you and your opponent are contesting the ball, but this time the ball was well away from us.' Collins finished his pint.

'So, anyway, I hit him back. Harder. And I knocked him out. Well, he went down and didn't get up. Nothing wrong with the fucker, he was putting it on. But one of the umpires saw me hit him and told the referee and I was sent off.'

'But he hit you first!'

'Yes, but that doesn't matter if it's not seen. Anyway, we lost the match by one point. One solitary point. So the blame for it was put on me. And I still get asked to this day, almost twenty years later, why did I hit him? Why could I not just have played on? I wasn't hurt.'

Collins went to the bar to pay for and collect the two drinks. The barman said he'd drop the Beamish down.

'What do you say? When they ask you,' Violette said.

'Mostly, I tell them to fuck off and mind their own business. But when I do talk to somebody I respect about it – a hurling person, I mean – I tell them that I *had* to hit him back. When you're hit, you have to hit back. It's the only way.'

He thought for a moment, twirling a beer mat on the table.

'I told you earlier that my father taught me about birds. Well he also taught me how to fight. I don't mean physically fight, he wasn't much good at that, especially when I got bigger than him. I mean *any* fight. Any contest or confrontation.'

The barman came with the Beamish and the change.

'He taught me that when you are in the fight, there is only the fight. It's the only thing. And you have to win. You have to. You either win or you lose, there is nothing else. Nothing in between. When it's over, you can move on. But while it's on, it's the only thing. And you cannot lose, whatever it takes.'

'Whatever?'

'Whatever it takes.'

She watched him intensely, her bottom lip sticking up.

'What do you think the most important thing is in a fight or a contest?' he said. 'Say an athletic contest, like hurling, but it's true of all contests or struggles. Is it size, speed, fitness, strength, skill, luck, intelligence.' He paused. 'Confidence, ruthlessness, calmness, experience? What?'

'All of those?' she said.

'No. All of those can be important and they usually are at the high levels of sport. The most important thing is *will*. The will to win. And it's not desire. You can desire something as much as you want, but the sheer willpower or resolve to win brings all the other factors into play. And it enhances all of them. Without it …' He shrugged.

'And what that *will* means, essentially, is that losing is not an option. It is not acceptable, it is simply not going to happen – no matter what. No matter *what* the cost, *what* the fallout, whatever it takes: materially, spiritually, ethically, physically, reputationally, financially. It doesn't matter. The will to win is the single most important thing – by a long, long way. And all the great players, all the people who have achieved – in any sphere – writers, artists, musicians, you name it: they have it. The person with the biggest will to win, wins. And that's that.'

His mouth was dry. He took a sip from the fresh pint. He entwined his fingers in a clasp and rested his elbows on his knees. He didn't know why he was talking so much.

'And, the moment your opponent realises it – that your will is bigger than his – he's beat. He's finished. What most people don't understand is that the very part of me that caused me to hit Treacy that day was the same part that won me man of the match, and Cork the All-Ireland, the previous two years. I'd been hit and hit back in those matches too, but they didn't go down and I wasn't sent off.'

He paused.

'Now. I *should* have been smarter, and picked a better time, or not hit him as hard. But I had to hit him back. There is no other way. And that's what I learned from my father. And that's who I am.'

He met her eyes again. He was embarrassed.

'Now you know,' he said. 'So, what do you think?'

'What do I think? That I've never seen you so passionate, even in bed and you are not so bad there. Also, when you were talking just now you looked ten years younger.' Another Gallic shrug. 'I don't understand sport. I don't like it. To me, it's crazy – men trying to be better than each other, chasing a ball. But there is no denying the emotion.' She pulled at the stud in her right ear, a habit of hers. 'You should have heard the – I forget the word – something sacred in his voice when he was talking about you outside,' she said.

'Holiness?'

'No, it begins with "r".'

He thought for a moment. '"Reverence?"'

'*Oui, révérence.* I think maybe that is what sport is. A religion for men. So, does that make you a god, Collins?'

'Sounds like a good plan to me. I'm all for it.'

'Oh yes? Be careful. You know what Victor Hugo said about God?'

'No. Tell me.'

'He said, "The eyes cannot see God clearly except through tears."'

Collins saluted Eamonn on the way out of the pub. Eamonn grinned and waved his phone.

'Legend, Collins. Twenty retweets! I'm going viral, man.'

Collins winced.

28

Collins and Violette sat on the couch listening to Anouar Brahem. Violette was reading and taking notes in her pyjamas. She was writing an academic paper on ethics using Fritz Lang's *M* as a case study – a 1931 film in which a man called Beckert, a serial killer of children in Düsseldorf, is captured by a criminal gang and put on 'trial'. They had watched it together on YouTube the previous night.

'I'm using different ethical systems to interrogate the film,' she said.

'How do you mean?'

'I'll give you an example. If the ethics is a simple rule, like in Christianity: "you shall not kill". This means the criminal mob have no right to kill Beckert.'

'Yes, but in Islam the children's families *would* have the right to have him killed, or to forgive him if they get compensation,' Collins said.

'Yes, but in this case it is clear they would kill him. That is obvious by the first trial, when the mothers want Beckert to die.'

'Okay. What other systems are there?'

'The next one is …' She flicked back over her notes. 'Consequentialism – this is the greater good for the greatest number of people. Here maybe you could say that he should be killed, in case he escapes or is freed because of Paragraph 51.'

'I thought Paragraph 51 was the rule that he wouldn't be executed because he was insane and was compelled to kill the children.'

'Oh yes, but because of it he cannot be executed in the film. So he lives. But still, the greater good for the greatest number says that he should die.'

'Yes,' Collins said. 'But it depends on your definition of greatest good. The Nazis thought that the greater good allowed them to exterminate six million people.'

'Hmm. I do not want to involve the Nazis. Anyway, they banned the film. And Lang had to run away to America.'

'And Peter Lorre.'

'*Oui*,' she said, writing. She took a sip of wine. 'Then there is the virtue ethics system, or ethics based on a series of values. For example, in modern democratic society, the murderer, even when found guilty, has fundamental rights, just like the victim.'

'Hence the end of capital punishment in Europe.'

'So in this system, Beckert would be sent to the asylum where he was before, when he was "cured" and released to kill more children.' She made the two-finger gesture of air quotes.

'Yes, it has happened in Ireland too,' Collins said. 'There is a prison for the criminally insane and some people have been "cured" and released, only for them to kill again.'

She thought for a moment and read her notes.

'The question is about Lang's view of what is justice and what should be done with Beckert,' she said. 'And it is not clear in the film. In the end, it's obvious that he will be sent to the asylum, *non*?'

'But why doesn't Lang make that clear?' Collins said. 'We just see the judges sitting down and one of them says "In the name of the state" or something. Maybe he is leaving it up to the viewer and not recommending one sentence over the other.'

'"In the name of the nation." Yes, it is not clear,' she said. 'I think he tells his view in the comment of the mother at the end.

She says "this too won't bring back our children". So it does not matter whether Beckert is locked up or killed. It will not bring back the children.'

'Is there a class issue in the film?' Collins said.

'What do you mean?'

He put down his wine glass.

'Is there an implication that it doesn't matter if Beckert is killed or not because the kids were poor? Or it was the mothers' fault because they didn't take proper care of their kids? Because I often think that's the case in Ireland. The kids up in Knocknaheeny don't matter as much as the kids in Bishopstown. And if it was the rich kids dying from drugs, you can be sure something would be done about it.'

'No. No, no, no. Pfftt,' she said, flicking her hand in the air. 'You and your class issues, Collins. Oh là là, it's all you think about.'

'No it isn't! And another thing: if it was men and not women being trafficked and forced into prostitution, there would be a lot more done, too.'

'Well, we agree on that subject,' she said.

'Getting back to the moral-based system,' he said. 'When I was in school a priest told us that the end never justified the means. And we used to test him on this. So, for example, if you could have killed Hitler in 1930 in Vienna, wouldn't it have been the right thing, preventing the Second World War and saving fifty million lives? Taking one life and saving fifty million?'

'And what did he say? The priest.'

'He said "no". It would be wrong. It would be murder. You would go to hell. And that's about the time that the Catholic Church lost me. Because I think that if you can take one life to save many, then you are duty-bound to do so. Especially the life of a mass murderer, or somebody who might kill again.'

Violette laughed. 'Is that you being God, again, Collins?'

Collins stood, put his hands in his pockets, and moved to the window. He looked at the statue of the Blessed Virgin Mary on the church across the river.

29

It was early, still not bright, when Collins stepped out onto Lavitt's Quay and turned towards the Opera House. The day's Christmas buzz was yet to come. Opera Lane glittered under lights. He saw the reflection of his stooped father in a shop window and stopped. He straightened his shoulders and walked right up to the glass until he saw himself again.

He crossed a quiet Patrick Street and strode down Winthrop Street. He realised his feet were carrying him; he was on auto-pilot. Just another man on his way to work.

The results of his fitness-for-work medical with the CMO had come through the previous week. He had torn open the envelope in the downstairs hall of his apartment building, suspecting what it was.

One photocopied sheet of paper and nothing else. A form, with his name and details at the top. The box 'Medically fit for duties' had been ticked and the Chief Medical Officer's scrawl was at the bottom. He had stared at it for a long time, the wind whistling under the big hall door.

Now he was standing on Anglesea Street, staring at the garda station across the road. Somebody watching him might think he was making a decision. The neo-fascist pillars of the building seemed as soulless as ever. The huge telecommunications mast on top of it was just as ugly.

He crossed the road and pulled open the large door, which gave a cranky creak. He stopped in front of the desk sergeant, whose glasses were perched on the end of his nose, his head bent, buried in a document.

'How'ya Tom?' Collins said.

Tom's head shot up and his eyes opened wide and were filled with something Collins could not read. Tom removed his glasses, slowly put them on the desk and took a step back. His heels shot together and he raised his right hand in a formal salute.

Collins, nonplussed, saluted back.

'Tom …?'

'Welcome back, Detective Collins,' Tom said, lowering his hand. He leaned towards the glass and said, face darkened, in a lower voice: 'Go get the fuckers, boy.'

Collins smiled.

'Busy, Tom?'

'Hectic here, Collins.'

PART 3

15 DECEMBER 2016

30

Claire Halvey stepped from the black BMW 5 Series car on Merchant's Quay, lugged her backpack out the door, and said a perfunctory 'Bye' to her father. She heaved the bag over her shoulder and walked towards the traffic lights to cross the street.

As if she were going to her school, Coláiste Bhríde, today. As if she were a good, studious and obedient eighteen-year-old daughter. As if she were not preparing to meet her boyfriend, Dave, to have sex with him in his friend's flat in College Road. As if she had not been meeting him there for that purpose since 20 October. This was their fourth time – well, not their fourth time doing it, they'd done it a lot more times than that, obviously – but their fourth time meeting up there. And she had loved every minute of it, every touch of it, every smell and taste of it. And could not wait until the next time. The next time, sweetly, being today.

Claire had texted the school from her mother's phone earlier, saying she was sick. The Vice-Principal, Miss Connolly, was so organised that she replied immediately, which allowed Claire to delete the reply as well as the original text before her mum could see them.

Claire stopped at the lights, waiting for the green, and crossed to the bridge, glancing backwards. Seeing no sign of her father's car on Patrick Street, she turned around and made her way into the shopping centre and up to Rosie's Café. She went to the toilet and changed out of her school uniform and boring shoes into the short black skirt he liked and her denim jacket and her Docs.

She reversed the backpack from the 'girlie' red design to the grungier black adorned with the badges Dave had given her. Muse, Pearl Jam, Nickelback and her favourite, Biffy Clyro, whom they had seen together at that amazing gig in June in the Marquee, when she had taken her first tab and flown like a bird above the world all night long.

Claire sipped her Coke for almost an hour, checking her feeds on Facebook and Instagram. A picture of Rihanna with a glass of wine reminded her of her mother, who seemed always to have a glass of wine in her hand and always to be slurring and unsteady by bedtime. She shivered at the thought of the fights between her parents. The silences. She moved the straw around in her Coke. How could they do that to her? Christmas was, like, going to be *so* boring.

On the way down the escalator, her phone beeped with a text. *On my way, can't w8.* From Dave.

Me2, she replied.

She entered the Beauty section of Debenhams. It was alright and they had Chanel, Givenchy and Tom Ford, but it wasn't a patch on Brown Thomas. She couldn't risk BT this morning, in case she'd meet one of her mum's friends. Still, she could picture it all so clearly. The feel of money and class everywhere.

The MAC corner, with all the beauticians in black and the black walls, then out into Lancôme with their Flash Bronzer Tanning Gel. Then Estée Lauder – so fab, through Benefit, Nails.INC, where she got her nails done for her cousin Lucy's wedding. Chanel on the left and Giorgio Armani beside the escalator, and Tom Ford. Oh. My. God. His stuff is, like, so cool. Back to Bobbi Brown near the door and Dior behind them and Yves Saint Laurent next, and Sisley – she didn't really like them. Aveda, so boring, and then Clinique and Molton Brown, where she got her wonderful shower gel.

The girl at the Benefit counter was happy to do her eyes with mascara and shadow, though she never stopped talking. Claire enjoyed the pampering and sprayed herself with the Dolce & Gabbana Light Blue on her way to the 205 bus stop outside.

It was so great being a woman, not a girl anymore. She could do anything she wanted. Fuck them.

31

Gerry Halvey drove through Patrick Street, vigilant for pedestrians crossing. He was early. For some reason Claire had been ready on time that morning. He drove mindfully, letting two indicating vans pull out in front of him.

He was trying to do everything mindfully now. With compassion, awareness and a lack of judgement. This was his last hope of getting through it all. His sanity had been slipping away piece by piece over the past eight years. He wasn't sure how much there was left.

After her affairs he did not really care about the marriage. The money and houses didn't matter, either. But he would not lose his home, Claire's home – no way. He needed to shield her from the last of the financial crisis fallout. And he needed to keep his mental health to achieve that. Just a few more years and he could take his package from the bank.

It was over with Elaine, he was sure of it. She would hardly notice if he never came home again as long as the Pinot Grigio didn't run out. Minister's sister or not, the marriage was finished, just a question of when that was formalised. Maybe when Claire went to college.

At least his mother was dead – that made it easier.

He enjoyed the city's early morning calm before the bustle began. Shop assistants and office workers walking purposefully. Van drivers delivering. A street cleaner with his barrow, cleaning. The city awakening, ready for another day of trade, moving money around.

At Singer's Corner he felt the familiar urge to turn right and escape west to his beloved Baltimore and the sea. Especially on such a beautiful morning. He could only guess for how much longer he would have his summer house there. Not long, once NAMA and the bank forced their terms. He would be lucky to hang on to anything. But he would never give up his home. Claire's home.

He parked in the car park at the back of the bank on the South Mall and used his staff-card to enter the building. It was still quiet, thank God, nobody around, his steps the only sound as he trudged up the stairs to his office.

Thankfully he did not have to share it with anyone. He thought he noticed a whining, begging tinge to his phone voice these days, and he was glad nobody else could hear it. Day in and day out, he was attempting to rein back in the same money he had distributed in huge amounts before 2008 – on good commission. Calling the same people that he had called then; people no longer interested in answering his calls.

He missed working in the old bank, being in the midst of the counters and the floor. The buzz of people, the physical presence of the small but real money being passed around – its lovely metallic, dirty smell. Unlike electronic money, numbers on a screen, the unseen flow of million after million, unreal and distant, issued with the clicks of mice and the taps of computer keys.

The money was long gone, of course. It would never return. He knew it and they knew it, but everybody played the game. And some of the people still had assets and the bank wanted those. Needed those.

And the shares. All his lovely Allied Irish Bank shares. Worthless.

His mother had not believed him at first, on that day when he told her that everything his father had worked for and saved was gone. That she was penniless, the pension fund empty.

He winced at the memory, it was like a needle in his side.

When he'd shown her the figures, there in black and white, how she had sat up rigid in her chair, in front of the fire in her sitting room, surrounded by the tat her brother, the priest, had brought home from Peru. And then, looking at him like he was dirt, she said, 'I'm glad your father isn't alive to witness this fiasco. He'd be ashamed of you.'

How she had risen stiffly from the chair and gone out the door and up the stairs to her room. He had not spoken. He had not defended himself with the excuses so often rehearsed. He just sat there and took it and stewed in it, before putting up the fireguard, closing the door and leaving the house.

She was dead in eighteen months. Cancer. Nobody could convince him it wasn't brought on by the crash.

He thought about his father, a decent man. Went too soon, only weeks after retiring – that's a lesson for everyone. Built that business up from scratch. There'd never have been a commerce degree if it wasn't for his father, or that job in the bank. He had pulled strings in the golf club, that was well known. Straight in as deputy manager too. Almost thirty years ago now, where did they go?

As he approached his office door, he re-ran his daydream of getting out of bank shares and property – saving the day – just before the wipeout. He, the only one to see it coming. Selling off all the properties except the house, clearing out all the portfolios, just in time. Putting it all into Facebook or Apple or YouTube or something crazy that has quadrupled since. Convincing all his friends to do the same. They would be forever grateful – he'd have been the hero. He'd have saved the day.

He sat at his desk and powered up his desktop, his heart racing, his shoulders tense. Since the day he got that first message from NAMA with the numbers and the demands, he had felt this rising panic every time he opened his email. He had disabled the ping for new email because it was like an electric shock when it sounded.

He unlocked his desk drawer, opened the folded tissue and selected a bitten-off piece of fingernail from the bunch. He kept them there because his nails were now so short as to be useless. He put the piece of nail in his mouth and moved it with his tongue between two lower teeth. And then between another two – forth and back, back and forth.

He gazed out his window at the South Mall. The glorious early morning light worked its way down over the roofs of buildings. If only he could appreciate it. To be present in the moment. He typed in his username and password with unsteady fingers. He closed his eyes and began his first three-minute breathing space of the day.

He told himself that these feelings were just feelings. They were not him. They did not define him. It was up to him how he responded to any message, any situation. Not react, that wasn't the mindful way. Respond – *his* choice, *his* decision. He was free. His mind a sea, now tumultuous, would soon be calm. He would be whole again. The storm would soon be over. Soon.

32

Dave McMahon sauntered down the stairs of the home he shared with his mother and entered the kitchen. He picked up the cornflakes box, and poured a large portion into the bowl that had been laid on the neatly set table. He smiled. He needed his strength today. He took a carton of milk from the fridge, poured some on the cornflakes and picked up the spoon that had been placed beside it.

As if, at the age of nineteen, he needed his mother to set the table for him. As if he were going to tidy it up after himself. As if he were going to his crummy class in that crummy portacabin in CIT, to listen to those thick lecturers drone on about load-bearing walls and structural strains. As if he were ever going back to that dump when he'd soon be making five, ten times the money of any builders in the city.

He began to noisily eat the flakes, relishing every mouthful. He checked the condoms in his pocket – three should do. He propped up his phone against the cornflakes box and watched a clip from his favourite porn film. He imaged Claire as the woman in the video. He imagined himself as one of the men.

Dave smiled, not believing his luck. Sweet rich pussy, and all his.

His phone buzzed, a text from Damien.
WU@ CIT?
He replied.
Bootie 2day
Nice 1

Or 3

Give hr 1 4 me

#Mad4it

He checked himself in the mirror before leaving the house. *Killer dude, no wonder she's gagging for you.* He hesitated at the front door, wondering if he needed a coat over his hoodie. He decided against it, coats are for wimps. He remembered his backpack before he closed the door and then realised he didn't need it – no college today. No shithole CIT, no bald fat culchie useless lecturer Gilligan on his case the whole time.

He stepped out into Fairmount Park, its neat terraced houses arranged on three sides of a square. Most of them unremarkable and drab, a few proudly kept pin neat, two derelict and sad.

Marie Donoghue, a neighbour from three doors up and a friend of his mam's, was getting out of her car with a shopping bag.

'Hi Dave, off to college?' she said, cheerily.

They said she was a total ride when she was younger.

'Hi Marie, how's the going?'

'Not bad, Dave, quiet night on the ward, thank God. Looking forward to a nice cup of tea and a good sleep.'

'See you later,' Dave said.

'What time is Sharon home?'

'Eh, around ten, I think.'

'Grand. I'll send her a text in a minute.'

Dave strolled past old cars in the sunlight, chilly in his hoodie. He didn't notice the two men in the blue van, the driver tapping on his phone screen, the other – a big man – reading *The Sun*. Dave glanced to Number 8, where Jessie still lived with her mam and kid brother. Definitely going to give her one when she breaks it off with Hannigan, which she will any day now. Awesome pair of tits.

He saw that Deckie's bedroom curtain was still closed in Number 3. Lazy git. He had been good in soccer training the night before, though. What a header. Dave thought about his own performance. He knew he should cover midfield more, but why should he be the one always chasing back when Adam never even made a tackle? He was going to say it at training on Friday night.

He took out his phone to text Claire.

On my way, can't w8

She replied, *Me2*

He grinned. Un-fucking-believable.

He crossed Blarney Street, thinking about his dad in Spain. The big house in Madrid behind all the gates and the security guards. The bar in Alicante, the Audi with the driver, the models, the sunshine. What a life, bring it on.

He passed five schoolgirls. Two of them glanced back at him. He grinned again at the thought of the morning ahead and was immediately rock hard. A blue van passed him at the bottom of Shanakiel and turned right.

There was ice on the old wood of the Shaky Bridge so he took his hands out of his pockets. The light through the bars of the Fitzgerald Park was like a strobe, flashing in his eyes. UCC students gathered at the traffic lights on Western Road, on their way to lectures. Stuck-up cunts, the lot of them. Thought they were it. He walked through the university grounds, checking his Facebook page again.

His mate Darren had slagged him the night before when Liverpool lost to Chelsea, but he couldn't think of a good reply.

Zach and Joey had posted some selfies from a nightclub in Melbourne – having a gala, them. A text came through.

U on for tonite?

Jimmy Mul about later. Dave would be able to sell €300 worth of yokes for €800 easy peasy in The Pod. That's five hundred yoyos for three hours' work – if you could call it work. Probably get off with one of the randy freshers there too. More posh pussy.

4Sure 7@Deans?

8 will do

Cu then

It was okay money, but it was only for a while, anyway. When his dad brought him over to Spain, he'd be in the big time. Serious moolah.

On College Road he checked in his back pocket for the condoms again. Sorted. He did not see the man in the newsagents, watching him through the window.

33

Sharon McMahon shivered in the smoking shelter on her second break of the morning. She texted Dave.

You up?

Yeah.

She shook her head. That was about the most she ever got from her son, unless he wanted something. He probably wasn't up, either.

Her thin jacket was okay around the computer factory site but not outside in those stupid wide-open shelters with a December wind trying to take the face off you. You'd think they'd make them warmer, anyway.

She was proud that she was down to only two cigarettes at work now. Time was, she would be on her sixth fag after four hours of cleaning and be well into her second pack after tea, before *Coronation Street* came on. And she wasn't fit for much after Corrie with such an early start, but it was an okay job, she could keep her headphones on until eight when her boss came in. *And* she was drinking almost nothing, just a few glasses of wine on Saturday night.

She felt better than she had in years, and she knew she looked it too. With her own house and her own job and her own cash. No thanks to that prick of an ex-husband, who'd done a runner off to Spain with Molloy's money. Good riddance to bad rubbish – she didn't need him. If he'd any decency he'd send a few quid more, but no surprise there. What he did send she squirrelled away in the Post Office for a rainy day. If Molloy knew that … she shivered again.

With her mam getting Alzheimer's and Dave in college there was never enough. The second job minding Mrs Matthews some nights was a big help – cash in hand – and she didn't want Dave to be working when he should be studying – if he ever did a tap. Still, he'd passed his first-year exams, anyway.

She wondered if Jimmy would help out – he *was* Mickey's brother and Dave's uncle, after all, and he had his own business. But it would be too much like him paying her for the sex. And since she'd been giving it to him for free for almost five years now, why would he bother? Probably had other women on the go too, knowing him. Still, nice to think he was interested. Of course it all only happened because of that stupid sibling rivalry – whatever Mickey had, Jimmy wanted. And Mickey had been in jail a lot, and she was entitled to a bit of fun too. But Jesus, if Mickey ever found out …

How she ever got mixed up with them she'd never know, but of course she did and she remembered the first time she saw Mickey, his denim jacket and tight hair and jeans and Doc boots. And his long legs and his wide grin as he strutted into the basketball club disco, like the king of fucking Cork.

Sharon smiled. She didn't put up much of a fight that night. Or any other night, either. Not that she was normally like that. She was just crazy for him and his charm and his quick smile. Those broad shoulders, those big brown eyes.

And then she was pregnant and married and that was all she wanted. Only she knew she wasn't trapped into it, and he wasn't either. It was good, then, and could have stayed good, until Molloy got his claws into Mickey with promises of more this and more that and more the other. There was no such thing as enough with Mickey. And the langer thought he'd never get caught. Never go to jail. Never get hooked. Could walk away any time. Stupid fucking tool.

There wasn't much smiling after the first time he got out of prison. Or any time after that, either. He was never the same after prison.

She stubbed out the cigarette viciously in the big metal ashtray, and threw the butt into the bin. Fuck him and all belonging to him, now look at the mess he's left behind, and he sunning himself in Spain.

Nothing to do with him now anyway, she thought, it's all about Dave and her mam.

No, it's all about Dave, really, and him never, ever, *ever* ending up like his father. Getting a qualification, getting a good job and a future. Somewhere nice. With someone nice who'll take care of him so she won't have to anymore. She smiled. It could happen anyway. Why not?

She took the mirror out of her handbag and examined herself. Still got it, girl. Still got it. She put on a little bit of gloss, smacked her lips.

God, she thought, it'll be so nice to put the feet up later in front of the fire and read a magazine with a cup of tea. Listening to Marie's gossip, and having a snooze.

34

Molloy hopped from the bed to the floor to put on his pants.

Jackie Buckley reached to the bedside locker and took a drink from an open Coke bottle.

'Five quid, wasn't it?' Molloy said, removing his wallet from a pocket.

'What? It was fifty. You said fifty.'

'Fifty? You must be joking. For that? You were crap.' Molloy smirked and dangled a five-euro note.

Jackie faced up to him.

'You said it was fifty. Tommy Tan …'

'Tommy Tan me hole, I own the little bollix. And I own you too …' He reached and caught her by the chin. 'And don't you forget it.'

He took two twenty-euro notes from his wallet and threw them on the bed with the fiver. He could have had her or one of thirty other women for free. He knew it and she knew it, but he didn't approve of freebies, so he paid like the other punters.

She grabbed the notes and nimbly moved back to finish dressing.

Molloy zipped up his pants, stepped into his slip-ons and strode from the room.

'Tan?' he shouted as he began to stride down the stairs.

As if by magic, a dark-skinned and shrivelled man in a cheap brown suit materialised.

'Dom? Everything okay? She do what she was told?'

'She's useless, like all the rest of them. And cheeky. Fifty quid, fucking robbery.'

He lowered his voice. 'Any more tapes?'

'I have, Dom. Two. Here they are. One works in a bank in town, the other's in the council. Not very senior, but still.' He held out a memory stick.

'With the same young one?'

'Oh yeah. The council guy was rough, too. Hurt her.'

'Did he? Could come in handy that: the council. What bank?' He put the memory stick in his pocket.

'TSB. On South Main Street.'

'Good. Shouldn't be a problem getting a loan there, hah?'

Jackie listened from inside the open door on the stairs. She stuffed the five-euro note into the tongue of one of her Superstar runners. She put the other forty into the bedside locker drawer to give to Tommy Tan.

That fiver's for you, Kyle. Help you pay for that dog in Farranree, she thought. *The other fellas will pay for you to get high tonight, Jackie.*

She went down the stairs to meet the next man.

35

Molloy strode out the front door with what seemed like a chirpy air. Collins watched him from the window of a house at the end of the road. Molloy's driver, Sean Brady, had parked on the busier Chestnut Drive around the corner.

Clarke's Drive, a once thriving council estate, was now almost deserted. All except three of the houses had been discarded, and the air of abandonment and neglect in the park was palpable. The former lawns were knee-high banks of weeds, with debris strewn about them. Some of the houses were boarded up, desultory graffiti on the walls. There was little sign of life, other than the comings and goings of prostitutes and their 'clients', as Tommy Tan liked to call them.

The room in which Collins stood was blanketed in dust and cobwebs. There was no furniture apart from a well-wiped kitchen chair by the window. Mould covered one whole wall and the window he looked through was grimed over with years of dirt. He had been impressed that none of the guards on watch had wiped the glass.

Collins had been back at work for two weeks. This was the first time he had seen Molloy since the poisoning and he had been unsure how he would react.

Michael O'Mahony, the guard who had been watching the brothel since early morning, glanced at him nervously. He was fresh-faced and reddish in complexion with traces of old freckles. One of those men who would always appear younger than his age, which Collins knew to be thirty-five. Collins envied him that.

'He came in about an hour ago,' Michael said quietly.

'Why hasn't it been shut down?'

'I dunno. I heard Jonno's been asking the same question, in case it gets into the papers. Clancy has some theory that people are being blackmailed and he's trying to build up evidence for a case, apparently.'

'Is he now?' Collins said. 'Where's Molloy off to? The pub?'

'Probably. He eats there in the morning before it opens. He only allows Mary Brady to cook for him. Afraid of being … ' Michael looked at Collins in horror, realising what he had been about to say.

Collins smiled and patted him on the shoulder.

'No worries, Michael.'

'Jesus. I'm sorry, Collins. Me and my big mouth.'

'Run me through his usual schedule would you, please?'

'He normally gets here between nine and ten, and leaves after half an hour or an hour. Then he goes to his pub and, like I say, he has breakfast there. She even brings the baby with her, for God's sake, to that place.

'He stays there most days, watching videos and stuff. He drinks a lot and we think he's using a lot of coke too. Acts like it, anyway. We think he's on the phone a lot, but it's all pay as you go mobiles and we can't pick up anything. We put a bug in the pub last month, but they found it and we didn't hear anything useful.'

'What else? The pub busy?'

'Yeah, people coming and going all the time – a lot of them are locals – just to drink and watch the horses and the soccer. Some scumbags, but he doesn't have any direct contact with any of his pushers anymore and there's never any drugs in the pub, either. Apart from his own coke, I suppose.

'Oh. Some days he goes out to his parents' grave in Killumney. Or he goes to Youghal and walks on the beach when it's fine, with Mary and the baby. Or shopping in town, buying computer games, clothes and stuff. He's forever buying baby stuff, he dotes on him, in fairness.'

'Is he ever alone?'

'Nah. He brings Corcoran and the Brady brothers with him whenever he goes out. He sits in the back of the car for fuck's sake, like he is the president. In the evenings he's usually in the pub too, or at home. He never misses a United game. He never goes out anywhere else at night, to other pubs or anything. He always has two of his minders with him at home.'

'Visitors at home?'

'Nah, never, really. Only Mary Brady, she's coming and going a lot.'

'Are the Bradys running all the dealers now?'

'Yeah, but they're as slippery as shit. We can't nail them down and they shut up totally when we bring them in. Can't get at them at all. The nephews do their own thing, apparently,' he said. 'But we haven't been able to pin anything on them, either; they never have any drugs on them.'

'A tight ship, alright,' Collins said. 'Always was. He might slip up, though, if he's on the hard stuff. Any idea how he cleans up the money?'

'Not a clue. Those guys are off the radar a lot. Maybe England or the North. I doubt the money goes near Molloy's house or the pub. He has these Polish guys in tow too, brothers. Very good at computers, apparently.'

'They anything to Mazur?'

'Don't think so, you better ask Clancy. Couple of the usual lowlifes but tech-heads, apparently. Maybe that's how they launder the money.'

Collins knew about the Morawiecki brothers. He would have words with Clancy about the brothel and why it had not been closed and Molloy charged. For soliciting prostitution, if nothing else.

'Where's Lisa?' he asked.

'She just went over to her mam's, she'd only gone two minutes before you got here. She'd normally never –'

'No worries, Michael, none of my business. How is her mam?'

'Okay for eighty-four, I guess, but, you know …'

Collins looked at O'Mahony. He had been newly promoted to detective the year before. Like most of the Kerry people that Collins knew, he was intelligent and ambitious. He was from Tralee, and, as was the case for so many guards, the son of a guard – a well-known sergeant down there, constantly battling with the Provos, and now some new bunch. Collins wondered where and what Michael would be in fifteen years' time. Settled, he hoped, and balanced, unlike himself.

He had heard that Michael and Lisa were an item, on and off. He wondered if it was awkward for them. When Collins first met him, he thought that Michael might be gay, but he wasn't sure where that had come from.

'Good woman, Lisa. Good guard.'

'Oh the best, the best, Collins,' Michael said sheepishly.

Collins was about to say something else, but Michael spoke first.

'Em, Collins, are you supposed to be here? You know with Molloy, and everything …?'

'Probably not, Michael,' Collins said, smiling. 'Probably not. You finishing up now?'

'Yeah, three days off, thank God. Clancy doesn't have anyone to replace us here, there's a few out on sick leave. Once I write this up, I'm out of here, back home for a bit.'

'Grand. I'm going up to the house by the pub. I'll drop you off to the station first. It's Tom and Jim covering the pub, yeah?'

'I think so.'

'Lisa knows you're off now, she won't come back here or anything?'

'No, no. I'll ring her now anyway. Thanks for the lift.'

They left the room and went down the dusty narrow stairs. They went through the back door, which Collins locked, and into an overgrown back garden. He glanced up at a neighbouring window and saw blinds being pulled apart. They walked into an alleyway leading to Lee Gardens, a small estate, where he had parked the unmarked car.

36

Molloy got into the battered Ford Mondeo on Chestnut Road and scowled at Sean Brady in the driver's seat.

'Did you sweep it?'

'I did. Nothing here. The car's clean.'

'Did you get that English guy to give the,' he waved his hand, 'the scanning yoke a going over? Calibrating it, like?'

'I did that yesterday. Took him nearly three hours. He said it's perfect.'

'Alright. We're going to the pub.' He took a phone out of his pocket and dialled a number.

'It's me. Are they there yet?' he said.

'Yes,' Pat Brady said. 'He came first, around half-nine. She was here around ten. Riding now, probably.'

'How long are they normally at it?'

'They go up to Jackie Lennox's on the Bandon Road around twelve, and bring their food to the Lough if it's dry. Then she heads for town and he usually goes back to the flat.'

'Right, that's when ye'll do it. Wait for him when he's on his own. Make sure she's not around, got that?'

'Okay, I got it.'

'If he doesn't go that way, don't do it. Or if she's with him. Sean's dropping me at the pub, then he'll go over to you. Is Corcoran there already?'

'Yeah, he's in the van.'

'Dump that SIM card now. Use the other one.'

'Okay.'

'Don't fuck this up, okay?'

'We won't. If he goes up the lane we'll get him. We know what to do.'

Molloy hung up.

He spoke to Sean Brady, who was driving.

'Don't let Corcoran lose the rag, okay? You know what happened with Buckley.'

'Okay.'

Molloy removed the SIM card from the phone, broke it and threw it out the window. He quickly replaced it with a new one. He took a grubby bit of paper out of his pocket and dialled the number. It rang for a long time.

'Hello?' a man answered cautiously in a thin Dublin accent.

'It's the Dom,' Molloy said. 'Are ye nearly there?'

'It's him,' he heard, more quietly. There was the sound of a car. Another voice, more confident. 'About time you got back to us, we're on our way.'

'Yeah, yeah, sorry about that, Slim. Problem with phones. What time will ye be here?'

'About two hours.'

'Okay. Do ye want food? A bite to eat?'

'No, we're alright. See you then.'

Molloy sat regally on a high seat in the Avondhu Bar. Back to the wall, facing the door. The whole man.

Three tough-looking men sat around the table with him. Tattooed, young and fit. They glared at everyone.

Molloy had thought about how to impress the Dublin gangland boss Slim Keaveney and his brother Patrick, who were due to arrive any minute. He decided the best thing to do was not to try making an impression at all. He could have shut the pub, or met them somewhere else in private, but why should he bother? This was a meeting of equals, on *his* turf, and if his pub wasn't good enough, they could go and fuck themselves.

Crazy that this should be going down the same day as they were grabbing McMahon, but that's the way it happens sometimes. The Keaveneys wouldn't change the date and it was their best chance to get the young fella, get the information out of him, teach him a little lesson, and send a message to his prick of a father at the same time. It would take an hour, two at the most.

The décor in the pub was grubby. Two of the lights on the wall did not work and one on the ceiling flickered. The lampshade tassels were tatty. There was a small fake Christmas tree in one corner. Three strips of silver tinsel had been spread around it. A long line of electric lights hung behind the bar, but they hadn't been switched on that day, as yet.

People did not go to the Avondhu for its style. Nor its locale. Derelict or semi-derelict houses surrounded the pub and the green area across the road was covered with old broken furniture and half-burned rubbish. The marks of 'bonnas' – the traditional St John's night bonfires – pockmarked the grass. A burned-out car mounted the footpath down the street, the rims of its back wheels on the road, its front crushed against a wooden lamp post. A boarded-up shop adjoined the pub, long closed. The windows of the pub were fronted by shutters.

There were twenty customers present, mostly regulars who came and drank, talked, kept their mouths shut and their eyes averted. One lone drinker was asleep, his face on a small round table. It was rare for a person not known to come in. Or stay long. The two bar staff, Frank and Shannon Fitzgerald, were nervous and watchful. Two televisions showed the Racing Channel, with the sound turned down, attentively watched by a few excited men.

A callow youth approached Molloy and one of his minders stood up to intercept.

'Not now, Jonesy,' Molloy said distractedly. He had watched the *Godfather* trilogy eight times and *The Sopranos* series five times and he liked to see himself as a benevolent, if tough, father figure for the community, dispensing justice and largesse in equal quantities.

Not one other person in the pub saw him in the same light.

The door opened and a nondescript man in a suit with no tie entered. He was about fifty with tightly cut grey hair, but he could have been older. He moved with economy and purpose. He was lean, not tall. He looked around the room, taking in Molloy, his henchmen, the customers and the bar staff. He took out a phone and made a call. He stood beside the door, all eyes on him. He did not seem awed, meeting eye with eye. He was calm. Not hostile. Attentive.

Thirty seconds later, the door opened and two men in their sixties or early seventies walked in. They were both smiling as if just having shared a joke. Both wore suits with no ties, and both were tall and well built. One wore glasses. Obviously brothers, the older of the two went straight up to Molloy's table and spoke, holding out a hand.

'Dom. Good to see yez.'

Molloy had risen, holding both hands out to his sides. His goons got up too, and moved away, making space.

'Slim, welcome to my humble abode.' He shook hands with them both.

'How are yez, Dom? Jesus, you haven't changed a bit since the Joy. Haven't put on a pound, fair play to ye.'

'How's the going, Patrick, how's tricks?'

'Not too bad, Dom, not too bad. Nice place yez have here,' he said, sitting down slowly. He looked around. 'I see a lot of Man U stuff on the wall there.'

'Oh yeah, this is a United pub, big time. Are ye soccer men?'

'Patrick used to kick around a bit with Drumcondra in the day. Played with Giles, didn't you, Pat?' Slim answered.

'Long time ago, Dom. Long time ago.'

'Giles was good, lads,' Molloy said. 'But he was no Keano, in fairness.'

The two men smiled.

'Will ye have a drink lads? Will ye have a Midleton Rare? Can't get better now, liquid gold.'

'Bit early for us, Dom, thanks. But work away yourself. I'll just have a water, sparkling,' said Slim.

'I'll have an orange juice,' said Patrick.

'Jesus, is that all?'

The two men smiled. The barmaid had appeared from nowhere.

'Sparkling water, Shannon. Orange juice, and I'll have a large Rare with ice.' She scuttled away.

The two men smiled.

Molloy kept his face neutral. He didn't like the way they were smiling, the way they were looking down on him and the pub. They wouldn't be smiling soon. By Christ they wouldn't.

37

The house being used by the gardaí as a lookout for Molloy's pub was not derelict like the one in Clarke's Drive, but the family had been relocated quietly to a house in Glanmire. It was two streets away from the pub, so that it required spotting scopes to watch the front door.

Collins took the stairs three at a time and entered what had once been a small bedroom. Detectives Tom Kelleher and Jim Murphy turned as the door opened. He knew them well. They had worked closely with him when he led the investigation into Molloy's murder of Dinny Buckley a few years previously. An investigation that neither charged nor convicted anybody. They couldn't even find his body.

The cramped room, the men, the watching and the sense of purpose flooded Collins with memories. It seemed to him right then that he had spent most of his working life just watching. Watching murderers, watching rapists, watching drug dealers, watching republican extremists. All that time he would never get back. All that time he could have been doing something with his life.

Murphy was drinking tea. Kelleher was typing on a laptop connected to a large screen on an office table. A cable snaked from a small camera attached to one of the scopes to the screen. The screen showed the front door of Molloy's pub.

Both men rose to their feet and exclaimed simultaneously.

'Collins!'

Collins smiled at them and shook their hands.

'Tom,' he said. 'Jim.'

'How are ya, Collins?' Kelleher said. 'I heard you were back.'

'Oh I'm fine, Tom. Can't get rid of a bad penny.'

'You're looking well, lad.'

'Thanks, Jim, but Fiona always said you were a bad liar. How's all the clan? I was sorry to hear about your uncle.'

'Oh, fine, Collins, thanks. Ah, he was sick a long time.'

'I know, but still. Tell your father I was asking for him, will you? Tell him I said the All-Ireland is Ballygunner's for the taking.'

'Ha! He'll be delighted with that. It's a religion with him.'

'Don't I know,' Collins said. 'How are you, Tom? How's Theresa and the kids?'

'Never better, Collins, thanks. Bigger and bolder. Theresa especially.'

'Still fighting the good fight, lads?' he pointed to the screen.

'Oh I don't know, Collins. Cooped up here all day with this farter,' Tom said.

'Even though …' Jim said, holding up a finger. 'Show Collins who just called to visit.'

Tom sat down and moved the mouse to open up a new screen. A video.

'Just ten minutes ago, would you believe.'

He pressed play. The video showed two cars pull up outside the pub. Dark Mercedes, Dublin registrations. A smallish man in a dark suit got out of one car and spoke to somebody in the back of the other one. He then turned and went through the pub door. Some moments later, the back doors of the second car opened and two tall men got out.

'Recognise anyone?' Tom asked.

'Oh yes. "Here, here, the Dubs are here,"' Collins sang.

The video showed the two men entering the pub. The cars moved around the corner, behind the building and out of sight.

'Do you know the small guy?' Jim asked.

'Oh yes. They call him the SEAL. Joe Duffy is his real name. He was a US Navy SEAL, they say. Verrrryyy dangerous man,' Collins said. 'We couldn't get near his military file, but it was thick, apparently. Dublin Castle really want to pin something on him, but no luck, yet.'

'He doesn't look like much.'

'They tend not to apparently,' Collins said. 'Who's out the back?'

'Mattie and Tooler,' Jim said.

'Would you give them a call, Jim? I'd say they'll all troop out the back soon and head away. Can't see them talking much business in the pub, even the back bar. Molloy probably just wanted to show them off a bit. Surprised the Keaveneys agreed.'

Jim made the call. 'They're just going out the back door now, would you believe,' he said. He and Tom glanced at each other.

'Are the boys under orders to follow?' Collins said.

'No, they can't anymore, after that woman got killed out by Tower,' Tom said.

'Not much point anyway,' Collins said. 'The second car would just hold them back. You'd need three or four cars to follow them properly and even then it's hit or miss.'

Tom's phone buzzed on the window sill. He glanced at it but didn't answer.

'It's Brennan,' he said. 'Probably to give us a bollocking for letting you in here when you're supposed to be on desk duty. Cup of tea, Collins?'

'I'd love one, Tom.'

'Well, get me one while you're at it,' Tom said, peering through the scope and adjusting the lens. 'Did you bring biscuits?'

Collins pulled the packet out of an inside pocket and held it up.

'Custard creams?' Jim said. 'Good man yourself; two sugars for me, and not too much milk.'

Collins smiled.

38

Gerry Halvey looked around the bustling café. It was a mistake to meet in such a public place, even if Eric O'Donovan was his brother-in-law. The clock on the wall said just after eleven. Over thirty minutes late – again.

The cappuccino in front of him was cold now. He knew it would play havoc with his dyspepsia, but he could not forego his morning coffee.

He reached for the antacid pills in his pocket. The bottles and packets and sleeves of drugs rattled and rustled there until he felt the familiar shape. He removed a tablet from the bottle and reached for the glass. His hand shook when he picked it up and held it to his lips. He put the pill in his mouth and drank some water.

He closed his eyes and was about to try a three-minute breathing space meditation – he didn't care if people thought he was sleeping. Perhaps he *would* fall asleep. He had slept so badly again the night before.

He heard Eric's stentorian voice at the counter, ordering his usual: the full Irish, white toast and a pot of tea. He opened his eyes as the bane of his life bore down upon him.

'Christ, Halvey, were you asleep? Is Elaine keeping you up all night riding or what?' O'Donovan said.

'Ha fucking ha, Eric, and can you say it a bit louder please, some people on North Gate Bridge didn't hear you properly.'

'Excuse *me*. Somebody got out of the wrong side of the bed this morning. But wait 'til I tell you. Did you hear this one?'

And he was off, engrossed in the telling of his own joke. Halvey looked at him, half-listening, and tried to raise some compassion and non-judgemental thoughts. He failed but did not blame himself for it.

When O'Donovan had apparently finished his joke and he had smiled at it, he prepared himself and said, 'NAMA were on again. They want to meet.'

'Jesus, can you not give it a rest? Let me get my breakfast in peace first anyway, will you, for the love of God?'

'But what will I tell them? They're demanding ...' Halvey stretched his neck forward. 'They're demanding the books on the Anterior account.'

O'Donovan blanched. He glanced left and right.

'I told you,' he said in a lowered voice. 'And I told you to tell those fuckers. There *is* no Anterior account as far as I'm concerned. *I* never heard of it. *You* never heard of it. I don't know where they got wind of it, but it does not now, nor did it ever, exist. Is that clear enough for you?' He hissed the words, looking around him again.

'Yeah, but how *did* they get wind of it, then?' Halvey asked. 'And, as you well know, I never even knew about it until you told me about it *after* their letter. You went to that crowd to set it up.'

'Yes well, you'll have no trouble denying its existence then, will you? You still never heard of it as far as I'm concerned.'

Halvey grimaced. He was only glad that it couldn't be traced back to him or the bank, even if he had stupidly agreed to become Eric's financial representative during the boom years.

O'Donovan's breakfast arrived, brought by a young woman in a short black skirt.

'Full Irish, toast and a pot of tea.' She smiled sweetly at the men and turned back to the counter with a swagger.

'Fuck it, would you look at the arse on that,' O'Donovan smirked as she sauntered away.

Halvey flinched.

'For God's sake, Eric. She's only Claire's age.'

'Sorry! Jesus, we can't open our mouths these days. Num, this potato cake is good. Did you not have something? Don't tell me she has you on another diet.'

Halvey sighed. *Compassion*, he thought. *Respond, don't react. Acceptance.*

O'Donovan speared a sausage and cut a piece off, stabbing it into some white pudding. Halvey began to salivate.

He moved the sliver of fingernail between two teeth and began to push it back and forward rhythmically, jabbing the sharp end of the nail with his tongue, hurting it.

39

Claire and Dave left the flat in Laurel Hurst and crossed College Road towards the chip shop. They were sated, and a little embarrassed; neither of them still quite believing their luck. They knew they were luminous.

Claire would have liked a shower, but the state of the bathroom in the flat precluded that. Her jaw ached a little, but she did not care. She massaged her chin with her hand as they went down Wycherley Terrace.

The sun was still out. Dave chatted amiably about how much he hated his course in CIT, how stupid the whole thing was and how great Spain had been when he'd visited his father.

'What does he do out there?' Claire asked.

'He owns a bar. Well it's kind of a restaurant too. Near Alicante. But he lives in Madrid, you'd want to see his place, it's massive.'

He turned suddenly to her at the door of the chip shop.

'We could work there. He'd get bar work for us, no problem. Imagine that, just the two of us. No hassle, no stupid lectures, no nagging mother.'

'No cold,' she replied and smiled at him. She would not like working in a bar. She wondered about Dave sometimes. He was hot, but he wasn't the sharpest knife in the drawer.

They gingerly bit into the chips, puffing air in and out of their mouths as they walked down the Lough Road. Claire looked at the time on her phone. Just after twelve, two more whole hours before she had to get the bus home. A lovely shower then with her new Molton Brown shower gel. Bliss. But her mother would be well into her first bottle of wine by then. She shuddered.

'You cold?' Dave asked.

'Not too bad. The chips will warm me up.'

They sat on the swings by the Lough and ate their chips and chatted. Dave had gotten on to his favourite topic: soccer. He was obsessed with it. She didn't care. She sipped her Diet Coke, her skin still tingling in the low sunlight.

They kissed and parted and Dave headed back up Croghtamore Square and Claire walked along the Lough's water towards the city centre. It was only then she noticed that her bracelet was missing. The one Granny Jan had given her.

She turned around.

At the sharp corner halfway up Croghtamore Square she almost ran into them. Two masked men were tussling with Dave at the back of an open-doored van. One of them was huge, his massive arms were clasped around Dave's torso, as the other man punched him and tried to lift him off his feet. Dave was making a growling sound, struggling, and he freed his arms, pulled the mask from the smaller man's head and kicked him.

The man twisted, his face set in rage. He picked up the mask and put it back on. He saw Claire. She was rigid, her mouth and eyes wide open. 'Fuck.'

She turned to run, but he grabbed her and clamped his hand around her mouth. He lifted her, twisting her around and she could see the giant pummelling Dave's head on the ground.

The engine of the van roared as the driver put his foot on the accelerator, but it did not move. The man carrying Claire put one foot into the van, lifted himself up and fell forward onto its floor, with her underneath him. The impact winded her and she began to hyperventilate.

His hand around her mouth smelled of cigarettes and piss. His fingers dug into her cheek. She tried as hard as she could to scream, bucking her head from side to side, but his weight pinned her down and now he could hold her head with both hands. The sound that she heard herself make was a high-pitched moan.

She saw the giant carry Dave into the van. Dave did not move, his eyes were closed, and his face was covered in blood. Blood flowed from his nose and mouth onto his lovely hoody. His head drooped.

The giant held him in one hand and closed the doors with the other. He banged his head against the roof of the van and grunted.

'Go! Go!' the man holding Claire shouted and the van accelerated loudly down the lane, tyres screeching. They rolled around its floor as it careered around the corner onto Glasheen Road. He held her tight.

'Fuck it,' he shouted. 'Fuck, fuck, fuck.'

His breath stank.

'No,' she said, whimpering. 'Please, no. Please.'

Igon Zatarain, an Erasmus student in University College Cork, stared out the window of his living room as the van sped down the narrow lane and swung around the corner. He could see the backpack that the girl had dropped on the ground.

He went out onto the street and picked it up. It was black, with badges on it. Two other people emerged from their terraced houses. His next-door neighbour Trisha and the old man who never spoke, three doors down.

'What happened, Igon, was it joyriders?' Trisha said. She wore a dressing gown with glossy pictures of Elton John emblazoned across it.

'What?' he replied, still stunned.

'What happened? Did somebody steal the van?'

'No. They took them,' he said in his strong Basque accent.

'They took who? Who took who?'

'Two men. With hoods. They took the boy and the girl. In the back of the van.'

He held up the backpack as if in proof.

40

Molloy got into the Mercedes thinking that only he and one of the Keaveneys would be sitting in the back seat – that the other would sit in the front. But Patrick quickly followed him and Slim got in the other door. The small grey haired man sat into the front passenger seat, leaned over and said something to the driver that Molloy did not hear.

Molloy realised that there were four of the Keaveney people in the car now with him, while his two men were in the other car with two more of the Keaveneys' crew.

Fail to prepare, he thought.

'You can drive straight on there,' he said to the driver, to restore some authority. 'There's a few nice pubs just out the road here, lads. Do a nice bit of grub.'

'Ah that's okay, Dom, we'll just drive around, keep the heat off and that, while we chat,' Patrick said.

Slim looked out the window, grimly. He had been repulsed by the burned-out furniture and rubbish on the green in front of the pub and the crashed stolen car. The hopelessness reminded him of where he had grown up, in Ballymun, in the 1960s. It had revolted him and he vowed the first time he returned home from prison that he and his family would move. Now Patrick and himself lived in adjacent gated properties in Clontarf.

He wondered what his wife would get him for Christmas this year. Last year she had bought a week's golf in North Carolina for himself and Patrick. She had been talking about a cruise. He hoped it wasn't that. Her obsession about having their youngest son, Charlie, home for Christmas worried him. There was no way he was getting out of prison on good behaviour. Good behaviour was never his strong suit. He would be lucky to be out by July, no matter how much pressure they put on the solicitor, or how many political strings they pulled.

Slim wondered about the man beside him. Molloy did not appear as stable and focused as he had been a year before when they planned the delivery of cocaine from South America. Molloy had steadily schemed, beat, blackmailed and killed his way to the top in Cork, but his usual cunning and viciousness seemed to be giving way to notions of grandeur and invulnerability. Slim wondered if the rumours of drug taking were true. He'd never seen any criminal who snorted his own cocaine survive for long. And when people like Molloy went down, they usually went with a bang and took others with them.

It was all about planning and preparation. Discipline. Sticking to the plan. Most of the guys who end up in prison did so because they didn't plan or they didn't stick to the plan. Impetuosity – that was the enemy. Winging it. It was all about strategy and trusting the process. Waiting, not lashing out.

He and Patrick had three plans. A short-term plan – the next six months. A medium-term plan – the next three years. And a long-term plan – the next ten years. That would see them out. They could retire already if they wanted, but the vacuum would come back at them. Dealing with that was part of the long-term plan. Molloy was only in their short-term plan, as of now. As soon as the shipment arrived and their seventy per cent was delivered, it would be over with him. Slim was sure of one thing – that careless man was going down and going down soon.

He returned his thoughts to the task at hand.

'Is there much heat around?' he said. 'It looked like two of them in that Hyundai.'

'Oh don't mind them,' Molloy said. 'They sit there near the back of the pub. And they watch the front from a house down the road. Muppets. They couldn't find their arses without a map.'

'So they know we're here,' Slim said.

'Maybe, but so what, sure?'

'The less they know the better. They only need to get lucky once. We could have met somewhere quiet. Out of the way.'

Molloy scowled.

'And nearly killing one of them doesn't help either,' Slim said, looking directly at Molloy. 'What we don't want now is any headlines, you get my drift?'

'There'll be no headlines and the fucker had it coming,' Molloy said. 'He's been a pain in the hole for years.'

'Yeah, but it's very bad for business, Dom,' Patrick said. 'Gets them all worked up and motivated – lots of overtime. Gets politicians and judges on their side, giving them extra powers. The newspapers start getting brave. Remember what happened after Veronica Guerin?' He wheezed, breathless.

'Fuck the politicians and the judges. This is *my* town, lads, not yere's, last time I checked.' Molloy sat more erect and pushed his legs out.

'Yes, but we've made a huge investment in this product and its delivery. Five million, that's not loose change. We don't want any more surprises, Dom.'

'There won't be. And it *will* be delivered. I guarantee it.'

'It better, Dom, it better. Or we're all in the shit,' Patrick said.

Both brothers looked out the windows.

Molloy, stuck in the middle, stared firmly ahead. His body had gone rigid with temper.

Slim sensed it. He reassessed what they had come down from Dublin to achieve in this sad excuse for a city and what they needed from this sad excuse for a businessman.

'You know what?' he said. 'Maybe we will go to that pub after all. Where did you say it was, Dom? A pint might be nice.'

41

The van seemed to be going more slowly, stopping every now and then. Claire could hear other cars and, once, the sound of voices. She thought about shouting, but the man who had thrown her in the van was sitting back in the corner, swaying slightly and staring at her. He had blue, bloodshot eyes. His face had been puffy, his nose a bit bent and one of his front teeth was bigger than the other. She didn't think she'd ever forget that face and the anger imprinted on it.

Conscious of her short skirt, she shuffled up against the other corner, her knees together, her feet to the side, and pulled it down as far as she could. She hugged herself and whimpered, eyes down.

'Oh, God,' she said. 'No, please no.'

'Shit,' the man said. 'What a mess. Shut up, you.'

Dave was unconscious on the floor of the van. She thought for a moment that he might be dead, but she could see his chest moving up and down. She was too terrified to speak or ask them to help him. She felt better when she closed her eyes. If only Dave would wake up, she would not be alone.

The man who had taken her was talking to the driver through a little shutter. She could hear only his voice above the engine noise.

'She saw me,' he said. 'He pulled the balaclava off and she saw me … *I* don't fucking know. She was just standing there … We can't. I told you. She saw my face. I'm not going back in there … Well, ring him then, but we're not letting her go. No way. She saw me.'

He slammed the shutter closed and cursed under his breath.

She glanced at the giant near the doors. He was staring at her. She could see his hungry eyes in the balaclava's holes. His fat belly was bulging against a tight tracksuit top. His long legs stretched almost across the length of the van, out through leggings and into massive black boots.

'Can I ride her later?' the giant asked in a guttural voice.

She froze. This could not be happening.

'What? No you can't ride her,' the other man said. 'You don't touch her, you hear?'

'What about after we find out where McMahon is?' the giant said.

'Shut up, will ya? She's not even supposed to be here. Stop talking.'

The giant grunted and lapsed into silence.

The other man opened a black refuse sack. He spoke to Claire.

'Turn around. Put your hands behind your back.'

She said, 'My uncle is the Minister for Justice. If you let us go now we won't press charges. My dad will get the guards to drop it.'

'Shut up. "Press charges", do you think you're on the fucking telly or something? Minister for Justice? Yeah, right.'

She cowered further into the corner.

'Turn around, I said. Where's your phone?' He pointed at Dave. 'Get his phone,' he said to the giant.

'Please let me go,' she said, crying. 'I won't say anything, I promise, I didn't see anything.'

'Shut up. Where's your phone?'

'It was in my backpack. I dropped it.'

'What?' he said. 'Where?'

'On the road,' she said.

'Take off your jacket.'

'No. Please. No please, I swear ...'

He lunged at her and threw her on the floor of the van, face down. He rummaged in the pockets of her jacket. He pulled up her skirt and pawed at her tights and panties. She tried to push his hands away, but he was too strong. He flipped her over on her back, pressing his forearm into her neck.

'Where is it?' he snarled, his face only inches from hers. She couldn't speak with the pressure on her throat. He felt along her breasts and stomach, searching for the phone. He tugged up her skirt again and groped her crotch. He got off her, cursing.

'Fuck,' he said. He opened the shutter and spoke to the driver again, more quietly this time.

Hysterical, Claire backed into the corner on her knees and lowered her head, her hands over her face as if worshipping him. Her head rocked up and down as she gulped for air, moaning 'no' over and over.

'Give it to me,' she heard him say and then there was a loud banging noise. She looked up to see him smash a SIM card with a metal bar and then batter Dave's phone, breaking it into pieces. He put all the pieces into a plastic bag. He opened the shutter again.

'Here, throw that out the window.' He passed the plastic bag to the driver and slammed the door shut.

Although she had not raised her head, she could feel him staring at her again.

'Turn around,' he said, quieter now. 'Put your hands behind your back.'

She sidled around, head still bowed. She put her hands behind her back. She was shaking.

'Please, please,' she said.

She wanted to say more, to say something convincing, but she couldn't think straight.

He grabbed her wrists and she felt something sharp tighten around them. It bit into her.

'Wait. They won't bargain with you. They can't,' she said.

'What bargain? What are you on about? I told you to shut up.'

He put a cloth bag over her head. There was some kind of dust or powder in the material and she thought she might suffocate. She tried not to make a noise, to draw attention to herself.

'Is he okay?' the giant said.

A pause.

'Yeah, he's fine. We'll wake him when we get there.'

'I thought we weren't supposed to take her,' the giant said.

'Shut up, will you? Just shut up. She's here now, and we have to deal with it.'

Claire tried to breathe. If only she could breathe.

42

Collins passed the two queues in the vestibule of Anglesea Street Garda Station.

Immigrants lined up on the right, trying to get visas or to extend them. A mixture of races and features, most people trying not to appear worried or guilty. On the left, the queue for driving licence and passport signatures and people who wanted to report something.

He waved to the desk sergeant.

'Quiet, Tom?'

'Hectic here, Collins.'

The open-plan office area on the first floor was empty. Christmas decorations bedecked the far corner where June and another female colleague had hung them. He took off his coat and draped it over his chair. He walked to June's desk and saw that her coat and handbag were there too.

She worked with Clancy's team now that Collins had been removed from active duty. She was running down the time until her early retirement in a few months. He went outside and noticed movement in the Incident Room down the hall. Four people stood around Clancy, who was seated and talking on speakerphone.

Collins entered the room. June, O'Regan, Mick Murphy and Michael O'Mahony all turned to him. Clancy ignored him.

'Did he get a reg?' Clancy said into the phone.

'No,' came the reply. '"A big blue van" is all I'm getting.'

'Any descriptions?'

'The girl is maybe twenty, dressed in a black skirt with black tights and blue denim jacket and black boots. Long blonde hair, thin face, he says. One hundred and sixty centimetres in height, whatever that is – she's fairly small. The boy is taller, one hundred and eighty centimetres, longish dark hair, thin, wearing a grey hoodie and blue jeans. He says he'd recognise them again.'

Collins couldn't place the garda's voice, but it was an East Cork accent. He got it: Jim O'Toole.

'Any description of the assailants?'

'They wore balaclavas. One was about one seventy or one eighty – I've no idea how tall that is, five-eleven I think. He said he was the same height as Jones here, who's about that. He had jeans on and a black jacket. Well built, a bit of a gut. The balaclava was pulled off him at some point, but he didn't get a good look at the face.

'He says the other guy is very big. He says well over two metres and fat. He was wearing some kind of a grey tracksuit and boots. He's very fat, the witness says.'

'What are those heights?' Clancy said.

'The girl is five-two,' Collins said. 'The boy six feet. The two men are five-eleven and over six-six.'

Clancy glared at him and returned to the phone.

'Where's the witness from again?' he asked into the phone.

'Bilbao, he says. The Basque Country.'

'That's Spain, isn't it?' O'Regan said.

'Don't we have a South American woman doing some place-ment on the first floor?' Collins said to June.

'Yes, she's on work experience. From Peru, I think.'

Clancy reasserted himself. 'Bring him in; we need to quiz him a bit more here and get Finbarr to stay and organise the door-to-door. We need his prints too. I'm sending June and Michael out there now with the tech gang. Don't touch anything, will you? Did you go through the backpack?'

'I did, yeah.'

'Any ID?'

'There's two. An ATM card with the name Claire Halvey and a UCC ID card with the name Laura Moore. I'd say that's fake, they all have fake IDs to get into clubs and stuff.'

Something in the name 'Halvey' made Collins's attention prick up. He moved closer to the phone.

'Jim, will you ask him how much over two metres the big guy was?' Collins said.

Clancy scowled at him again. There was a pause.

'He doesn't know, but he was over two metres for sure.'

'Could be six foot eight,' Collins said quietly. He looked meaningfully at June.

'No way, Collins,' said June.

'What?' said Clancy.

'Collins thinks it could be Corcoran.'

'I didn't say anything,' Collins said. 'But how many men that tall are out there capable of something like this?'

'We don't even know what happened yet.' Clancy stood up and stretched. 'Let alone speculate who could have done it. And Collins … last time I checked, you were on desk duty.'

'Fuck you, Clancy,' Collins said, staring at him.

Clancy laughed and pointed his thumb towards the door. 'Out.'

Collins left the room.

When June arrived at her desk to get her bag and coat, he was sitting in her chair.

'All set for Christmas?'

'Collins, don't start. And no, I'm not going to keep you in the loop. Get out of my chair.'

Collins shook his head wryly.

'I wasn't going to ask you that.'

'Yes you were, and the answer is no. You're on desk duty for another month at least. And Collins …' She paused to put on her coat. 'Not everything is down to Molloy. This whole thing is probably nothing. Some student prank.'

'Would you just let me know who she is? That name rings a bell.'

She looked at him. 'I don't know. I don't fucking know,' she said, walking away. 'Maybe.'

It was good enough for him. For now. It smelled like something to him: two metres.

He returned to his desk and switched on the computer. Two email responses to enquiries he had made about foreign investments in Cayman Islands accounts. Neither of which was of any use.

He was reading a report on offshore banking when he had an idea. Halvey was an unusual name in Cork and so he looked it up in the online phone book. There was only one Halvey family in the city. His eyes widened when he saw the address in Douglas.

'Wow,' he said.

June burst into the office. She rushed to Collins.

'It's Mickey McMahon's young fella.'

'What?'

'The boy who was abducted. He's Mickey McMahon's young fella: David.'

Collins stared at her.

'Molloy,' he whispered.

43

Hunched up in the corner of the van, Claire concentrated on not vomiting. She knelt to prevent her short skirt from riding up her thighs. The ridges of the van floor bit into her knees.

She closed her eyes and pretended that none of it was happening. She cried and imagined that she was eight again and that she was crying because her mother would not let her wear her best dress. Or when she was six and afraid of the dark and her father put on the light in the hall and comforted her. It wasn't happening, it just wasn't.

'Daddy, Daddy,' she said.

The van stopped again and the driver opened the shutter.

'We're here,' he said. 'Stay there till I open the door and we can get them in. Why isn't his hood on?'

'Because he put it on her, that's why,' the giant said. 'Anyway, he's out of it.'

'Well he could be faking it. Put something over his head before we move him, I don't want him seeing me.'

The van door opened, and Claire could see light through her hood.

'Carry him,' the driver said to the giant.

She was grabbed roughly by the arm. Her knees scraped the door of the van.

'Please, please, my father will pay. He's a bank manager; he'll pay. I have his number, I can give it to you …'

'Shut up. "My father's a bank manager." Get up, for fuck's sake. Come on.'

He pulled her towards the door. He stopped her and she was lifted down to the ground.

'This way.'

He pulled her roughly.

She scrunched her eyes together and made up her mind to fight. She tripped and banged her head on something hard.

She was pushed into a chair and a rope was pulled tight around her chest, waist and legs, tying her to it. It cut into her. She was sure that she would faint. She listened. Only the sound of an engine in the distance and a bird outside. The engine stopped. It was quiet for a while. The bird began to sing again. The sound of a crow.

'Dave, Dave?' She thought he was nearby.

'He's in another room. Shut your mouth. If you try to shout or run away we'll let *him* do what he wants to you and that'll fucking hurt, I guarantee it.'

The door closed and there was the muffled sound of voices from another room.

She wept and then she prayed. Her breasts hurt, her wrists hurt, her legs hurt. Time passed.

The voices got loud sometimes and sometimes there was silence. The snot from her nose was all over her face. She could feel it, like a crust. Her head was all itchy from the hood. She felt she would go insane; if she hadn't already. She didn't know how long she had been there. She needed to go to the toilet.

'Daddy. Help me. Help me, Daddy,' she whispered.

44

Molloy sat opposite the Brady brothers in the kitchen, dimly lit from a single bare bulb. They had run a cable from the show house, which was still, amazingly, connected to the grid. The floor was bare concrete; the walls were bare cavity blocks. The window opening was covered over with a sheet of chipboard and a cold draught blew through the gaps at the edges.

They sat on fold-up chairs, the Bradys beside each other near the door. They were holding cans of beer, Molloy was drinking from a glass of whiskey. Some food and a kettle on a countertop nearby, a stack of dirty dishes in the sink.

It was almost dark out; the Keaveneys had been keen to get back to Dublin, which suited Molloy just fine. Good riddance to bad rubbish, it would be the last time he'd ever clap eyes on them.

'A total disaster,' he said. 'But it ends here and now.'

'She saw me,' Pat said. 'What was I supposed to do?'

Molloy kept his calm. The Bradys had a look of determination that he didn't like and he knew they were far more loyal to each other than to him.

He wanted to say: 'Ye were supposed to grab the young fella on his own and give him a hiding and find out where his prick of a father is holed up in Spain. An hour at most, maybe two. Ye weren't supposed to kidnap the niece of the fucking Minister for Justice. How thick are ye?' Instead, he said, 'It doesn't matter now, it's done, but we have to let her go.'

'She saw me,' Pat said again. 'She can ID me. I'm not going back inside.'

'We don't know that,' Molloy said. 'We can scare her off, we have plenty of options to make sure she won't open her mouth.'

Pat shook his head. His face was set firm.

'We can't let her go,' he said. 'And Sean will back me up one hundred per cent. Mary too.'

Molloy exhaled. He didn't want to involve Mary, but if he had to, he would. He knew she would take his side against the brothers, for Luke's sake if nothing else.

'Look,' he said, 'her uncle is the Minister for Justice. She's eighteen, from Douglas, her father is a bank manager. If we don't let her out right now, the shit will totally hit the fan. We'll be finished, completely fucked. Don't you get it?'

Pat glared at him. Sean appeared less angry, but he shook his head, too. Molloy decided to change the subject.

'Did we find out where McMahon is, in Spain?' he said.

Sean replied. 'We didn't get that, yet, he's a bit out of it. We wanted to talk to you first, sort it out about the girl.'

'Well, it's sorted now as far as I'm concerned. We let them both go, this minute. He'll have learned his lesson to deal without my permission and we'll get McMahon when we get to Spain.'

'She saw me,' Pat said, more emotion in his voice. 'I'm not going back in there, no way.'

Molloy thought about the three Micro Uzis on the table to his left, but he did not move. He'd have to get around the Bradys some other way, but quickly.

'Okay, let's go and have a chat with the girl, how about that?' he said, standing up.

The Brady brothers moved to the table, put down their cans and picked up an Uzi each. They kept them pointed down. They both met his eyes, waiting for him to react.

He readjusted his thinking. If the girl and boy had to die, they had to die. He'd have to make the best of it, and get out of the country within days. The girl's death would concentrate Eric O'Donovan's mind, that was for sure. He had thought the threat of it would be enough, but this would seal the deal and make sure O'Donovan continued to do what he was told.

He'd deal with the Bradys afterwards. It would have to wait but deal with them he would, whatever Mary had to say about it. He'd make it look like the Limerick crowd did it.

45

Claire heard the door open. She felt the chair being lifted, with a grunt. There was a horrible smell of body odour. She assumed it was from the giant. She was carried for a bit and then put down. The atmosphere in this room was different; there were some people.

'Hello, Claire, we're going to have a chat now and you're going to answer a few questions.'

It was a new voice, full of confidence. A country accent, but somewhere in Cork.

'Isn't that right? You're going to answer our questions.'

'Yes,' she said in a whisper. 'Please, my father, my uncle …'

'I know all about your father and your uncle, Claire, and they can't help you now. Only you can help yourself – it's all up to you and what you're willing to do for us.'

'Please don't hurt me,' Claire said.

'We don't want to hurt you, Claire, but we have to get one thing straight in our heads first. So I'm going to ask you a few questions and you have to think carefully before you answer.'

She forced herself not to cry. She heard a chair being pulled along the floor towards her. He was closer, his voice right in front of her.

'First question,' he said, 'is this: tell us what you saw earlier today on the street before you and Dave were put into the van.'

'Nothing,' she said.

'Nothing? You must have seen something.'

She swallowed. He seemed to want her to say something and she figured out what it was. The face, the man's face.

'I saw the fight,' she said. 'The … the men with Dave and then one of them grabbed me and put me in the van. Then he put the thing over my head.'

'And did you see anybody's face?' The voice was almost gentle but too close. She could almost feel his breath on her.

'No,' she said. 'No, they had masks on. I didn't see anybody's face, I swear.'

'For fuck's sake,' another man said, loudly. She thought it was the man in the back of the van with her. She heard him walk away and a door closed.

'Never mind him, Claire,' the voice said again. 'The important thing is that you never saw anything, anybody's face.'

His fingers were suddenly pressing her cheeks. She whimpered. The tone of voice changed and his fingers tightened on her face.

'Because if we let you go and you say something different, or you identify anyone, we'll find you, Claire, and we'll hurt you in ways you can't even imagine. Stop crying and listen, are you listening?'

'Yes,' she said.

'Say it. Say you're listening.'

'I'm listening. I'm listening, I swear.'

'They will try to persuade you that you saw something, that you can identify somebody, but you can't. Right? Isn't that right, Claire?'

'Right,' she said in a whisper. She could do this. She could.

'Nobody knows what you saw, except you. There was nobody else there, no witnesses, am I right? Right?'

'Right,' she said more loudly.

'That's right,' he said. 'You think about that, Claire, and we'll talk again, later. You think very hard what you want for the rest of your life. Am I right?'

'Yes,' she said, crying.

She was picked up and carried. As she was put back down she felt a hand on her breast, kneading it. A low laugh.

She screamed and then there was nothing.

46

Collins stared at June.

'How do ye know it's Dave McMahon?' he said.

'We traced the bank card to the girl,' she said, breathless. 'The account is registered in her father's name, Gerry Halvey. He's a manager in AIB on the Mall. McMahon is her boyfriend. We were able to retrieve text messages on the phone. We checked the number and the address came up on the system linked to Mickey McMahon.'

'What home address did ye get for her?'

'Somewhere in Douglas, Beechmount something.'

'Wow. What were they doing over in Glasheen Road?'

'On the lang, I suppose. *I* don't know.'

'Wait a minute,' he said. 'Don't ye know who she is?'

'I just told you, her father is a bank manager.'

He turned to leave. They didn't know. He shook his head in disbelief. This was too good to be true.

'Unbelievable,' he said.

She followed him down the corridor.

He grabbed her by the arms, grinning. 'We have the bastard. We have him.'

The Incident Room was packed with gardaí, talking in groups and on the phone. At the top of the room, Superintendent John O'Connell, Chief Superintendent Sean Geary, Inspector Gerard Brennan and Clancy were standing deep in conversation.

Collins strode up to them.

'Chief Superintendent,' he said.

'Not now, Collins, we have to get this thing under control and moving,' Geary said.

Chief Superintendent Geary was a political animal and rarely involved himself in the workings of individual cases. Collins guessed that the abduction of two teenagers in broad daylight in front of witnesses was serious enough to merit Jonno informing him. Collins owed him a favour from a major case the previous year, when he could have been hung out to dry, although he was not naïve enough to think he was supported by Geary for his own sake; he knew it was for reputational reasons.

'Chief Superintendent, you need to know who the girl is,' Collins said.

'We know who the girl is, Collins,' Clancy said. 'You stay out of it.'

'No you don't, Jack. Chief Superintendent, if I'm right, her mother is Elaine Dempsey, the Minister's sister.'

The three men stared at him. Geary's mouth opened.

Jonno managed to speak. 'You sure about this, Collins?'

'No, Superintendent, but if she's from Beechmount Dale, that's where Gerry and Elaine Halvey live. Unless there's another Halvey family living there …'

'Why didn't you know this?' Geary said to Clancy.

'We … we just identified her, Chief Superintendent, we're confirming now in the school.'

'They'll know there for sure,' Collins said.

'What school is it? I'll ring Heather,' Jonno said. His wife had been a school principal. He took out his phone.

'Coláiste Bhríde,' Clancy replied. 'Sean and Jerry are on their way, I'll call them now.' Clancy took out his phone and looked for the number.

'John, walk with me,' Geary said, moving towards the door. 'Jack, you too. And you, Collins.'

The four of them left the room and headed for the top floor, towards Geary's suite of offices; Jonno and Clancy in conversations on their phones. Collins was thinking hard.

'Jack,' Geary said, and Clancy took the phone from his ear. 'Who's breaking the news to the parents?'

'One of the FLOs, sir. Nora, I think. I don't know who she brought with her.'

'Call them. Get them to hold off until we confirm. I need to plan this.'

'I'll do that, sir,' Collins said, taking out his phone.

Jonno took the phone from his ear. 'Sir, Heather says that Gerry and Elaine Halvey have one daughter, about eighteen – she doesn't know her name. She knows the Principal of Coláiste Bhríde too. Will I get her to phone her?'

'No, let the lads do it,' Geary said. 'We need to keep this under wraps for a bit. Jack, tell them to go straight in to the school. Under no circumstances are they to tell anyone what happened. This is just a general enquiry, alright?'

'Yes, sir.'

'Collins, where are the Liaison people?'

'On the Douglas Road, sir, ten minutes away from the house.'

'Right. Tell them not to go into the house until I give the go-ahead.'

They arrived on the top floor, and Geary barged through the door of his personal assistant's office. She stood up, startled.

'Linda, can you get me the Minister, please? It's urgent, top priority. If he's in the Dáil, he needs to get out now and talk to me. It's that serious. Tell the Departmental Secretary it's an urgent personal family matter. And if you can't get him, get the advisor, whatshisname.'

'Yes, sir,' Linda replied and picked up the phone on the desk.

'And will you put a call through to Number One? And Daire Foley in Corporate Communications. And get Noel and Dermot up here now. Straight away,' Geary said, walking into his office.

'Yes, sir.'

Jonno, Clancy and Collins followed Geary, who sat on his chair and pulled it into the desk. He looked at his watch and glared at them.

'Clancy, Collins, I want this girl back in her own bed in her own house tonight by ten o'clock, do you hear me?'

'Yes, Chief Superintendent,' Clancy said.

'Yes, Chief Superintendent,' Collins said.

There was a moment of awkward silence.

'Will ye pull in chairs and sit down, for fuck's sake!' Geary said, pointing.

Clancy's phone rang and he answered.

'Sir,' Clancy said. 'The Principal confirmed that the girl's uncle is the Minister. She's eighteen, in her Leaving Cert year. She was off school sick today; they got a text from her mother.'

'Not that sick, it appears,' Geary said. He shook his head. His phone rang. He picked it up. He listened.

'Okay. Will you try Smith too, the advisor? He's the only one he listens to. It's critical I speak to him in the next fifteen minutes. Critical. Did you tell him it was a personal matter? … Okay … And Number One? … Oh, okay.' He put the phone down.

He looked at Collins. 'What are their chances?'

'It depends, sir,' Collins said. He rubbed his chin. 'My guess is that Molloy wants to get at Mickey McMahon. But he could just have kidnapped the boy in retaliation, holding him as hostage or something. Word is that McMahon took a few hundred thousand of Molloy's when he did the runner to Spain that time last year. But the longer it goes on, the worse, either case. I doubt Molloy knows the identity of the girl, even though he has been acting recklessly lately, as we know.'

'Sir, this is all conjecture,' Clancy said. 'We don't even know who …'

The Chief Super silenced him with a raised hand.

'Let's assume it's Molloy's gang for now. Collins?'

'*Assuming* it's Molloy and he did this for information, sir, it doesn't look good. I know the boy went to Alicante recently and that's where McMahon has his bar.'

'How do you know this, Collins?' Jonno asked.

'I … I have a source close to the family, sir. They keep me informed about the mother and the boy. I was actually in the bar last summer myself, just for a look. He isn't there often, apparently, and the rumour is that he actually lives in Madrid and only comes down the odd time.'

'And the girl?'

Collins considered his answer.

'If she isn't released soon, I think she's in grave danger. Our best bet is to get the news out as quickly as possible who she is, and also to get Molloy in here straight away.'

In for a penny … Collins thought.

'I also think we should shut down his bar immediately and bring in all his known drug dealers and anybody associated with him. He and Tommy Tan have a brothel in Clarke's Drive and another on Killarney Hill. And he's selling drugs out of two other pubs in Fair Street and The Close. We have to hit him hard now to let him know how badly he's fucked up.'

'Sir,' Clancy tried to interject, but Geary again raised his hand. It was clear that Collins hadn't finished.

'If the kids can identify the Bradys or Corcoran, or worse, Molloy himself,' Collins said, 'he won't risk it. He might with the boy but not with her. Also, Corcoran – and it was probably him and the Bradys who took them – he's a known rapist. I wouldn't bet against them raping and killing her and killing the boy too. The only way he might hold back is if he thinks it's bad for business, a Minister's niece and everything. Or if they get what they want, quickly. I can't understand why they took her.'

Collins continued. 'One more thing, sir. My information is that there's a big drug shipment coming in and that the Keaveneys are funding it. And they were seen at the Avondhu Bar today, sir, and left with Molloy at about eleven o'clock.'

'Did you know this?' Geary asked Clancy.

'Yes, sir, but again that's all conjecture about the shipment. And without evidence that Molloy is involved …'

'I know what you're saying, but this is a Minister's niece,' Geary said. 'The usual niceties don't apply. And we need to be seen taking strong action.'

'Sir,' Collins said. Clancy was glaring at him, but he couldn't care less. 'I need six detectives, including Carroll, O'Mahony, Kelleher and Murphy. And I need six squad cars and twenty-four uniforms. We need to hit him now, straight away, and I need to get to one or two people who might know something. But we'll have to stir it up first.'

'Sir, you should know that Collins here is on desk duty and hasn't been cleared for active duty yet,' Jonno said.

'I'm perfectly fit, sir, and if you want to find this girl alive, I think I'm your best bet.' Collins locked eyes with the Chief Superintendent.

Geary paused. Collins watched the intelligence working behind the cold grey eyes and tried not to appear too eager. Or worse, desperate. Geary looked at Jonno, who nodded briefly.

'I hear what you're saying, John, but this is a crisis situation. I'm reinstating Collins and giving him what he wants for now. You will head up the operation with Gerard second in command, but we have to act now and act decisively. Collins, I don't want to hear about anything illegal, am I clear? But I want this girl back tonight.'

'You won't, sir,' Collins said, picking up the delicate inference.

The phone rang again. Geary took a deep breath and picked it up.

'Yes? ... Yes, Minister, thanks for getting back. Minister, I have some grave news. It's about your niece Claire.' He looked at Collins and Clancy and waved them away. He looked at Jonno and pointed down indicating for him to stay.

'Minister, we have some information to indicate that she has been abducted this afternoon ... Yes, I'm afraid so. No doubt about it ... No, no, it's not political at all, we think it has to do with her boyfriend and that she was an innocent bystander. But the investigation is at a very early stage.'

On the stairs Collins realised he had to act quickly and shrewdly to prevent Clancy stymieing him. Before they entered the Incident Room he spoke to Clancy earnestly.

'Jack. I know you don't like me being involved, but if we work together on this we might actually nail the prick. You *know* that I have the contacts out there and I know him better than anybody.

I think he's fucked up this time with the Minister's niece and we might have a chance.'

Clancy scowled at him and turned away.

'Wait. Jack.' Collins put his hand on Clancy's shoulder. Clancy stopped and looked down at the hand. Collins withdrew it as if scalded. He knew he'd have to make a gesture and had no problem doing so. He held his two hands before him, as if pleading.

'Listen. The main thing is we get those kids back alive. I can't make that happen if I don't get the resources. I don't blame you that you didn't nail him for the poison – you had next to nothing to go on. But we do now.'

He could see Clancy thinking hard.

'We do now,' Collins repeated.

They stared at each other.

'Please,' Collins said. 'I'll beg if I have to. I don't care as long as we nail the fucker down. And you can take all the credit, I couldn't give a shit about that. But I need your in – not just Geary's. I need *yours*. We both know how this works.'

Again the stare. Collins tried to fix his thoughts.

Somebody was running up the stairs. Noel Dunne and Dermot Clifford, the Communications people. They shuffled past, knowing a battle when they saw one, and bounded up the next flight.

Clancy's expression changed. 'You can have whatever you want, tonight. That's it, then, you're out,' he said and entered the room.

A wave of relief flowed through Collins. It was on. He was back in the fight.

47

Claire awoke. She was lying on a bed. She could feel a cold wetness on her thighs and on her bottom. She had wet herself. She began to cry.

It was dark. Her hands were still tied behind her, but the hood had been removed from her head. She could barely see the outline of a blanket over a window. She shivered.

She could breathe again. Her nose was clear. The side of her head hurt from when she had fallen, and her face stung.

Her father would come. Uncle Sean would come. He was a government minister, he'd find her. The guards would come and find her.

She whispered to herself: 'Mummy loves me. Daddy loves me. Granny Jan loves me. Ciara loves me. Debs loves me. Saoirse loves me. Auntie Susan loves me. Uncle Sean loves me. Uncle Eric loves me. Auntie Sinead loves me …'

She heard footsteps approaching.

'Mummy loves me Daddy loves me Granny Jan loves me Ciara loves me Debs loves me Saoirse loves me Auntie Susan loves me Uncle Sean loves me Uncle Eric loves me Auntie Sinead loves me …'

She heard the door creak open.

She began to silently weep.

48

When it came to abductions and murders, Collins often reminded June of the cliché that the information acquired in the first few hours had a direct correlation with the success, or failure, of the case. It was absolutely critical for them to get up and running quickly and in the right direction, for the teenagers to have any hope.

And this time it was up to him.

While he knew there could be several reasons for the abductions, he was certain that they were all linked with Molloy, through his relationship either with Mickey McMahon or with Eric O'Donovan, the dentist/developer. Molloy was the key, either way. O'Donovan could wait, for now.

Collins entered the Incident Room and told June what had happened in Geary's office, that he was in charge of the case, under Jonno and Brennan. He was itching to get going but had to wait for Jonno to announce it.

When Jonno purposefully entered the room and made his way to the raised dais at the top, Collins followed him. The room quietened when people saw that Jonno was about to speak.

'I've just had a meeting with Chief Superintendent Geary,' Jonno said, pausing to garner more attention. 'And he has asked me to take charge of this very serious case, aided by Inspector Brennan. We both agreed that Detective Collins here will lead all activities in this phase of the investigation.'

Brennan, who was standing to one side, tried not to show his ignorance of this development.

'Now. I don't have to tell you how vital the first few hours are, and it's 16.50 now, so we're a few hours behind already. So we need to act quickly and decisively. There are lives at stake. So I'm handing you over to Detective Collins.'

'Right,' Collins said, loudly. 'We have a double abduction in Croghtamore Square, off Glasheen Road today at …' He looked at June.

'12.35,' she said.

'12.35. Two young people were taken. Claire Halvey, aged eighteen, a sixth-year student in Coláiste Bhríde. She is five foot two, with long blonde hair, was last seen wearing a blue denim jacket, white blouse, black skirt, black tights and black boots. The other person is Dave McMahon, aged nineteen, a student in CIT. He is described as being six feet in height, thin, longish dark hair, last seen wearing a grey hoodie and blue jeans. We'll have more details shortly.'

Collins looked at June. She was waving two photos. How she got them so quickly he didn't know, but her real worth came out in situations like this. Sharp as a pin. Collins noticed a few disgruntled faces and a bit of confusion as to why *he* was the person addressing them. He saw Clancy's crony Johnny Barry walk out. Good.

'We have some photos here, we'll get them distributed. We'll have some more shortly,' Collins said.

'Now. As you probably heard, Claire is the niece of the Minister for Justice and Equality and Dave is the son of Mickey McMahon, former associate and right-hand man of one Dominic Molloy. While it's early in the investigation, it appears that there is a link to Molloy in the case and we are going to act accordingly, for now.'

Collins watched his audience, scanning for resentment. The usual suspects, but he didn't care.

'We're going to hit Molloy hard and fast,' he said. 'The Chief Super has given the go-ahead. But we need big numbers, so all leave is cancelled. Everybody on duty now stays on duty until further notice. Nobody goes home without Superintendent O'Connell's permission. Two lives are at stake here.' He thought for a moment about what else to say.

Jonno nodded his approval. Collins continued.

'We're also calling in all staff from all other stations in the division. And we'll be getting extra assistance from around the county.' Jonno did not react, as though this had all been agreed.

'We'll also probably be getting help from our betters in Dublin, God help us,' Collins said. This elicited a groan.

'If anybody enquires about the overtime, it's guaranteed, the Chief Super has laid it out. This is the Minister's niece so there won't be a problem. Mick, would you mind ringing around the other stations, it's just you know everybody and they know you? We'll also need secure units and vehicles, we're going to be bringing in a lot of people, too many to handle here.'

Collins looked beseechingly at Mick Murphy, who nodded assent and left the room. Whatever else, he was a professional.

'Okay, this is going to go ballistic and communication is vital. June is going to set up a hotline and we're going to have five different phones linked to that, so we need five people to person those phones. June, will you arrange that, please?'

'On it,' June said, handing him the photos. She walked away.

'One more thing, June. I want an operational line too, with three more people on that, and everything important to be siphoned through you before it gets to me. If the Comms Room isn't big enough you can use the big desk room.'

'Three more?' she said. 'Alright. We can rotate them.'

'Now, we're going big on getting this out there quickly and I see Noel and Dermot from Communications have just entered the room. What have you planned lads?'

Clifford replied. 'We're running up releases this minute, using those photos, and we'll take the lead on the 6 p.m. news, if the parents agree. This is going to be huge on social media, so we're getting some tweets ready now, a hashtag and a Facebook page.'

Collins spoke up again. 'I think Facebook could be useful, given the age of the kids – some of their friends might know something useful and that's the best way to reach them. Will you monitor all the comments, too?'

'Yeah, we're on it,' Clifford said. 'We'll need Instagram as well as Facebook. Phoenix Park have promised us their social media people. Two of them are staying on tonight to help with that. The main reason we dropped in is to emphasise the need to stay on message for this one. It's going to be huge. International. And during the, ah,' he glanced at Collins, 'big case last year there were leaks and … unhelpful information being released. Detrimental to the operation of the investigation.' Clifford paused. He cleared his throat and continued. 'Basically, we don't want anybody talking to the media on or off the record. Definitely not *on* the record but either way. We know you all have media contacts and we know how useful they are, and how much they are going to pressure ye, but stick only to what's been issued by the Press Office.'

Everybody in the room knew this was not going to happen, but Collins butted in. 'As I said, lives at stake here, everybody. Anything else, Dermot?'

'No, that's it. The statement will be ready in ten minutes. We're hoping the parents will do the press conference in time for the 6 p.m. bulletins. They will rerun them all night and that will keep the media happy till the morning. They'll be crawling all over the place within the hour so be aware of that too.'

The Communications men turned to leave the room.

'Before you go, two things, lads,' Collins said. 'I want to see the release *before* it goes out. Also, has Dave McMahon's mother been notified and asked to come in? I don't want her to hear it from the media. And she may have some important information.'

'That's up to Liaison,' Dunne said.

'I'll call them,' Clancy said, taking out his phone. This was an important gesture, Collins knew.

'Thanks, Jack,' he said. 'Her name is Sharon McMahon and she lives in 24 Fairmount Park. I have her mobile if they want it. I want to talk to her as soon as she's in.'

Collins spoke up again. 'We're going to be here for the foreseeable future, so I want food and drinks set up for everyone. Kevin, can you ring Jan and see that Catering are on top of that? I want everybody to eat every three or four hours through the night. Otherwise we make mistakes. We'll have hot and cold options.

'Also, I want everybody to charge up your phones when not using them. Nobody's runs down tonight, is that clear? We are going into some red zones and we need to be able to stay in touch at *all* times. We'll get some spares for people here too, if they're needed.

'Now, we're going to break up into groups. June will facilitate it. We will be bringing in all known associates of Molloy. Our three current suspects, based on very little information, are Sean and Pat Brady and Jim Corcoran. We have photos, we'll print them up. You all know them. We're going to raid Molloy's house and their three houses ASAP once we can get the legal stuff tied down. Has anybody seen Jerry?'

'He's on his way, he had to pick up the kids from school, but he's coming back in now. He'll know which judge is on,' Michael O'Mahony said.

Collins tried to get it out of his head that at least one person in this room was going to pass on this information to Molloy. He couldn't deal with that now.

'Okay,' he said, winding down. 'It's going to be a busy night. We're going to bring in all Molloy's associates, and I want Mary Brady in here ASAP. I want Molloy's two brothels on Clarke's Drive and Killarney Hill raided in a couple of hours before they are cleared, and I want the Avondhu shut down and his two pubs on Fair Street and The Close, and all his dealers arrested. I want Tommy Tan too; he'll be in one of the brothels. And we're going to need checkpoints. A lot of checkpoints. Do we have a reg for the van yet?'

O'Regan replied. 'Yes, we got it from CCTV. Stolen. Blue Volkswagen Transporter. I'm heading out now to see if I can trace where and when it was taken.'

'Okay, and we should appeal for dashcam footage anywhere near Magazine Road, Dennehy's Cross, Wilton and Bishopstown. By the way, any ID on the driver, from the CCTV?' Collins asked.

'Not really, he had a peaked cap and his head down. Could be one of the Bradys. IT are working on it. Last image of it was in Wilton heading for the South Link, but we don't know after that. A couple of the lads are going through the cameras now.'

'Right. June will form groups and we can get ready. I see Ray Halloran there from the Emergency Response Unit – will you have all your units on standby, Ray?'

'We are locked and loaded, ready to go,' Halloran replied. 'All off-duty personnel are on their way in.'

'Right. I don't have to tell you that these people are armed and very dangerous. Full protection and follow all procedures. But I want to scare the shit out of everybody, especially the dealers and junkies. Everybody is going down. I want the word out that Molloy is finished – get that message out to everybody on the street. Then we might get some co-operation and get these kids back alive. We need information, now.'

Collins noticed Tom Kelleher beckoning him urgently from his left.

'You got something?' he said.

'You need to talk to the witness,' Tom said.

'The Basque kid?'

'Yes,' Tom said.

'Now?'

'Now.'

Collins paused at the door and spoke to June, who was just coming back in. 'I want nine simultaneous hits on the houses, pubs and brothels. Will you form the groups so they can prep up please? You can divide up the ERU into each unit, until we have the locations sorted. Clancy's gang can do two of them, but keep them separate.'

'Okay,' she said. 'On it.'

49

Igon Zatarain was sallow-skinned, thin and small, with shining dark hair. He was unshaven with a prominent cleft chin. He had a hoop in his left ear and his brows were furrowed with worry. He was sitting at the desk with a mug of coffee when Tom Kelleher and Collins entered the interview room.

'Igon, this is Detective Collins, he's leading the case. Will you tell him what you told me, please? What you saw.'

Collins shook hands with him.

'Start at the beginning, please, Igon,' Collins said, sitting down.

'Okay. I was in the kitchen when I heard some kind of shout on the street …'

'Could you describe the shout?' Collins said.

'It was like somebody shouting "Hey" or something like that. So I went into the living room and looked out the window.' He stopped, as if to recall.

The two detectives nodded and said nothing.

'Three men are fighting in the street. *Were* fighting. Two of them had masks on. Balaclavas. One of them was *very* big, over two metres. And they were trying to pull the other one – the young man – into the van.' He paused again.

'Then the girl came around the corner and the young man pull the mask off the head of one of the men. He put it on again and he grab her. Grabbed her.'

Again Collins nodded. He wanted him to finish in his own words.

'The big man is beating the boy on the ground. He hit him a

lot in the face and the head. The other man pick up the girl and throw her in the back of the van and the big man throw the boy. Then the doors close and it drive off.'

Collins realised why Tom had wanted him to hear this.

'So the girl was not with the boy at the beginning?'

'No, she come after, when they are already fighting.'

'And when the balaclava was pulled off the man, did she see his face?'

'*Sí*, she is very close, and he was looking at her. Then she turn around, but he grab her.'

'Did you get a look at his face?'

Igon squirmed and shook his head.

'Not really. He is looking away from me at the girl, then he put it back on very quickly.'

'How far away from the window is this happening?'

'About fifteen metres, maybe.'

'But she definitely saw the man's face?'

'For sure, they are very close, and she is looking at him. It all happen very quick, but I am sure of that.'

'Thank you Igon, that's very helpful,' Collins said and left the room with Tom.

'They never planned on taking her,' Collins said, outside.

'Seems like it,' Tom said. 'Like they were taking him and she came upon it.'

'Molloy fucked up,' Collins said. 'That means he might let her go.'

'Yeah, but she's a witness. She can identify one of them, pro-bably one of the Bradys.'

Collins grimaced. Just then, Jonno and Kate came up the stairs into the corridor.

'With me, Collins,' Jonno said. 'The Halveys are here.'

'Will you phone me please, in ten minutes?' Collins said to Tom. Tom nodded.

Meeting the parents of victims is the part of a police officer's job that nobody wants – facing the rage, fear and misery of people whose worst possible nightmare has just befallen them.

Collins climbed the stairs beside Jonno and Kate, wondering how to approach the Halveys. He asked Kate several questions about them, none of which she could answer. Jonno would probably lead, but Collins wanted to suss out the parents too. You never know.

He assumed the privileged background of the sister of a government minister, especially this particular minister, would have formed a certain type of woman. He expected an air of entitlement and someone accustomed to being in control, being obeyed. A bank manager and a father would also be a handful, outraged that somebody could hurt his baby girl and furious with the possibility that he had not protected her enough.

Collins set his demeanour and prepared the standard responses that he had learned the hard way in the face of such horrors. Appearing determined, strong and in control, but at the same time sharing their outrage. Giving the impression of knowing what he was talking about. Concealing that he was hiding anything from them, but hiding as much as he possibly could. Looking them in the eye but not for too long. Not volunteering anything he was not asked. Getting away as quickly as he could but 'reluctantly'.

Even if there was very little hope, it was always better, initially at least, to give the family as much optimism as possible, to let the shock wear off. In this case, any hope was a challenge.

Jonno gave a cursory knock and entered the room. Collins and Kate followed. A heavy-set bearded man was standing at the round table and pointing his finger close to Geary's face. His wife, the girl's mother, was also clearly fuming, but she was also swaying a little and her eyes were glossy as well as being raw from crying. She was clearly drunk or high.

'How can you allow a man like that to walk the streets?' Gerry Halvey was shouting. 'What kind of a police force are you running here, for Christ's sake? With, with, with *children* being kidnapped in broad daylight on the streets of Cork?'

Geary was well used to being abused by the families of victims and he was balancing the appearance of being simultaneously sympathetic and focused. He saw Jonno and Collins with relief.

'Mr and Mrs Halvey, this is Superintendent O'Connell, Detective Collins and Sergeant Browne, our Chief Family Liaison Officer. Superintendent O'Connell is supervising the case and Detective Collins is our leading detective. Collins is one of our most experienced officers and he successfully brought the serial killings to an end last year, you probably read about that.' Geary was about to go on when Halvey cut him off.

'What are ye doing to get my daughter back, eh? I want to know this minute!'

Collins knew he had to be quick and decisive.

'We have just mounted the largest search and rescue operation in the history of this division, Mr Halvey. I will have almost fourteen hundred gardaí at my disposal within hours and we are on our way to simultaneously raid the homes and known haunts of the four suspects. We are also bringing in all known associates of the chief suspect and we will be questioning these and all other potential sources. We have cancelled all garda leave and we are bringing in …' Collins had pulled up a chair to the side of Geary's desk as he spoke and sat down, so that the two parents would sit down too and hopefully calm down. But Halvey cut him off.

'How can ye allow this kind of individual to have the run of Cork, that's what I want to know!'

'Mr Halvey, I would gladly lock up this individual and throw away the key,' Jonno answered. 'But, unfortunately, the law won't allow us to do it.' Jonno held out his hands in a gesture of regret.

'We don't make the law, but we have to obey it,' Collins said. He needed to get this over with quickly. 'Now, I need to ask you some very important questions about Claire, these could be absolutely vital.'

This quietened Halvey and he sat down.

Collins noticed he did not make eye contact with his wife and there was little or no communication between them. Probably not relevant, but you never know.

'Do you know what Claire was doing in Croghtamore Square near the Lough this afternoon at 12.35?' Collins said.

'We, we … don't,' he admitted. 'We only found out a while ago that she wasn't at school.'

'Did you know about her relationship with Dave McMahon?'

'We … heard there might have been somebody. She told us it wasn't serious, just a couple of dates.'

'So you hadn't met him? You had no idea who he was?'

Halvey squirmed. Collins sensed he was the kind of man who could beat himself up about such a lapse.

'No,' Halvey said, and ran his fingers through his thinning hair. He looked at his wife for the first time. Collins didn't see his expression, but it could have been accusatory.

She shook her head from side to side.

'We were told by the school that they received a text from your phone this morning, Mrs Halvey. Excusing Claire from school due to illness …'

'What?' Mrs Halvey said. 'I *never* texted the school, I would *never* …' The penny dropped. She whipped out her phone and began to check her messages.

'She probably deleted the text and the reply, Mrs Halvey. It happens all the time, I'm afraid. But we have her phone and we have found some messages to the boy confirming they had arranged to meet. Can I ask you when you both saw Claire last?'

The father answered. 'I dropped her on the way to school at about half-eight. She was on her way to *school*.'

'And where was that?'

'At the corner of Merchant's Quay and Patrick Street. The school is just …' He stopped. He put his hands to his face and let out a sob. 'If anything …'

'Mr Halvey, can I ask you what she was wearing?'

'Her uniform, of course. It's dark blue.'

'Right,' Collins said. That was certainly not what she was wearing when abducted, but he did not mention it. 'And did she have her schoolbag with her?'

'Yes. Yes she has a, what-do-you-call it,' Halvey said.

'A backpack,' Mrs Halvey said. 'It's red. Adidas.'

'Thank you,' Collins said. 'We think we have that, if you can identify it, it would be helpful. Did you notice anything different about her this morning?'

'I … She was in good form. She was up early and …'

He paused and Collins noticed the realisation. She was in good form and up early, not for school, but to meet a boy.

'I presume that the Chief Superintendent has told you the

suspected motive behind the abductions,' Collins said, trying to raise their hopes.

They nodded.

'Well then, you know that Claire was not the focus of the attack, so there is a possibility that they might be focusing on the young man. We're almost certain they did not intend to take her, but she may have been in the wrong place at the wrong time.'

'It's his fault!' Mrs Halvey said, standing up. 'The little gurrier! Oh Claire …' She burst into tears and sat down again.

Halvey ignored her and looked at Collins, his eyes full of pleading. 'Will you get her back? Will you?'

Collins faced him squarely, holding his eyes. 'We are going to do *everything possible* that we can to get them both back, Mr Halvey. The fact that we have a very good idea who is involved helps us a great deal.'

'Mr and Mrs Halvey,' Jonno jumped in. 'We think that the best chance we have of successfully and speedily concluding this case is to make a strong media statement as soon as possible. We will need your co-operation in this and there will be huge media interest in any case, due to Claire's uncle, the Minister.'

Jonno coughed, choosing his words. 'Would you and Mrs Halvey be willing to do a press conference and make a statement in time for the six o'clock news? This would be a great help to us and we'll help you in every way – we have two experts on media issues here and we're getting in some outside advice too. This could be very important.'

'It's quite possible,' Collins said, 'that those involved didn't know Claire's identity and we hope that by getting that message out there as quickly and dramatically as possible, we can spook them and get them to release the kids, Claire especially. Also, we can use this to … motivate other potential information sources to co-operate.'

'Yes, yes, of course,' Halvey spoke decisively. 'I'll …' He looked at his wife. '*We'll* completely do anything, anything at all.'

Collins's phone rang. It was Tom, on cue. Collins apologised and answered, and then realised his mistake: the two Halveys regarded him expectantly, as if he were receiving news of Claire's safety.

'Yes?' he said.

'You asked me to phone you,' Tom said. Collins paused a moment, as if still listening.

'Okay, thanks, I'll be right down.'

He stood. 'Excuse me, I have to go.'

'Go ahead, Collins. Do you have everything you need?' Geary asked, loudly.

'Yes, Chief Superintendent, but we have to make sure that all the other stations get their people on board immediately.'

'That's in hand. Is the legal work done for those raids? Did Jerry get hold of the judge?'

'I'm just going to check now. June is putting together the teams.'

'Right, right. Let me know if you need anything,' Geary said, rising. 'One moment, please,' he said to the Halveys and went to Collins, who was standing by the door.

He whispered into Collins's ear. 'Get this sorted, I don't care how.'

'Yes, sir,' Collins said. Message received. If they had to crack skulls, so be it. He was pleased.

50

There was bedlam in the Incident Room. June was struggling with gardaí looking for instructions and answers to questions. Collins took charge.

'Okay, quiet everyone,' he said, loudly, from the dais. 'We're getting nowhere here.'

'Collins, Collins,' two men said – he vaguely recognised them. They were detectives from other stations, wanting in on the action.

'I said *quiet*.' Collins stared them down.

When the room had quietened, he continued. 'Now. The nine raids are the current priority and what we want are the leaders of those teams in here and everybody else out.'

There was a moan of protest and curses.

Collins spoke above it.

'June, do you have the nine names?'

'Yes,' she said, handing him a sheet with the list.

'Okay, everybody, listen up. These are the nine names. Everybody else will leave and await instructions from each of them. They will contact you when we're ready. There's food in the cafeteria, go and eat something or have a coffee.'

Collins called out the names and June wrote them on the whiteboard at the same time. Collins realised that they would need more whiteboards and beckoned Cathy up to tell her. He also asked her to get somebody to stand at the door and prevent anybody other than the nine team leaders from entering.

Clancy sidled up to him.

'Yeah?' Collins said.

'You said you wanted to question Sharon McMahon,' he said.

'Did you get her already?'

'No, I was just going out when I saw her below screaming blue murder. She must have heard.'

'Fuck, how did that happen?'

Clancy did not answer.

'Where is she?' Collins said.

'They have her in one of the first-floor offices, I'm not sure which one.'

'Right. Thanks, Jack. June, will you get the rest of them ready, please? I have to talk to Sharon McMahon.'

Collins knew Sharon McMahon from the two times he had put her husband away. Mickey had been impulsive and overconfident. And greedy – they were nearly all greedy. He remembered her as being smart and fearless. Face a regiment, as his mother would have said. Collins knew the kind of reception he'd get from her and he tried to think how to handle it. Very different from the Halveys, that was for sure. He had to put her on the back foot immediately and he knew how.

On the first floor he met Nora, one of the FLOs.

'Nora, did ye break the news to the Halveys, earlier?'

'We did, yeah. Well, to Mrs Halvey. The husband was at work, I think Brennan went over to the South Mall and told him.'

'Really?' Collins was surprised that Inspector Brennan would dirty his hands with such a menial and challenging task. He was a very important man, as he had told Collins more than once.

'Yeah, his brother-in-law ...'

'I know, but still. Didn't she ring the husband when ye told her?'

'No, she rang the brother first, the Minister.' Nora lowered her voice. 'Slugging wine back to beat the band. He knew already, I think the Chief Super told him. He was on his way back from opening some new factory in Clonakilty. Eventually the husband rang her on the landline and it was Mags who took the call.'

'Did she come in on her own?'

'No, she has a sister living next door, a painter. Not a painter decorator, an artist painter. A bit of a queer hawk.'

'What was the mother's reaction?' Collins said.

'She screamed bloody murder. We were fools, we'd made a mistake, she was at school. Then she rang the school and they told her she was out sick. Well, she fucked them out of it too.' Nora looked at her watch.

'Anyway,' she said. 'When we told her we found the backpack with her school uniform and everything, she realised we were right and she nearly lifted the roof with the screeching. Never heard anything like it, Collins, and I'm doing this shit for four years now. I think the sister heard her 'cos she came barrelling in through the back door, giving out she couldn't paint with the racket.'

Nora shook her head.

'Couldn't fucking paint, Collins. Jesus ... I'm in the wrong job.'

Collins braced himself and entered the room.

Sharon McMahon sat at a small round table, red-faced and tearful, in a blaze of anger and fear.

Another woman sat beside her, patting her hand, trying to calm her. A bit older, shabbier, big-boned.

Kate sat opposite them. She must have come straight down from the Halveys. She had probably been giving Sharon the usual spiel, that it was early in the investigation, too soon to come to any conclusions; that a detective would be along soon to answer questions.

Sharon jumped up when she saw Collins.

'Collins! Who has him, Collins, who has my baby?'

'Sharon,' Collins said, moving to the table. 'Sit down, Sharon, sit down, I'll tell you what we know.'

'Don't tell me to sit down, you prick. You put Mickey away, you *framed* him, so you did. Who has him? Who?' She was shouting, near to hysterical. He decided to shut her up.

He looked her in the eye. He spoke loudly and clearly. 'Molloy. *Molloy* has him, Sharon. Right? Molloy. So we need your help. Now.'

She staggered back as if struck. The other woman stood up and held out her hands in support.

Collins sat down and scrutinised Sharon's reaction. She had paled, all the blood gone from her face.

'Oh, no,' she said, gasping. 'Oh, Jesus, Jesus. Poor David.' She sat down.

'How do you know?' she said, hoarsely.

'A few things. I can't give you operational details, but it definitely looks like it was him. I have over a thousand guards on active duty this minute trying to find them.'

'"Them"? Who's "them"?'

'Dave and his girlfriend, did nobody tell you?' He glanced at Kate.

'His *girlfriend*? He doesn't have a girlfriend. Where did you get this from?'

'I … There was a young woman with him when he was taken. She's eighteen, her name is Claire Halvey, do you not know her?'

'Never heard of her, must be some mistake. No way.' Sharon glared at him and Collins felt her ignorance was sincere.

He decided to draw her out. He held her eyes, reading them.

She gave that shake of the head and hands movement for the other person to speak.

'She's eighteen, as I said. From Douglas,' Collins said. 'She's in sixth year in Coláiste Bhríde, rang in sick to school apparently. We found her bag at the scene; she'd dropped it. There was a lot of messages between them on her phone.'

'That means nothing. Was she involved?' Sharon said.

'Involved?' Collins said.

'You know, did she set him up or something?'

'Sharon, she's eighteen, her father's a bank manager.'

'What's that got to do with it? Maybe Molloy got to her.' She looked at him again for a response. 'Well?'

'Sharon, we think Molloy took him because of Mickey, because of what Mickey did. And Dave was out in Spain lately visiting him …'

'What? He was not! Bullshit. No way.'

Collins said nothing for a moment; he let her stew.

'He went to Spain with Brendan Crotty and some of the soccer crowd. But, they, they …' She was suddenly unsure.

She must have already suspected something about that trip, Collins thought.

'What do you want to know?' she said.

'Where was Dave supposed to be this morning?'

'At college. In CIT. He's doing structural engineering, second year.'

'And what time did he leave home?'

'He usually leaves around eight.' She looked at the other woman, who spoke.

'He left around quarter-to-nine. He … he … I was just home from my shift.'

'And what's your own name?' Collins said.

'Oh. Marie Donoghue. I'm a neighbour of Sharon's.'

'Fairmount Park?' Collins said. 'What number?'

'Oh, em … twenty-one. God, nearly forgot there for a minute.' She smiled, embarrassed.

'And what was he wearing, Marie? Do you remember?'

'Oh, em, em. A grey hoodie, yes that's it. And jeans, I think.'

Collins nodded. A good witness, for a change.

'Did he have a bag, a rucksack, anything like that?'

'No. No. I don't think so anyway.'

Collins looked at Sharon. She was thinking hard.

'He normally has a bag. With his books and stuff,' Sharon said.

That was what he had wanted to hear. Something she had said about Claire put a thought in his mind. She suggested that Molloy had gotten to the girl. Not impossible given that he was controlling her uncle, but it was far more likely that Molloy had gotten to Dave. That Dave was somehow involved in selling or taking drugs, or had been some kind of go-between for his father and Molloy and it had all gone wrong. Mickey would be well capable of involving the young lad if it suited him. If so, that could change things.

'Sharon, would you mind if we could get access to his room, his stuff? It might help us figure this out. Does he have a laptop? That often gives useful information.'

She paused. Collins was sure he knew what she was thinking. On the one hand, her son was in great danger and she wanted to help. But on the other, if he had done something stupid and gotten involved with his father and drugs, or even Molloy …

'Yes, you can do that. Anything that helps bring him back.'

Right answer, Sharon.

'Okay, I'll have someone do that immediately. And we'll have our IT people go through his laptop. What's his mobile phone number? We might be able to trace that too, if he still has it.'

She gave him the number and he wrote it down to check if it matched with what they had. 'Grand. Thanks. Sharon, do you have any idea if he knows somebody living around College Road, or the Lough? That's where they were taken. About half-twelve today.'

She shook her head. 'No. I don't know. But …' She let loose another sigh. 'Looks like there's a lot I don't know.'

His heart went out to her. She knew Molloy and what he was capable of, the danger that Dave was in.

'Here's what we know,' he said. 'He went for chips with this girl just before twelve on the Bandon Road. We think they went to the Lough with the chips. On the way back, in a small lane called Croghtamore Square, two men, one of them described as extremely tall, grabbed them and put them in the back of a large blue Volkswagen van, which drove off towards the South Link.' He said nothing about Claire not being with Dave when the attack happened or that Dave had been badly beaten.

At the words 'extremely tall' her eyes widened. She knew as well as he did about Corcoran.

'That's all?' she said. 'How do ye know it's Molloy?'

'I can't say any more for operational reasons, but we need your help, Sharon. We're hoping to have a strong, fast media presence to raise the stakes for Molloy. The girl is a niece of the Minister for Justice, Sean Dempsey, would you believe, and obviously the media are going to go crazy for the story, so we need to use that to our advantage. To the advantage of Dave and Claire.'

He paused. He would have to choose his words carefully.

'It would be a big help, Sharon, if you appeared on TV and made an appeal. Our Communications people will help you and tell you what to say, it won't be much, just a couple of minutes, no questions or anything, but it makes a huge difference, believe me. Claire's parents will be doing the same. It's really important.'

She looked at him in alarm, putting her hand to her mouth. She closed her eyes and opened them.

'Yes. Okay,' she said, determination in her voice. 'When?'

'We're aiming to have it finished for the six o'clock news, so in the next thirty minutes or so. If you don't have any more questions, Kate here will bring you down to the Communications people and they will help you get ready and tell you everything you need.'

He stood up to leave.

She looked at him beseechingly.

'Collins. What I said earlier, I'm sorry. I … Will you get him back, Collins? Will you bring him back to me?' She blinked once and tears spilled down her face. 'He's all I have, Collins, he's all I have. If anything happens to him …' She broke down.

'Sharon,' he said. He approached her. 'Sharon. Look at me.'

She looked up, as vulnerable as anyone could be.

'We're getting him back,' Collins said. 'I firmly believe it. But if you think of anything else, be sure to let us know. Any friend of his who might know something. Anything. Be sure to tell Kate.'

Christ, he thought, *the responsibility you have now.*

51

The nine team leaders were prepped and ready when Collins arrived back in the Incident Room. Gerard Brennan was lecturing them about the importance of firearm procedures during the operation. Collins was tempted to cut him off but instead let the inspector have his say. Not a good time to make another enemy.

Brennan stepped down from the dais and said, 'All yours, Collins.'

'Thank you, Inspector,' Collins said. 'Okay everyone, listen up. We have nine targets, all classified as red. Safety first. You heard the Inspector about best practice. You all know your target and your team. Any final questions, anyone?'

'Yes. Collins, tell us why did you get sent off against us in '97?' Kevin Tuohig said, with a big fat grin splitting his big fat face.

Everybody laughed.

There wasn't much that the veteran Tuohig had not seen. He had battled against the IRA all along the border in the eighties and nineties and an operation like this didn't faze him.

'Fuck off, Tuohig,' Collins said, smiling. He spoke to June as the gardaí were leaving the room.

'Did Jerry get sorted by the judge?'

'Yeah, yeah,' she said. 'All above board. Jonno has given the go-ahead.'

'Good,' he said.

And now for the hard part: the waiting. It would be an hour at least before everybody was in place and they could co-ordinate the raids. He decided to eat something and figure out who could give him the information he needed to find the kids.

Talking to the right people was more important than the raids. Essentially they were just a show of force – to pressurise Molloy into letting Claire and Dave go. And to send a message to others that Molloy was finished and they could co-operate. Appearing proactive was vital to keeping the Minister and the media onside. He didn't envisage they would find anyone or anything useful from the raids, but you never know, too. Shit happens.

As he was about to leave the room, Linda, Geary's personal assistant, approached him.

'The Minister is here,' she said, glumly. 'The Chief Super says you're to come up.'

'Fuck,' he said. 'Fuck, fuck, fuck.'

In many ways Collins preferred criminals to politicians because you knew where you stood with them. Sean Dempsey, the Minister for Justice and Equality, was a pet hate, holding forth about family values while having an affair with one of his office secretaries in Dublin. And then toddling off to Mass every Sunday with his perfect blonde wife and their two perfect children.

Hypocrisy didn't come into it, but Collins knew enough to be a good boy as he trudged up the stairs to face the politician's judgement and patronising. Otherwise he'd be out.

He put on the face and knocked hard on the door.

Jonno opened it and gave him a stern look. *Behave*, it said.

The Minister was sitting opposite the Chief Superintendent at Geary's large meeting table. Claire's father, Gerry Halvey, was sitting beside him. Although a good ten years younger than his brother-in-law and not the girl's father, Dempsey was dominating the conversation. He didn't deign to look up or acknowledge Collins as he approached. Halvey looked utterly miserable.

Groomed to perfection in an expensive pale suit and tan shoes, with his hair slightly gelled like a teenager, Sean Dempsey epitomised the ruling class. Tall and well kept, composed and in control, arrogant and intelligent – he looked born to rule. And he was venomous enough to make it happen.

The top student in a private primary school by the age of twelve; a sailing and rugby prodigy at fourteen; out-half and captain of the rugby senior team at sixteen; screwing the prettiest girl in Blackrock at seventeen; president of the Students' Union in UCC at nineteen; first-class honours degree in commerce at twenty-one; a TD at twenty-three; a government minister at twenty-nine. Easy peasy.

Now, at thirty-eight, he was destined for nowhere else but the very top. One slip by the Taoiseach and he would have the reins of power in his surprisingly small but very well-manicured hands.

'Ah, Detective Collins, I was just briefing the Minister here on the case,' Geary said, glad for the attention to be diverted elsewhere. He beckoned to a chair.

Dempsey briefly looked Collins up and down.

'Detective,' he said. 'Would you mind telling me why you think you are the best person to lead this case? I understand you are just back from sick leave. And wasn't Molloy the chief suspect for that too?'

Just as Collins was about to respond, the Minister turned to the Chief Superintendent and said, 'Sean, this doesn't look good at all, does this animal have the run of the city?'

Collins thought for a horrible moment that he was referring to him, but Geary began the same speech that he had given to Halvey earlier: evidence, the DPP, the system, etc.

Dempsey held up an imperious hand and cut the Chief Super-intendent off. He looked at Collins.

'Can you give us an update, Detective?'

So he did. In the middle of his little speech, a phone rang and Dempsey took it out of his pocket, looked at it and then answered. His hand went up again, this time in Collins's direction.

'Yes?' he said, then listened for a while. 'Is that confirmed? ... Right, see that you do, Seamus.' He hung up.

'The Commissioner. He is sending Denis down now to take over. He will have thirty detectives with him. Most of the Organised Crime Bureau. Sean, it's still your division, of course, but Denis will be making the main decisions regarding this investigation himself. God knows we pay him enough. Seamus has also authorised a CRI alert so we can use the 112 number and give this the profile it needs. Technically Claire is over eighteen, but they're both teenagers – children, essentially. Will you get that out there, John?'

'Yes, Minister, I'll do that now,' Jonno said and left the room.

'Detective, can you tell me again why ye are going on the Molloy connection?'

'Well, the boy is closely linked to him. His father ...'

'Yes I know all that, but why now?'

'We don't know that for sure, yet,' Collins said. 'But the lad went to Spain a few weeks ago, I suspect to meet his father, so it could be related to that. But with Molloy you never know; he's grown unstable over the past few months and we think he's using himself now too. We've heard of a large new shipment coming in. Two major Dublin drug dealers, the Keaveneys, visited him today. The description of the abductors fits very closely with some thugs who work for Molloy and ...' Dempsey cut Collins off.

'Have you completely ruled out a connection to myself?'

'It's very unlikely, Minister. Who would do something like that now? I don't think the Continuity IRA have the people and if they did, they'd probably target one or both of your own children. I understand they are in primary school here in the city.'

Dempsey was startled by that.

Collins continued. 'Molloy's exact motive is unclear, but it could be one of several. Simple revenge for what McMahon did to him. They could be hostages for McMahon to pay back what he's supposed to owe Molloy. He could be looking for information from the boy about his father, or it could just be a warning to him – he has several potential motives.'

'What are their chances?' Dempsey said. 'Seriously. Will they make it?'

Halvey gave a little sob and put his head in his hands. Dempsey patted him on the arm and said, 'We need to know this, Gerry. I'm sorry.'

Collins paused. This was tricky ground.

'To be honest, sir, with Molloy's track record, I personally would be very fearful for their well-being. We're almost certain that Claire was not the focus of the abduction, but our witness has just told us that she may be able to identify one of the assailants. That wasn't great news, to be honest. In the past Molloy has limited his killings …'

'Alleged killings,' Geary broke in.

'His *alleged* killings, to other gangland people, but now, I think he's a bit out of control. Our best bet is to give a major show of force and a large media campaign to … persuade him that this is a step too far and that he's finished if he doesn't return them unharmed. But if revenge is the motive, who knows?'

'What do you know about the boy? Is he involved in drugs? This looks very bad I must say; to have Claire involved with a drug-dealer's son.' Dempsey glanced at his brother-in-law.

Everybody in the room knew what the political consequences could be for the Minister, but Collins suspected that only one person there cared about them.

'We have no indication that he is,' Collins said. 'He's never come up on our radar, anyway. I've contacted the garda who covers CIT and watches for drugs and so on there and he says he's never come across him. The local gardaí where he lives don't know him. He plays on a soccer team and that doesn't fit the profile for drugs or crime, so my gut feeling is that it's just the connection with the father that got him into this.' Collins gathered his thoughts, he needed the Minister to go with the Molloy angle.

'But I'm concerned about the recent trip to Spain. The father is well capable of using the young lad and he might have dragged him into something to do with Molloy. We're looking further into that.' This reminded him to check who went with Dave to Spain and question them.

'What are you expecting tonight?' Dempsey said.

'Well it's hard to say. Time is critical,' Collins said. 'Every hour they don't turn up somewhere leaves the outcome looking less optimistic. That's why it's so important for us to make a big splash so soon. The next twenty-four hours will tell a lot.'

'Well, then. You better make sure that they do turn up, hadn't you?' Dempsey said.

Silence. Collins did not react.

'Right. That's all. You can go back to your operation,' Dempsey said.

As he walked slowly away, Collins reminded himself that

Dempsey's niece was in danger, his precious career on the line, and it was hardly a time for the niceties. But still it rankled. The ruling class was a bugbear for him, their self-entitlement. It always had been and always would be, he knew.

On the first-floor landing he passed Nora escorting Elaine Halvey and her sister Susan Jameson into her office. All three women turned to him hopefully, as if he might have good news. He kept moving. He was halfway down the flight of stairs when Susan caught up with him.

'Wait,' she said.

Collins looked at her impassively. He didn't have time for this.

'The day you came to my house,' she said, quietly.

'Yes.' *Where is she going with this, now?*

'Did that have anything to do with this?'

'With Claire being taken?'

'Yes. Was it the same people? Were they staking out the house or something?'

'They weren't staking out the house for Claire. I'm sure of that,' he said.

'But was it connected?'

What's bothering her? Collins had wondered how much she knew about her husband's financial dealings, and any possible links to Molloy. He had assumed nothing, but now he wasn't so sure.

'What do you know?' he said.

'What do you mean?' She was prevaricating, fishing.

'I don't have time for this,' he said. 'If you know something, tell me. This is your *niece* we're talking about.' *Jesus, what are these people like?*

As he reached the corner of the stairwell, Collins glanced back. She was sitting on the stairs, her shoulder pressed against the bannister. She was bent over, as if in pain. A look of grief twisted her face, making it appear old and lurid.

52

Collins went straight to the Incident Room, which was calmer now. June said everything was under control, the units were en route, the raids were all set up and would be executed within thirty minutes. Somebody had christened it 'Operation Rescue'. *How original*, thought Collins.

He told June the news about Claire witnessing the abduction, seeing the face of one of the men, presumably one of the Bradys.

'Jesus,' she said. 'Talk about being unlucky.'

'I think he'll let her go,' Collins said. 'I can't imagine he'll want all the shit that's about to land on him. Especially if there's a shipment of coke due in. He's not stupid, whatever else he is.'

'I hope you're right,' she said. 'I'm going for food, want some?'

'I'll follow you over. I want to check on the press statements.'

The statements looked fine, nothing that could come back to haunt them, or give Molloy anything to use. They comprised the usual banal declarations and requests for assistance. 'Definite line of enquiry' was the term used to indicate they knew who did it but were still looking for them. Of course that would prompt the obvious question: who? He decided to leak that out later, if it wasn't already obvious to the media.

The press room was chaotic, a feeding frenzy. On the following day, if the kids were not found, he knew it would be much worse.

It had obviously been leaked that the missing girl was the Minister's niece. A scatter of journalists approached him, looking for quotes.

He'd begun to get phone calls from other journalists he had previously used, but he had no intention of talking to any of them until he'd figured out what 'leak' would be most beneficial.

'Collins, what's the story? Is it true the Minister's niece has been kidnapped?'

'Is there a ransom request, Collins?'

'Who's the young fella, Collins? We heard it's Mickey Mc-Mahon's son. Is he her boyfriend? Is there a connection to Molloy?'

'We heard they've been killed, Collins, any truth to that?'

Some of them had already been briefed off the record by gardaí, that was clear. Favours were being called in.

Collins said he didn't have anything yet for them today, maybe later. The stock answer. He got some dirty looks. He met the eyes of a friend of his, Jimmy Croke, and held them to let him know he'd be in touch.

Once things settled down, the media event itself was well orchestrated. They'd had some experience the previous year with the serial killings, and Dunne and Clifford were efficient and thorough.

Jonno walked confidently to the lectern and began to speak.

'Good afternoon ladies and gentlemen. I'm going to begin by reading a statement. Then I'm going to introduce you to some people who will also make statements. We won't be taking questions today, but we have a press release that's being passed around the room with more details.' He cleared his throat.

'Today at approximately 12.35 two young people were abducted in Croghtamore Square near the Lough, in Cork city. They are: Claire Halvey, from Douglas, aged eighteen, a sixth-year student in Coláiste Bhríde. She is five foot two, with long blonde hair, blue eyes, and was last seen wearing a blue denim jacket, white blouse, black skirt, black tights and black boots. The other person is Dave McMahon, aged nineteen, from Blarney Street, a student in CIT. He is described as being almost six foot tall, thin, long dark hair, brown eyes, last seen wearing a grey hoodie and blue jeans.

'Both were taken and put in a dark blue Volkswagen Transporter van, registration number 12 C 14599, which then sped off in the direction of Wilton and onto the South Link towards the west on the N40 and possibly the N22. The van was stolen last night in the Little Island area.

'Needless to say, we are very concerned about the well-being and safety of these young people and are appealing for assistance from anybody who might have seen something in the Lough/ Glasheen Road area today from 11 a.m. onwards. We're especially keen to get dashcam footage of any roads in the western parts of the city.'

Collins watched the assembled media. He wondered how much pressure he could put on Mary Brady and how he could use Molloy's child as a pressure point. Probably not very much, she was a tough cookie.

'We consider this situation to be of such concern that a Child Rescue Ireland or CRI alert has been issued,' Jonno said. 'If anybody has any further information, we would like them to dial 112 immediately and they will be put through to us.

'We have some photos of the two young people, which we are now distributing along with the press release. And now I would like you to give your attention to Mr and Mrs Halvey, Claire's parents, who are also going to make a statement.'

The Halveys entered the room, holding hands. Mrs Halvey

was holding a photograph of her daughter by her side. Collins noticed she had changed her clothes and was now wearing neat black shoes, black tights, a plain charcoal dress with a small black jacket over it and pearls around her neck. No earrings. Mr Halvey was holding a sheet of paper, which, no doubt, contained his statement.

They sat down at the table before several microphones and he began to read. Mrs Halvey held the photograph before her, facing out, her hands shaking badly. She looked stone cold sober now but was having difficulty keeping her composure. Gerry Halvey spoke, in a low, hoarse voice.

'Our daughter, Claire, was taken from us today and we are appealing to whoever has her to return her immediately.' He looked up at the flashing cameras and blinked.

'Claire is the light of our lives, a happy, quiet and friendly girl. We love her so much. She never harmed anybody in her life and she doesn't deserve this. She is an innocent schoolgirl who has never been away from home before, she must be very frightened, and we are appealing to whoever has her to return her to us immediately. We just want her home.

'If anybody has any information, we are asking them to contact the gardaí by dialling 112. Anything, however small, could be vital to secure Claire's release, so please please, we are appealing for your help.' He bowed his head.

Elaine Halvey then spoke. Collins strained to hear her above the din of the cameras. The flashing must have been blinding to the couple, but they just looked ahead morosely.

'This is a picture of our beautiful Claire,' she said, in a surprisingly clear voice. 'We just want her home. Whoever has her, can you please just let her go so she can come home to us. We love her so much.' She hesitated and then stopped. Collins could see that she did not trust herself to speak again.

A journalist tried to ask a question about the Minister, but Jonno talked him down.

'As I said earlier, we're not answering questions right now. Please respect Mr and Mrs Halvey's situation. We will be issuing a statement within the hour.'

Dunne approached the Halveys, who seemed to be rooted to the spot, transfixed by the cameras' racket and the flashing lights. Eventually they stood up and left the room with him.

Shortly afterwards Sharon McMahon came in, with Clifford beside her. She also held a sheet of paper and sat down at the seat that Halvey had just vacated. Jonno spoke.

'Now we are going to have an appeal from Sharon McMahon, Dave McMahon's mother, so once again, please, no questions.'

Sharon stared at the page. She was breathing quickly, her chest rising and falling inside a grey blouse that she had somehow acquired to replace the hoodie. She looked pale and wizened. The din and flashing of the cameras started up again.

'Today my boy, Dave, was taken from me and I am appealing to whoever has him to release him immediately and let him come home.' She swallowed and continued, the paper shaking in her hands. 'Dave is a wonderful son and a loving nephew and grandson, and he means everything to myself and all my family. He has never done anybody any harm, he's never been in trouble. He loves his soccer, and Liverpool ...' Her voice broke and she had to compose herself '... and he's a good student. He's only nineteen and I love him and I just want my baby home.'

She broke down and began to weep. The room was silent except for the sound of her heaving. Even the cameras stopped flashing.

Clifford approached her and said something in her ear, holding her elbow.

She lifted her head again and blurted, 'Please don't hurt my baby, please. I'll do anything, anything …'

Clifford looked up at Jonno. She had gone off message. Clifford leaned over her and pointed at the page and Sharon looked down and began to read again. Collins wondered if there was a hidden message in her last comment and then dismissed it. But you never know. He decided to make sure to follow up on her phone monitoring and bank details.

'If anybody has any information, I am asking them to contact the gardaí by dialling 112. Anything, however small, could be vital to secure Dave's release, so please, I am appealing for your help.'

She stood up suddenly, pushed the chair back with her legs, and wobbled. Somebody in the media give a gasp. Clifford held her around the shoulder and helped her from the room.

Her departure prompted another chorus of questions at Jonno, and it was obvious that the connection between the Minister's niece and the exiled drug dealer's son was the main story.

Typical media, Collins thought, *the kids' abduction and imminent death were secondary.*

He imagined the headlines in the morning. He resolved to make sure that Molloy was front and centre of attention, if he could at all. He'd have to make some calls off the record later.

Collins went to the Comms Room and looked at the five gardaí wearing headsets, answering the deluge of phone calls. Gillian Jones looked up at him and smiled, threw up her eyes, and drew circles in the air beside her ear.

He met June there.

'Anything from the phone lines?' he said.

'We got three anonymous messages that he was dealing drugs around town, in some clubs. A few possible sightings of the van we're checking up on but nothing promising. But we have positively identified Pat Brady as being in a shop in College Road a few hours before the kidnapping. He was acting suspiciously, according to the shopkeeper.'

'Nice one, June. Every little bit counts. That could be important, about him dealing. Any news on Jackie Buckley? I think we really need to talk to her.'

'Jesus, give me a chance, Collins. I have to fucking do everything around here.' She stormed off.

'Sorry!' he shouted after her. 'I was only asking. Thanks!'

Twenty minutes later, she approached him in the Incident Room and said she had an address for Jackie – a drug squat in Windsor Hill.

'You're a star,' Collins said. 'I really mean that.'

'Right,' she said. Apart from two burgeoning dark bags under her eyes, her skin had the complexion of a washed-out cloudy sky.

53

The raids were a damp squib, as Collins had expected. Both brothels were empty of prostitutes and punters, which may have been just as well, as the paperwork to charge all the women would have been a distraction as well as a nightmare, and none of them would know anything. Most of them spoke little English and, when confronted by authority, pretended they spoke none at all.

Various known drug dealers and thugs were arrested and they made the usual song and dance about harassment. At the closing of the pub, a few bottles were thrown and some drunks were dragged away to sober up in a cell. There was nobody at home in Molloy's house. A subsequent search revealed nothing.

Mary Brady was taken from Sean Brady's house and was brought in with her and Molloy's toddler son. There was a scene in Glanmire Garda Station when Tusla tried to take the child away to be cared for – Mary had raised the roof, which woke the sleeping infant and set him off.

Collins wanted the leverage, so he made the decision for the toddler to be taken and for her to be restrained. He decided not to talk to her for a few hours, in order to let her stew and in the hope that the news would get out to Molloy.

Corcoran's mother, who was seventy but as strong as a mule, had to be subdued immediately, having run out of the house and attacked two gardaí with a baseball bat. Collins had come across that woman before – and he'd never met her like.

There was little point in questioning her, but Collins wanted Corcoran to hear that his mother was in custody, the Bradys to hear about their sister, and Molloy to hear about his child. And Molloy would hear about it, from his informer if not from one of his own crowd – of that, Collins was certain.

The team that turned up to an empty brothel went on to Tommy Tan's home and there he was ready and waiting for them. When he was brought to the station, the solicitor, O'Callaghan, was already there, insisting his client was being harassed.

At eleven o'clock, after all the teams were back and had reported, Collins decided to go to Windsor Hill to talk to Jackie Buckley. He knew she would be high and probably uncooperative, but he had to give it a shot. He was running out of options and time and he didn't trust anyone else to talk to her. He also wanted to escape from the growing sense of desperation in the station. Jonno was doing the rounds, looking for updates and peppering him with questions every fifteen minutes.

Jackie's squat was near the top of Windsor Hill, where the slope eased and it was possible to park a car. The derelict house that she shared with some other junkies was obvious among the neat bungalows on either side.

Collins and June took stab vests and two large flashlights from the boot of the car and went around the back of the house – a massive sheet of plywood had been nailed over the front door. There was a strong odour of human shit at the side of the house and he checked the path carefully before each step.

He had been in many such places, but he could still feel the surge of adrenaline as they approached the back door. He hadn't brought a weapon and suddenly regretted it. Junkies are usually pitiful and pathetic creatures but, from time to time, one can rage with a drug-induced recklessness. He went ahead of June and pointed behind him to indicate where she should be. She poked him in the back with the flashlight.

The first room was a former kitchen with rubbish strewn across every surface and much of the floor. The smell was revolting.

There was a man passed out on the floor of the next room. A discarded syringe, some tubing and a spoon lay on the floor beside him.

Jackie was in the third room they entered, with another woman. Collins knew her: Patricia Corkery. Daughter of a GP from Macroom, she had grown up in a difficult household and ran away at sixteen into a life adorned by one catastrophe after another.

Jackie was sitting on a mattress, wrapped in a grimy sleeping bag, her back against the corner. Her knees pulled up tight against her, she appeared comatose until the lights made her wince and screw up her eyes. She looked up, squinting.

'Great,' she said, hoarsely, and closed her eyes again.

June bent down to her. 'Jackie, something's happened, we have to talk to you.'

Her eyes shot open.

'Is it Kyle? Is he hurt?'

'No, it's not Kyle. Kyle's fine, and your mam. But we have to talk. Get up now, Jackie, we have to go out to the car.'

'No.' She closed her eyes and flopped down on the bed, putting her head into the sleeping bag.

'Get up, Jackie, or Collins will pick you up and carry you out,' June said.

'Fuck off.'

'Jackie, we're going to talk one way or another and we don't have to go down to the station if you make it easy.'

A muffled groan. Then a definite 'No!'

Collins bent down and picked her up, sleeping bag and all. She stuck her head out of it and glared at him.

'Fuck you, Collins. Put me down.'

As he moved towards the door she squirmed and then gave up the struggle.

'Bag,' she said, pointing to the small rucksack that was behind her in the corner. June picked it up.

The best time to talk to a heroin addict is when they have almost come down from a high and can still feel the bliss in their bones, before the mental and then the physical craving for another hit overwhelms their wits. They were lucky with Jackie, they seemed to have timed it well.

June opened the car door and Collins placed Jackie inside on the back seat. He went around and sat beside her. June got into the front and removed the headrest from the passenger door. She held out a bottle of Coke. Jackie looked at her balefully and then grabbed it. She opened it, took a swig and screwed the cap back on.

'Get on with it,' she said.

Collins smiled. He liked Jackie.

'Jackie, two kids were abducted today near the Lough. An eighteen-year-old girl and a nineteen-year-old boy. The boy is Mickey McMahon's son, and we think it was Molloy who took them,' he said.

She took another swig of her Coke. She glanced at him as if to say 'What's it to me?' She was far from out of it. And he could tell she was interested.

'Thing is,' he said. 'The girl is the niece of the Minister for Justice so the shit has totally hit the fan. We shut down Molloy's brothels tonight, and a couple of his pubs, and we raided his house and the Bradys' houses and Corcoran's. We've arrested most of his dealers and over the next few weeks we'll be completely shutting down his operation. He's finished.'

He looked at Jackie for a response. He could sense her assessing the implications for herself and the habit she had to feed.

'There's the best part of a thousand gardaí out there looking for those kids and we won't stop 'til we find them. Roadblocks all over the city. We've another fifty organised crime detectives coming down from Dublin – this is big, and it's not going away.'

He paused to let it sink in. Still no response. She tapped a forefinger against her thigh.

'He fucked up, Jackie. He's finished. History. We know he did this and we'll prove it, one way or another. The Minister's niece. Ha! He never knew. "The Dom" himself, Mr "Fail to Prepare". He'll probably run off to Spain if we don't catch him in a day or two. Either way, it's a matter of time.'

This time she did speak. 'So?'

'So we need to know where those kids are, Jackie.'

'*I* don't fucking know!'

'Does Molloy have any safe house? Any place he brings women for parties and stuff like that?'

She shook her head. 'Nah. I dunno it, anyway.'

'Who would know?'

She shrugged.

'Anyone you can think of?' he said.

'That prick Sullivan, maybe.'

'Wayne O'Sullivan? The guy who drove for him? Who cracked up?'

'Yeah. Cracked up, my hole. He let that on to stay out of jail.'

'And do you know where *he* is?'

She smiled. It was a nasty smile.

'He's in his aunt's house in Mahon. With his mam. The aunt is gone off to England or something.'

'Where in Mahon?'

'*I* dunno.'

'What's the aunt's name?'

'I don't fucking know; you're the guard, aren't ya?'

'Does his mam still work in the shopping centre?'

'I don't know. Jesus, Collins, what am I, the Golden fucking Pages?'

'And you're sure you can't think of a place the kids could be?'

'No! How the fuck would I know that?' She took another swig from the bottle and squirmed.

She was getting restless, coming down. Collins knew he wouldn't get much more out of her.

'Anyone else, besides Sully?' he said.

She thought about it.

'Mary Brady, maybe. Or that barmaid at the Avondhu. Molloy's fucking her too.'

'The English one? Shannon something?'

'Yeah, she goes off with him sometimes. The husband is too afraid to do anything about it. Coward.'

Collins looked at June, her arms on the passenger seat. She shook her head, no questions.

Sensing it was over, Jackie said, 'That's worth fifty anyway, like. At least.'

'I'm not giving you money for drugs, Jackie,' Collins said.

Her expression turned combative. 'I gave ye Sullivan.'

'Yeah, well.'

'Prick. Got a fag?'

'I quit.'

'I didn't do it for the money, anyway. I know what you done for Kyle.'

'What?'

'That boxing thing.' She fidgeted. Her feet tapped on the car floor. 'I know you got that trainer to look after him, like. Got him into those competitions.'

Collins didn't react. 'Where'd you hear that?'

'Some guys like to talk, know what I mean?'

Silence. June was looking at Collins and Jackie, back and forth like it was a tennis match.

'Why'd you do that, Collins?' Jackie said. She was picking at the plastic wrap on the bottle.

'I dunno. Kid deserves a break.'

'Yeah, well. Don't we all.' She started to shuffle out of the sleeping bag. She was fully clothed underneath it. In fact, it looked like she had two jumpers and two pairs of jeans on.

'Jackie,' Collins said. He took a fifty out of his wallet.

She smiled. A lovely smile this time. It made her look girlish. She could almost have been the Jackie Buckley she once was: a friendly shop assistant in Centra, with a boyfriend and a possible future.

'Ya big softy,' she said, grabbing the money, the sleeping bag and the rucksack. She got out of the car and lugged the sleeping bag over her shoulder.

June smirked at Collins.

'What?' he said. 'She gave us Sully, didn't she?'

He hopped out of the car. Jackie hesitated at the footpath and then began to walk away.

Collins followed her. 'Jackie,' he whispered.

She stopped. He caught up.

'I haven't given up on finding Dinny, either. I'm convinced if we can get Molloy, somebody will squeal. I think we have the prick this time. Imagine it, Jackie.'

She looked sideways at him, then glanced back at the car.

'You know Molloy owns some guards, don't you?'

Collins nodded.

'Do you know how many, or who?' he said.

She shook her head.

She turned around and began to trudge up the hill. Sleeping bag over one shoulder, rucksack over the other.

Collins wondered where she was going.

54

In the kitchen, Molloy and the Brady brothers sat around the table looking at their phones. The three Uzis were back on the table, along with a bag of coke, two mugs of tea, a half-finished packet of biscuits, a fresh bottle of whiskey and an empty glass.

Text messages and phone calls had been coming in thick and fast. Eventually, Molloy stopped everyone taking the calls, in case somebody's phone had been hacked. He'd already changed his SIM cards twice.

He watched the video of the news conference from the garda station again. At one point during Sharon McMahon's statement, the camera panned and lingered on Collins's scowling face. Molloy paused the video and looked at the image. He took a screenshot of it.

'That fucker,' he said, pointing to the phone. 'He's behind all this. One of my sources just confirmed it.' He didn't tell them what else had been passed on: there was a witness saying that Claire had seen Pat's face. He didn't want Pat to know that.

The Bradys looked up at him.

'Question is: What are we going to do?' Sean Brady said, taking a sip of tea.

'We have to let them go and we have to do it right now,' Molloy said. 'It's our only chance before we're totally fucked. Tomorrow morning might be too late. There are roadblocks all over the place and this is all over the news. Half the detectives in Dublin are on their way down.'

Pat Brady shook his head.

'She saw me,' he said. 'That was bullshit before, she'll say anything to get away. They'll make her talk, you fucking know they will.'

Molloy didn't react. He had to get Sean alone to convince him to change Pat's mind. And he'd have to get out of the country himself within a couple of days. Otherwise he'd have to call in the Poles to take out the Brady brothers now and cut his losses. It would be tricky with Mary, but he couldn't see any other way.

'Even if she does,' Molloy said, 'and I don't think she will once we scare the fuck out of her, we'll have an alibi for you and everybody else. And we'll have the best barrister in the business to contest it and make a liar out of her.'

'No,' Pat said. He went to the table and picked up the Uzi again. 'No fucking way am I going back in there.'

'Calm down, Pat,' Molloy said. 'Just calm down and put the gun away. Sean, calm him down, we'll sort it out.'

Sean stood up and took the gun from Pat's hand and put it on the table. He led him outside and Molloy could hear them talking.

Three hours later, Pat was dozing on a blanket on the ground. Molloy nodded to Sean to go outside with him. It was dark. The wind moaned through the ditch behind them and they turned their backs to the rain. Water dripped from a roof into a puddle by the door.

'You have to talk him down,' Molloy said.

'I don't know. I never saw him like this before. He's not going back inside.'

'I tell you what. What if I head to Spain in a couple of days and he comes with me? I have a boat lined up. We'll get him a new identity, plastic surgery, the works. If we let the kids go now, the whole thing will blow over, but if we don't, the shit will really hit the fan. We're out of business, Sean. Finished.'

Sean grimaced.

'I don't know. A minister's niece. Did you know who she was?'

'No, I didn't, but it doesn't matter. Once they turn up it'll all go away, but if we kill them, it'll be a complete shitstorm. We'll be finished forever in Cork. And ye'll have to do it, not me. Kill two innocent kids.'

He let that sink in.

'It's one or the other and ye'll have to do it now, this minute. The morning is too late, ye'll have to bury them somewhere, we can't transport them. Ye'll have to find a place and dig the holes and ye'll have to do it in the dark somewhere near here, but not too near, either, in case they find this place.'

Sean did not reply. He looked towards the fields beyond, and up at the dark rain.

'Think about it, Sean,' Molloy said. 'What's done is done, but it's about survival now. And if Mary was here she'd agree with me. I know she would. When they release her, I guarantee you she'll back me one hundred per cent. It's the smart play.'

'I'll talk to him,' Sean said.

'Good man, do that. I'm going over to the grave for an hour. When I get back, have yere minds made up. We'll find somewhere to leave them where they'll be found tomorrow on the side of the road and the whole thing will be over.'

55

Collins strolled past the main desk of the station and saluted the night-duty garda.

'Any news, Tom?' he said.

'Go get 'em, Collins.'

Mick filled him in, upstairs. No new developments. A huge amount of information had been received from the social media sites and the phone calls, but nothing useful apart from the fact that Dave had been dealing drugs. And that didn't help them with the location of the kids. Any credible suggestions as to where they might be hadn't panned out.

A friend of Dave's had come forward and said that he had loaned out his flat on College Road to him, so the young couple could have sex. He said it was the fourth or fifth time they had used it. Mick had sent around a couple of uniformed gardaí and they found two used condoms in a bin in the kitchen. A street camera on Western Road showed Dave walking towards Gaol Cross at 09:08. The shopkeeper on College Road was 'one hundred per cent sure' that the man who had been behaving suspiciously in his shop was Pat Brady, when shown a photo of him. The shop window looked out on the street just down from the flat where Dave and Claire had spent the morning.

There was nothing new on the van after the last camera had picked it up going west at Wilton. No witnesses at its theft the night before. It had been taken from a small garage with lax security. No dashcam footage showing the van.

Facebook, Instagram and Twitter had gone ballistic, as they

had expected, with most people posting in a way that implied the two kids were dead. The hashtags #SaveClaire, #SaveDave and #SaveClaireAndDave were trending. Rumours of a €500,000 reward to get Claire back were also out there, but nobody seemed to know the source.

Collins wondered if O'Donovan had anything to do with it, out of a guilty conscience about his niece, if nothing else. Probably just another false trail, but he decided to talk to that man sooner rather than later. 'Follow the money' wasn't a cliché for nothing.

June and Collins headed for Montenotte, a northside suburb, where Emily Creedon, Molloy's ex-girlfriend, lived. She had been going out with Molloy for a while, but when she learned the extent of his criminality she would have nothing more to do with him. She now ran a hostel for abused women and ex-prostitutes. For some reason nobody could figure out, Molloy never interfered with the place. Collins suspected she had some information on him that kept her safe.

When you are ringing somebody's doorbell during the night and they don't want to answer, you have to keep pressing it in a way that gives the impression you will never stop. Nobody can stand a doorbell ringing incessantly and eventually the person inside will convince themselves that there is a good reason to answer.

In Emily Creedon's case, it took only five minutes, though she was smart enough to talk to them from inside the door before she opened it. June did the talking and once she had slipped her badge through the letterbox, the door opened and a wary-looking woman in her late thirties, holding a poker in her right hand, eyed them up and down.

She shook her head when she saw him.

'I heard about those kids,' she said. 'Ye must be desperate to be looking for information off me.'

'Hello, Emily,' Collins said. 'Yeah, we are, really. Can we come in?'

She waved them into the living room. She wore a light striped dressing gown over her nightdress and comfortable slippers. She dropped the poker into its stand by the fire.

'Do ye want tea?' she said. 'Sit down, sit down.'

'No thanks, Emily, we're on the clock.' Collins sat on a two-seater sofa, June sat beside him. Emily sat in her own armchair beside the fire and crossed her arms.

'So,' Collins said. 'Dave McMahon was the target, but his girlfriend got caught up in it. Molloy didn't know that she was the Minister's niece. Looks like he fucked up big time.'

'How do you know it was him?' she said.

'Corcoran was one of the guys who grabbed them.'

Emily shook her head. 'God love her,' she said, sadly.

'She's only eighteen,' Collins said.

'A lot of his girls are eighteen – some of them are younger – but if they're from Moldova or Nigeria or Farranree, there isn't nearly as much fuss,' she said.

'That's true. But you know that's not down to me.'

'Fair enough. What do you want to know?'

'I know you have no idea where they could have gone, but I was wondering if there was somebody you could suggest who might know. An ex-prostitute or somebody who might be willing to talk.'

She looked at the fireplace, then at him and then she looked at June.

'You never heard this from me, right?' she said.

They didn't respond.

'Right?'

'Right,' they both answered, simultaneously.

'I heard he's fucking that barmaid in the Avondhu, the English one. Try her. He always liked to brag in bed, I think it made him think he'd perform better or something. Apart from the Bradys, she's your best bet.'

'What about Mary Brady?' Collins said.

Emily laughed. 'Good luck with that. She's tougher than both her brothers put together, runs that whole family. Not a hope, especially since the baby.'

Collins did not mention that he had ordered Mary separated from her child or why.

'Anything else?' he said.

'One thing. You said that Molloy fucked up.'

'Yeah? Well he did, she's the Minister's niece.'

'Are you sure about that? I heard he's coked up half the time these days, but there's not much goes on in this town he doesn't know about. Don't underestimate him, Collins. A lot of people have made that mistake and paid for it. Including me.'

Collins had wondered about this: if the abduction was a message to O'Donovan, to play ball or else. If it was a kidnapping with a ransom in the offing. But the witness was fairly adamant that Claire had happened upon the scene by accident.

Collins stood up. A wasted trip, really. He held out his hand.

She shook it and led them to the front door.

'Oh, one more thing,' she said. 'I heard your old pal Jason Townsend is in rehab in Cuan Dé. I heard he's clean these days. I facilitated some counselling for him, I think he's serious about it. He might be worth talking to, he probably knows a thing or two.' She hesitated. 'If he'd talk to *you*, that is.'

56

Molloy paced up and down beside the grave. Up and down. Four steps each way before he turned. There was an indentation in the grass from all the times he had done this. He half-mumbled, half-talked.

The light from his phone shone on the ground and his feet. It made the wet grass glisten and cast eerie moving shadows over nearby headstones.

The graveyard was exposed to the south-westerly wind and rain, but he didn't feel any cold.

'I can't stay,' he said. 'I can't stay, Mam. I have to go away, they're after me.'

He stopped and directed the light out into the distance. Headstones. Stillness.

'Sean and Pat are after crossing me. They crossed me. *He's* stirring things up, telling lies about me. It's all over the news.'

He took a pinch of white powder from a small bag and sniffed it. He wiped his nose with the back of his hand.

'I have to go, I have to. I have to get Luke away.'

He sobbed and kneeled beside the headstone.

'I'm sorry, Mam, I'm sorry,' he said. 'I'm sorry.'

He ran his fingers along the writing on the headstone, feeling every etched-out letter of his mother's name. Pressing his cheek against the edge of the granite, he clutched the headstone with both his hands and wept.

57

Collins drove down the hill, away from Emily's house. Near the entrance to the estate, he pulled the car into the side of the road.

'What?' June said.

'I think we should go up there.'

'To Cuan Dé? Now?'

'Yeah,' Collins said. 'He might know something.'

'If he does – and that's a big if – do you think he's going to tell you, of all people?'

'Yeah, but we have to try. We're running out of time. And options.'

She looked at her watch.

'Okay. So let's go. But I'm going in with you.'

'Sure, no problem,' Collins said.

Cuan Dé was located on the Middle Glanmire Road, only a mile away. It was a converted Dominican monastery on large grounds overlooking the river and the south-eastern suburbs of the city. Collins had done a silent mindfulness weekend retreat there the previous year.

'You sure about this?' June said at the old stained-glass door. A proximity light had come on when they were a few yards out.

'No,' he said. 'But what choice do we have?'

'Let's get it over with so,' she said, and pressed the doorbell.

A young volunteer – probably a former inmate – answered. She was tall and sleepy-looking and was wearing a heavy navy dressing gown over baggy pants and soft flat shoes. Her hair hung in long dreadlocks down her back. Her skin was pockmarked from teenage acne and there was a hole in her left nostril where a nose ring had been. She had large greenish eyes with the brightest sclerae Collins had ever seen.

'Yes?' she said. 'Is it an emergency admission?'

'No,' Collins said. 'But it is an emergency. We have to speak with one of your clients straight away. It's a matter of life and death.' He explained the situation.

The volunteer – her name was Sasha – bargained with them. She said that they could meet with Jason, but only if he agreed; there was to be no coercion, Cuan Dé was a place of medical treatment. Otherwise, they would have to come back in the morning. Collins agreed, not for a moment intending to keep his side of the deal. He toyed with the idea of following her up to Jason's bedroom.

He and June were shown into a large, cold, high-ceilinged room, with foldable chairs stacked around panelled walls. Old windows rattled in their frames. A flip chart rested against a wall. The words 'Respond not React' were written in large red letters on it. Collins set up three chairs in a circle in the middle of the room and they sat down and waited. He thought about all the healing that had happened in that room, including some of his own.

He was surprised when Sasha and Jason appeared five minutes later. They stood in the doorway and Sasha spoke.

'Jason has two stipulations. That June remains during the interview and that I am here too.'

'That's fine,' Collins said, rising. He unfolded another chair and widened the circle to accommodate it. 'I have very little time, Jason, so I'm going to have to rush you a bit. I'm sorry about that, but I'll explain straight away.'

Collins watched Jason closely, noticing a slight limp. He

looked different. He had grown a dark beard, which made his face appear less hollowed. His hair was cut tight, highlighting slightly protruding ears. He was wearing slippers, pyjamas and a similar heavy navy dressing gown to Sasha's. Collins noticed his fine angular hands, which showed a slight tremor when he sat down and placed them on his thighs. The smoking fingers of his right hand were stained by cigarettes.

'First off,' Collins said, 'I want to apologise for what happened in the van. That should never have happened and I'm sorry. I was upset about Kelly and …' He held up his hands in admission.

'She's the reason I'm here,' Jason said. He spoke in a soft voice, but it was clear. 'The reason I went to bed sober last night and hopefully again tomorrow night.'

Collins noticed that his teeth were still brown, but his eyes looked healthy, as did his skin.

Jason continued. 'I've been sober and clean now for six weeks. After … after my leg, I started going to NA meetings, a doctor in the hospital sponsored me. But I started my journey before then, really. When … when Kelly died.'

Collins wanted to rush him but held his impatience in check.

'I'm glad to hear it, Jason. Really.'

'I'm trying to fix things with Mam. But … I dunno, like. She blames me,' he said. 'She's right, too. Kelly dying was down to me.'

Sasha put a hand on his arm. 'We can't change what we can't change, Jason. Acceptance with serenity, remember?'

'I know, Sash,' he said, smiling at her.

'Anyway, you said it was a matter of life and death, so I'll tell you whatever I can.'

'Okay,' Collins said. 'Two teenage kids were abducted by

Molloy, the Bradys and Corcoran earlier today. They haven't turned up yet and we think their chances are slim if we don't get to them in the next few hours. The boy is Mickey McMahon's young fella and we think he was the main target, but the girl may have seen something she shouldn't have. Do you have any idea where he might have taken them?'

Sasha's eyes widened in shock, but Jason just wrinkled his brow.

'I'm not surprised,' he said. 'He's been off the rails the last few months. I, eh … I heard what happened to you, too; I'd nothing to do with that.'

'I know,' Collins said.

'I don't know where they might be, but I heard he's headed to Spain. I think he's going to take the Keaveneys' coke with him. He's going to bring the Poles with him too, I hear, but I don't know much else.'

'How do you know that?' Collins said.

'I overheard a couple of the Poles a while back, Mazur and one of the Morawiecki brothers. I have a bit of Polish – I used to be going out with a Polish girl in London.'

His expression changed. 'I'm sorry I don't know more, but I really doubt if they're still alive. He's …' He looked up, his eyes filled with sadness.

'I know,' Collins said. 'Thanks for your help. Is there anybody you think might know where he is?'

'Some of the Polish guys might know, but they're hard. Mazur is crazy, had it in for me, big time. I heard ye got him.'

'That's right,' Collins said. 'Anybody else who might know something?'

Jason shook his head, thinking.

'I dunno. I don't think so.'

Collins stood to leave. June stood too.

'We better be going,' Collins said.

'Not that it matters now,' Jason said, looking up at Collins. 'But I plugged out the camera that night in the van. Before you came.'

Collins stared at him.

'It was a set-up to catch you on video attacking me. He used me as bait. And then he expected me to … well it doesn't matter now. But I was going to tell you everything I told you, anyway. Before … I just wanted you to know.'

'Why?' Collins said.

Jason looked at him questioningly.

'Why did you unplug the camera?'

'I … I wanted out by then. Away from *him*,' Jason said, his eyes welling. 'I wanted to get clean and I thought you were our best shot at getting rid of him.'

'But why didn't you tell me?' Collins said. 'On the night? Before I …?'

'I wondered about that after,' Jason said, his voice breaking. 'I think I wanted you to hurt me. For what I done to Kelly.'

'Oh, Jason,' Sasha said and put her arm around him. He bowed his head to her.

June looked at Collins, her eyes wide.

'Thank you,' Collins said, putting a hand on Jason's shoulder. 'I'll tell Niamh what happened. How you're in rehab and what you did for me. I'll put in a good word for you. If you want.'

Jason raised his head and smiled. 'I'd like that,' he said, quietly, wiping his eyes.

Collins smiled back and headed out the door.

'What did you make of that?' June said, back in the car.

'I dunno,' Collins said. 'Means we're not much closer to getting the kids.'

'I know, but of all people in rehab: Townsend?'

'I guess stranger things have happened,' Collins said. 'I hope he makes it.'

'And that camera?' June said. 'Fuck me, you dodged one there, Collins.'

'I know. Better off being lucky than good, I guess.'

'That's if he's telling the truth, of course. He might just be bigging himself up or something.'

'Maybe,' Collins said. 'I dunno, though.' He looked to his right, pulling out onto the Middle Glanmire Road.

'What now?' June said.

'Back to the station for me. You should head home. Get some sleep. Tomorrow is going to be shit when that crowd takes over.'

'Do you think they're still alive?' June said.

'Not looking great,' Collins said. 'But we have to keep trying. What else can we do?'

58

Collins often said, to anybody who would listen, that the guilt or innocence of a professional criminal in a country like Ireland was close to being immaterial. The gardaí usually knew within days, if not hours, who did what crime, and why. But the only thing that mattered was being able to prove it in court. For sure, it was good to know who did what, because it helped in gathering the evidence required to make it matter. But without that evidence, the knowledge wasn't worth a whole lot.

Inside information was the Holy Grail – what every detective craved. Once you had a source, you had a good shot at a conviction, but you didn't want to compromise the source, either.

It was only in the case of amateurs that third-party witnesses offered worthwhile assistance. Some crimes – like theft, murder and assault – were committed by amateurs and first-timers. But that type of crime – one of passion, especially – was usually solved and convictions came quickly unless there was a mistake during the trial or with evidence.

Dealing with professional career criminals was different. Organised crime would always flourish in a modern democratic society. There was a hint in the word 'organised'.

Within that ecosystem, people were loyal or getting rich, or they owed debts. Criminals hated the gardaí and what they had 'done to them' and they knew the consequences of ratting. They were beyond any sense of remorse or morality. They were guilty of something themselves. They were afraid.

In Molloy's case, the gardaí had been deprived of two cast-iron convictions by witnesses recanting. Tommy Roche, a small-time pusher, was persuaded to give evidence against Molloy until his mother and father had a petrol bomb thrown through their front window. Kerri Burton, a prostitute who wanted out, and who had overheard something she shouldn't have, also retracted her statement. When Collins asked her why, she calmly said she needed her face to get by, and she was fond of her fingers too. They offered her witness protection, but she said it was a joke.

Back at the station, Collins phoned Rose. She answered quickly. Gardaí do, if they answer at all.

'Yeah?' she said, no sign of sleep in her voice.

'Rose, it's Collins.'

'Collins. What do you want? Is it about the abductions?'

'Yes. I need some information about a Shannon Fitzgerald, lives in that new Sunview House apartment block. She's English and I wonder if there's any dirt about her over there. Also, if there's anything on her here, but I don't think there is. I think she's from London.'

'Okay, get back to you. The Brits owe me some favours. You don't have her PPS number do you?'

'No.'

'Never mind, I'll get it myself.' She hung up.

He checked into the Incident Room while he was waiting for Rose to reply. June had gone home. Jonno was sitting near the door, in conversation with Kevin Tuohig. Tuohig was eating a breakfast roll, even though it was just turning 2 a.m. Probably the first of many, he must be pushing twenty stone, Collins reckoned.

'I was just telling Tuohig here that we have one hundred and twenty checkpoints in place now all over the county,' Jonno said. 'I think it's a record since the Border Fox. And there are checkpoints all over Kerry, Limerick, Tipperary and Waterford, too.'

'Good to hear, sir. It makes it impossible for him to transport them, if nothing else.'

'Anything at your end?' Jonno said.

'Not yet. I'm going to talk to Shannon Fitzgerald as soon as I get some background info. We might get something from her if I can convince her Molloy is finished – she might be glad to see the back of him. I've one other source at around seven and then we regroup and have a briefing at eight. The Dubs will be down by then, probably.'

'You can't question her now, Collins, it's two o'clock in the morning. Any judge would throw it out.'

'I'm not that interested in judges to be honest, Superintendent. If we don't find those kids soon … ' He held out his hands in a gesture of helplessness.

'Well, you never told me about it. And *you* didn't hear anything either, Tuohig.' Jonno said, and left.

Tuohig rolled his eyes.

'What do you think?' Collins said.

Tuohig swallowed a bit of his roll and took a sip of tea. 'Doesn't look good.' He examined the roll and picked out a piece of black pudding and put it into his mouth.

'He's a stubborn fucker, is Molloy,' he continued. 'He won't admit to himself that he messed up, and he's too arrogant to cut his losses and let them out on the side of the road somewhere.'

'Yeah, but he's finished either way,' Collins said. 'The media are going to go crazy for this. Upper class, blonde, eighteen and pretty would be enough for them. But the Minister's niece?'

'I wouldn't count my chickens, Collins. We need evidence.'

'Yeah, but surely Dempsey will push something through and we can take the handcuffs off ourselves. They did it for Veronica Guerin.'

'He's the Minister for Justice and Equality, Collins,' Tuohig said. 'The opposition will crucify him for this. Can't even protect his own family. He'll want to distance himself from the whole thing, I'd say. His niece going out with Mickey McMahon's son? Wouldn't hold my breath if I was you.'

'What's it going to take?' Collins said. 'Molloy's been riddling Cork with drugs for years. He kills anyone who crosses him. He tries to kill me. Then he *does* kill two innocent teenagers. Jesus fucking Christ.' He went to the board and looked at the pictures of Dave and Claire.

Tuohig put the roll on the desk.

'Depends how the media runs with it,' he said, wiping his mouth with a napkin. 'Helps that she's pretty and well-off, for sure. If we get the bodies it would be a big boost – all those crying teenagers at the funeral, the grieving parents. Speeches about crime and a drugs epidemic and a line in the sand. Can't trust those politicians, though. Bunch of chancers at the best of times, the lot of them.' He stood up and stretched. 'I hope Geary brings his A game tomorrow.'

Collins's phone rang. Rose, already. She had surpassed herself this time.

'Collins,' he said.

'Okay, get a pen,' she said.

He sat down, pulled a notepad towards him and picked up a pen.

'Fire away.'

Collins also wanted some information for the morning. It hadn't been difficult to trace Wayne O'Sullivan's aunt's address. As Jackie said, they *were* the guards. And it wasn't hard to confirm that his mother still worked at the Tesco in Mahon Point and was due to start work at seven on the following morning. The proximity to her work was probably why she moved there. And Sully, the leech, had moved in with her, though why she allowed him next or near her was beyond Collins, considering he had robbed her blind for years to pay for his habit.

So he knew the address where Sully would be, but he didn't know the lie of the land in that particular estate. And he wanted to surprise him in the morning. There was only one person who could help him with that.

Collins found the number and pressed the screen. After four rings there was an answer.

'Wha?'

'Hega?' Collins said.

'Yeah.'

'Hega, Collins here, can you talk?'

'Yeah, but I'm riding the girlfriend here so you better speak up, she gets noisy, like.'

'What?' Collins said. He could hear grunting.

'I said I'm giving her one. Hold on, I'll put you on speaker.'

'Hi, Collins, Jen here.'

'Oh, hi, Jen. Hega can you stop for a minute and put me off speakerphone?'

'No can do, Collins. She's in the zone, man and …' There was another grunt and then a moan.

Collins hoped they were nearly finished.

'This is kind of hot, Collins, I always fancied you, like,' Jen said, panting. 'Want to come over and join in?'

'Yeah, Collins, we have a huge bed, and she's mad for three-somes,' Hega said.

'No thanks. I'm a bit … busy here right now. But I need to talk to you, Hega, I need a favour.'

'No worries man, fire away.'

'But not you, Hega,' Jen tittered.

'Hega, I need you to check out a house for me in Mahon, I'll text you the address. I need to call there on the QT tomorrow morning around seven.'

'No bother,' Hega panted.

Things seemed to be heating up, Collins held the phone away from his ear.

'We're doing it from behind Collins,' Jen shouted. 'Oh fuck, it's good. Go on, Hega, give it to me!'

'That it, Collins?' Hega gasped. 'Only …'

'Eh, yeah. I'll send you the address now.'

'Don't hang up, Collins,' Jen cried, 'I want you to hear me coming. This is so hot. Fuck, fuck, that's it. Oh, God –'

Collins hung up. He looked at the phone. Sometimes he thought he wasn't living at all. He texted the address, and told Hega to ring back before seven in the morning.

59

Garda Theresa Byrne was sitting in Interview Room 4 with Shannon Fitzgerald when Collins entered. Theresa was experienced and he had briefed her fully on what he wanted. She got it, even if her tight lips indicated disapproval. He didn't react to that, he didn't have time to discuss ethical niceties when lives were at stake.

She spoke into the microphone that was attached to the video recorder: 'Detective Collins entering the interview room at 2.25 a.m.'

Collins sat down opposite Shannon. She looked sick, her skin had a shiny pallor and her eyes were wide open and staring as if she were in shock. She had the sunken cheeks of a seasoned smoker and a jumpy wariness that spoke of a tough life.

Her head darted around in quick movements, like a bird. The collar of her powder blue blouse was tucked in on one side, at the neck. Her short hair stood up on the top of her head.

'Hello, Shannon,' Collins said. 'My name is Detective Garda Collins and I want to ask you some questions.'

'I want a lawyer, I know my rights. I'm not talking to no one without a lawyer.'

She spoke with a strong south London accent, pronouncing the word 'without' as though it had a v in the middle. She looked Irish, one of the so-called 'black Irish' who are dark-haired and complexioned. She tried not to meet his eye, but Collins just waited until she did look at him.

'A lawyer?' she said.

'You can have legal representation anytime you want, Shannon, it's just your children … if you have a solicitor present when I talk to you, it's official and I'll have to act on it. I'll have no choice.'

She stiffened. 'What do mean my children? What's this got to do with them?' He had her full attention now.

'Theresa, will you please phone the free legal aid people and get someone to come over for Shannon?' Theresa stood up. Collins said, 'It'll take an hour or so before someone arrives at this time of night, but they're usually very good, I must say.' He looked at his watch.

'I'll be back in twenty minutes or so,' Theresa said, and then: 'Garda Byrne leaving the interview room, 2.28 a.m.'

'What do you mean my children? What you on about?' *Abaht.*

'We can talk about it when your solicitor gets here, Shannon. There's no rush.'

'We'll fucking talk about it now. They're *my* kids and you'll tell me what this is about.'

In other circumstances Collins would have felt sorry for her.

'It's okay, calm down,' he said, with feigned concern.

'Don't fucking tell me to calm down. I heard about you. You come in here and start talking about my children. They're not even in this fucking country. What the fuck?'

She stood up, and made for the door. He stood up and blocked her way. She moved to step around him. He moved and blocked her again.

'My kids,' she said, shaking her head. 'You can't do nothing to my kids. You can't.' *Nuffink.*

'Sit down, Shannon. I can talk to you about it if you want, but you have to sit down.'

He was taken aback. He'd expected her to call his bluff for

a while at least, but he had clearly hit the right nerve. She was strung very tight. He could smell cigarettes from her when she came close to him near the door. She could be on something else too, but the craving for a cigarette is as bad as many other drugs. He knew it well himself.

She stood stock still, her face downcast. She seemed to compose herself, glanced at him, returned to the table and sat down. She began to pick at her nails. She pointed at his chair, and then at the microphone. He got the message. He sat down and switched it off.

He looked at her. Silence was the most difficult thing for weak or inexperienced people to deal with in these situations, especially when there was something they wanted to know. Many people found talk to be comforting. It meant they didn't have to think. Collins was in a desperate rush, but he wanted Shannon to think he had all night and was just going through the motions. That he couldn't care less what she said or when she said it.

Molloy had groomed the Bradys to be as doggedly silent as he was when questioned, but he had not trained this woman.

'Please tell me,' she said. He was not taken in by her plaintive tone, but he pursed his lips in a false regret.

'Look, it's complicated, but they'll have to go into care for the moment,' he said.

'Care? What care? What happened? My dad is looking after them.'

'That's the problem isn't it? He has a record, he's not fit, Shannon.'

'What record? He's off the drink for nearly twenty years, he never did nothing except drink.'

'Why do you think he left Ennis in the first place?' Collins said.

'To emigrate. To get a job. To get out of that shithole. Why do you think?'

'He never told you? I suppose he wouldn't,' Collins said.

'Never told me what? What you on about?' She was getting desperate.

'His job in the school, why he got sacked, and had to leave?'

'What about it? Was he drunk or something?' *Somefink.*

'Oh no, it was a lot more serious than that. Wasn't proved, but still ...'

This was the delicate bit, it all hinged on this.

'Did he ever ...?' Collins said. He winced and moved his head as if to ask something delicate or embarrassing. 'Did he ever ... *touch* you or anything like that, when you were young, Shannon. Or your sister, Maura?'

She jumped up from her chair as if electrocuted.

'No, you fucking prick. He never. He never. That's a lie.'

Collins held his hands up facing her, in the 'I surrender' pose.

'Shannon. Shannon. Look, it doesn't matter, anyway,' he said. 'I'm going to have to report it to the police in Deptford. They'll have to know now, and Donal and Saoirse are going into care. That's it.'

She stared at him, shaking her head, vehemently.

'No fucking way. No way, man. Not going to happen. I'll go over there myself and look after them. Soon as I'm out of here later today. Or the minute I get my lawyer.'

He looked at her pityingly. He shook his head.

'Don't you know what happened, Shannon? Didn't they tell you?'

'Tell me what? About them kids? I'm just a barmaid, what do I know?

'They're just kids, Shannon. The girl is only a couple of years older than Donal.'

'But it doesn't have nothing to do with me.' *Nuffink.*

'Yeah, but it does, Shannon, it does. Molloy did it and we know that you and him are an item.'

'An item? Bullshit. I'm married. I'm married to Frank, don't know what you're on about.' She sat back, arms folded, her face rigid with fury.

'Well we have witnesses that say different, Shannon. They tell us you and Molloy are like that.' He held up two fingers, crossed. 'They tell us that Molloy told you everything and that makes you an accessory to kidnapping, murder maybe by now, if they're dead.'

'Fuck off!' She almost laughed when she said it, but he could detect a hint of panic in her voice.

'Very serious crime, Shannon. Ten years minimum, especially with the girl being the Minister's niece. They'll throw the book at you,' he said. 'They'll be gagging to put someone away. Who better than you, riding a gang lord behind your husband's back?'

She snorted. 'You're having a laugh. I know what you're up to. Trying to scare me, I'm not having it. No way.' *Larf.*

'Okay, well. You can discuss it with your legal representative when she gets here. See what she thinks. That's up to you,' Collins said. 'We'll be charging you sometime tomorrow and making a statement to the press. It'll probably come out about your criminal record in London and your father's removal from the school in Clare.'

Collins paused for effect. He looked at her. In fairness to her, she met his stare. He reminded himself there were lives at stake.

'But it doesn't have to, Shannon. The microphone is off now. If there's something you want to tell me it doesn't go on the record and nobody knows, and you can go home and we needn't call the Met.'

She glared at him, arms still folded across her chest. Her left knee was jumping up and down. She coughed. A smoker's cough. Collins said nothing. All the time in the world.

'The solicitor will be here soon,' he said, looking at his watch. 'Then it's all on the record.' He smiled broadly. If looks could kill, he'd be a dead man. Not for the first time. He took out his mobile phone and called a fake number.

'Anything new?' he said, and paused as if hearing a reply. 'Okay, right, keep me posted. Don't do anything without checking with me first.'

He 'hung up'. He looked at the phone, and pretended to check his messages. He looked back up at Shannon as if he'd forgotten she was there. He checked the time on his watch.

'Oh yes. Before the legal aid comes I want you to know this,' Collins said. 'Molloy is finished. He's history. The Minister's niece is a step too far, even for him. Her funeral is going to be huge. If he's not out of the country in a couple of days, he'll be hunted down like a dog. We have two hundred checkpoints set up already. There's no escape. And it's a small country, Shannon. The media are going to go wild for him and we'll have new powers of arrest and seizure by the end of the week. It's going to be a cold, cold Christmas for him, that's for sure. But the good thing is … anybody who wants to get out from his clutches can do it now. He's finished.'

'I don't know nothing about this. I wouldn't hurt kids, I swear.'

He tapped an index finger on the table, as if impatient. He looked at his watch again.

'Well, what *do* you know?' he said, giving her an easy option to begin with. She took it.

Mostly, of course, she wanted to paint herself as the victim – he made me do this, he made me do that, he threatened this, he threatened that, Frank got beat up. Which was fine by Collins as long as she began to talk. Once some people begin to talk they often can't stop, so all you had to do was to get them going.

When Theresa arrived back he waved her away and told her there was no need for a legal representative. She hadn't phoned one anyway, so it didn't matter.

And in the end, after ten minutes of rambling self-pity, Shannon had told him almost nothing of use in finding the kids. *Almost* nothing.

He learned three things of value.

One: Molloy's mind was unravelling – he was snorting coke twelve hours a day and drinking the best part of a bottle of whiskey; he was irrational most of the time and paranoid.

Two: he was planning on getting out of the country at the same time as the shipment of drugs arrived. He spoke about a boat, so she assumed that was how he was leaving.

And three: he visited his mother's grave in Killumney every day. *Every day*.

'I think …' Shannon said. *Fink*. 'I think it's because he's off, isn't he? He's off to Spain or wherever? That's why he's going to the grave every day. Because he won't be able to go when he's gone, isn't it?' *Innet*.

Collins couldn't care less why Molloy chose to visit his beloved mother's grave and in other circumstances he'd be happy to hear that he was on his way out of the country. But he knew that the moment he ran, the kids were dead. He also knew where that graveyard was, and he could think of worse plans than to stake it out the following day.

60

Collins went down to the Incident Room. A few gardaí were looking at computer screens and phones.

He phoned June and she answered immediately.

'Sorry if I woke you.'

'No, just heading up to bed now. Anything new?'

'I just interviewed Shannon Fitzgerald. Not much use really,' he said.

She was silent for a while.

'June?' he said.

She didn't reply.

'What time will you back in? In the morning?' he said.

'Around six, I'm going to sleep now.'

'Okay, see you then.'

Collins hung up and told Tuohig that he was going to get some sleep at his desk and to wake him at six. Tuohig didn't appear to need sleep.

'Come get me if there's any development,' Collins said, hoping against hope that a phone call would come in from a motorist who had just picked up two cold and shocked teenagers on the side of the road.

He took an old sleeping bag and a pillow out of the locker room in the basement and lay down under his desk. He thought about the fact that he didn't tell June about the graveyard or going to Wayne O'Sullivan's house first thing in the morning.

He fell asleep.

61

Collins awoke to Tuohig kicking the sole of his foot, telling him to get up. He extricated himself from under his desk and looked at his watch: 6.10.

There was coffee and buttered toast on the desk. Apparently, Tuohig could make food appear anywhere and anytime.

Collins sat down and took a sip of coffee. It tasted good, hot and reviving. He didn't like other people buttering his toast but made an exception. It was going to be cold and dark out there.

'Well?' he said. He'd had an idea in his sleep. It was just out of reach now, but he didn't force it, that would just frighten it off. It would come back to him.

'Nothing. Not a dickey bird. They're dead, Collins,' Tuohig said.

'Well then, we have to catch the fucker who killed them,' Collins said.

'The crowd from Dublin have started arriving.'

'Who?'

'Some of the Drugs and Organised Crime gang, trying to steal desks and complaining about the Wi-Fi.'

'Won't be long so 'til Sweeney and his entourage arrive,' Collins said.

He took a bite of the toast.

'Is June in?'

'Yep, with a big puss on her.'

'What's wrong with her?'

'How do I know? She's your partner.' Tuohig looked at his phone.

'Hmm. Okay, let's do this,' Collins said.

'What?'

'Better if you don't know.'

Collins picked up a slice of toast and the coffee and headed for the door.

'I'll be back in an hour or so, unless I get lucky,' he said, over his shoulder. He knew Tuohig was eating the other slice of toast; even without turning around, he just knew it.

Hega phoned him at 6.45. Collins and June were sitting in an unmarked car parked at the end of Daly's Road, around the corner from Sully's house. It was a typical Irish winter's morning. Dark and grey and dry. A breeze from the south-west pulling black clouds in from the sea, bringing rain.

'You in the blue Hyundai?' Hega said.

'Yes, where are you?' Collins said.

'I'm in the white van down the road.'

'Okay, you can walk over.'

Hega got into the back of the car, behind June, who was driving.

'You can talk, it's only June,' Collins said.

June did not respond. She glanced in the rear-view mirror then turned her head away. She had hardly spoken three words on the drive to Mahon.

'Okay,' Hega said, all business. 'Number 4 is the second-last house on the right. His mother left for work at about quarter-past-six. There's a key out the back under the blue flower pot, and the gate around the side is open. The front gate doesn't squeak, but you have to lift the wooden gate at the side a bit, it's fairly rotten. The back door opens out, but there's a bin just inside so watch that. He's in the first room on the left at the top of the stairs, beside the bathroom. The stairs are quiet. None of the doors squeak.'

June moaned and put her head in her hands. Collins ignored her.

'Anything else?' he said.

'No,' Hega said.

He looked tired. Collins wasn't surprised.

'Okay, thanks,' he said.

Hega got out and headed towards his van.

'You okay?' Collins asked June.

'Yeah, fine. Tired.'

'You sure?'

'Yes I'm fucking sure. What are you going to do in there, Collins? I don't want to be hearing about another broken ankle.'

'Okay, June. Okay. But there are two lives at stake and it's our last chance before the Dublin gang take over and make a bollox of everything. I'll be back in twenty. If a squad car arrives, don't let them in, okay? Ring me first.'

She didn't answer.

'Okay?' he said, louder.

'Okay. Alright,' she said, still looking away. Collins could hear tears in her voice, but now wasn't the time to pursue it.

He took a pair of thin grey latex gloves out of his coat pocket and put them on. He got out of the car, pulled a woollen hat out of his other pocket and pushed it down low over his head. Crossing the road as casually as he could, he opened the small front gate, went through and closed it again, as if he had done this often. He opened the side gate, lifting it and closing it after him. The only pot he could see in the gloom at the back door yielded up the key. The door opened out silently. He took out the key, put it in the keyhole from the inside, closed the door quietly and locked it again. Avoiding the bin, he stepped into the kitchen. The room was warm and a light from under some presses illuminated it. He felt the kettle with the back of his hand – lukewarm. He felt the top of the toaster – cold. A loaf of sliced pan, some butter and marmalade were on the countertop. Otherwise, the kitchen was neat and content. A clock ticked.

He stopped and listened to the house. Nothing. The fridge purred. He looked around the kitchen and picked up a chair and moved it away from the table and faced it towards the door. He passed through the hall and into the living room. Through the blinds he could just make out the Hyundai and see that June had her phone to her ear.

The stairs were quiet, as Hega had promised. On the landing he could hear the faint sound of snoring from behind a door. The room on his left was the bathroom, the room at the front was the box-room and the other room was Sully's mother's. He checked all three: empty.

He turned the handle and pushed. It was dark inside, and it smelled of beer and chips and farts. Collins turned on the light and went straight to the bed.

'Wakey, wakey, Sully,' he said, pulling the cover back. He grabbed an arm and dragged him onto the ground with a thump.

'What?' Sully said. 'Ow!'

'Up and at 'em,' Collins said, helping him up. 'Downstairs, now.' Sully's belly hung out from under a T-shirt and over his boxers; he'd put on weight since he got clean – that often happens, due to the medication if nothing else.

'Jesus, you're after getting fat, Sully,' Collins said. 'You'd want to get some exercise, boy.'

'You can't do this. Fuck you,' Sully said.

'The fuck I can't,' Collins said, putting something into Sully's hand. A plastic Ziploc bag containing white powder. Sully held it up to see and then dropped it with a gasp.

'No, no!' he said, in horror.

'Your prints are on it, Sully,' Collins said. 'You're fucked.' He picked it up and put it in his pocket.

'No, no, this is a set-up. No fucking way, Collins.'

'Yes fucking way,' Collins said pushing Sully out of the room. Sully pushed back against him at the top of the stairs and they wrestled for a moment. Collins banged Sully's head against the wall.

'Oops, be careful there. Don't want you getting hurt,' Collins said and pushed him down the stairs.

In the kitchen, sitting on a hard chair, Sully gathered himself.

'This is bullshit, Collins. This is a complete set-up. No way am I having this.'

'We had a call,' Collins said. 'Somebody reported a huge argument at this address, the threat of violence, and I came to investigate. I found the coke, with your prints on it. If I look, I'll find more. Heroin too. Enough for possession for sale or supply. With your record, you'll get seven, maybe nine. End of.'

'No way. This is breaking and entering. I'm clean. You can test me. Bring me in and test me, I'm clean, Collins. I got out. I got out, man.'

'Tell it to the judge, Sully,' Collins said. 'I'll have a court order in an hour to search the place and we'll find a lot more, I can guarantee you that. I'm also putting the word out that you co-operated. Gave us a rake of names.' Collins paced back and forward in front of him.

'No! No, you can't!'

'It's your poor mam I feel sorry for. Very sad.' Collins tut tutted. He picked up an old wedding photo from the dresser, Sully's mother and father, young and full of joy.

Sully groaned and put his head in his hands.

'Did you like prison, Sully?' Collins said. 'Good sex life in there? I'd say you were fierce popular in the showers.' Collins moved a net curtain aside and looked out into the back garden.

'Jesus, Collins, please. Please.' Sully began to cry, snot dripping from his nose, his head bowed, bobbing up and down. It hadn't taken long, Collins thought, if he wasn't faking.

'Or you might end up back in the loony bin,' he said. 'Did you like it in there with all the other nutters, or were you bluffing?'

Sully squeezed his eyes shut, as if in pain. Collins bent down in front of him, lifting his face.

'Look at me. Look at me, Sully,' he said.

Sully looked up at him, still blubbing.

'One piece of information and I'm out of here.'

Sully groaned.

'Where did he bring the kids? I know you know, Sully. Don't tell me you don't know what went down yesterday.'

'I dunno, I dunno.' There was a pleading in Sully's voice, in his eyes. He wasn't faking. But he knew something. Collins grew excited with the realisation.

'You drove him for nearly a year. You know where he went. He's fucked, Sully, he's going down. He's probably on his way to Spain already, and he's not coming back.'

'No, no, no,' Sully begged. *Don't make me tell you*, were the unspoken words.

'Tell me now and I'm out of here,' Collins said. He pulled up another chair and sat down, his head only inches from Sully's. 'You'll never see me again. Nobody will ever know. You can go back to your life, Sully. Your mam will never know. I'm giving you a second chance.'

Sully wept, his eyes closed, his head shaking from side to side.

'You have five seconds, Sully, or you're back inside, getting reamed by every horny fucker in the prison.'

'Aaah!' Sully said, as if he'd been struck. He lifted his head and opened his red raw eyes and he looked at Collins. He swallowed. He sniffled loudly. Collins held his breath – now or never.

'There's a housing estate near Killumney,' Sully said, in a flat tone. 'Those ones, what do you call them, that were never finished.'

'A ghost estate,' Collins said. He didn't trust his own voice.

'Yeah. After the graveyard, down the road to the left.'

'You sure?' Collins said.

'Course I'm not sure! How the fuck should *I* know? But when I heard on the news last night, that's where I thought of. He used to bring girls there. Young ones.'

'And you didn't think to tell us?' Collins fisted his hands. Sully recoiled.

'Jesus, Collins. I don't want nothing to do with this. I'm out, man. They mightn't even be there.'

'They fucking better be, for your sake,' Collins said. He jabbed Sully in the chest. 'And if you think of anything else, you ring me. Do you hear?'

Sully glared at him, stood up and went to the counter. He switched on the kettle. 'Get out of my house,' he said. 'You got what you came for.'

Collins looked at him, deciding. He turned and went out the front door.

62

When he got back to the car, Collins asked June to move to the passenger seat – he wanted to drive.

'Well?' she said, walking around the car. 'You weren't long. Jonno phoned, looking for you. We're to go straight back to the station.'

Collins didn't reply. He was thinking.

When he reached the Skehard Road, traffic was heavier. He switched on the siren and flashing lights and put the foot down.

'Belt on,' he said.

'What did he say?' June said. 'Where are we going?'

'Belt on, I said.'

He overtook a line of cars by the Central Statistics Office and broke the lights.

'Who did you phone when I went into the house?'

'What?' June stared at him.

'Fuck!' Collins said, narrowly missing an elderly man who was crossing the road. 'Idiot.'

'What do you mean who did I phone? Are you *questioning* me?'

'It's a simple question.' Collins wove through traffic approaching the Mahon Point Shopping Centre.

'I phoned Mícheál. To remind him about Maeve's medication, she has to take it with her breakfast. WHAT THE FUCK, Collins?'

'Show me your phone.'

'What?'

'I said show me your phone. Show me the number.'

'Fuck you, Collins. Is this it? *Is this fucking it?*' She slammed her hand against the dashboard and then kicked it with her heel. 'Is it? Is it, Collins? Are you fucking serious? Eight years, and now this? You *fucking* prick.'

'I need to see it, June. Just show it to me. Please.' He accelerated down the ramp onto the three lanes of the South Link. He held out his hand.

'Why?' she said. 'Just tell me why.'

'Because I need to see it.'

'Why? Why do you need to see it? Who do you think I was calling? WHO, COLLINS?'

'Show me the fucking phone, June.'

'No.'

'If you don't show me, I'm going in alone,' he said.

She looked at him for a long time.

'You fucking prick, I'll never forgive you for this.'

She activated the phone and found the list of recent calls. She handed it to him. He looked at it. *Micheal Mob* was the only call since Collins had phoned her the previous night. It was timed at 6.55 a.m. Other calls she made were to him and some 021 numbers and to other colleagues. He handed her back the phone.

'Sorry,' he said. 'I just had to see it. I don't know what we're going into. Do you have your weapon?'

'Fuck you. Pull in and let me out here.'

'No. I need you for this,' he said. He grabbed her forearm. She tried to pull it away and couldn't. She hit him on the face with her left fist. The car wobbled. Collins flexed his jaw and ran his tongue along the inside of his gum, checking for a cut.

'Jesus, June, I'm doing one-sixty here, you'll get us killed. This Hyundai handles like shit.'

'Pull in, I said.'

'He told me that they were in a ghost estate near Killumney. I know it – it's a good bit off the main road. There's thirty or forty unfinished houses there, it's perfect. And his mother is buried down the road. I should have known it would be out there.'

June looked out the passenger window.

'You've lost it, Collins. Finally, you've gone off the fucking rails.'

'I want those kids, June.'

'You want Molloy, Collins. You don't give a shit about those kids.' She spat the words at him. 'You want to beat Molloy, kill him, for all I know. This is all one "who has the biggest dick" contest, isn't it? The two of ye are as bad as each other.'

'No. That's bullshit. They might still be alive, June.' He swerved to the left and passed a car on the inside. 'This is our last hope. Jesus Christ! Are they deaf or what?'

June pressed the screen of her phone.

'I'm calling it in. We need the ERU.'

'No. No, June, we have to go in alone.' He held out his hand to grab her phone. She pulled it away.

'Bullshit. Just the two of us?'

'That's the way it has to be,' he said. His own phone rang and he looked at it. A number from the station, probably Jonno calling him back in for the briefing and the handover. He put it back in his pocket.

'Why?'

'Because if we call it in, somebody in the station will alert Molloy. There's a traitor in the station. Maybe two.'

There was a pause. He didn't like the sound of it. He wished he could take a good look at her.

'Bullshit,' she said.

'There is. Townsend told me. Jackie too.'

'Ah,' she said. 'So that's why you wanted to see my phone. You thought it was me.' She licked her lips.

'Jesus, he thought it was me,' she said, softly.

'I never thought it was you. But I had to check. We're going in, June!'

'You fucking bastard.'

'I said I'm sorry.'

'We need backup, Collins. I have two kids. And a husband. Ever think about that?' Her voice was breaking.

Collins didn't answer. He was thinking.

'Collins! Ever fucking think about that?'

'Yes, yes I did. That's why you'll stay back, and then call it in when I've made contact. When I've pinned them down.'

She slammed the dashboard again.

'Fuck! You want to kill him, don't you?'

'What? No!'

'You do. You want to go in there and kill him and you can say it was self-defence. It's what you've always wanted. Admit it.'

'June, he has the kids. I want to save them.' He pulled off the dual carriageway onto a narrow country road. '*If* they're still alive.'

There was a long tail-back of cars. He passed them, siren blaring.

'It's a checkpoint,' Collins said. 'Probably the Ballincollig crowd. Say nothing, we're just following up on something. No backup needed.' He pressed the button to open the window. Decelerating, he avoided cars coming against him and switched off the siren.

63

A few kilometres after the checkpoint, Collins slowed the car. They were getting close. Bungalows appeared on the right-hand side of the road as they approached the village.

'His parents are buried in there,' Collins said as they passed a graveyard. 'We should have thought of that, he was very close to his mother.'

June opened the glove compartment and took out a Sig Sauer P229 pistol and looked at it. She pulled the slide and checked that there was no round in the chamber. She took a magazine from the glove compartment and examined it, testing the spring. She loaded the magazine and checked that there was now a round in the chamber. She holstered the gun.

'You're staying in the car,' Collins said.

'No fucking way.'

'You said so, yourself,' he said, craning his neck to look into the entrance to a farm. 'You have two children and a husband. I'm going in. Once I confirm they're in there, I'll text you and you call the cavalry. I won't make contact first. I can't guarantee the kids' safety that way.'

She looked at him sceptically. She didn't speak.

'But if they're still there, it probably means the kids are alive,' Collins said. 'A big if. Sully might have been lying, too, or he mightn't have a clue. The whole thing is just a hunch.'

She bit her lip.

Gerry and Elaine Halvey sat across from each other at the large kitchen table, unspeaking, looking at their phones. He sipped a coffee, she drank tea. He looked up at her and he was moved. He had loved her so much, once. Her face was the colour of blank newspaper. The radio played *Morning Ireland*, an RTÉ news programme. Every so often, they both lifted their heads from their screens to listen. Every so often, they looked at where Elaine had set a table place with a plate, bowl, small juice glass, spoon, knife and Claire's favourite mug.

'More tea?' he said.

'No thanks.'

His phone buzzed with a text and she sat up. He looked at it.

'Anything?' she said, swallowing.

'No. Sean saying there's no news.'

He pressed a number and held the phone to his ear.

'Sean, it's Gerry. What have you heard?'

'Oh, nothing,' Dempsey said. 'The Dublin crew are down now and they're sorting things out. Sean Geary has let things slide badly there, he'll pay for that, I guarantee you. Denis Sweeney will put the investigation on a proper footing. I don't know why Sean put that Collins in charge – I heard he had a breakdown after that serial killer incident last year.'

'We're running out of time,' Halvey said.

'We don't know that, Gerry. Hold your nerve, man.'

'If we don't find her soon ...'

'Listen, I have to go. I'm going into the station now. Apparently this Collins character has gone missing; they can't find him. Typical.'

'Missing?'

'Off on some wild goose chase, apparently. It's a disgrace, the state of the force – there's going to be big changes, I can guarantee you that, letting that animal Molloy have the run of the place.'

'He told us he'd find her,' Halvey said.

'These fellows would say anything to further their careers, Gerry, but I'm expecting major progress today. Major progress. I have to go now.' He ended the call.

'Anything?' Elaine said.

Halvey looked her and shook his head.

'He said the Deputy Commissioner is at the station. He's taken charge. He said he expects major progress today.'

'Major progress,' she said, spitting out the words. 'Oh God.'

'I'm going in there to meet him,' Halvey said. 'You should come too, if you're up to it. Better if we're doing something, not sitting around.'

'Yes. Yes, I'll just get dressed. Major progress,' she said again, as she opened the door.

'There it is,' Collins said as they passed the entrance to the ghost estate. It led to a large pillared opening, about twenty metres in, high walls on either side. There was a series of metal gates attached to the brick columns, barring entry. Beyond that, an array of semi-detached houses in various states of completion. It was perfect, Collins realised. He could feel a tightening in his chest.

He drove past at a steady pace. After about two hundred metres on the left, he pulled into a farmyard. He parked out of sight of the road, beside the house, lowered his window and looked around. No visible sign of life and no car, but the sound of a milking machine hinted at where the farmer was. Collins noticed a ball in the lawn and two children's scooters against a wall. A small hurley on the grass with a tennis ball and football nearby.

'The wife is probably bringing the kids to school,' Collins said. 'If she comes back, keep her calm – let her give you tea if they have reception inside. Or him, when he comes back from milking. Don't say anything about the estate. Do you have reception here?'

She checked her phone, not looking at him. 'Yes.'

Collins checked his phone. Three missed calls, two voicemails. He put the phone on silent. He took the gun out of his holster and checked it. He got out of the car and faced her.

'June?' he said.

She looked at him, her lips a white angry line.

'I'm sorry, okay? I'm … I'm just paranoid. It all just got to me.'

He hesitated.

'How do I know you're not going to call the station?' he said.

'You don't,' she said. 'And maybe I will. But if I wanted to, I'd have done it already. If I don't hear from you in twenty minutes, I'm going after you.'

'Jesus, June. We'll end up shooting each other if you creep up on me. I'll text you every ten minutes, okay? If I don't, then call it in – DO NOT come in on your own.'

She did not respond.

'June?'

She did not respond.

'June, I've enough on my conscience,' he said.

'Good,' she said, looking at him. 'I hope it fucking plagues you.'

He closed the door and climbed over the gate between two farm buildings. He trudged away through the mud, the first glimmers of dawn emerging above the fields to his right.

June watched him, found a number on her phone and pressed the screen.

'Hi,' she said. 'Everything okay? … No, no, I'm not checking up on you, I just wondered if you needed anything. Good. Did Maeve take her medicine? … Grand … No, I just wanted to hear your voice. I love you … No, no, everything's fine. Can you put them on? … Hi love, how are you feeling? … You did? Great, good for you. Don't forget to have that satsuma during your break … I know that, love. I love you too. Put Jack on, please, pet … Hi love? … Oh you do? How much do you need? … Dad will give it to you. Okay. I'll see you later. I love you. Bye. Bye, love.'

She put the phone on her lap and gasped.

She put her hand into her coat pocket and took out the other phone. An old Nokia. She took a huge breath in through her nose and tried to hold it. She tried to clear her head. She began to weep, then she typed in the passcode, her hand shaking.

Sharon McMahon lit another cigarette and flicked it towards the ashtray on the Superser. She couldn't get warm, even wearing her pyjamas, a pair of Dave's football socks, slippers and the good winter dressing gown.

'More coffee?' Marie said, though Sharon was already wired.

Sharon did not reply.

'Or maybe some toast. Would you like some toast?'

'He hardly ever cried as a baby,' Sharon said.

'He was only gorgeous. Remember that little Sesame Street dungarees he had? I've a picture somewhere.'

Sharon took a puff from the cigarette. She checked her phone for the umpteenth time. She had it plugged in constantly, in case the battery went down.

Marie was looking at her phone, too. Scrolling down the Facebook page that had been set up yesterday by one of Dave's friends. It had 4,256 followers already. She checked Twitter. *#SaveClaireAndDave*, *#SaveClaire* and *#SaveDave* were all trending in Cork.

'Should I phone the station again?' Sharon said. 'Something might have happened last night.'

'You phoned them a while ago, Sharon, remember?'

'Oh, yes, that Liaison woman, what's her name?'

'Nora.'

'Nora. Useless bitch, like the rest of them. Should I go in?'

'If you like. I'll drive you. They can't hang up on you then. You need to talk to Collins, I'd say.'

'Okay, I'll get dressed so.' Sharon stood up. When she reached the door she stopped. She leaned against it and heaved in great gulps of air.

Marie held her and tsked. She said, 'Shhh. Shhh. They'll find him. They will, I know they will. I just know it.'

Collins moved along the edge of a field, near the ditch, for cover. He was close to the estate now. Some of the unfinished houses were just yards away, on the other side of the barbed wire fence and the briars and bushes. He seemed to remember that the most complete houses would be near the entrance, but he couldn't imagine them using one of those – too close to the road. He listened. Nothing. A tractor in the distance. Some rooks and robins. It began to rain – that soft rain that can go on all day.

He found a hole in a ditch and climbed through. His jacket snagged on thorns and he had to drag it free. He had pulled up his socks outside his pants to make walking through the mud easier.

He was at the back of a terrace of houses, or the shells of houses. The block-work had only been done to about ten feet, but it was perfect cover from the rest of the estate. He eased through a door opening at the back and moved carefully to where he had a view. He crouched down and peered out.

Half-finished houses and empty spaces surrounded a grim, weed-littered central area. Weeds had prospered at the edges of the foundations, and bits of wood and lumps of unused concrete lay around in mounds. Some stacks of breeze blocks. Weeds were also coming up through the tarmac on the road. To his right, another ditch and a field beyond. To his left, more complete houses, several with roofs, their windows boarded up with plywood. If they were here at all, that's where they would be – in one of those.

He thought about going right, towards the back of the estate, and looping around to the front, but he'd have to go across an open area to get there. No way. There must be a different way in. He turned around and went back through the ditch whence he'd come.

He felt his phone buzz. A text from June.

???

Fuck, he'd forgotten to text her. He replied.

Ok

Molloy stretched his arms expansively, stood up, and walked around the kitchen. He sat back down and took another sip of tea. He was getting restless. His senses told him that something was wrong, and he trusted them. That's why he was still alive. A message came through on his phone and he checked it.

Sean Brady looked at him sleepily from a kitchen chair. Pat Brady was in the house opposite, on lookout. Better be paying attention. Corcoran was in the room next door, keeping an eye on the boy. Probably asleep, but the boy was well tied up and not going anywhere – even if he could walk.

Molloy tried his phone again to read the news, but the

reception was so bad it took the pages forever to load.

'Go up and check on the girl, then get the rest of the stuff out of the van,' he said. 'We're leaving soon.'

Brady got up and left the room. Molloy looked at the closed door and rubbed the stubble on his cheeks. Those two would pay for crossing him, but now was not the time. He pressed the screen and held the phone to his ear.

'Yeah?' he said.

'Roadblock on other side of Killumney is just gone,' Karol replied. 'I am 5k to west.'

'Okay,' Molloy said. 'Have you got the two plumbing vans?'

'Yes, like you said, but is very risky now. Better to wait a few days.'

'What's the news from the city?'

'Everybody still in police stations, everybody scared. Many roadblocks, my friends tell me. All around city. Cop cars everywhere. Pavel said some of the Keaveney guys and the SEAL are around too, asking questions.'

'We'll worry about them later. Mary and the baby?'

'I don't hear nothing. I think she is still at the station, the baby is still in care.'

'He'll fucking pay for this, however long it takes. Be here in one hour, we're going to move then.'

'Is too dangerous, I think.'

'We have to finish this and move. Put on your work clothes as if you're going on a job. They don't know you or the van. One hour, right?'

'Yes, boss.'

Molloy picked up the Micro Uzi on the table and checked the mechanism. He felt the remembered satisfaction of the recoil the time he tried it out in Slovakia when he went there to buy twenty of them.

Wouldn't waste it on the kids. Too noisy anyway. Corcoran can use a knife – he likes the knife does Jimbo. He can have a go off the young one first if he wants. It was too risky to let them go now. The damage was done.

Wouldn't be coming back here again, anyway. Pavel can torch the place when they're in the safe house in Kerry, destroy all the evidence. Bury the kids somewhere down there, they'll never be found.

Molloy thought about doing a line of coke, then decided against it. They could be hours stuck in that hidden floor compartment in the van. Must remember to have a piss before they get in.

Fail to prepare, he thought. *Prepare to fail.*

He thought about the Keaveneys. Fuck them; they were yesterday's news, SEAL or no SEAL.

All the coke was going with him on the boat to Spain and that was that.

Collins was trying to find another gap in the ditch to skirt around the back of the estate when he heard the sound of a car door closing, followed by footsteps.

He jogged along the edge of the field, scanning the direction the sounds had come from. No sign of movement. There was an opening beside a big beech tree and he made his way through. He crossed some rough open ground and crouched behind a large mound of earth. The footsteps had gone in the opposite direction, towards the more finished houses. He took the Sig Sauer from his holster and rushed behind the wall, near where he'd heard the sound of the door.

The van was parked in the opening for a garage. He approached it from the side. Very smart; the angle of the garage meant it could not be seen from the open area. Three of the houses here were close to being finished, roofed and plastered with more plywood covering the windows and door openings. He heard a sound to his left. From one of the houses on the far side. He saw a tall sheet of plywood being closed in the middle terrace house, like a door. There were holes in two of the sheets of plywood over the windows on the first floor. Probably lookout spots. He had them. Sully had been right.

He took out his phone and texted June.

Ok, no sign yet

He ducked in beside the van, into the garage area, and opened the driver's door. The key was still in the ignition. He took it out, thought for a moment, put it in again, then broke it off, throwing the plastic covered bit on the ground.

He went the way he had come, to flank them from the other side and get close, with cover from the ditch and the trees. He tried to stay calm as he clambered back through the briars.

Claire, her skin glowing, her legs tanned, steps out of the summer sun and into Brown Thomas. Slowly, she moves slowly. There's an older woman in charge of the MAC corner and she smiles at her. Claire smiles back. A blonde woman in a white outfit stands by Lancôme. She looks like Jennifer Lawrence. She asks Claire if she would like a make-over.

'Not that you need one,' she says. 'Your complexion is flawless.' She smiles and reaches out a finger and touches Claire's face with the back of its perfect, moistened skin. Flawless, she said.

Next, she'll go up to the first floor, where the clothes are. She loves it there. That Victoria, Victoria Beckham lace dress for her debs.

Claire awakes by the pool. She can feel the heavy heat of the sun through the umbrella by her bed. Her right foot is in direct sunlight so she pulls it back into the shade. She sips a Diet Coke. She wonders if she'll stroll back to the hotel and decides against it. That total babe of a waiter, the one with the brown eyes, might come around again. She loves her aquamarine bikini, the cups make her breasts look larger.

She imagines kissing the waiter and wets her lips. She has her cherry red gloss on, it's so cool. Hôtel du Cap-Eden-Roc – even the name is exotic. Juan-Les-Pins. Antibes. All the names have, what's it called? *Je ne sais pas.* No. *Je ne sais quoi.* That's it. *Je ne sais quoi.*

She closes her eyes again. These Ray Bans are the best thing ever. She smiles. Soon it will be time for lunch. She'll have the *Salade Niçoise* and a glass of rosé. They never ask her age. She's been practising saying *Niçoise – neesewaws.* That's how you say it. *Neesewaws.*

Dave gives it and goes. *Give it and go, that's how you pass the ball,* Brendan Crotty says. That's the way Steven Gerrard used to do it. Always moving, always looking for the return. It's a team game, let the ball do the work. Dave's on fire tonight.

It's Turners Cross. It's the Intermediate Cup Final, against Temple United. Fucking Temple, have to beat them. There's a huge crowd.

Last minute, just going into time-added-on. 2–2. Dave's on for a hat-trick.

Dave runs up the left and Deckie side-foots it to him. He cuts inside, the defender falls.

'Shoot, Dave!' his Dad shouts from the sideline.

'Shoot, Dave!' Brendan shouts from the bench.

Everything slows. Dave touches the ball with the outside of his foot and takes the shot. It flies into the top corner.

'Great shot!' his Dad shouts.

'Great shot!' Brendan shouts.

The crowd cheers. It's a huge crowd, to be fair, the biggest he's ever played in front of.

The Liverpool scout takes his programme out of his pocket and writes something on it. All Dave's teammates gather around and congratulate him. The final whistle blows.

Collins realised that the only way of getting close was via the house next door – if he went through the ditch into what was going to be the back garden, he'd be seen thirty metres away. A sitting duck. He had to use the other building as cover.

He sidled along the front of a house, crouching low, and had almost reached the corner when a plywood sheet was smashed out and Sean Brady pointed an Uzi at him and began firing. Brady fired high and Collins ducked into a doorway. He could hear the gunfire coming closer, bullets tearing gouges of concrete from the walls. After a burst, when he judged that Brady was in the right spot, he pointed out the window opening and fired three times, in a tight sequence. The Uzi stopped and Collins looked out. Sean Brady was on the ground; he'd been hit once, looked like just below the eye. A satisfying pool of blood was welling under his head on the concrete.

Collins came through the doorway of the house, holstered his pistol, and picked up the Uzi. He tried to recall his automatic weapon training in Templemore. He heard a crash from one of the houses opposite and Pat Brady appeared, roaring, and ran towards him, another Uzi spraying bullets. Collins moved behind a mound of earth, steadied himself on one knee and held the gun in both hands, pointing low, firing in intervals. Brady went down in the weeds, bellowing like a bull, the weapon skidding along the tarmac. Collins aimed lower and fired three more bursts into where he thought Brady was lying. He dropped the Uzi, took his Sig Sauer out again and faced the house next door.

'Molloy!' he shouted. 'I know you're in there.'

Nothing. Collins heard sirens in the distance. June must have called it in.

'Molloy! Come out with your hands up. Armed gardaí!'

Corcoran burst out the door of the house, the Uzi firing on automatic. He was pointing directly in front of the house, away from Collins. Collins aimed and fired twice but missed. Corcoran turned towards him, shooting all the time and Collins pulled the trigger again. He heard gunshots from behind him and Corcoran's face burst into a mess of red and white and he went down.

Collins swung around and saw June on her knees twenty yards away, her hands on her neck, blood pouring through her fingers. He ran to her. She looked blankly at him, her eyes glazed, her breathing fast and shallow.

'June!' he said. He held his hand over her hands to staunch the flow.

'I'm sorry,' she said with a gurgling voice. The sirens were close now.

'It's okay, it's okay, June,' he said, pressing his hand over hers. 'They're coming.'

He heard an almighty crash and an Emergency Response Unit Audi 4x4 smashed through the loose gates at the front of the estate and screeched to a stop beside them. Masked officers in helmets and dark uniforms poured out of the vehicle.

'Ambulance! Ambulance!' Collins shouted, and one of the men returned to the car and spoke hurriedly into the radio.

'In there,' Collins said, pointing to the house. 'They have Uzis. Man down over there, he could be alive.'

Other vehicles pulled up and more men with automatic weapons swarmed past, speaking into mobile radio sets.

'Stay with us, June,' Collins said, hoarsely. 'It's gone through, just a flesh wound. Look at me, look at me, June.'

June stared at him, her eyes glazed over. He eased her to the ground. The ERU garda – it was Halloran – began to work on her, while Collins, on his knees, held June's bloody hand and rubbed her hair. He whispered: 'It's okay, June, it's okay.'

64

'Looks like it missed the artery,' Collins heard a paramedic say to a colleague as she put an oxygen mask over June's mouth. 'But we have to watch the airway. Keep a bit of pressure on there.'

Two more paramedics rolled a trolley beside her and lifted her onto it. She seemed to have lost consciousness. They strapped her in and rolled her to the doors of the ambulance. Collins walked alongside, his hand on June's arm. As they lifted her in, he looked around and saw Halloran conferring with another ERU man.

'You coming?' a paramedic said to him, before closing the ambulance door. 'You'll have to stay out of our way.'

Collins shook his head and went up to Halloran.

'Did you find him?' Collins said.

'Find who?'

'Molloy? Did you find Molloy?'

'We didn't find anyone else, yet,' Halloran said.

'Well, keep fucking looking,' Collins said and he ran towards the house and unholstered his gun. A big ERU man at the front door raised an arm to hold him back.

'Just let them bring the kids out first,' he said. He looked closely at Collins's face.

Dave was on the first trolley, covered by a blanket. He was unconscious. His mouth and nose were bloody and there were bruises and a swelling under his left eye.

Moments later, they carried another trolley down the stairs. They had to manoeuvre it at the door and the ERU man helped them. As she passed, Collins saw that Claire's eyes were wide open, but she wasn't focusing. She swung her head from side to side, looking towards the sky. She, too, was blanketed and a female paramedic was comforting her. 'It's okay, Claire, you're safe now,' she said as the trolley was lifted past, then rolled away.

Collins fought off a sudden urge to follow and ask her if Molloy had been there. He noticed that Halloran had caught up and was standing beside him.

Collins went into the house and Halloran followed him.

The first room, on the left, was empty except for some over-turned chairs and a sleeping bag crumpled up in a corner. There was some rubbish – cigarettes, crisp bags, tissues, pizza boxes and pizza ends – piled up in the fireplace. Some bits of narrow acrylic rope, a cable tie and a cloth hood lay on the ground beside one chair.

'Looks like they kept one of them in here,' Halloran said.

The kitchen was large with more of the same folded chairs. A kettle, teabags and milk on a countertop. Sliced pan and butter and cheese. An open packet of biscuits. An open coffee jar. Dirty plates and cups in the sink. A whiskey bottle and cans of beer. A large carton of water. A roll of toilet paper. More cigarette butts in an ashtray. Two phones plugged in at the wall.

A blow-up mattress in the corner, a duvet. A large bag of white powder on the table. A cardboard box under the table. Collins pointed at it for Halloran to take it out, as he had gloves on.

Halloran pulled it from under the table and lifted the flap. Under three layers of polyethylene foam an Uzi and a spare magazine. Under that another, and then another.

'Plenty of weaponry, anyway,' Halloran muttered.

'Upstairs,' Collins said. 'Are your men searching for him?'

'If he's here, we'll find him, Collins,' Halloran said. 'Why didn't you call it in earlier?'

Collins did not reply.

The large bedroom had a double bed. Stained sheets and pillows. A dirty blue duvet cover on the ground beside it. Another hood, more cable ties.

'They probably kept her here,' Collins said. 'Did you check the attic?'

'We checked everywhere, he isn't here,' Halloran said. 'If he ever was.' He looked closely at the stains on the bed. He picked up and shook the duvet, then bent down and checked under the bed. 'And you didn't answer my question.'

Collins stared him down.

'No sign of clothing,' Collins said, leaving the room. 'I'm going to look for him.'

Collins met Tom Kelleher and Jim Murphy outside the front door. They stared at him.

'What?' Collins said.

'Come on,' Tom said. 'Let's get you out of here.'

'I'm going to look for him,' Collins said.

'No, you're not,' Tom said. 'We need to get to the hospital. Check on June and get your face looked after.'

'June,' Collins said.

'She'll make it,' Jim said. 'She's tough out. Let's go, Collins. Holster that, would you?' He pointed to the gun. Collins hadn't realised he was still holding it.

At the entrance to the CUH Emergency Department, Collins and Tom jumped out of the car and rushed through sliding doors. Collins went to the front desk, pushing an old woman aside. The woman recoiled.

Collins pressed his badge against the glass.

'June Carroll, just admitted. A garda. Gunshot wound.'

The young woman behind the glass stared at the badge, then at Collins and asked, 'Do you want treatment? You'll have to wait.'

'Treatment? No. Where did they take June Carroll?'

The young woman's forehead furrowed. She looked at his hands, then back at his face.

'Where is she?' Collins said.

He heard his name being called. Tom was at the door of the unit. It was open. Collins rushed inside with him.

They stopped a doctor. He was young, fresh-faced. Looked no more than eighteen, his stethoscope wrapped around his neck.

'Detective June Carroll has just been admitted with a gunshot wound to the neck,' Jim said. 'Where is she?'

'They've taken her over to Resus, she might need surgery,' the doctor replied, looking closely at Collins. 'You need to have your face treated,' he said.

'Which way?' Collins said.

'You can't see her, she's being stabilised,' the doctor said.

'Which fucking way?' Jim said.

'Out that door and down the corridor, follow the blue line, but you –'

Tom and Jim headed for the door. Collins said, 'I'll follow you on.'

He turned to the doctor.

'Where are her clothes? I need her clothes as part of an urgent ongoing investigation.'

'I don't know,' the doctor said. 'I'm sorry, I'm busy right now.' He made to move away. Collins grabbed him by the arm.

'Find out now,' Collins said and glared at him. 'Now!'

'Alright, alright,' the doctor said and went to the desk.

Two nurses had been staring at the confrontation.

'Down here,' one of them said, and walked past Collins. 'I bagged them after she was triaged.'

Collins followed her. She went to the end unit and found a large black plastic bag in a corner, with a blue tape wrapped around its neck.

Collins crouched down, ripped it open and pulled out the contents. June's shoes, underwear, a bloody white blouse, black pants and her overcoat spilled onto the ground. Collins dug into the pockets of the coat. He found her iPhone, and then the Nokia. He groaned and lowered his head. He felt his throat tighten and a weight pressing on his chest.

'Oh, June,' he said.

'Are you okay?' the nurse said. Collins lifted himself up, unsteadily, and leaned against a bed.

'Shit,' he whispered. He bowed his head.

'You need to have those cuts cleaned,' she said.

Collins ignored her.

'Hello?'

He looked at her.

'What cuts?'

'Your face is all cut. And your hands are covered in blood, are you injured somewhere else?

Collins held up his hands.

'No. How long before I can talk to her?'

'Depends,' the nurse said. 'Hours probably, if she needs surgery. Sit up there now like a good man, and I'll give those cuts a wipe and we'll get you to wash your hands too.'

'Is she going to live?' he heard himself say.

'They seem to think so,' she said. 'The artery is okay anyway. Cervical spine, too, I think. That's the main thing. Is she a friend of yours?'

'Yes,' Collins said. 'Yes, she is.'

He sat up on the bed, passively. He put the phones in his inside coat pocket. He took out his own phone. He found the number and pressed the screen.

'Hello, Sharon?' he said.

'Hello, who's this?' A woman's voice.

'He's alive. He's going to be okay, Sharon. This is Collins. I'm at the hospital.'

He heard a gasp and then she cried out. He heard her say 'He's alive, he's alive!' to somebody.

'Oh, Jesus. Oh, Jesus,' Sharon said. 'Thank you, thank you, Collins. Oh my God.'

'One second,' Collins said.

'Where's the boy they brought in?' he said to the nurse.

'He's gone up to X-ray, he might have some fractures,' she said, wiping his forehead with a wet piece of material.

'He's in X-ray in CUH,' Collins said into the phone.

'Oh thank you, thank you, Collins. God bless you. Wait, is he hurt?'

'I have to go now,' he said and closed the call. He put the phone down by his side and let the nurse wipe his face.

'Where's the girl?' he said.

'She's in a room down the corridor,' the nurse said. 'She's in shock, they've sedated her.'

'Was she raped?'

'No. I don't think so, anyway.'

Collins closed his eyes. The nurse applied ointment to his face.

His phone rang. He shut down the call.

'How did you get all these cuts?' she said. 'They're mostly superficial, but there's so many.'

'Briars. I had to go through some briars.' He stood up from the bed.

'Thank you,' he said. 'The blue line, was it?'

She tut tutted but stepped back. 'Yes, but it could take hours.'

'I know,' he said and he looked at her. 'I know.'

He tried to smile. Her eyes were the softest of blues, very like his mother's. He took out his phone and found another number.

'Hega,' he said.

'Collins,' Hega said. 'Any joy with those kids?'

'Yeah, we got them. Can you get out to CUH? I want you to look at a phone for me.'

'No bother, Collins. I've a new Chinese fella, he's a dinger. Where will you be?'

'Text me when you get here,' Collins said, following the blue line down the corridor.

It took him past the entrance to the Oncology Unit. Sunlight was streaming in through skylights, the rain had stopped. A little girl, maybe six years old, skipped gaily past him, with bright orange boots and a plastic raincoat. She clutched a sodden piece of paper, a get-well card she had made for her mother. The sunshine lit her up when she passed through it, transforming her hair from ochre to gold.

PART 4

17 DECEMBER 2016

65

'Well, lookit, the main thing is she's going to be fine,' Jonno said. He had monopolised the previous ten minutes in the meeting room off Chief Superintendent Geary's office, but he was fading a bit now.

Collins sat beside him, directly opposite Geary. Deputy Commissioner Denis Sweeney was the fourth man at the table. He sat on Collins's other side, his face livid. He had not yet spoken, Collins noticed. Waiting for the right moment.

Collins was restless; he wanted to be elsewhere, away from this bullshit. He could do with a drink, or a long drive up the west. Or around Italy. God, Italy would be so good. His face itched something terrible, but he resisted the urge to scratch it.

'And the kids are safe,' Geary said. 'We got the kids alive, remember.'

'Absolutely,' Jonno said. 'Thanks to Detectives Carroll and Collins here.'

'Yes,' Geary said. 'That's the way we should push this to the media too. The kids were saved by the heroic actions of two brave officers, putting themselves in extreme danger. And we should emphasise the Uzis too.'

'I'm not so sure about that, Sean,' Sweeney said. 'Maybe just mention they were armed. We don't want to make it known that there are Uzis on the streets of our cities and towns.'

'Yes, yes,' Geary said. '"Armed".' He made a note on a sheet of paper.

'When are the two victims expected to be interviewed?'

Geary said.

'We're not sure,' Jonno said. 'The girl probably not for a while. Young McMahon today or tomorrow, probably. Do you think he'll talk, Collins?'

'Hard to know, sir,' Collins said. 'Now that fingerprints have confirmed Molloy was there, he might clam up.'

'Well, the fingerprints prove he was in the house at some stage,' Sweeney said. 'We still haven't confirmed he was there recently.'

'The girl will confirm it in due course, sir,' Collins said. 'In the meantime I think it's best to continue the manhunt.'

'Oh, we haven't stopped looking for him, Collins,' Sweeney said. 'Although if you had called it in sooner, we'd have had the place surrounded.'

Collins did not reply. He'd been through all this at the debriefing. He knew that if he'd been smart, if he'd really been prepared, that all he had to do when Pat Brady came out shooting was to retreat around the back of the house and he'd have caught Molloy sneaking out the back. He'd have had a clear shot and June wouldn't have been hit. And it would be all over. He still couldn't figure out how the bastard got out and away without transport. No point in brooding on it. God, he needed a drink.

'What time is the press conference?' Geary said.

'Twelve hundred hours, Chief Superintendent,' Jonno said. He turned to Collins. 'Well, Collins, you'll be getting your second Scott Medal for this. I think it's the first time a garda has received two medals – I must check that up.'

'Depending on the GSOC investigation of course,' Sweeney said. 'And our own internal inquiry too – two fatalities and a member shot. Internal Affairs have been on to me already. Number

One wants John Doyle to head that up, he's on his way now. So you better get your story straight, Collins.'

'Yes, sir,' Collins said.

'There's going to be pressure from all sides,' Sweeney said. 'Sinn Féin are already trying to put down a question in the Dáil, the hypocrites. And the usual loony lefties were all over the radio this morning. Not to mention the opposition – they'll want their pound of flesh too. Number One is very concerned, he told me. Very concerned.'

Sweeney paused.

'And we very nearly lost a member, Sean,' he continued. 'A fine garda, and the mother of two children.'

'Yes, well, we didn't, thankfully,' Geary said. He began to gather up his papers, to bring the meeting to an end. 'Now, if you'll excuse me, I have to talk to our Communications people about this press conference and square things away with Phoenix Park. You won't attend, Collins. I'll make up some excuse. Best if you don't talk to the media at all.'

'Yes, Chief Superintendent,' Collins said.

'When are you heading back to Dublin, Denis?' Geary asked, casually.

'Later today,' Sweeney said. 'John has asked me to sit in on his conversation with Detective Collins. He mentioned fourteen hundred hours.'

'I'll see if my rep is available,' Collins said. 'Obviously, I'll have to have representation. My solicitor too, probably. I'll phone her now.'

'Oh, there's no need for that,' Sweeney said. 'Sure, it's just a chat.'

'I'll go and discuss things with them now,' Collins said. 'If that's okay, Chief Superintendent.' Sweeney took him for a fool, that was clear.

'Yes, yes, off you go, Collins,' Geary said. 'I want to have a quick word with Denis anyway, before he heads back to Dublin.'

Jonno left the room with Collins.

'Oh, by the way, Brady came out of the coma last night,' Jonno said.

'Right.'

'Yes, and he wouldn't let O'Callaghan near him. Wanted to talk to us, would you believe. As soon as the doctors give the go-ahead.'

'I'd like to interview him,' Collins said.

'Oh, I don't think so, Collins. Seeing as you're the man who shot him and killed his brother.'

A coffee would have to do for breakfast today, Collins realised, but he'd better talk to Michael O'Leary, his GRA representative, first. And phone Debbie, his solicitor.

'Quick word of advice, Collins,' Jonno said, moving into a doorway. He lowered his voice. 'If I was you, my solicitor wouldn't be available for a couple of weeks. Get my drift?'

'Yes, sir,' Collins said.

'And then, if I was you, I'd take some leave. Maybe a bit of sick leave, after … you know. Let things sit for a couple of months. Know what I mean?' Jonno scanned up and down the corridor. 'Let the Communications people do their thing for a while; get the media on board. Hype up the "heroic actions of two gardaí" story.'

Collins scrutinised Jonno, trying to read between the lines.

'Then,' Jonno said, looking around him again, 'Sweeney can go fuck himself.'

Collins blinked, shocked.

'This is *our* division, Collins. *Our* district, *our* city. Nothing to do with those Dublin fuckers,' Jonno said. 'Oh, and another thing. If the Unit are going across to the pub tonight tell them to be careful who they're talking to. We still have a member seriously ill in hospital and we have to respect her and her family. I don't want to read anything in the papers tomorrow about this except what the Press Office have given them. Clear?' Jonno gave Collins the eye and walked away.

'I'll spread the word. Thank you, sir,' Collins said, to his back.

66

Collins pressed the 'up' button on the hospital lift. He counted back. Four months since he had been in the Intensive Therapy Unit himself, when June had visited him every day. Now it was his turn.

An oldish, bearded, doctor in blue scrubs looked at him for a long time, obviously trying to recollect how he knew the face. The newspapers had been full of his picture that morning. Collins had seen one headline in the hospital shop. 'Hero hurler saves kids'. What a load of rubbish, but if it kept Geary happy and Jonno off his back …

Collins did not make eye contact with the doctor.

The doors opened. Two nurses emerged, deep in conversation, followed by Gerry and Elaine Halvey. Gerry saw Collins and started. Collins thought about going past them into the lift but decided against it.

Gerry had a washed-out look; the cardigan and check shirt he wore seemed incongruous. Elaine appeared very different from when Collins had seen her at the media event. She stood erect and poised, purposeful. Her hair shone and she was wearing a bright-red woollen overcoat.

'How is Claire?' Collins said.

'She's … still very shocked,' Gerry said. 'It was a terrible ordeal. She'll be coming home tomorrow, they say.'

Collins nodded.

'But we have her back,' Gerry said. 'We thought she was gone.' He looked at his wife and smiled. Her eyes filled with tears.

Collins did not know what to say.

Gerry took a step forward and held out his hand to shake. 'Thank you,' he said, hoarsely, 'for saving her life.'

Collins took his hand and shook it. He held out his hand to Elaine, but she brushed past it and hugged him.

'Thank you, *so much*,' she said into his ear. She stepped back. 'We can never repay our debt to you.'

Collins smiled and shook his head.

'How is your colleague?' Halvey said.

'I'm just going up to see her now. She's out of danger.'

'Please pass on our gratitude to her too,' Gerry said. 'She was very brave.'

'I will.'

Collins was about to say something else, something consolatory about Claire, but he changed his mind. 'I will.'

The lift doors were open again. 'I better …' he said, pointing to it. The Halveys smiled as he entered the lift. The doors closed behind him.

'Well, well, look who it is,' Norma said by the nurse's station outside ITU. 'I was hoping we wouldn't be seeing you here again.'

'Hello, Norma,' Collins said. 'How are you?'

'Oh, understaffed, underpaid, under-appreciated,' she said, appraising him up and down. 'And you? You've put on a bit of weight. What happened your face?'

'Oh, nothing. A scratch.' He hesitated. 'How's June?'

'She's very weak,' Norma said. 'I don't know if she's up for visitors.'

'I just wanted to see her, to let her know I am here for her. Like she was for me. Two minutes.'

'I'll check if she's awake. Two minutes max – you know the routine. Wash your hands,' she said, pointing to the alcohol foam dispenser.

She marched through the double doors. Collins put his hands under the dispenser and rubbed them together. Norma appeared back after a moment, and beckoned him in.

'She's in the last bed on the left. Literally two minutes, and don't upset her, right?'

'Right.'

He shuddered as he entered the room, the sounds and smells bringing back memories he would prefer not to have.

He approached the bed, warily. June's face was almost invisible behind the oxygen mask. Her eyes were closed. She was sitting up, her head resting on thick pillows, her neck swathed in bandages, her finger caught by a clip. A drip flowed from a plastic bag of clear fluid into her arm, and a wire from under the blanket was connected to some electrical device. He felt the back of his hand, where they used to attach his own cannula.

She opened her eyes, facing straight ahead, and then at him. Her eyes widened.

Collins smiled at her.

'You look great, June. A million dollars, girl.'

She blinked several times, tears welling. Collins put out his hand, enveloping hers.

'You're going to be just fine,' he said, gently. 'Everything is fine.'

She tried to say something from under the mask.

'No,' he said. 'No, no. Don't say anything. You always talk too much.'

Her eyes searched his, looking for something.

'Everything is fine, okay?' he said again. 'Don't worry about a thing. I found the phone. I got rid of it. You're safe, okay? It's all over. Nobody knows. Nobody will ever know.'

She closed her eyes.

'Hey, look on the bright side, you'll lose a load of weight.'

This time she did smile.

'Don't worry about a thing,' he said, squeezing her hand. 'I got ya.'

June moaned and one of the machines began to beep more insistently. Norma appeared in an instant, adjusting the machine.

'Jesus, Collins, what did I tell you?' she said. 'Out. Now.'

Collins squeezed June's hand again, his eyes never leaving hers. He smiled, and nodded his head.

'Out, I told you, Collins,' Norma said, pointing to the door.

In the corridor, he took out his phone.

'Mr O'Donovan, this is Detective Collins again, please ring me back at this number. This is the third message I've left you. I need to talk to you urgently. I'm not going to stop until I talk to you. I assure you it's in your best interest.'

67

The rigid inflatable boat began to lurch on the deep swells once they went out past Mizen Head. Water sprayed up over Molloy and he swallowed some of it. Why was the fucker going so fast and how could he even see in the dark? Pure madness. He felt his stomach heave and he put his head over the rubber side and vomited. Much of it was blown back into the boat. He spat after it and more sea water drenched him. His eyes stung. He was freezing with the cold.

Waiting all night in that stinking Land Rover and now this. He could just as easily have sneaked on board the yacht in Baltimore in the middle of the night and who would have known? That captain was one weird bastard. A college friend of O'Donovan, apparently. After sailing across the Atlantic from Martinique to the Canary Islands and then to West Cork with a hull full of cocaine, it was a bit late to be getting paranoid now. The RIB could flip over or sink, then they'd be completely fucked. He pulled at his lifebelt to make sure it was securely tied around his chest. Christ, but it was cold.

The noise of the engine was deafening. Wind whipped at his wet face and hair, making him breathless. Thankfully there was nothing else to throw up. He could feel water sloshing around his feet, he was completely soaked.

He turned his face from the wind, looked back, and could just make out the dark mass of land behind in the pre-dawn gloom. He wondered if he'd ever return to Ireland. Probably not, thanks to that prick. It wasn't over between the two of them, that was for sure, however long it took. It never would be.

The local guy steering the boat shouted something and pointed. Molloy looked to the left – the yacht, a dim blur in the distance. Thank fuck. In three days they'd be in France, on dry land again. Two more would get them to Spain, where everything was arranged.

The villa outside Malaga was all set up, the pictures and video had been amazing. The Thais were arriving in February and then he'd be made for life. Ten million clear profit a year, minimum.

Luke and Mary would follow in March, just as the weather got really nice.

Getting out of that shithole of a ghost estate had been a nightmare, dragging himself through the muddy hole in the ditch and then Karol taking ages to find the right field. That bitch hadn't warned him Collins was coming, either; she'd pay for that. Pity that bullet hadn't gone through her head instead of her neck. Not one of those useless morons could get a round into Collins. But his luck wouldn't last forever.

The Poles would get on top of things again once all the hassle settled down. O'Donovan would get the message and keep on laundering the money. Didn't matter what the girl said, now they had Pat. He better keep his mouth shut. That little pup McMahon too.

As the RIB slowed and approached the yacht, Molloy felt that all his planning had finally paid off. It would all sort itself out. He was home and hosed.

A fresh start was just what he needed.

He smiled.

68

Collins knocked on the hotel-room door. Number 221. No answer. He looked at his watch: 10.20 p.m.

He knocked again. Maybe the fucker was out drinking somewhere, but he'd checked the hotel bar.

He put his ear to the door, dialled the number again and heard the faint sound of a phone ringing inside the room.

'Room service,' he said, loudly, knocking again. 'Room service for Mr Dineen.'

The door swung open. 'I didn't order –' Eric O'Donovan stopped in his tracks, his mouth open, shock written all over his bleary face.

O'Donovan went to shut the door, but Collins pushed past him.

'You can't come in here,' O'Donovan said, keeping the door open. 'That's breaking and entering.'

'Close the door,' Collins said, holding up a document, title side out, so that O'Donovan could see it. On the front page it said, in large writing: *Assessment and Report on Shane Eric O'Donovan, (DOB: 21 May 1995) by Alan O'Regan MB BCh MRC Psych. June, 2016. The Well Centre, The Meadows, Kildare, Co. Kildare. PRIVATE AND CONFIDENTIAL.*

O'Donovan shut the door and grabbed the document.

'Where did you get this?' he said. 'This is stolen property. You can't –'

Collins looked him up and down. O'Donovan's eyes were dilated and bloodshot, his face bloated. His skin was slick with a sheen of moisture. He was stubbled and dishevelled, with sweat stains under the arms of a wrinkled blue shirt, which hung out over his suit pants. His shoes were off. He had a slight residue of white around one side of his mouth. Collins guessed that he had been asleep when he knocked. Good.

The room was not untidy, except for the bed, though it smelled of sex and stale food. He guessed that O'Donovan had had some company earlier. He could see two towels on the bathroom floor. The remains of two meals were visible on a trolley beside a low table and two armchairs.

'Have a seat,' Collins said, sitting down in one armchair and beckoning to the other.

'This is bullshit,' O'Donovan said and he began to rip up the document. 'Bullshit. All lies. Now, get out.' He opened the door and stood aside.

'Out. Now,' he said.

Collins laughed and picked up the empty bottle of red wine.

'Châteauneuf-du-Pape. Not bad.'

'Out!' O'Donovan, said. 'I can phone the Minister for Justice and have you thrown out of the guards.'

'Do you think that's the only copy I have of that report? I can email it to every newspaper and blogger in the country. Or put it up on Twitter. Take about five minutes,' Collins said. 'And do you want everyone in the hotel to hear our conversation?'

O'Donovan slammed the door shut.

'You won't get away with this. That document is private. How did you get it?'

'Never mind that. The question is what I'm going to do with it. But that's not all. Sit down,' Collins said. 'I'm not going to tell you again.'

O'Donovan glowered at him. He ran his tongue over his teeth, under his lips. Collins guessed he was coming down off a cocaine high and wanted another hit.

Collins took another thinner document from inside his coat. He unfolded it and handed it to O'Donovan, who was still standing.

'What's this?' O'Donovan said, waving it at Collins.

'Sit down and read it. It's all legal and above board, fully witnessed and signed by myself and the witness. And Shane, who is fully compos mentis,' Collins said. 'And very pissed off with you.'

'What?' O'Donovan plopped into the armchair and began to read. He flicked a page forward.

'Oh, no. Oh, Shane,' he said, after a few moments, horror etched into his face. He turned a page. 'Oh, Jesus Christ.'

'There was no coercion; he's over eighteen. It'll all stand up in court,' Collins said. 'I have it all on video too, it'll look great on YouTube.'

O'Donovan groaned and seemed to fold into himself. His head moved slowly towards his knees and for a moment Collins thought he was going to be sick. He sniffled, wiped his nose and looked Collins in the eye.

'Is it money you want?' he said. 'I have to warn you, I'm more or less broke.'

'No money. Just information.'

'What information?' O'Donovan scratched his face, and looked away, feigning nonchalance. He was a good liar, Collins guessed. With lots of practice. He'd have to tread carefully, sceptically.

'I'll come to the point,' Collins said. 'I know you've been laundering money for Dominic Molloy. I know too, that you are somehow involved in the smuggling of several million euros' worth of cocaine into Ireland.'

O'Donovan didn't quite hide the shock. Maybe not as good a liar as expected.

'What? This is bullshit. What are you on about?'

'Look, I don't have time for this,' Collins said. 'If you don't start talking now, I'm going to call some media friends I know and wait for them to get here with cameras. Then I'm going to arrest you and drag you out of the hotel in your socks and into a squad car. I'm sure I'll find cocaine in this room for starters. I'm sure that the Criminal Assets Bureau will be interested in a certain account called the Anterior account, and that it will show up some very interesting information linked with money laundering. Then I'll leak this document and the video and drop some hints that your son got his paedophile tendencies from you. Maybe you even taught him.

'Do you know what happens to paedophiles in prison? Whatever about you surviving, how do you think Shane will do? Oh, and your brother-in-law – the Minister? When he hears what you've been up to, he'll drop you like a lump of dogshit he picked up off the ground by mistake. And so will his sister. You're fucked, O'Donovan. I own you.'

O'Donovan swallowed. He coughed, or cried out – Collins couldn't be sure which. He scratched his face again. With trembling hands, he placed the document slowly on the coffee table. He looked desperately at the open window.

'Don't even think about jumping,' Collins said. 'If you even try to get out of that chair I will drag you down and dislocate both your thumbs. That fucking hurts, I can tell you.'

O'Donovan began to cry. He was an ugly crier.

'He made me, he blackmailed me,' he blubbed. 'I had no choice.'

'Start at the beginning,' Collins said, quietly. He poured a glass of sparkling water and pushed it across the table.

At 11.45 p.m. Collins left the hotel room and walked down the stairs to the vast lobby area, where the spill-out of a Christmas party was in full swing. He avoided the drunken revellers and looked to his left, inside the bar. They were still serving. He decided against a pint and kept moving.

He took his phone from his pocket and selected a number. He crossed the road to Lapps Quay, a northern wind cutting across him. The air felt like there was snow coming. *Surely not*, he thought. *A white Christmas?*

The phone rang out. He didn't leave a message.

On Crane Lane his phone buzzed.

'Hiya Christy, happy Christmas,' Collins said. 'How's the going, boy? Thanks for ringing back.'

'Hi, Collins. Many happy returns. We're in Counihans, are you coming in for one?'

'No, Christy, but I need a favour.'

'No probs, boy, what do you need?' Collins could barely hear him, with the din. A man and a woman were singing a duet in the background. 'Girl from the North Country'. Christ, it would be that – his favourite Dylan song.

'I need a car,' Collins said. 'Something reliable.'

'Now?'

'No, but I'll need it around five in the morning.'

'Jesus, Collins. Tomorrow is Christmas Eve, I'm on the tear, like.'

'I know, I know. Sorry about that.'

Nothing was said for a time. Christy cleared his throat.

'The usual place? Full tank?'

'That would be great, thanks, Christy. Have a good one.'

Collins hesitated outside the open door of the pub. He could smell the beer and feel the heat of the bodies from inside. He could hear the music from inside, too. A harmonica solo had ended and the woman was singing again. One of those high throaty voices whose clarity raises the hair on the back of your neck.

The music faded as he moved down Pembroke Street, under the Christmas lights, past a large group of 'twelve pubs' kids in Christmas jumpers and hats, smoking and laughing on the footpath.

69

Traffic was light on the motorway, the odd truck. Collins drove fast through the morning darkness. He had the heating on high. It was a silver Avensis, solid on the road and unobtrusive – just what he needed. He took the exit at Junction 8 at Cashel to get coffee at the Topaz. The coffee was tepid and weak, the croissant was stale.

The usual build-up of cars as he approached Dublin. The sky brightened to his right. He was expecting congestion in the city on the day that was in it, so he parked at the Red Cow park and ride and took the Luas. A crowd was gathered at the tram stop, people's breath appearing, then disappearing, in the biting air. A watery sun had risen to the south-east, and was tracing its low arc over the Dublin Mountains. The platform heaved with Christmas Eve shoppers. Excited children, on their way to visit Santa, chattered and peppered parents with questions. The air was heavy with their expectation – feelings he could not share. A black official with a peaked cap told the queuing passengers not to worry about a ticket, they could get it on the way back. Nobody argued. Collins stepped out of the queue and turned away from the CCTV cameras pointed at the platforms. He boarded the tram at the last second, head bowed, and stood by the door.

He checked his phone: 08:55. Three messages, the most recent from his mother: *What time will we see you tomorrow? Dinner around 2.*

He replied: *Before 12, I hope.*

An immediate response: *Flight in at 6.25 this evening.*

He replied: *Thanks.*

His brother and his family were due in that evening, from JFK, via London. He'd hoped to meet them at the airport and drive them to his mother's, but Paul insisted on renting a car, so that he could escape to his friends whenever he wanted. Collins didn't blame him. He wasn't so sure he'd make their arrival now. He wasn't so sure he'd make anything after today.

His eye was caught by a small girl wearing a red and white Christmas hat sitting on a nearby seat, her mittened hand clutching that of her father. Her cheeks and impossibly red lips shone, her eyes glittered with the excited wonder of it all. She glanced up at him and he saw Kelly O'Driscoll in her, how she had looked at that age. He felt an almost irresistible urge to stroke her cheek with the back of his hand. He lowered his head and concentrated on what he was about to do.

Google Maps showed him the address and he decided that the stop he needed was the one at the Collins Barracks Museum on Benburb Street. He wondered about the irony of that.

He extricated himself from the Luas at his stop, took the next left and walked northwards. The streets were familiar to him from his time in Store Street Station. On Phibsborough Road he passed a woman in a sheepskin jacket over pyjamas and Ugg boots at a bus stop. She was furiously smoking a cigarette and staring down the road. Her two daughters, smaller, fatter versions of herself, shuffled beside her, frozen with the cold in identical pyjamas, slippers and light Adidas jackets. One of the girls glared at him as he passed.

'The fuck are youse looking at?' she said. 'Fucken pervert.'

Dublin, Collins thought.

He was glad of his gloves and woollen hat. He rehearsed what he was planning to say as he went. After Doyle's Corner he passed a café serving breakfast, and the smell of bacon made his stomach growl, but he didn't have time. He had been there with Christy and Paulo in September 2013 at the All-Ireland Hurling Final against Clare and the replay that Cork lost. He wondered if he'd see another one. He ventured into a McDonald's and took a double espresso to go.

A left onto Connaught Avenue and into a more residential area – typical old Dublin, two-storeyed, red-brick terraces. He concentrated here, checked the App on his phone again.

Five minutes later, he saw the small entrance. He made a call.

'How's the going, Anto? Happy Christmas,' he said.

'Season's greetings, Collins. How's tricks?'

'Never better, boy. What's the story? I'm just on Connaught Avenue now, at the entrance.'

'She went out earlier to the Spar, but they're both inside now.'

'Sound, thanks. You head home, I owe you one. Love to Sarah.'

'No bother, Collins. Here, what's up, man?'

'Oh, nothing much, just a courtesy call. You'll keep this to yourself, yeah?'

'Sure thing. Call up after Christmas, will ya? Herself would love to see you. We could go to a Bohs game, have a few pints.'

'Will do, Anto, thanks.' He closed the call.

It was a narrow street, two-storey semi-detached houses either side. Cars and vans parked half on the road, half up on footpaths, allowing just enough room for passage. He followed the numbers down from 38 to the one he was looking for: 12. On the left. A house like any other, red and white bricks on the ground floor, a greenish pebble-dash above it. Bay windows at the front. *Rather mundane*, he thought, *considering who is living there.* A neat garden, a few perennials in the lawn, low-cut hedges either side, a 04 D

Ford Focus in the drive – the wife's, he guessed. His watch said 9.56, not too early to call to somebody like him.

He stood on the footpath and looked at the house.

This is your last chance to pull out, he thought. *You can still walk away, nobody would ever know, nothing would change.*

She answered the knock quickly, smiling, probably expecting a neighbour. Her face hardened immediately – she was in the know. A fit-looking woman in her early fifties, short blonde hair, medium height. Those perfect teeth and glowing skin that only Americans seem to manage. Scandinavian facial features, blue eyes. Not to be underestimated, Collins remembered. Ex-military, too.

'Yes?' she said.

Collins removed his hat – women always appreciated that, and it made him appear less threatening. Not that this woman was threatened by much, he guessed.

'Is himself in?' he said, smiling, hat in hand.

'Who's asking?' The accent had a touch of Boston he thought – they didn't have much information on her, apart from her nationality, not even through immigration.

'My name is Collins. I'm up from Cork, he knows me.'

'Does he?' she said and closed the door. Collins took two steps back, to give himself room. The door opened and a slim man about five foot eight inches tall stepped out, closed the door behind him and walked up close to Collins. Grey hair tightly cut. Black polo-neck, cord pants and hard brogues. His hands were empty, but Collins didn't like the look of the shoes. At six foot two he had a distinct reach advantage, but those shoes could do real damage.

Real name: Denis Joseph Duffy, known mostly as the SEAL. Aged fifty-three. Dublin born, emigrated to the States in his late teens, and joined up. The United States military knew an asset when they saw one and they had spent a lot of time and money teaching him to how to kill and hurt people in many different ways.

'Fuck do *you* want?' Duffy said, eyes narrowing – behind the Dublin accent a slight mid-Atlantic twang.

'I apologise. I'm sorry,' Collins said, backing away and raising his hands in apology. 'But I need to meet them urgently and if I went to Clontarf I wouldn't get near them.'

Duffy stared Collins down.

'I have some information for them,' Collins said.

'What information?'

'I know where Molloy is. And the coke. I thought they'd want to know.'

'Don't know what you're on about,' Duffy said and he walked quickly out to the footpath. He looked left and right. Reassured, he returned to the front door.

'In here,' he said. He opened the door with a key and pointed to the first room on the right and said something quietly to the woman who had been standing in the hall.

Collins went in. A living room, with a Japanese feel. Solid wood floor with a rug. A bookcase, a large flat-screen TV, a gas fire, a sofa, two armchairs, a coffee table. Three Samurai swords hung, pride of place, on the side wall. Sheathed, two in black and gold, the other a lacquered olive green. Two prints over the fireplace. One of Mount Fuji, the other of that famous Japanese wave.

'Take off your clothes,' Duffy said, closing the door of the room behind him.

Collins watched him, but did not move.

'Take them off, or get the fuck out.'

Collins began to undress.

'Give it to me,' Duffy said, taking his coat, emptying the pockets and feeling the lining. He took Collins's phone and put it on the coffee table. He examined the jacket and pants pockets and felt up and down the legs.

The woman came in with a foot-long, hand-held scanner. She gave Collins a dirty look and left.

'Give me the shoes,' Duffy said, and examined the sole and heels. He moved the scanner around them. It gave off a slight beeping sound. When Collins removed his boxers, Duffy said, 'Turn around.' He waved the scanner over Collins's clothes on the sofa.

'The watch,' Duffy said. Collins removed his watch and handed it over. A stronger beeping, but Duffy did not appear concerned by it.

'Get dressed,' Duffy said. He sounded like a man used to giving orders. He picked up Collins's phone and turned it over in his hand.

'Put in the code,' he said. Collins did so. Duffy flicked through it, handed it back and said. 'Turn it off. Fully off.' Collins did so, and resumed dressing. Duffy put out his hand again, and Collins gave him the phone.

'Satisfied?' Collins said.

'Wait here,' Duffy said and left the room. Collins put on his coat and gloves again and examined the books on the shelves. Almost all of them were military history, thick self-important tomes, except for some biographies of country and western singers – the wife's, Collins guessed, but you never know. He picked out one: *American Caesar: Douglas MacArthur 1880–1964,* sat down and opened it.

Several minutes later, Duffy came back in.

'We're going,' he said, and took the book from Collins and put it back on the shelf. He walked out and Collins followed.

The Ford Transit van smelled of oil, the kind used for metal lubrication, and Collins wondered about that. Duffy pulled out onto the Navan Road and accelerated towards the city. He opened the window and threw Collins's phone onto the road.

Collins opened his mouth but didn't speak. Where the fuck would he get a new phone on Christmas Eve? He looked out the window. *Worry about that later.*

They headed east, towards Drumcondra.

In a maze of small terraced houses near Croke Park, Duffy suddenly braked and parked. A few cars overtook them and Collins noticed one, a silver Audi, pull in twenty metres ahead. Duffy took out his phone and made a call.

'Well?' Duffy said. 'Okay. Follow us again and keep your eyes peeled.'

They drove through a maze of housing estates and narrow streets. Collins could see the Audi in the side mirror, following them.

The van turned into a small dead-end street with mostly derelict buildings on either side and Duffy parked and switched off the engine.

'Out,' he said to Collins. 'Fast.'

They walked quickly. Collins noticed the silver Audi pull up at the entrance to the street, blocking it. Two men sat in an old Merc parked up on a footpath, watching him. They looked the type.

Collins tried to get his bearings. He knew the canal was on his right somewhere, so he was north of it. And he could see the top of Croke Park straight ahead, so that was east. Halfway down the street Duffy pushed at a green door beside a lock-up and Collins followed him inside, to the concreted back of a decrepit terraced house. Duffy stood back.

'In,' he said, pointing at the slightly ajar door. There were jagged openings in the door near its base, where the wood had rotted and fallen away. Collins put his hand on the rusted old-fashioned latch and went through into a dusty kitchen. It was tiny and had clearly not been used in years.

Duffy pushed Collins into a dark hallway with stairs on the right, and for the first time that day he almost lost control of his temper. What drew him back was the sight of two large, fit-looking men standing at the other end of the hall, by the front door. They both held pistols downwards, Glocks it looked like; fingers outside the trigger guards, like professionals. The house smelt musty. Duffy pushed him again.

'In there,' he said, and Collins went into the second room on his left – what had once been the front room.

The two Keaveney brothers sat in small armchairs on either side of a small unlit fireplace. An old wooden kitchen chair faced them. Slim, on the left, had a bemused, almost sardonic look on his face. His brother, Patrick, was clearly angry, mouth tight, eyes cold. They always reminded Collins of an English actor who played bad guys. An older man with slick grey hair and a peaky nose and chin – he was a prisoner in the series *Porridge*. Collins could never remember his name.

'This better be fucking good,' Patrick said.

'Detective Collins,' Slim said, smiling all the while. 'You have five minutes, beginning now.'

'I'm sorry for doing this on Christmas Eve,' Collins began. Duffy pushed him towards the chair.

'Sit,' Duffy said.

'Molloy is on a yacht about a hundred miles south-west of Cornwall,' Collins said, sitting. He slowed down his speech. 'On his way to France with your cocaine. And I wanted to let ye know as soon as possible.'

Patrick sat up. Slim stiffened. He had their attention now. Patrick's expression changed, but Slim kept the smile. Collins noted that for future reference.

'Don't know what you're on about,' Slim said. 'But go on.'

'He's headed for an island called Île de Ré, near La Rochelle. Place called Saint Martin de Ré.' He pronounced the name as if in English. The two men's eyes glinted, piercing, in the half-gloom. Collins continued.

'It's a Panama-registered yacht, *The Fairest Lady II*. It's due in port in two days if there isn't any bad weather or anything.' Collins swallowed and licked his lips.

'There's three men on the boat: the captain, one sailor and Molloy. Probably armed, Molloy anyway. It's the same boat that brought the drugs from the West Indies to Ireland, but it was never unloaded in West Cork.' Collins scrutinised the Keaveneys, trying to find something he could use later. He couldn't read them and it rattled him. Slim had a smile painted on, Patrick a scowl. Collins wondered if it was an act.

Time seemed to slow.

Collins noticed dark stain spatters on the old, greenish wallpaper to his left. He didn't want to think what caused them.

'And that's it,' he said. He held up his hands. 'That's my information, take it or leave it.'

Slim smiled more broadly. 'As I say, I have no idea what you're talking about. Why are you giving *us* this so-called information?'

'I thought it might be useful, that's all. Oh, and I have a website you can track the boat on too,' Collins said. 'I have it on a bit of paper here.'

He hesitated, this was the tricky part. If they were recording the conversation he was already fucked, but there were different degrees of fucked.

'You thought it might be useful,' Slim said. He pursed his lips. He glanced to his brother and something passed between them. Collins could not interpret it.

Slim took out a pen and a small notebook from the inside pocket of his jacket and handed them to Collins.

'Write down what you just said – everything.'

Collins did so, trying to keep his hand steady. A car drove slowly past the window. He wondered for a moment if he'd leave the building alive, if the window would rupture with enough force. He wouldn't make it halfway there with Duffy behind him.

He flattened out the bit of paper with the website address and copied it carefully, especially the slash and numbers at the end. He handed back the notebook and the pen. It was an expensive pen.

'What do you want?' Patrick said. 'You want money? Is that it? Want to go on the take?'

'No,' Collins said. 'No money. That's it.'

'That's it?' Slim said. 'I don't think so. Anyway, we're off. Grandchildren to spoil and that.' He stood up. He smiled broadly at Collins. He really was very like that actor, with his narrow nose, long chin and evil grin. The very caricature of a bad guy.

Patrick stood up slowly, clearly in pain. He was the older one. He was glaring again. Slim looked at Duffy and shrugged – Collins couldn't read what that meant. He stood up too, but Duffy pushed his shoulder back down.

'Happy Christmas, Detective,' Slim said, on the way out. 'I

think we'll be seeing more of you in the new year.' He stopped in the doorway. 'Oh, I forgot to ask: how's your partner, Detective Carroll? Is she on the mend?'

'Yes,' Collins said, looking straight ahead. 'Yes, she is.'

'Good,' Slim said. 'That's good, glad to hear it.' He chuckled and left the room. Collins heard some shuffling and whispering in the hall. A door creaked, and then was closed.

It was done, Collins realised. Whatever happened now, happened.

Duffy stood behind him, silent. Collins had no sense of his presence at all, he really was impressive. He waited for the blow to the top of his head or the pressure of a gun's barrel.

'You know,' Collins said, 'I don't think you were ever a Navy SEAL.' He stood up to face Duffy, whose brown eyes indicated absolutely nothing.

'Is that so?' Duffy said.

'Yes,' Collins said. 'I think you were Special Forces. Too small for a SEAL, but Special Forces like them wiry and fast.'

Duffy blinked. Nothing.

'Let's go,' he said, standing aside. 'Out the back again.'

Collins went outside. The gunmen were gone from the hall, he noticed with relief.

Duffy drove the van towards Croke Park, a place Collins knew well. He went right at Jones's Road, then onto the North Circular Road and left down Dorset Street. Traffic was heavy with Christmas shoppers.

Near Capel Street, the van pulled in. Duffy turned to him.

'Next time you come to my home, you're a dead man,' he said, with an edge in his voice.

Collins held his eyes for a moment and got out. He slammed

the door of the van and Duffy pulled away. Collins steadied himself by putting his hand on a lamp post. He thought his legs would give, then he thought he'd be sick. He took deep gulps of air until his head stopped spinning and he could straighten again.

A dark-haired woman with a plump face was standing outside a shop on a smoking break. She had her hair done up like Imelda May with that curl at the front – she even looked like the singer.

'Y'alright mister?' she said. 'On the gargle last night, wha'?'

She smiled at him, some gum showing through her teeth. She bent down, stubbed out the cigarette on the footpath, and went inside the shop.

Collins looked at the cars and the people on the footpath. He'd thought everything would appear different, somehow, now. But it didn't.

70

Amazingly, Collins managed to get a replacement phone in a shop in Jervis Street, amid the Christmas chaos. The shop assistant synced his contacts from iCloud and charged it enough to get him home, while Collins wandered around the shopping centre buying presents.

His phone rang when he was walking to the Luas stop on Abbey Street Upper. He winced when he saw the caller ID.

'Hi Violette,' he said. 'I'm really sorry about this morning, I had to go to Dublin with work at the last minute.'

'You couldn't text me?' she said. 'I was sitting there for nearly an hour, I phoned you five times.'

'I'm really sorry,' he said. 'I'll make it up to you when you get back.' He checked his watch. 'Are you in the airport?'

'Yes, I'm just boarding,' she said and he sensed a sadness in her voice.

'What's wrong?'

'I wanted to tell you in person, Collins, but now you messed that up too.'

'Tell me what?' he said. He stopped on the street and leaned into a wall away from passers-by. He stuck a finger into his free ear to block the sound of a tram. 'What's wrong?'

'I'm going back to Paris,' she said.

'I know that,' he said.

'I'm not coming back to Cork,' she said and the line went quiet. Collins pressed the back of his head against the wall behind him.

'Why not?' he said. 'Your research isn't finished. You said the summer at least.'

'I … My mother is getting frail,' she said. 'I told you she fell and I need to make sure she's taking her medication.'

'Bullshit,' he said. 'What's the real reason?'

'Philippe is talking about a reconciliation,' she said. 'I have to meet him to discuss it and I … I don't know if Cork is right for me anymore.' Another long silence. Collins looked at spots of chewing gum on the footpath.

'I don't feel safe, Collins. They poisoned you, and then the foxes and those kids …'

He looked up and down the street. Christmas shoppers left and right, full of the joys, not a care in the world.

'I understand,' he said. 'I get it. I really do.'

'I'm just so confused. Last week I thought somebody was following me.'

'There's nothing more to say, Violette. You don't have to explain. I get it.'

'I'm sorry, Collins,' she said and her voice caught.

'I'm sorry too, Violette,' he said. 'I wish you well.' He held the phone away from him and looked at the red icon with the white phone on the screen. He pressed it.

A Luas was coming in his direction. He put the phone in his pocket and picked up the shopping bags he had placed on the ground. His ears were buzzing. He crossed the road and got in the queue to board the tram.

It wasn't until he saw the man in uniform checking tickets that he realised he didn't have one. He got off at the next stop, which was Museum again.

He riffled through pockets to get coins and put them into the ticket vending machine. He pressed a button, not knowing if it was the right one. The machine ejected a ticket and some change. He grabbed the ticket, picked up his shopping bags and waited for the next tram.

Cork Airport was a frenzy of homecoming and eager faces. Decorations hung along the walls and a gigantic Christmas tree stood by the Arrivals gate. Christmas music was playing in the background. People smiled and kissed and hugged each other. Children ran up and down the concourse with excitement. People shed unexpected tears and laughed through them.

Collins stood with all the others to face the flow of incoming travellers, as they pushed their trolleys forward. He had a sheet of paper in his hands and when he saw his niece, Tara, and his nephew, TJ, coming through the doors, he held it up.

'COLLINS. NYC BRANCH,' it said, in large blue letters.

The children smiled their beautiful American smiles and ran to him.

71

The man known as Sarge – bearded and dark-featured – sat at the bar counter of the brasserie Le Sextant in La Rochelle. He sipped his red wine and ostensibly read from the football pages of *L'Équipe*. He could overhear some of the conversation of the target, Molloy, and the captain of the yacht, whose name was Elwood. They were sitting at a nearby booth, under a replica of a three-masted schooner.

Elwood looked in his early sixties. He was overweight, with a thinning head of grey hair and a grey beard. His face was tanned and well-lined. He was doing most of the talking – mostly stories of nautical exploits in South East Asia. Molloy was watchful and looked at his phone screen regularly. He was thin, bleary-eyed and pale. It was definitely him, even with the stubble – the photos had been clear.

Molloy had a battered backpack on the seat beside him. At one point, he opened it and put a hand inside, as if to feel for something. Sarge tensed; he didn't have a weapon with him. Molloy withdrew his hand and picked up his glass. He was on his fourth whiskey, as far as Sarge could tell; Elwood was drinking white wine.

When their food arrived, Sarge paid for his drink, went outside into the dark, and walked away through steady rain.

Chief was sitting at the steering wheel of the large van on the nearby quayside. He was big and fresh-faced and looked younger than his forty-two years. Three more men waited in the back:

Mancs, Guy and Didi, checking and rechecking weapons and night-vision goggles. All four men were wearing black latex gloves.

'Contact,' Sarge said in a northern English accent, getting into the passenger seat. 'Positive ID. They're eating now so we should have thirty minutes, at least. Possible weapon in the target's grey backpack.'

'Okay,' Chief said. 'You, me and Mancs will take them first. Guy, Didi, recon the boat; we'll do that, afterwards.'

'Roger that,' Sarge said and pulled open a small panel door behind his head.

'Weapons?' he said, through the panel.

'Check,' a voice said.

'Guy, Didi, you'll need night vision.'

'Check.'

'Radio test,' Sarge said, putting on a headpiece. 'Alpha.'

'Bravo,' Chief said.

'Charlie,' Mancs said.

'Delta,' Guy said.

'Echo,' Didi said.

'Mission is a go. Repeat, mission is a go,' Sarge said. He looked at his watch. 21.11 local time.

Chief started up the van and it crawled forward.

An hour and forty-five minutes later, Molloy and Elwood were walking down a narrow, ill-lit side street, headed for the Quai du Bout Blanc. Boats in dry dock on either side behind railings. Molloy was using his mobile phone to light the way. Their heads were bowed against the drizzling rain.

Chief approached them on the street, wearing a yellow oilskin coat and sou'wester hat. He had a powerful torch in his left hand, pointed to the ground. His right hand was in his pocket, gripping his Heckler & Koch VP9. As he came close, he looked up and smiled.

'*Bonne nuit, messieurs*,' he said in a hoarse voice. '*Il va pleuvoir toute la nuit, je pense.*'

Molloy and Elwood did not reply but turned their heads to watch him as he passed by. As they did, he lifted the torch and shone it into their eyes. At the same time, from the opposite side, Sarge emerged from behind a large trailer.

The four short bursts made suppressed metallic sounds, not unlike large staplers. A momentary silence, followed by two double shots.

Chief switched off the torch. He and Sarge looked around them and listened. Wind and rain, a vehicle in the distance. He shone the torch on Molloy's face, what was left of it.

'Target confirmed?' Sarge said.

'Confirmed,' Chief said. 'But we'll get fingerprints all the same.' He took out a phone, pressed the screen and held it to his ear.

'Yeah,' he said, and a van started up nearby.

After midnight Guy and Didi stole aboard *The Fairest Lady II*, wearing night-vision goggles. They quickly overpowered the sleeping deckhand, who felt the knife as a burning punch in the chest.

It took them almost two hours to dismantle the panels behind which the cocaine was stashed in smallish bales with thick black polyethylene wrapping. Sarge reversed the van along the quayside. He, Guy and Didi quietly loaded the bales while Chief and Mancs stood guard on either side.

At the rendezvous point at Angoulins, twelve kilometres to

the south, they were joined by the women and kids. The kids slept through the whole thing. Didi and Mancs went in one camper van. Guy went in the other.

Chief drove the van to the safe house down the coast, followed by Sarge in the rental. They stashed the weapons and equipment in a garage at the back. They unloaded the bales into a small delivery truck parked beside the house. Its driver, a monosyllabic Irishman with clipped grey hair, helped them. They drove to the cliff they had selected, near Fouras. Just before dawn they pushed the van over the edge into twenty metres of raging Biscay sea. They settled down for the drive to Nice and the flight home.

72

Things were hotting up in the Carbery Arms when Collins got the phone call. The night after St Stephen's night was always hectic.

'That you, Collins?' Rose said. 'Happy Christmas!'

'Rose?' Collins said. 'One second, I'll go outside.' He made his way through the packed bar to the smoking area at the back.

'Happy Christmas. How was it?' he said. 'Did Suzie like the Lego I sent her?'

'Oh, she did,' she said. 'She was delighted. And Santa did the biz, so happy days all round.'

'Did you and Alice get some time off?'

'Alice got two days before and after. I'm actually on tonight, which is why I'm ringing.'

'Oh? What's up?' Collins paid attention. He moved away from a crowd of drinkers sitting under a heater, and put a finger in his left ear.

'We just got word in from France. There was a shooting last night in La Rochelle.'

'Where?' said Collins, though he had heard her perfectly.

'La Rochelle. Down the west coast. It appears that a certain Dominic Molloy got his comeuppance.'

'He's dead?' Collins asked.

'As dead as he'll ever be. The Gendarmes say it was very professional. Traces of cocaine in the hull of a boat where another body was found, nearby. Looks like they got that too. They put Molloy's body on display, would you believe, tied up on a fence, just outside the town.'

Collins gritted his teeth. He put his shoulder against a wall and closed his eyes.

'Can't say I'm sorry,' he said.

'Fuck, no. Scumbag had it coming for years,' Rose said. 'How's your mam, and Paul and the gang?'

'Oh, fine thanks. Paul is ready to go back, I'd say, but the kids are loving it. They ... they were in Cork today shopping, and Mam is delighted with the company. I'm in the Carbery Arms with Paul right now.'

'Right. Well, I better go. Say hello to everyone.'

'Okay, Rose, will do. Love to Alice and Suzie, I might come up for a night soon.'

'You'll be welcome any time, Collins. And you know what? I'm glad the fucker is dead, after what he did to you. I hope he died roaring.'

Collins smiled. He loved that woman.

'Thanks, Rose. And thanks for the heads up.' He paused.

'Definite ID?' he said.

'Definite. The fingerprints showed up on the Europol database.'

'Okay. When does it go public?'

'Should be on the news in the morning.'

'Right. Thanks, girl. See you soon.'

'See you, Collins. Have a pint for me. Have two, it's a night for celebration.'

'I will. Thanks again.'

He closed the call. He looked around him.

Did everything seem different? Were the colours of the Christmas lights more vivid? Was the music less schmaltzy? Would the beer taste better, would he sleep sounder tonight?

He tried to decide. He thought about it for a moment, then

caught Katie's eye as she was collecting glasses. She smiled at him. The gap in her teeth was very sexy, he had decided months ago. He smiled back.

'Hi, Katie,' he said.

'What about ya, Collins?' Her accent was fairly sexy too.

'Busy?'

'Yeah,' she said, picking up another glass. 'Up the walls.' Her hands full, she blew a strand of hair away from in front of her eye.

'Are you off any night this week?' he asked.

Her eyes widened. She considered him. 'Are you asking me out, Collins?'

'I am,' he said. 'Is that okay?'

'About time,' she said. 'Jesus, youse southern men are very slow.' She turned away and spoke over her shoulder: 'Thursday. Dinner and a film in Cork. Café Paradiso. I'll give you my number before you go.'

Collins smiled. Then he didn't.

He thought of Kelly O'Driscoll, the first time he saw her on that sunny day at the Na Piarsaigh grounds. Her chipped tooth, her rosy cheeks. He thought of the last time he saw her, on the quayside. Her eye eaten away. Her dead baby inside her.

He looked at the high old stone walls of the beer garden, speckled by the drizzling rain. The Christmas lights illuminated the myriad of tiny drops of water, which were falling gently on the wall and gently on the ground near where he stood. He pursed his lips. He said, 'Fuck him.'

He went back to the bar for another pint. Or two.

73

Collins pulled the car into the large driveway of 12 Elmdale Drive, a small estate in Bishopstown. He swung it around and backed up to face it out again. Mícheál's car wasn't there, which meant he wasn't home – probably by design.

He got out and stood in the rain. Unlit lights hung from the two large shrubs in the front garden. He could see the Christmas tree in the living room, and a TV screen showing a cartoon. A typical Christmas scene, the picture of normality.

The house two down was lit up with an array of gaudy, flashing, multi-coloured concoctions. Strips of bulbs were hung along the gutters, over the crown of the roof and down its front. Depictions of Santa and a reindeer shone out under the chimneys. It looked like the garden was full of bright statues too.

June answered the door. She looked unkempt in a grey tracksuit – so unlike her. Her eyes were raw and ringed. Her hair was straggly, unwashed. Her face was drawn. There was a small dressing on her neck.

'Collins,' she whispered, smiling wanly.

'Hi, June. Happy Christmas, girl,' he said. He hugged her and pulled her into him and held her tight, and he didn't let her go. He swayed her from side to side, until he felt the ripples of her body from the weeping.

She sniffled and then half-laughed. 'Look at what you're after doing now.'

He followed her into the warm, homely kitchen he'd always loved, where he'd had many a meal and glass of wine with her and her family. She sipped some clear liquid from a long glass, through a straw. It looked suspiciously like a gin and tonic, with the ice and lemon, but surely not.

She took a bottle of whiskey out of a press and poured him a measure and pushed the glass under a dispenser in the door of the fridge, releasing some ice. He didn't refuse it.

'Cheers, Collins,' she said. 'Happy Christmas.'

'Many happy returns, June,' he said, holding eye contact, clinking his glass to hers.

'I'm surprised they let you out so soon,' he said.

'Me too,' she said. 'Not as much damage as they thought at first. Of course, I'm supposed to be in bed.'

It hurt her to talk so he waffled on about his family, the Yanks, his mother complaining that the turkey was dry, his hangover from the previous night. And she smiled through it all until, at the end, when he was flagging, he noticed a tear wander lazily down her cheek.

'Don't, June,' he said. 'You're safe now. He's gone.'

'I'm so sorry,' she said, sniffling. 'He … he picked Jack up from school one day. Just drove him around, but …' She shook her head from side to side. 'Jack thought he was a guard. He told him he was a guard.' She wiped her eyes with a tissue.

'If anything happened to them,' she said. 'Anything.'

'Shhh,' he said. 'No.'

He put his hand on her arm.

'I destroyed the phone,' he said. 'He's gone now, and all his dirty work with him. And I saw the text you sent him that morning, I know you didn't warn him. Not only that: you saved my life out there. Only for you, Corcoran had me. You saved my life, June. Don't ever forget it, because I bloody won't.'

She looked into her drink. She began to cry again; but this time he thought it was with relief, not guilt, and he let her at it. He patted her shoulder and went into the room next door to say hi to the kids.

They were growing fast, already past the stage where they felt the need to please. Jack was eight and fair and the image of his father. Maeve was twelve and growing tall, but skinny from the Crohn's. They were engrossed in their screens, so after some half-hearted responses, he wandered back into the kitchen where June was making spiced beef sandwiches.

He sat back down and sipped his whiskey.

'Maeve is getting tall,' he said.

'Mhmm,' she said, her back to him.

'June. I have only one question.'

She looked up, stopped buttering, and turned around.

'All you have to do is nod.'

Her eyes bore into him.

'Do you know who the other garda was? I think there were two.'

She shook her head from side to side.

'And was there another one?' he said.

She shrugged her shoulders. She didn't know.

He was satisfied. He told her about his hot date the following night, with Katie. That Violette had phoned him on Christmas Eve to tell him she wasn't returning to Cork to finish her research. He didn't tell her why.

June smiled and whispered, 'What are you like, Collins?'

She placed the plate of sandwiches on the table and he said, 'I don't know, girl. I just don't know.'

He took another sip of whiskey. He picked up a sandwich and bit into it.

74

'That is one bad hoor of a day,' Kevin Tuohig said, releasing another sweet from its wrapper and lobbing it into his mouth. He hadn't offered Collins one, though he seemed to be on his fifth or sixth.

Collins couldn't disagree. The rain was being flung horizontally through the trees by a gale of wind. But he felt more sorry for the four people of the Technical Unit who were trying to dig through the muck in what had once been white polypropylene boiler suits. The small marquee they had placed over themselves had blown away twice and careered off down the hill, so they were now just digging under the lights, but carefully. Pat Brady had been very exact with the location, and the cadaver dog they brought down from Dublin seemed to agree that there were human remains in situ.

Collins tried to adjust the umbrella again to keep off the rain. It appeared to be changing direction every few minutes.

Tuohig scoffed at him and said, 'You and your umbrella. Jaysus ye Corkies are fierce soft, trying to dodge a drop of rain. No wonder ye haven't won an All-Ireland since 2005.'

Tuohig ducked his chins in towards his neck and sucked on the sweet. He adjusted his back to the wind and leaned against a tree.

'Yeah, well I don't have your fucking insulation,' Collins said, which he knew was a bit lame.

'What insulation? Sure I'm in tip-top shape. A mean lean machine.'

'Are you going to offer me a sweet or what?' Collins said.

'Oh, sorry, that was my last one.'

Donal Fogarty, the head of the Technical Unit, waved them over. Even ten feet away the smell told them that they were in business. The forensic technicians were using their little garden trowels to scrape and scoop away the soil from what seemed to be a body. Cora Keohane was taking photos, her flash going off regularly.

'Looks like human remains alright,' Donal said. 'Doesn't appear to have been scavenged. Which is surprising considering how shallow the grave was.'

Bits of frayed clothing, decayed flesh and bone became obvious. Collins and Tuohig stood just close enough to see, in the flash of the camera, what appeared to be parts of a sternum and perhaps a clavicle. The buckle of a belt with an ornate motorbike was uncovered and Collins murmured: 'That's Dinny Buckley's, alright.'

'Thanks, Cora, thanks, men,' he said and walked away.

Tuohig followed, surreptitiously popping another chocolate into his mouth.

Collins took out his phone.

'Hi, Mick. Collins here.'

'Detective,' Sergeant Mick Murphy replied. 'Any news?'

'Yes, they found a body. Looks like Buckley, there was a belt buckle I recognised.'

'Well, good. Right. Of course it will take a while before we can get a DNA test completed.'

'Yes,' Collins said. 'But I want to tell the family that we may have found him anyway. Unofficially, off the record, like.'

'I'll talk to the Super and Kate and see what they say. I don't see a problem, though, as long as it's all unofficial and they don't go to the papers.'

'Right, thanks, Mick.'

At the bottom of Lota Hill, they sat into a car, out of the rain.

'Thanks be to Jesus,' Tuohig said, slicking his fingers through his wet air. 'Turn that thing on full blast, like a good man.'

Collins engaged the engine and put the heating and air-conditioning up high.

'I'll drop you at the station,' Collins said.

'Right,' Tuohig said. 'Or I could go up there with you, if you like.'

'Nah, you're alright,' Collins said. 'Thanks. But I know them and I want to have a bit of a chat with Kyle, the young fella. Don't like who he's been hanging around with.'

'Right. Is the sister back at home? The prostitute?'

'So I've heard,' Collins said. 'However long that lasts for.'

He wiped the windscreen and pulled out on the road carefully. The wipers thumped out a quick beat.

'Still. If she can quit that shit, she might be in with a shout.'

'Big if,' Tuohig said.

'Yeah,' Collins said. 'Big if.'

The wipers worked away against the rain. The screen demisted and he could clearly see the road ahead.

EPILOGUE

5 OCTOBER 2017

Claire Halvey walked through the front door of Waterstones. She made her way past tables piled with books. Head bowed, hands in the pockets of her leather jacket. Her head shaved on one side, showing the piercings in her left ear; her dyed night-black hair cut short on the other; the tip of her new cobra tattoo peeping above her Ramones T-shirt; her septum-ring silver and ebony.

She looked to her right and saw that policeman, Collins, in the history section, but he didn't look up. Almost a year now. Since the interview with that woman cop, Kate – she was nice, never made her say anything she didn't want to. When, near the end, after the worst of it was over, he had quietly entered the room and sat down beside Kate and asked her some questions about Dave, about if she knew anything about him dealing drugs. Which she didn't, it was another thing he'd never told her, the prick.

Nearly a year since a different life, a different her. Now, in St John's College, with her film-friend students, she couldn't even imagine what she had been like then. Brown Thomas make-up; pretty girl clothes; Molton Brown shower gel; Pandora bracelets and charms – how all that superficial shit had meant anything to her, she would never know.

And yet.

And yet here she was making for the YA bookshelves that she used to love when she was fourteen. She was aware of the irony.

Here she was reading the first page of *The Hunger Games*, about Katniss and her sister Prim and the ugly cat Buttercup. Katniss Everdeen, who could save the world but couldn't save her sister. Childish stuff, saving the world, saving anything. But she read on, not noticing the tall man approach.

'Hello, Claire,' he said quietly, startling her. There was something different about him when he was up close, when he looked straight at her. His eyes were a mix of green and brown. They were knowing eyes; they didn't let you go. He had on a heavy navy coat, with a jacket and open-necked shirt underneath.

'Oh, hi,' she said. She didn't know what to call him.

'I'm Detective Collins,' he said. 'I'm not sure if you remember me.'

'Yes. No. I mean, yes, I remember.'

He smiled more broadly and then his face became serious again.

'How are you?' he asked. 'I hear you're studying film-making.'

She resented his knowing that – was he keeping an eye on her? Though some part of her felt glad too.

'I'm fine,' she said, not adding anything. Was it a lie? When she thought about that residential home during the summer, it did seem like a lie to say she was fine. What a stupid name: *home*, too, when it was everything except a home – the opposite of home. Of course he probably knew that as well, and why she ended up there, and why she dropped out of school without doing her Leaving Cert.

He looked at her shrewdly and she was angry now. *What did he know? What would any of them ever know?*

'I hope you don't mind, but I bought you a book,' he said, holding out a small brown Waterstones paper bag. 'I hope you'll like it.'

She was taken aback. She didn't want his stupid present, but she did want to know what it was. She softened her face and took it. She said thanks and realised she was blushing. Blushing! How fucking ridiculous is that?

'It's ... a wonderful book,' he said. 'And it meant a great deal to me when I was your age.' He looked away for a moment. Into the past, she thought. She wondered what he was like then.

'When I didn't know who I was, or what I wanted to be, it was a big help to me,' he said. 'Because the truth is – and Hemingway knew this – you can be anyone you want to be, and you can do anything you want to do. And you can take the good things with you, wherever you go.'

She looked at him as he spoke and she thought she might cry, but she wouldn't cry, not here, not in front of him. She opened her mouth to say something, but nothing came out.

He said, 'Take care, Claire,' and he touched her arm lightly and turned away.

She watched him walk towards the back door of the bookshop.

She put the child's book back on the shelf and took the adult's book out of the paper bag. There was a picture of Paris on the cover, a narrow street in black and white, with the Eiffel Tower behind, almost in fog.

She opened it and on the title page he had written: 'To Claire, the bravest person I know. Take the good things with you, always. Collins.'

She looked towards the back of the bookshop, but he'd gone.

She re-read the words he'd written and then she closed the book.

The title on the cover was embossed and she ran her thumbs along the letters. *A Moveable Feast*. She wondered what it meant.

She looked at the picture again. Her mother had been promising her a trip away and she'd been thinking about New York, but she knew now that she would go to Paris. And read this book there.

She put the book back in the bag and walked past the counter, down the little carpeted slope and through the tables near the front door.

She walked out onto the cold bright street.

ACKNOWLEDGEMENTS

First, thank you for taking the time to read this book. Without readers like you there wouldn't be books in the first place.

Thanks to everyone at Mercier Press for publishing *Whatever It Takes*, especially Deirdre Roberts who commissioned it. Thanks to Patrick O'Donoghue for the support and Wendy Logue for bringing the work to fruition. Thanks to Sarah O'Flaherty for the wonderful cover. A special thanks to my editor Noel O'Regan – it's been such a privilege to work with Noel again.

Some of this book was workshopped during my MA in Creative Writing in UCC a few years ago. Thanks to all my fellow writers there and to the author Mary Morrissy who facilitated the workshops. I also received advice on it from Lisa McInerney in a workshop at the West Cork Literary Festival some years ago – thanks, Lisa.

Parts of the book have also been critiqued by my friends, the writers Anna Foley, Mark Kelleher and Eileen O'Donoghue, to whom I owe so much.

I've received great support for my writing over recent years. Huge thanks to Madeleine D'Arcy, Danny Denton, Danielle McLaughlin, Mary Morrissy and Donal Ryan for providing cover quotes for my first book, *The First Sunday in September*.

Thanks to everyone who read that book, especially those kind enough to let me know how much they enjoyed it. Thanks to those who wrote reviews or otherwise supported it. Thanks again to Mercier Press for publishing it.

A big thank you to Kieran Scanlon for his advice on garda elements of *Whatever It Takes*, to Peter O'Sullivan for advice on medical issues, and to Barry Roche and Frank Lingwood for insights on aspects of crime and policing in Cork. Thanks to the writer Mary Rose McCarthy for a great idea about Molloy. Thanks to Ashling Costello of Good Day Deli for Claire's septum-ring.

Thanks to everyone in my book club, of which I've been a member for over twenty-five years. I've learned so much about reading and writing from them. They are: Jacque Barry, Valerie Coogan, Betty Dineen, Eleanor Goggin, Brigid McLoughlin, John MacMonagle, Mary Morrissy, Paul Mulvany, Kim Murphy, Maeve Saunders and Tom Sheehan.

Thanks to Ciara for beta-reading and proofreading the book – her suggestions were invaluable, as ever. Special thanks to Anna Foley and A. N. Other for their brilliant proofreading, along with Jennifer Armstrong of edit365.com.

Many thanks to all the publications that have published my stories, sports writing, essays and other work, including the *Irish Examiner*, *The Stinging Fly*, *The Holly Bough*, *Honest Ulsterman*, *Silver Apples*, *Quarryman*, *From the Well Anthology 2017* and *The Cine-Files*.

Thanks to all those who support literature in Cork, too many to list individually – you know who you are!

Love and thanks to Ciara, always.

Finally, love and thanks always to my wonderful family, all three generations, to whom I dedicate this book – they have done so much for me. Never forgetting the generation just gone, especially my parents, Tim and Kitty Coakley, to whom I owe everything.

ABOUT THE AUTHOR

Tadhg Coakley is from Mallow and lives in Cork city with his wife, Ciara. His debut novel, *The First Sunday in September*, was shortlisted for the Mercier Press fiction prize and published in 2018 to much acclaim. Donal Ryan described it as 'vibrant and authentic, brimming with intensity and desire'. *Whatever It Takes* is Coakley's second novel. His short stories, sports writing and essays have been widely published. He is a graduate of the MA in Creative Writing course in University College Cork. For more about Tadhg and his work, see www.tadhgcoakley.com.